GODDESS OF FIRE

Bharti Kirchner is the author of six critically acclaimed novels, four cookbooks, and hundreds of short pieces which were published in magazines and newspapers. Bharti has written for *Food & Wine*, *Writer's Digest*, *The Writer*, *Fitness Plus*, *San Francisco Chronicle*, and *The Seattle Times*. Her essays have appeared in ten anthologies. She has won numerous awards for her writing, including a Virginia Center for the Creative Arts Fellowship. Prior to becoming a writer, Bharti worked as a systems engineer for IBM and as a systems manager for Bank of America, San Francisco. She has also worked in Europe and other continents as a computer systems consultant. Bharti lives in the US with her husband. Visit www.bhartikirchner.com for more details.

PRAISE FOR *GODDESS OF FIRE*

"Lush with historical detail and tense with dramatic emotion, *The Goddess of Fire* is a page-turning story of ambition, luck, love, betrayal, and, finally, the hope that comes from having survived the most desperate of circumstances."

Kim Barnes, author of *In the Kingdom of Men*

"A compulsive addition to Indian, or indeed international, historical fiction."

Farrukh Dhondy, author of *Bombay Duck, Rumi: A New Translation* and *Prophet of Love*

Reviews of *Darjeeling, Shiva Dancing* and *Sharmila's Book*

"Witty, sensitive . . . Kirchner deftly weaves an intricate tangle and then gradually unties the knots toward the end . . . The language is elegant."

San Francisco Chronicle on *Pastries: A novel*

"Interwoven with themes of family, unrequited love, and forgiveness, *Darjeeling* is as strong as the tea itself and just as satisfying."

Booklist

"A novelist and Indian cookbook author mixes a sensual and at times suspenseful transcontinental family saga as two sisters vie for the same man."

Kirkus Reviews

"[Kirchner] reveals a tremendous faith in her characters and their love of their homeland . . . she does infuse her work with a genuine Indian spirit."

Review in *Publisher's Weekly*

"*Darjeeling* is poetically told, artfully rendered story of the true test of blood loyalties, bringing a family to the brink and back again. There is a lot to love here."

India Currents

GODDESS OF FIRE

Bharti Kirchner

This first world edition published 2015 in
Great Britain and India, and 2016 in the USA by
SEVERN HOUSE PUBLISHERS LTD of
19 Cedar Road, Sutton, Surrey, England, SM2 5DA,
in association with Harlequin, an imprint of
HarperCollins *Publishers*, Uttar Pradesh, India.
Trade paperback edition first published 2016
in Great Britain and the USA by
SEVERN HOUSE PUBLISHERS LTD.

British Library Cataloguing in Publication Data

Kirchner, Bharti author.
  Goddess of fire.
  1. Kolkata (India)–History–17th century–Fiction.
  2. East India Company–Fiction. 3. Historical fiction.
  I. Title
  813.6-dc23

ISBN-13: 978-0-7278-8550-0 (cased)
ISBN-13: 978-1-84751-659-6 (trade paper)
ISBN-13: 978-1-78010-713-4 (e-book)

All Severn House titles are printed on acid-free paper.

Severn House Publishers support the Forest Stewardship Council™ [FSC™],
the leading international forest certification organisation.
All our titles that are printed on FSC certified paper carry the FSC logo.

Typeset by Palimpsest Book Production Ltd.,
Falkirk, Stirlingshire, Scotland.
Printed and bound in Great Britain by
TJ International, Padstow, Cornwall.

For

Didi, Rinku, Tinni and Tom now and always

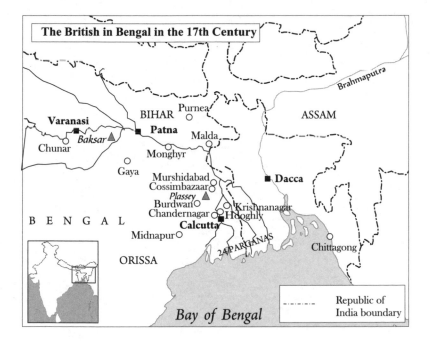

The British in Bengal in the 17th Century

"How blessings brighten us as they take their flight!"

— Edward Young

"In this world, full often, our joys are only the tender shadows which our sorrows cast."

— Henry Ward Beecher

INDIA IN THE 1680S

ONE

Village of Rampore, Bengal

The day after my husband died, my brother-in-law and his son came to my door. They dodged the copper bowl I had thrown at them and dragged me by the wrists to the funeral pyre. The blazing afternoon sun bore down on my bare scalp and oiled body as we headed toward the river. Tendrils of ochre dust, carrying the smell of death, rose from the earth around my bare feet. A dog howled in the distance.

Years later, I'd remember how I had winced from the clutching fingers of Bipin. "Take his land," I said, trying to pull away, "but please let me go. I will live as a ghost in my parents' home. I am only seventeen."

His skin rough as a tree bark, Bipin gave my forearm a vicious twist; his foul breath triggered a wave of nausea in my already queasy stomach. "Hold your tongue, Moorti. Now that I am the head of the family, I've decided you're going to be a goddess."

A fresh wave of humiliation coursed through my body. The voice of my schoolteacher father shot out from my throat. "You've twisted what our sages prescribe to serve your selfish intent. Abuse a widow, throw her into the fire, and take her property. You ought to be punished, not me."

Eyes red from the palm wine he'd drunk, Bipin once again tightened his grip. "You, the lowest of the low, a village girl who could pay no dowry, what do you know?"

My father had taught me at home. "You learn faster than the boys in my school," he would often say. To Bipin, I said, "Baba might be poor, but he's better educated than you are."

"You miserable little wretch!"

Bipin and his twenty-eight-year-old son Jadu were momentarily distracted by a procession of people at a distance—shadowy figures—beyond a bank of trees. Gritting my teeth and gathering all my strength, I kicked Bipin, yanked my greasy arm from his grasp, and kicked him again. He slipped and tumbled onto the ground. In trying to help him rise, Jadu, short and muscular, let go of my wrist. I ran along the rocky road. Bipin caught up with me, grabbed me by the neck with a fierce hand, and cursed me under his breath.

"Two days with you and my brother is dead. You're a bad omen. We want *you* dead."

Jadu plucked a white kerchief from his tunic pocket and stuffed it into my mouth. "Does that feel better?" He asked with mock concern.

I gagged and struggled to breathe as they pulled me by the arms to the public crematorium, a spacious open-air spot facing the river, surrounded by jungles and a few hills, far away from the residential section of the village. The place was bare save for burned logs, piles of ashes, and bone fragments. Several departed souls had recently been cremated here; the stench clogged my nostrils.

Father and son pushed me down onto a bamboo pallet placed on the ground, next to my husband's corpse. I was already dead and disposable. They stood there, muttering together, occasionally throwing malevolent glances at me. I pulled myself up into a sitting position, removed the handkerchief from my mouth, dabbed at my eyes with it, and tossed it to the ground. My feet hurt from the bruises, my stomach heaved, and eyes stung. Could I escape my fate? How?

A crowd of about twenty men had assembled around me. Where was my mother? She would have heard the news by now and do whatever she could to help me.

The solemn-faced men, huddling together, weren't here for the cremation of my husband. They'd come here to observe a young widow being burned alive in her husband's funeral pyre to join him in his next life.

Flee, I told myself again, slipping the cover of my white sari from my shaved head. *Jump into the river and swim to the other side.* Slowly, I stood and began to push away from the pallet, knowing my voluminous sari would hinder my attempts at swimming. Crocodiles infested the river. One could swallow me whole, like it might swallow a flower blossom or a sleek fish.

Holding a wooden rod under his armpit, Jadu advanced toward me. Any attempt to escape and he would tie my hands and feet. I sat down again.

This morning, in preparation for this forced cremation, my sister-in-law had rubbed my body with hibiscus oil and dusted it with sandalwood powder. Her two daughters had held my shoulders, pinning me down to the floor while she wiped the crimson vermilion dot from between my eyebrows and the black kajal from my eyes. Applying the kajal every morning had been a beloved ritual of mine; running a comb through my hair had always made me feel like a woman. They'd deprived me of that, my last shred of dignity, by shaving off my lustrous, waist-length hair. My husband's kin had also confiscated my colorful clothes and forced me to wrap myself up in a borderless, stark white cotton sari.

I cursed everyone present; I cursed my fate. *Why me?*

I looked at my deceased husband's body. Clad in a white cotton cloth and garlanded by white flowers, he, a broad-nosed, fifty-year-old groom with a weak heart, rested on a bed of sandalwood next to my pallet. I could have shown everyone the swelling on my left eye and the scar on my right cheek—beatings from him. An odd blend of sadness and disgust arose in me. Again, I looked around. Perhaps I could stand up and sprint into the woods.

Two young boys who stood nearby at the water's embankment stared at me and at the still body of my husband. "He died, that rich man, because of her," one boy said. "She killed him."

Not true. I could have related the full story. How my ill-tempered husband came to me the night after our wedding; drunk, naked, drooling, unsteady on his feet.

I was standing by the window. Turning, I saw his manhood flaring at me like an animal's tongue, and I pulled backwards. How could I feel amorous toward someone so crude? A stranger, he had practically bought me from my poor parents who couldn't feed and clothe me. In his dull monotonous voice, he'd told my father, "We'll forgo the dowry. I want her."

My husband, that foul-smelling man, leaned closer and fondled my breasts, his eyes bulging like those of a dead fish. I pushed him away. He spat on me, shoved me against the wall, and slapped my face. By the time I recovered, flinching in pain and feeling small, he had struck me above the eye with the back of his hand. I had barely regained my balance when he leaned over me, poised to strike again.

I turned into stone.

"You bitch," he murmured. "I'll finish you . . ."

Much to my relief, that third blow never fell, nor did he finish the sentence. His face first turned copper, then purple, and finally a sickly black. Veins bulging and throbbing, he struggled for breath and collapsed on the floor. His chest heaved for a few seconds, then became still.

I stood horror-struck, called for help, but by that time his heart had failed him. On that dark moonless night, the eighth day of the month of Baishakh in the Bengali lunar calendar, only the second day after my marriage, I became a widow. My husband's family blamed me for his death; I trembled at the ominous looks they gave me.

My husband's body, lying on top of a stack of fragrant sandalwood logs, was now ready for cremation. Why had I been given in marriage to a man so much older? Did I not deserve a better life? A longer life? Panic gripped me as I envisioned the terrifying prospect of what awaited me: blistering skin, burning hair, disintegrating bones, unimaginable pain, screams that would shake the hills, and then, death. A horrifying end. I was only seventeen. I had to find a way out. If only my mother would reach on time.

On my left, the Bhagirathi, a stretch of the River Ganges, flowed. *O, dear River Mother, please take me away from here. I want to live.* The river meandered on.

A row boat glided by. Leaves quivered on trees. A kingfisher dove into the water, intent on an unwary small fish. That's when I noticed the silence that had fallen over the spectators in anticipation of the approaching hour. The last few moments of my life. Would I be able to see my mother, hear her voice one last time?

A devout elderly kinsman, dressed in fine white garb, stepped forward, stood a few feet away from me, and began intoning words of praise in anticipation of my status as sati: "Our girl Moorti, pure, brave, and beautiful as a champa blossom, will ascend to heaven. Because of her sacrifice her husband, too, will be ushered into paradise. Her ashes mingled with his will cure ailments. The ground on which she's walked will become hallowed. On the anniversary of her death, we'll float oil lamps on the river in her name." He closed his eyes and chanted wholeheartedly. "She's a sati. She's a devi."

The chant sickened me; it was taken up by the crowd. "Sati devi sati devi sati devi sati devi . . ."

The kinsman continued, "*Sat* truth. And *sati* flesh purified by flame, leaving only blessings behind."

The chanting grew louder, the sound pressed on my chest. The frenzied spectators raised their arms to salute me. What glory was there in such worship? How much more insulting could it get? Again, I turned toward the river. *Ma Bhagirathi, please protect your daughter. Please. Hurry.* The river flowed on, calm, blue, impassive; a vulture flapped its wings, circling overhead, a crane stood on the bank.

"Lagao!" Someone shouted in the distance. I heard the splash of an anchor in the water.

A wooden houseboat, curved and wide, moored on the shore. A boatman hurled a long rope with bamboo stakes to the ground. My heart leapt foolishly at the sudden arrival of the newcomers.

About ten men, young, strong of build, spilled out of the vessel. Some were clothed in long tunics, skin-tight trousers, decorative vests, and round headdresses. Muslims. Others, Hindus, wore white cotton dhotis, like my father did. They each had a shawl thrown around their shoulders, as people did on social occasions. Among them was a tall Ingrej, Englishman. Dressed in tunic and trousers, his complexion white as the daylight, he moved with grace and ease. His eyes scanned the land, as though dazzled by its beauty, as though he wished to claim it as his own. As I sat staring at him, a distant hope fluttering in my chest, he looked toward me several times.

The Englishman and his crew strolled in my direction. Did they know they'd soon witness a young girl being burned alive along with the remains of her husband?

The voices of the villagers soared and fell over the chant, "Hari, Hari," until the words throbbed in my head. Holding myself rigid, still hoping for my mother's arrival, I tried to suppress a wave of nausea, but the spasms shook me and I couldn't calm the urge. Vomit welled up out of my belly and gushed onto the ground, a sickly yellow liquid with a rotten smell, the poison of an undesirable marriage.

The Brahmin priest, the most respected person in the village, made his way to the forefront. He wore a saffron loin cloth, his upper body bare save for a matching shawl and a three-strand sacred string placed diagonally across his chest. Everyone bowed to him. Stern-faced, eyes half-closed, his forehead marked with sandalwood paste, the priest chanted in Sanskrit, the sounds delivered in an ominous tone. The crowd fell silent. A drummer thumped a dholak. My heart beat fiercely. My schoolteacher father had educated me at home in the ancient rituals. I could pick up much of what the priest uttered. He was performing the last rites of a person. A chill coursed through my body.

"Moorti!"

Hope flooded over me as I heard the familiar plaintive voice.

"Moorti!"

At last! Ma had come here to save me. I saw myself in her—fair skin, big dark eyes, a small forehead, a tiny chin. Accompanied by a young cousin of mine, she pushed through the crowd, her threadbare blue cotton sari slipping off her shoulders. The creases on her forehead showed the strain of walking a mile from our house in the adjacent village of Kadampur. At home, about this time of the day, I would always massage herbal oil on her scalp to provide relief from frequent migraine attacks.

Weeping and shaking, standing behind the crowd surrounding me, she extended her spindly arms. "Please, have mercy," she gasped as she spoke to Bipin.

Glaring disdainfully at my mother, Bipin caught hold of her upper arm and thrust her back. "Women aren't allowed at a cremation," he growled. "You very well know that."

"Don't speak to her like that!" I shouted.

Mother lost her footing, but managed to grab the arm of a man standing nearby. "My only daughter," she wailed.

A murmur of uneasiness went through the crowd. Some shuffled on their feet, as though swayed by what she said. Others continued chanting. Bipin, sensing the slight change in the crowd's mood, passed an angry glance at me, then at my mother, and motioned to two men.

They stepped toward her menacingly. "You've gone too far," one of them said, grasping her arm. "We'll take you home."

"In the name of Goddess Durga," Mother said, "I refuse to go." She bit his hand.

He screamed; a dot of crimson appeared on his hand, and he yelled, "Miserable hag," and reached out with a fist.

The pair, now even more vengeful, pulled Mother along the dusty path. Her feet twisted on the rocks, loose pebbles rattled; the crowd was silent. I feared the punishment she would have to face when she reached home.

"Ma!" I shouted with love and desperation, wanting to protect her. "Ma!"

Mother turned back, eyes swollen, face pinched. "Moorti!"

For the last time I took in Mother's tormented face—the anguished eyes, puffy lips, high cheekbones bathed in tears—as much of it as I could store inside me. Soon she disappeared down a pathway, a blue speck through the green filter of the peepul trees, and then I could no longer see her. Only her laments echoed from the foliage.

The Englishman and his companions had positioned themselves at a discreet distance from me. Were they simply being respectful of the sati ritual and leaving me to burn or had they heard the anguished cry of my mother and felt motivated to act?

I strained to hear above the crisp, clear sounds of the drum as the

Englishman asked Jadu in broken Bangla, "What's going on here? Why did you drag that woman away?"

"Moorti has decided to go to heaven with her husband," Jadu replied, pointing at me. "It is her dearest wish and it will soon be fulfilled. Her mother is the only obstacle. We had to send her back."

I locked my gaze with the Englishman's and screamed, "He's lying!"

His blue-green eyes first brimmed with concern, then his face became a mask of fury, the corners of his mouth tightened.

Above the priest's chanting, I heard Jadu ask the Englishman, "What are you and your men doing here?"

"We're here to buy jute and cotton and have a look around. You have a pleasant little village."

"Our market is closed for a holiday. This is a private event. You're not welcome here. Go!" Jadu turned and joined Bipin a short distance away.

Years later, sitting under a Neem tree in a garden far away from this burning pyre, he would speak of the thoughts that troubled him as he stood undecided by the pyre.

Should he, a foreigner, get involved in a dispute over a local custom, however barbaric the practice appeared to him? For a moment he listened to the rhythmic chanting: sati devi devi sati . . . Why should he risk his life to save a stranger, even if she was a beautiful young girl whose eyes pleaded with him? The crowd could easily kill him. He had glanced back at the girl on the chita and realized that at that instant he was her only hope. The realization had galvanized him into action.

The Englishman stepped back and spoke in a whisper to his people; they turned and walked back in the direction from which they'd come. He stood nearby, strong, as though he had every right to observe the proceedings and question them. I'd seen English traders before. They would arrive in our village with their bodyguards and escorts, mostly native personnel, to shop for silk, jute, cotton, spices, and vegetables; at the village market, they'd haggle and pay ridiculously low sums for bundles of goods. Afterwards, they'd carouse and sing and march through our quiet streets, disturbing the peace. *They come here to steal*, a few elders insisted, but they tolerated their presence. *They're our guests and all guests are divine beings*, declared some others.

The priest, finished with his shlokas, accepted a burning torch, made circles in the air with its curling orange flame, and invoked the God of Destruction. As his invocation blended with the sound of the dholak, he beckoned to Bipin who swept the torch down and poked the oil-soaked logs beneath the shrouded body of my husband, thus releasing his soul, sending forth an explosion of red sparks and billowing black smoke. I regarded my husband for the last time; pot-bellied and bad-complexioned, with graying hair and a bulbous nose. I felt no grief; my eyes were dry.

Their faces drawn, the mourners folded their hands, shut their eyes, and mumbled a collective prayer for the deceased: "Haribol." Take the name of God.

The fire in the chita crackled and spat, more smoke snaked up, and the odor of burning flesh assaulted my nostrils. The priest continued his nasal incantation. Smoke and flame danced before me. The yellow heat blasted my arms, back, and feet. I thought the heat would dry up my blood. Beads of sweat gathered on my forehead, my heart pounded. *Should I run? What was better? To be burned or to be hacked to pieces by the crowd?*

The priest startled me to attention as he switched to Bangla. "It is your right to be a sati, a great honor for a woman, a sacrifice of the highest order, the ultimate act of devotion you'll show to your beloved husband. Together, you and I will recite your final prayer. Agni, God of Fire, will be our witness."

I shouted in a voice greater than my own, "I refuse to be burned. I was forced to marry that man. The marriage wasn't consummated."

The priest's eyes darkened with anger. "Do you understand the severe penance you'll have to undergo? People will spit on you no matter where you go. They'll try to take your life. When you die, you'll be sent to narak."

Tendrils of hungry flame crept toward me. "I have a right to live."

The spectators drew closer; more dried palm leaves were added to feed the pyre; as the flames leapt higher, they stepped back. Any moment now, my sari would catch fire, my skin would follow. Already the fire surrounded me, consuming the flesh of my dead husband, consuming the sandalwood and the bamboo pallet, and devouring the last the air that was left for me to breathe.

The Englishman was closing in on the priest with determined strides. His people, who had returned from the boat, had planted themselves behind him, each man clutching a bamboo baton.

The Englishman struck out at the priest's chest, a small but powerful strike delivered with an open hand. The priest slipped and staggered backward. I gaped, awed by the Englishman's boldness, by the violent light in his eyes. No one in our community, in that part of the Bengal province, would ever hurt a priest; they feared punishment from the gods. The chita was a raging inferno. Columns of smoke, ashes, and sparks swirled skyward.

Face twisted, lying on the ground, the priest screamed: "How dare you touch me, you beef-eater? You'll go to narak for this!"

Bipin lunged at the Englishman, but before he could deliver a blow, his adversary pivoted, grabbed him by his collar, and pushed him back. Bipin swayed and made a feeble effort to strike back, but the Englishman again took him by the collar and tossed him onto the dust. Bipin lost his balance and crumpled on the ground. Finally, I had a chance to escape, but the flames and the spectators blocked my path.

The crowd observed the assault, their eyes bulging in fear and shock, but no one advanced upon the Englishman. Drawing nearer, so near that any moment now he would catch fire himself, the Englishman plucked me from the pallet, draped me over his shoulder, and strode toward the river. Grasping his tunic, I clung to my rescuer's back. With each stride he took, my hips and belly bounced painfully on his broad shoulders, I found it difficult to breathe. His feet sank into the muddy earth and he fought to increase his pace. His bodyguards trotted along, forming a shield around us.

"Swine," someone screamed from behind. "Bastards! Thieves! Goondas! They're abducting our sati."

A wave of villagers came rushing behind us. What if they grabbed me and hurled me into the blazing fire?

The Englishman mumbled to me in accented Bangla, "Please be assured we'll protect you."

Before I could utter a word, his voice soared and he ordered his bodyguards to launch an attack. They turned and began to wield their bamboo batons, clobbering whoever came into range. I could hear shrieks of agony behind me.

A feeble voice cried out from among our pursuers: "Stop the goondas."

My husband's relatives rained down a hail of rocks, battering the ground around us, striking the guards. One hit my upper back and I cried out, but I still nursed a sweet sense of victory. I sent a prayer of gratitude to the River Mother for sending me this savior.

Although wishing to maintain my modesty, I clung tightly to the comforting shoulders of the Englishman. I could feel beads of perspiration penetrate the hibiscus oil that covered my body and dampen his tunic. My heart raced, my soiled white sari smelled of ash and smoke, I was scared, numb, but I was still breathing, could feel the breeze on my face, and admire the blue-black ripples of water lapping about the Englishman's shoes.

At that moment, he, a stranger in an irate crowd, felt a sense of victory as he climbed onto the boat and gently lowered the girl he had rescued on a bench under an awning. He was grateful to be alive.

Lying there on a bench on the weather-beaten deck, too ashamed to look into his face, I studied the Englishman's hands. Big and rough, they trembled; he, too, must have been petrified. He stepped aside, his milky complexion reddish from the exertion.

Flying rocks, splattering like rain, splashed into the river and struck the floor of the boat. Startled, I sat up, covered my head with the train of my sari, and craned my neck to look over the side of the boat. Shouting, shaking their fists, my in-laws hurled stones from the edge of the water. Hadn't they punished me enough? Everyone on the boat, including the white-turbaned oarsmen, ran here and there, seemingly disoriented. One rock barely missed me but thumped a crew member on the shoulder. "Bojjat!" he cursed.

The Englishman's eyes narrowed with mean delight. He cursed in English, picked up the fallen rock, and hurled it back toward the shore in a long arc. A yelp from the shore was followed by an exchange of insults. The crowd drew closer, some even waded into the water. What if they surrounded the boat? My stomach clenched.

"Chalo!" the Englishman shouted, his nostrils flaring. The two boatmen hurried to take their places. One of them muttered a prayer: "O God Shiva, please guide us on our journey." With grim determination, they slipped their oars into the water. With a groan and a clatter, the boat pulled away from the shore and into the fast-moving river. A few more rocks crashed on the deck. My persecutors, still yelling, remained assembled on the shore. Soon the burning pyre, peepul trees and coconut palm groves lining the bank disappeared from view, leaving behind only flecks of leafy green, the murmur of water, and a trail of foam in our wake.

I turned my head to view the yellow mustard fields and the mango tree. I remembered those times, carefree and rebellious, running through such fields, twirling in the sunshine, climbing the mango tree, plucking its ripe fruit and savoring its golden flesh, the juice sticky on my chin.

I saw myself feeding the shy, long-tailed monkey that hid near the river bed.

I slumped on the cold hard bench of the boat; the last thing I remembered was the monkey and the thud of my head hitting the wooden floor.

TWO

A perfume of spices mixed with sharp smelling salts under my nostrils brought me back to consciousness. Lying on the hard bench, I heard men's voices and snatches of conversation. A pair of eyes closely scrutinized me. My instinct was to stand up and flee from this odd dark gaze, but my legs wouldn't cooperate; they tingled in dreadful anticipation of what would happen to me. I trembled as I recalled how close I had come to dying.

"Sahib, sahib, the girl is waking up," said the young man watching me, as his hand, cupping the smelling salts, moved away from my nose. In a pleasant voice, he said, "Please don't try to get up too quickly. You've been unconscious for over an hour." With that he departed.

My stomach contracted from hunger; I slowly sat up, feeling dizzy from the rocking movement of the boat. The sun was directly overhead, beating down mercilessly on the boat. Where was I going? I took a look around the clean, well maintained boat. A deep-water vessel, both a row boat and a sail boat, large enough to accommodate at least fifteen people, it boasted a private cabin with windows. In the center, there stood a lofty mast on which a large square white sail was raised. No one in our hamlet could ever dream of affording such an extravagant vessel, made of fine wood and shiny metal, as elegant as a heavenly bird. Nor had I ever dreamed of finding myself in such lavish surroundings. But what must lie hidden beneath that shine? How could I trust the Englishman or anyone else on this vessel? One heard stories of women being kidnapped and sold to brothels in big towns, never to be heard of again.

The crew was scattered around; the Englishman stood nearby. I said in a voice loud enough for everyone to hear. "Ask the Englishman to please let me off the boat. I want to go home to my parents."

No response. As though they hadn't heard my plea. Or it didn't matter what I wanted.

A pair of crew members carried on a conversation in Bangla. "Thanks to our lucky stars, we got away," one said.

"Leave it to the English, those cunning fellows," a second replied. "My grandfather told me they came to our country at the turn of the century after the Dutch and the Portuguese. But it doesn't take them long to seize a situation. I only wish my tunic hadn't torn."

The oldest crew member, a tall mustachioed man with a glum face, pointed to a swollen spot on his shoulder and gave me a spiteful glance. He had only one eye, the right socket simply a pit covered with scar tissue. His skin was pockmarked. "I fought the hardest but got this purple beauty as a reward." He pointed a finger at me. "All this wouldn't have happened on our pleasure trip if it weren't for you, wretched widow."

"I feel bad for what you had to do for me," I said. "Kindly tell me who you are." I didn't ask the other questions on my mind: *Where do you come from? Where are we going?*

His one eye blazed. "You're asking *me* a question, you bald-headed country bumpkin. Do you know my position in the Company? I am the gomastah, supervisor."

He would have continued his tirade, but his English master held up a hand; a gold ring set with rubies blazed on his middle finger. Frowning, he said, "Bass!"

Once again, I was amazed by this Englishman who exerted authority with a light touch, who spoke my mother tongue, even if with an accent. I liked listening to his manly voice. I liked his supportive stance, like that of a shade-giving mango tree, despite the mean streak I'd noticed in him.

The suitably chastened gomastah bowed his graying head and said to me, "My name is Tariq. I am to be your interpreter. And this is Job Charnock, Esquire, Agent of the English East India Company. He's here to carry out the orders of the Crown, a charter from his King. But then you don't know what a Charter is. It's a contract between merchant adventurers and the Crown. Do you understand?"

What did all these terms mean? Through my ghomta, I scrutinized the Englishman. Tall and square-shouldered, he was attired in a fashion similar to his crew, only more lavishly. The pearl-embroidered vest spoke of his position of power. The gleaming white tunic splashed with silver stars was soiled in places. White trousers, tight around the legs, displayed his well-muscled limbs. His slippers, embroidered with spangles and mud-soaked, appeared finely crafted. How unusual for an Englishman to dress like that. Sharp-featured and oval-faced, he had wheat-colored hair cascading in loose curls over his shoulders. The smell of fine silk lingered about him. He seemed to accept his position without assigning too much importance to it.

As he stepped away to speak with a crewman, a history lesson from my father came to mind. "Our land is golden. Europeans have been crossing the seven seas for millennia to reach here. They want their share of our wealth. They kill, loot, burn homes, and take our freedom away. Already the Portuguese occupy land on the west coast and the Dutch have built trading posts in the east."

Seeing my questioning gaze, Tariq told me that the Englishman who cut such an impressive figure had embarked on a long dangerous voyage from his country, bidding farewell to his loved ones, knowing full well that ships were often lost at sea. He had first sailed to Sumatra, looking for spices to trade and arrived in India later.

"How old?" I asked, sounding foolish to my own ears.

Admiration and fear mingled in Tariq's eyes; he glanced over his shoulder at his superior who was still busy speaking with a crewman. "He left home at seventeen. You see, the sahib is a self-made man. He worked his way up to becoming a tradesman, landed on our shore, and opened up relations with the local Mughal Government. The sahib even studied Persian on his own so he could transact business easily with the Royal Court."

Again, I didn't follow much, except for the mention of Persian, which my father believed to be the language of culture. Job Charnock, the culturally inclined, high British official, joined us just then. He must have overheard snatches of Tariq's praise, for he glanced at him with pleasant acknowledgment. I looked at him again. I'd never mistake him for a mere merchant, this man who fairly radiated brilliance.

"The sahib is a kind man," Tariq said. "He's saved you from burning. You wouldn't be here were it not for him."

Tariq seemed extra deferential in his use of the word sahib.

His words annoyed me. My swollen, blistered feet were reminders enough of my experience. I tried to swallow, but my mouth was parched, my tongue felt like a dried leaf. I placed my hand at the base of my throat and tried to swallow again.

Job sahib stepped up to me and held out a tin flask filled with water. "Please drink."

I observed the calloused hands, powerful wrists, and the care with which he poured water into my cupped hands. I drank the sweet warm water, glancing at his features as I did. Many years later, I'd remember what I had observed. With his thick neck, oval face, and powerful legs, he was an intimidating figure. He must have been in his thirties, vigorous for his age. I had seen his capacity for violence, how quickly he'd changed, and I didn't fully trust him. If only I'd known then. It would take a rustic young girl like me months before I could begin to understand him or his actions. Yet, at that moment, in that boat, I had to admit that despite being a stranger, a foreigner even, he'd made a generally good impression.

My thirst somewhat quenched, I wiped my lips with the back of my hand and tried to hide my discomfort. Although I mumbled a few words of gratitude, what I really wanted to ask was: *Why did you save me? You could have been killed.*

The sahib glanced at me and then stood staring at the river. He must have sensed the question in my mind. "You're too young to die," he said.

It surprised me again that this foreigner could speak my mother tongue, although with some effort and not always correctly. "Drag a woman to the burning ghat to be sacrificed like an animal?" He continued. "What a horrible custom. I couldn't go along with that."

I put a hand to my mouth, stung by little tremors on my lips.

"I am a Muslim," Tariq said in a superior manner. "We don't burn our widows or take away their property. It's just as shocking to me, sir."

The sahib looked curious. As though feeling encouraged, Tariq continued. The sati practice was limited to upper caste Hindus only. A Brahmin widow, one whose husband owns property, had to undergo sati. Untouchables and those of low birth didn't observe it.

"And for those who escape sati?" the sahib asked me directly.

They were forced to wear the coarsest cotton, given only leftovers to eat, and shunned from all social and community activities. Speaking to such an important person, keeping my head bent, all I could say was, "They might as well be dead."

"Such a custom is outrageous, sinful, and criminal," Job sahib said. "We had to come to your aid."

Tariq turned to the sahib. Acting as though he was privy to inside information, he said, "Isn't there more to it?"

"No, no, of course not." Job sahib spoke quickly, above a whisper, as if wanting to guard his private feelings. "Besides, that was over a year ago and in a remote village, as you well know, Tariq."

Curious, I mumbled, "What happened?" It helped me to concentrate on his life, rather than my own misfortune. I only wished I didn't feel so awkward.

"Oh, dear God!" Job sahib exclaimed, his voice a tad shy and breathy. "I was riding my horse, galloping over a desolate farming area when a beautiful deer jumped in front of me."

This foreigner rode alone in the countryside? Brave, but also foolish. Noticing from the corner of my eye that Tariq had moved to the front of the boat, I asked the sahib, "You fell off?"

"Aye." His features crumpled. "The horse reared up, I was unable to rein it in and was thrown from the saddle onto a pile of rocks."

I could tell he still hadn't recovered from the shock of it.

"I was struck by a sharp rock and bled heavily." A farmer who was harvesting rice carried him to his hut and sent for the local physician. He and his wife gave him food, shelter, and loving care for over a month and taught him many words and phrases of the local dialect of Bangla they spoke. "They didn't ask for anything in return."

Job sahib turned his face to the distant shore. The strong wind ruffled his hair and threw him off balance as it rocked the boat. In that unguarded moment, through the symmetry of his features, I detected turmoil in his eyes, as though his mind had flown back much further in the past.

Job sahib turned back to Tariq who had come back to us and consulted with him in English before turning to me. "What are you called?" His voice had a gentle quality whenever he addressed me directly.

"Moorti." Saying my name helped me feel like myself, even though I wasn't sure where this was going. Who were these people? What would my husband's kin do if they found me in the company of strangers, moving gradually away from the place I'd known?

"Does Moorti have a meaning? I understand most of your names have meanings and even stories behind them, perhaps even an association with one of your gods."

"Yes, I am named after a consort of God."

I didn't tell him that Moorti was the consort of God Dharma, the deity who embodied order in the universe. Moorti exemplified serenity, luminosity, power, and harmony. That day, I couldn't lay claim to any of those qualities.

"You'll come with us, Pretty Consort," Job sahib said. "We're heading toward Cossimbazar, the 'Great Market Town' in the district of Murshidabad."

My father had once told me about the famous town filled with landmarks. How much I'd wanted to visit the sprawling bazaar where one could buy anything. "But, but my husband's relatives will come after me no matter where I go."

"They won't find you, or us," Job sahib said. "If they do, we'll know how to handle them."

"As a foreigner, the sahib doesn't have legal power in the town where we live, but he has much influence," Tariq said.

Legal power. What did that mean?

"What age are you?" Job sahib asked.

"Seventeen."

Years later he would tell me how my response had churned up an old memory that day.

Job Charnock sighed. How could he have told this stranger girl that he, too, had begun a new life at seventeen, kicked out of home with no place to go, no job skills, and no experience beyond his town? No, he told himself, he mustn't let that influence his thinking. He would simply offer her employment. Yet, he shuddered in the warm river breeze as he considered the hard labor she'd have to endure, the pittance she'd be offered in return. What other choice was there? She couldn't go back to her village. If cast out in a city like Cossimbazar, she'd end up in a brothel. Of course, it would be good for the Company too. His primary responsibility, as a loyal agent, was to run a profitable operation, keeping expenses as low as possible, even if that meant exploiting the poor servants.

He had looked back at the girl he had helped escape fate. She sat erect, waiting for him to speak. He'd never met a girl so resilient, so spirited. He looked again at her lovely, young face. She was elegant, had a way of maintaining her poise despite being traumatized.

"Do you cook?" Job sahib asked me.

I inclined my head in affirmation. I was capable of doing much more and was thankful to my father for it. He taught at a pathshala for boys affiliated with our village temple. There was no such facility for girls, so he taught me at home; Sanskrit, History, Literature, Geography, along with various Bangla dialects, so I would be better prepared to live my life. Under the shade of a tree, sitting on a low stool, he would often read classical Sanskrit poetry by Kalidasa to me. "You must develop both your head and heart," he would say. I would sit on a mat and practise arithmetic using pebbles. I would write sentences on dust with a twig because we couldn't afford to buy paper made of jute.

The sahib was again engaged in a muffled conversation with Tariq. I bit my lip. A cook? Gazing out at small silvery fish weaving through the blue depths of the water, I contemplated diving into it and swimming to the shore. Perhaps the river would cradle me, deliver me to safety. Then I'd sprint through the woods, but with these two men guarding me closely, that would be next to impossible. And then, there were crocodiles in the river. The very thought turned my blood cold.

A strong wave rocked the boat and broke into my thoughts, drenching my face. Job sahib and Tariq drifted away to consult with the oarsmen. The sahib walked with a slight limp, favoring his left leg over the right. "His heart is not in sync with his body," my mother would have said.

A cluster of white lilies released by devotees at a nearby temple floated down the river. Turning, I saw a young crew member approach, the one who had been watching me earlier, bearing a leaf plate heaped with rice, flat bread, and wilted greens.

He handed me the plate and said, "My name is Sal, short for Saleh." Thin and dark, with gentle eyes and a mole above his lips, he looked only a few years older than me. "Here, you must be hungry. Allah be praised!" He turned.

"Please wait." Feeling the weight of the plate, my mouth salivating, for I hadn't eaten since the day before, I gave Sal a thankful gaze. "I am a Hindu. We never eat on the river."

Sal surveyed my face; he must have noticed the confusion of pain in my gaze. "I've worked with Brahmins. You see the water as your mother and you show respect. But this is a most unusual situation . . ."

So my companions consisted of foreigners, Muslims, and various Hindu castes. Would I, a Brahmin girl, be required to cook meat or even forced to eat it? Rattled by the thought, I found it difficult to taste the food or even swallow it. Yet, touched by Sal's friendly approach, I motioned for him to sit.

He dropped down on the other end of the bench. "We have a long journey ahead against the current," he said. "We're going north to Cossimbazar, also situated on the Bhagirathi River, and a part of the Bengal province. Although Dhaka is the capital of our province, Cossimbazar is an important town because of its silk industry. If you

walk the streets where silk is being produced, you'll smell mulberries.
Silk means money and we have many rich people. On the streets you
can tell them by their brightly colored, embroidered silk robes. They
live in big houses, with lots of servants. The biggest house in town is a
palace that belongs to Haider Ali, our regional governor. It's the most
beautiful house I've ever seen."

I could hardly bear going so far away from my family and in an
environment more opulent than the one from where I came. Sal must
have understood, for he nodded gently and said, "You'll like it there;
the weather is milder. There's always a river breeze. In my village, which
is near Cossimbazar, we say that our land is a child of the rivers." He
further informed me that Job sahib's trading station was called a Factory
although no goods were manufactured there. The Englishmen were
called Factors or Agents. They were clerks and bookkeepers. They also
received and dispatched goods. "In the Factory, our job is to serve them.
We get one meal a day and a place to sleep. We can occasionally visit
the big market. But whenever I manage to get time off, I go back to
my village."

One meal a day. He did look rather thin. "It's all very strange to me,"
I said. "I don't know how I will manage."

"I'll help you, behen." Behen. Sister. I felt a little less scared. "I'll be
back presently," he said. Refreshed by the meal and the new friendship
with Sal, I settled on the bench and imagined the trees, fields, and the
river banks of my village. I could see it all clearly. By now, my wicked
in-laws had slunk back to their houses. Soon they'd pay a visit to my
mother who lived a mile away, carrying gifts of flowers, coconut, and
sweetmeats. Unable to admit defeat at the hands of strangers, they'd
cover up the facts of my rescue and concoct a story for her.

"Your daughter is a sati," Bipin would sing. "She left the earth in a
state of grace. We'll worship her for generations to come. Please accept
these gifts in her name."

Mother would stare blankly at Bipin. If only I could appear before
him, look him in the eye, and point to the door. "Not another lie! Leave!
Don't disturb my family."

My thoughts were interrupted as Job sahib and Tariq approached me.
Job sahib stood tall and impassive, holding much inside; Tariq, on the
other hand, gave away his intentions easily by his sour expression, sly
glances, and sneer. The empty space of his missing eye radiated mischief.

"Job sahib says Moorti is difficult to pronounce, especially our soft T sound," Tariq said. "Job sahib's great grandmother's name was Maria, which is what we'll call you. Isn't it a pretty name? Maria?"

My jaw tightened. How could they even consider asking me to make such a drastic change? My parents had chosen that name for me on the day I was born, after consulting with a jyotishi. When I was seven years old, the same astrologer had also created a birth chart for me. In an excited voice, he had recited a roster of good fortunes that awaited me: riches, progeny, a loving spouse, a shining position, and high regard from friends.

"Position?" my mother had asked in disbelief. "For a village woman?"

The astrologer's lips had parted in a smile. "Did you forget we have the tradition of valiant queens and women of high status in the Royal Court?"

Happily, my mother had paid him double his fee. How could she have known that he was delivering a false prophecy?

A butterfly blew past me. "I was given my name at birth," I said to Job sahib. "The name I was supposed to have according to the stars."

"Consider yourself reborn." He sounded as though rebirth was a natural phenomenon.

"Consider yourself lucky," Tariq added.

One day I would smile as I remembered the obstinacy of that young girl, "I answer to Moorti and Moorti only."

"You're a lovely girl, Maria." His one good eye flashing in anger, Tariq began speaking to me in a local dialect, which I presumed Job sahib wouldn't grasp. "Lovely but mouthy. You must impose control on your tongue if you don't want to be thrown into the river." He turned to his master, switched to a polite tone of voice, and translated what he'd remarked to me.

"Couldn't you find a local name for me?" I asked Job sahib.

He gave me a tender look. "Maria, beautiful Maria," he whispered in Bangla, "Welcome."

He strode away with Tariq scurrying after him.

I gripped the edge of the bench. As the boat plunged upstream, the oars dipping and making splashing noises, a light of realization burst inside me. They were right. I could never return home. What was that saying? Marriage was a woman's destiny. Her primary duties consisted of fidelity and devotion to her husband. End of marriage, end of woman. Moorti, a widow destined to die, had been reborn in the next life as Maria.

Henceforth, I would have to forge a new direction and make my way upstream, like this boat.

The river stretched before me, vast, blue-black, and turbulent. I watched its flow, a girl of seventeen, alone, in the midst of nowhere, with nothing left, not even her name. The back of a huge crocodile, sleek, dark-olive, deadly, parted the surface of water.

THREE

We climbed out of the boat, all ten of us, under a cloudy sky, and stepped into a vibrant town that stretched as far as the eye could see. Amazed, I took in the wide streets of Cossimbazar teeming with pedestrians and oxcarts. Food vendors crowded into whatever empty space was available to hawk their specialties. One man had set up shop only a short distance from the quay and did brisk business ladling a fragrant lime drink into clay cups for thirsty passengers. Close by, another offered chunks of delicate, milk-based sweetmeats on small leaf plates which were snapped up as fast as he could fill them. So many different kinds of fancy food items! In my village, they'd be served only on special occasions, if at all, and in limited quantities. Here anybody could buy them. Sal was right. This was truly a wealthy town. Some day, I said to myself, some day, I'd be able to afford these pricy items myself.

Listening to people's chatter and the rumble of carts, and still caught in the boat's rocking sensation, I walked behind Job sahib as he led the way along a footpath next to the river bank. We passed by an ancient sandstone pillar and a brick watchtower. Standing at a distance was a temple with a conical roof, its façade animated by carved deities. I'd never been to any place of this size or this historic importance. A pleasant wind brought in a pungent yet sweet smell, mostly mulberry mixed with that of seasonal flowers.

We walked past a field where cattle grazed, then a row of thatched-roof and mud-walled houses. The afternoon light had nearly faded when we arrived at the trading post, a large brick-walled compound, occupying at least a bigha of land, its sheer size frightening. A moat surrounded the compound's exterior walls. Inside, there stood a two-storey stone mansion, illuminated by large windows, and furnished with cannon. I'd only heard about cannons in stories, heard of the damage they cause, the horror.

Wrapping the sari train closer to my chest, I forced myself to look again. My fear at the time was understandable but in retrospect, it was unnecessary. The Mughal-style building was embellished with columns, archways, and eaves, adorned with a red-and-white flag and fronted by a four-quartered garden in which flowers bloomed in pink, white, yellow, and crimson. For an instant, I stared at an outer wall etched with fancy floral designs. Another fear of mine at the time was how I, a girl of modest means, would fit in the magnificent edifice taller than our village temple. I'd ask myself that question over and over that day and in the subsequent months.

Job sahib, accompanied by Tariq, walked ahead of me. As I held back, he turned to look at me and stopped. He must have noticed the bewildered look in my eyes, for he said, "Perhaps we should explain to Maria what this building is about, Tariq, what the English East India Company is about?" A trace of pride rang in his voice.

Silently, I repeated the name English East India Company, imitating the sahib's sounds.

"Yes, sir." Turning to me, Tariq said, "You've not heard of this bit of history, so let me tell you. It goes as far back as the early part of this century. On a day the stars were lined up right, the first English ship arrived on our shores with Sir Thomas Roe. He had brought with him a large number of gifts for Emperor Jahangir: pistols, knives, European paintings, an ornate carriage, and liquor. Of course you wouldn't know this either, but emperors can be childish. They have everything, but they still want more. Emperor Jahangir was flattered by the gift items from England. 'What do you wish in return?' He asked Sir Thomas. 'I'd like to open a Factory in Surat,' Sir Thomas replied. 'And I wish to conduct trade with you.' These weren't small wishes, but he had pleased our childish emperor. He got both."

"Of course it took years and years," Job sahib interjected. "My fellow countrymen established bases in Madras, Patna, Dacca, Ahmedabad, and Surat, about twenty of them. Now we have one in Cossimbazar as well." He smiled.

The smile would reveal itself one day.

Job Charnock was a man of few words. He could have elaborated upon the Factory's work and responsibilities, his role for its growth, its future potential as he thought about it, but he had said enough for the time being. The girl wouldn't quite understand the complexities; she didn't need to, he'd thought, little knowing what the future held for him and for her.

He wanted his trading station to be one of the three most important ones in Hindustan. Yes, he saw great possibility, here in the Bengal province, one of the richest in the land, with its fertile alluvial soil, abundant monsoon rains, several great rivers, well-functioning markets, expert craftsmen, and a friendly population. He could easily envision an enormously profitable trade route from here to England; ships loaded with jute, cotton, silk, indigo dye, opium, and saltpeter would arrive at regular intervals in London in exchange of gold and silver. Merchants would be excited by the prospect of introducing novel products from the East to the consumer. High profits and much rejoicing in the English parliament would follow, not to mention considerable personal benefit as well.

"This sahib is our Chief Factor," Tariq said to me. "He's new here, having recently been transferred from Patna. This mansion, which now houses our operation, was built by a Mughal prince but abandoned because it's too close to the river and open to attacks by pirates. Don't you think it's a beauty?"

I gave a half-nod. Beautiful, yes. Imposing enough to scare me? Yes.

A uniformed watchman, positioned at the iron gate, rose from his low stool. He flung the massive gate open; it creaked loudly. He stepped aside, gave me a condescending look, and saluted Job sahib. "Did you get some fresh air, sir?" He asked in Bangla. "Did you have a chance to shop?"

"Aye, it was a memorable trip. We didn't shop and I am happy to return. I trust all is well here."

Standing behind Job sahib, I hung on to every inflection of his speech; his words were like a lifeline extended to me. He put unnecessary stress on some Bangla words, but they sounded charming to my ears. Standing close by, Tariq kept an eye on me.

"I'm sorry, sir," the watchman replied glumly. "Something unexpected happened. I was taking a short break when a goonda managed to get inside the compound. I saw him running away with a sack of saltpeter. I ran fast, caught up with him, and we had a fist fight. He managed to escape, blood running down his nose but without the sack, ."

Saltpeter. Why would someone want to get a bloody nose for this thing? What was it? I followed Job sahib's eyes to the warehouse on the left. A uniformed guard patrolled it. Several laborers loaded plump jute bags into the building. Already, this place had taken on a menacing edge for me.

"Why didn't you have the gate locked?" Job sahib asked. "From now on, make sure no stranger gets in under any circumstances. Understand?"

He gave an explanation to the watchman, which I would recall and understand only when I was older, more familiar with the ways of this Factory and the world in which it functioned.

Saltpeter, a kind of rock salt used to make gunpowder and found naturally in our land, was loaded in big ships for England. There it was in demand as ammunition for war. To me, a young girl, as yet untutored in the ways of the world, war meant death, destruction, and the toppling of order. I who had already stared at death wanted to be as far away as possible, even from a skirmish. That day, as I stood behind Job sahib and listened to him instructing the watchman, I didn't realize that someday I'd find myself embroiled in a war that would forever alter my life.

Drops of rain burst from the clouds and pelted us, striking my forehead, my arms, my back; soon it was heavy enough to obscure my vision. Was the sky crying for me?

"This way," Tariq beckoned, his voice strained.

I looked toward Job sahib to see if I should follow Tariq, but the sahib and his escorts strode in the opposite direction, with no apparent concerns about me. Disappointed, I trailed behind Tariq.

We undertook a long walk, cutting through a beautifully tiled courtyard dotted with trees and flower bushes toward the back of the compound. Here the ground was bare, dusty, full of rocks, and so treacherous that I wobbled. The rain had eased a little, but looking around I wondered about where I was being led. A series of dilapidated, thatch-roofed huts loomed before me, small, uncared for, and hidden from the rest of the compound by a bank of bamboos, quite in contrast to the magnificence of the mansion, and well away from it.

A feeling of desolation swept over me. "Are these the servants' quarters?"

"You've understood correctly." Tariq pushed open the door of a hut and guided me to a tiny windowless chamber. "Go in."

Repulsed by the smell of cow dung, I took tentative steps into a dark, low-ceilinged room. Tariq swung away and returned in a short while, bearing a small wick lamp in the shape of a saucer. It threw a tortured dim yellow light on the walls. I remember thinking that these mud walls could cave in if it rained any harder. A snake could be hiding under the floor of bare earth. A wild animal could force its way through the flimsy door. A robber could break in. Even in my village, we Brahmins lived in better conditions. Job sahib? Where was he?

Unease prodded me to speak. "Women born in my caste . . ."

Tariq broke in. "Caste? You're lucky you don't have to sleep on the kitchen floor. We don't even know if you're any good at housework."

I bowed my head. Anger and disgust twisted Tariq's face as he swiveled around and went out of the hut.

Holding the wick lamp, its oily odor in my nostrils, I surveyed the meager surroundings: an uneven mud floor flecked by insects, a soiled mat, a thin worn sleeping rug not large enough to cover the mat, a few wooden pegs on the wall for hanging clothes, a pillow, a kantha no larger than a cradle cover, and a water pitcher.

My eyelids were so heavy that I didn't have either a word of protest or a word of prayer in me. Why should I expect any better, a woman who had no status left?

Arms heavy and lifeless, I made my bed. The night deepened outside, rain hammered the roof, the wind howled, and insects chirruped. I extinguished the lamp and tucked myself under the quilt, flinching at even the smallest sound. I shut my eyes, only to listen to a mosquito buzzing overhead. Soon the high-pitched whine of the insect was drowned out by wailing from the next room. Waves of laments rose and dipped, echoing the despair inside me. I listened as the cries filtered through the walls.

"How could you abandon me?" A woman sobbed. "How could you?"

I lay there, horrified. Was that an unhappy maidservant? A ghost? To whom was she speaking? What a scary, lonely, unlucky place!

Then I heard pounding, and I knew it was this unknown woman, slamming her hands upon the wall that separated us. She kept a beat, the rhythm of a disturbed heart. Worried that the wall might collapse, I dragged myself upright, my shoulders sagging with exhaustion.

The wailing continued, tearing through the space and lodging inside me, making me feel tenser than I already felt.

To divert my mind, I thought of the name Job sahib had given me. I took a deep breath and whispered: *Maria*. The music of this new appellation soothed me. It conveyed hints of the grandeur of a faraway kingdom, so much so that I fancied myself attired in a silk sari, dripping with jewels, perched on a throne. I laughed to myself at the absurdity of such an image, a laugh drenched with deep sorrow. After a while I fell asleep.

As the day dawned, golden sunshine flooded the room through the gaps in the door. Sal's voice boomed good-naturedly outside.

"Up yet, Maria?"

He sounded as gentle as when he'd fed me on the boat. Again my new name brought with it a glimpse of hope. Maria could do anything. At a minimum I could start this day afresh, in the company of a man who'd called me sister. I also made up my mind to search for Job sahib and speak with him about my concerns. His mere presence would comfort me.

As I rolled out from under the quilt, I noticed the mosquito bites on my arm. "I'm up, bhai." I called to my new brother.

"I could show you around this place. Will you come now?"

"I am not ready to leave my quarters yet, bhai."

"I'll come back in a while, then."

I folded the quilt and put it away, veiled my head, flung my sari tighter around my shoulders, and did my morning ablutions. A short time later, I emerged from my room. It struck me hard in the white clarity of daylight that I was in a strange place, with no one to call my own. Yet I also knew that if my in-laws traced me, they'd hack me to death, so being alone here with these strangers seemed safer.

Sal's all-white garment contrasted with the bronze of his skin. Appearing clean and well rested, he smiled as pleasantly as at the time we'd met on the boat. He led me across a large well-kept ground, past a well and a champa tree brimming with fragrant yellow flowers. Somewhere a pigeon cooed. I looked up momentarily at the bright sky where clouds floated soft and serene.

"The sahibs are in a meeting," Sal said. "Perfect time for you to get to know our Factory."

With his homely ways, Sal put me at ease.

Hearing the swish of a skirt, I turned to see a maidservant emerging from the servants' hovels wearing an ankle-length black dress and carrying a long-handled broom of twigs, the ornaments at her ankles jangling. Solemn-faced but graceful, a black scarf covering her head, silver armlets over her arms, she appeared to be young, about nineteen years of age. I was excited at the presence of another woman. She must be a stranger like me, I thought, thrilled by the prospect of making friends with someone who was in the same situation as I. No such luck. She marched past us without acknowledging my presence; my heart sank. There was nothing friendly about her. In my society, women usually sought each other's company, but this woman disappeared behind a rhododendron bush without even looking my way.

"That's Proteema, the sweeper," Sal said. "We call her Teema. She lives next door to you."

What had made Teema cry so pitifully the night before? Who had abandoned her? What secrets did this place hold? Secrecy bothered me, like a thorn stuck in my foot.

"Why didn't she stop to talk with us?"

Sal's gaze shifted. "She's late in getting started this morning. By now, she should have swept the yard. Here you must get your work done on time, or the sahibs will call you lazy, and you won't get your wage."

As we trooped through the tiled part of the courtyard, a pink-necked duck, which must have flown up from the river, appeared. It quacked and hurried off at our presence. I was about to chase the duck in a playful manner when Sal steered me away.

"Another house rule," he said. "The sahibs don't like us to amuse ourselves when we're on duty. We have to keep our heads low and behave like we don't exist. Maintain the place, take care of the sahibs' needs, and don't be seen or heard. If you do . . ."

Job sahib doesn't want me to be invisible, I said to myself, neglecting to listen to the rest of Sal's comment. *Job sahib had called me beautiful.*

We climbed a steep, stone staircase, reached a winding verandah, and glided through a door which led to an entrance hall, the 'public section', Sal said. We peered from behind silk curtains into a smoke-filled lounging area illuminated by several windows and smelling of tobacco and rose water. Several Englishmen reclined against yellow-and-gold bolsters placed on the carpet. They argued in English, taking sips of a beverage from ornate cups, their silver hookahs resting nearby. I searched the faces and every corner of the room. Job sahib wasn't there.

At Sal's signal, we slipped away into a covered passageway. "They were talking about being underpaid," Sal whispered. "Underpaid! They get room and board and luxury, and get to act like pampered princes."

A group of four Englishmen swept out of the hall, one humming a tune, another scowling at a shaft of bright sunlight. We stepped aside to let them pass. All wore breeches, broad hats, and unbuttoned doublets. I liked the air of freedom they had about them—open, expansive, unfettered—as though they were masters of their environment. Someday I would walk proud like they did.

I smiled at an Englishman as I would smile at anyone in my village upon meeting them and mumbled a greeting in Bangla. Short and heavy, with a scowling pink face, a wide linen collar round his neck, and carrying an umbrella, he cast a red-eyed glance at me.

"That's Arthur sahib," Sal whispered, staring at his back. "He always carries an umbrella to ward off sunshine or the lightest drizzle. He's been sick for days. English people always seem to be catching something or the other."

"Why?"

"They can't tolerate the water or the food. Our steamy climate is too difficult for them to handle. It kills whatever appetite they have. They die like flies, suffering from gout, bloody flux, fever, drunkenness. Poor creatures! Most of them are still in their twenties. They're supposed to serve for five years, but most don't survive more than three monsoons."

"Why do they come here then?"

"Some are lured by the prospect of not having any responsibility, you know, being away from home, drinking like the world's ending, and going to the brothel; but mostly they want money. Our silks and spices sell for high profit in the markets of London. Muslin alone can make an Englishman fabulously rich. They can return to their home in England, carrying with them textile goods worth a bagful of pounds, that's their currency, and retire with a nice little fortune. Some buy big houses and entertain titled friends. Some have the opportunity to serve the King."

"They get so much from here, but they treat us like . . ."

"Right." Sal interrupted. "You must know how to behave in front of a sahib; keep your head low when you run into one. Don't stare. Speak only when you're spoken to. Don't show your teeth when smiling. We're like specks of dirt. They can flick us off whenever they like."

My mouth tasted sour; I almost lost my footing but kept the turbulence I felt to myself. The palace had much going on behind the scenes, bad manners being the least of it. In order to survive, even in my constricted role, I needed to figure out what really went on here, and as I could already understand, proficiency in English was the key to everything.

I asked Sal if he'd teach me the language.

"Yes, sure, I'll help you, if we can manage any free time."

As we strolled further, I learned many other things from Sal. Emperor Aurangzeb, whose name meant 'Ornament to the Throne', ruled Hindustan, much of the northern and eastern regions and even parts of the south, from his palace in Delhi. An ascetic man, given to reading the Koran daily, he was known to be partial to Muslims. They were given the first chance at employment at the Royal Court; Hindus were left out. Though Sal was a Muslim, he found this unfair. On the other hand, our local governor, Nawab Haider Ali, who administered this district from his seat in this very town, Cossimbazar, was 'kind of heart'. He welcomed people of all faiths as his ally.

I had barely digested this bit of information, when Sal said, "Now let me tell you about your duties. You'll work as part of a team of four khansamas, male cooks. Tariq will come down shortly and show you what needs to be done. Follow his orders to the letter. He's the king among us servants. He has one eye, but double the ambition of the rest of us." Sal paused. "I'll now go to milk the buffaloes. Is there anything you need?"

The mere mention of Tariq turned my stomach. But I wouldn't let him stop me from pursuing what I had in mind.

"I can't help but think about my mother," I said to Sal. "She must be having a difficult time believing I'm dead. I'd like to send her a message."

"That might not be easy. Although we have an efficient postal system here and our couriers, dak runners, go all over, carrying dispatches to and from the Factory, we servants aren't allowed to use that service. You can well imagine what Tariq will do, can't you? Besides, the couriers charge a fortune. They need money for the passage and their job is dangerous. They could be attacked by a tiger or a robber. No, Maria, much as I would like to . . ."

"You have a family, you said."

"Oh, yes. Whenever I manage to get time off, I visit my parents. I'm blessed with three sisters. One is your age and the other two are older."

"Then perhaps you understand," I said.

He hesitated for a while, then reconsidered his stand. "Alright, I'll speak with Abidur who's a friend, but . . ."

I slipped my hands inside my sari, and fingered the perspiration-drenched, 'five-formed' pendant on a gold chain set with rubies, pearls, diamonds, emeralds, and lapis lazuli. My husband's kin had snatched all the jewelry bequeathed to me by my mother, aunts, and grandmother, save for a pendant that had remained hidden under my sari. Now I unfastened the gold chain, took it off my neck, and held it in my hand. The pendant seized the brilliant light of the day and shone like a miniature sun.

"Tell Abidur to show this to my mother," I said to Sal in a broken voice. "She'll know I'm still alive. He can then sell it and share the money with you."

"In the name of Allah! This is pure gold. Are you sure you want to part with it?"

I nodded, gazing longingly at the ornament, the only memento of home in my possession.

Sal closed his fingers reluctantly around the pendant and pocketed it. "Please don't speak a word about this to anyone. If Tariq hears about this, then we'll both lose our jobs."

Sal was about to turn when I stopped him. "Where is Job sahib?" I asked, even as I felt my cheeks flush.

"He's gone to the Royal Palace." I listened intently as Sal described Job sahib's daily life. The sahib had become a close ally of Nawab Haider Ali. The Dutch and the French, the sahib's competitors, also wanted the Nawab's ear. However, the sahib, who was always thinking how he could further the interests of the Company and would go any distance for that, had won. He often accompanied the Nawab on his hunting expeditions, mounting a royal elephant to go bird-shooting or tiger hunting. In the evening, they drank spirits and played cards. Sal looked me full in the face. "You won't see him much, if at all."

I cast my gaze to the ground. "But . . . on the boat . . ."

Sal gave a smile of derision. "You didn't catch everything. I overheard the sahib ordering Tariq to take good care of you in his absence. You'll have adequate food, shelter, and clothing."

"I thought I'd see the sahib once in a while."

"Don't count on it. Tariq, who is our supervisor, monopolizes the sahib, so he'll always be more powerful than us. If he sees you as a threat, he'll make your life miserable." Sal paused. "My dear behen, there's something else I must warn you about. Job sahib can't take a local woman as a companion, at least within this compound. That's a strict order from the Council of Directors—no mixing of colors, no getting close with the kala —the dark people." Sal explained that the Council of Directors sat in Surat and oversaw all English Factories in our land. "They're cruel authoritarians. Even Job sahib, who's a member of the Council, can't break a rule set by it. He cannot consort with you."

A sigh escaped me, but I managed to keep still. "I was a high-caste girl in my village. People looked up to me. They praised me for my light skin tone."

"Here you belong to the dark race and you're thought to be inferior."

"But Job sahib said he'd protect me."

"He'll soon be too busy for that, behen. A boatful of young, fair, and unmarried English ladies will be landing here soon." Sal talked of pale-skinned, pink-cheeked, and well-polished women arriving in Cossimbazar, smiling and flouncing in their fine gowns, hoping to catch a sahib's eye. Job sahib was the most eligible bachelor. "The boat is jokingly called the 'Fishing Fleet'. The sahibs are all waiting for it."

Dust and grime covered my body and shaved head. My homespun sari was stained, my face beaded with perspiration.

"There'll be a lovely young lady who will soon steal Job Charnock's heart." Sal said.

FOUR

A day rolled by.

At night, lying on my meager bed, the quilt wrapped around me, my eyes closed, I heard the noise of someone pushing through the door. A thief? A drunkard? A wild beast? Shuddering, I made an attempt to rise, only to be thrown back on the bed when a heavy body landed on top of me. In the pitch blackness, I couldn't make out the intruder's face. He reeked of alcohol. I tried to shout for help, but his hand pressed down hard on my mouth, nearly crushing my jawbone. I made an attempt to push him away, but I was no match for him in size or strength. With his free hand, he began to work up my thighs.

Although I had no weapon in my possession, my hand was free. I picked up the wick lamp lying next to the bed. It had been extinguished only a few minutes ago, so the oil was still hot even though the amount was negligible. Sensing my chance, I threw the hot oil in the face of my molester. He screamed and cursed in English.

A sahib!

He lurched to his feet and stumbled out the door, crying out in pain.

I rose to my feet, my heart thumping, and shut the door quickly, securing it with a piece of log, even though I wasn't sure it would prevent another incident of this kind. My mind buzzed, trying to address a stream of disturbing questions: Which sahib was it? What if he returned? I lay down again, pulling the quilt over me and making a resolve to leave this place as soon as possible. After only a few minutes of sleep, I woke with a start. No intruders this time, only a dog groaning. The night was cool, but my body was soaked with perspiration.

I rose before dawn and walked to the river ghat. Although my shoulders ached from lack of sleep, my mind began to work. With Job sahib out of reach, to whom should I relate last night's incident? What if the attacker returned?

I climbed down the steps to the water, still fully clothed, and waded in up to my chest, the tepid water bubbling about me. Ladling water with both hands and rinsing my face, I tried to wipe out of my mind the horror of last night. Not long ago, I used to descend the graying ghat steps of my village into the divine stream which always purified me. Giggling, I would swallow sweet-tasting, life-sustaining water, my face warmed by the sun. My mother would stand on the top step of the ghat and watch me play. I'd assumed those days of laughing, shouting, singing, and bathing would go on forever. But they hadn't.

My sari dripping wet and clinging to my body, I wandered toward a shack situated by the palm grove, used for the changing of clothes. I had no other clothes to change into, but I was happy for the privacy in which to dry my body.

I heard voices speaking English and looked around.

Hidden by palm fronds, two of our sahibs were talking with a local man. Clad in a chintz robe, a strand of pearls around his neck, he had a well-fed appearance and eyes that glinted with greed. Add to that the gold belt around his waist, and I knew for sure that he belonged to the wealthy merchant class. From the way the three men huddled together, the concentration on their faces dissolving into sneaky glances, I suspected they were up to some mischief. What if they spotted me? I could be severely punished for being a witness to a clandestine activity. I dried my body quickly. The morning wind warm against my face, I strove to walk past the group unnoticed, but one of the sahibs turned, spotted me, and gave me a disdainful sidelong glance. Keeping my head down, I headed toward the Factory.

I slipped into the kitchen, a spacious room crammed with cooking vessels, brass utensils, silverware, and several earthen stoves—chulahs— placed directly on the ground. Part of a low worktable was crammed with guavas, mangoes, pineapples, and a stack of cut sugar canes, the remainder piled high with freshly harvested herbs and other edible greens. A sweet scent emanated from the fruits, a pungent one from the herbs, and they mingled with the smoky odor from the chulah.

The four khansamas were already busy building the fire, rinsing the rice, grinding the wheat berries, and sorting through the herbs. They scarcely raised their eyes to me but continued chatting amongst themselves in brotherly closeness. I stood alone, the only female in the room, baldheaded and shrinking, my stomach fluttering.

The size of this kitchen, not to mention that of this entire trading post, unnerved me. How I wished I could sail back to my village and be amongst the members of my family, loved and known within the coziness of a small hut.

Hearing the sound of a greeting, I came back to the present. The oldest cook, he introduced himself as Idris, pointed to a pile of leafy greens on the work table. "You're to chop these, Maria." Short, sturdy, and gray-haired, he had a burnt-copper complexion. His mouth turned rigid as he added, "Tariq didn't like it that you were late."

O, Lord Shiva! What punishment would befall me now? I picked up the knife and minced the greens furiously. The male cooks, continued chatting amongst themselves.

Finally, when I couldn't bear the loneliness any longer, I asked in a voice that rose above the chatter in the room; I asked no one in particular, "So how do you like working for the English East India Company?"

No one replied. Didn't I deserve an answer? Well, I'd wait until the right moment came and insert myself into the conversation. Soon enough, the men began to babble amongst themselves, this time about the sahibs: who gave the most bakhshish, who drank the most alcohol, who smelled the worst, who had the foulest temper. My ears pricked up. Would these men reveal the molester among the sahibs?

Instead, I learned that the English East India Company was here to grab as many commodities as it could—opium, what they called their "dream drug", silk, cotton, black pepper, nutmeg, and vegetable dyes—to sell them at a profit in England. They would do so in exchange of gold and silver, much in demand in our land.

Detecting a gap in the conversation, I gave an account of what I'd seen this morning at the shore.

Idris raised his eyes to me. "Be careful," he said, lowering his voice to a whisper. "You might be accused of eavesdropping. You could even be shot dead."

"They were speaking English," I said quietly. "I didn't understand a word of it."

"Well, what she saw isn't unusual," another man said. He had wild curly hair, bronze skin, and keen eyes. "I am Jas," he said to me softly as he scrubbed a pot. "The sahibs have a strong personal motive for leaving their 'dear old England,' and coming to this 'dreadful, boring post'. They're here to fill their pockets. Believe it or not, the Factors have private businesses of their own on the side. Those bastards were haggling with the local merchants. They buy huge amounts of goods for a few coins and ship them to London on their own. Oh, the profit they make by robbing the local weavers, dyers, metal workers, and shopkeepers."

"Does Job sahib . . .?"

Before I could finish my question, Bir jumped in. He was thin-bodied, amiable, high-spirited, younger than the other three, and handsome. "I know it on good authority that Job sahib doesn't engage in such practice. They jokingly call him 'Honest Mr. Charnock' behind his back, those traitors to the Company. It's a pity he knows all about the smuggling, stealing and poaching of local merchants that goes on, but he still insists he can work through it all to make the Company prosper. He trusts people too much, especially his own. That's his weakness and I think that'll be his downfall."

"Our idealistic leader is cheating himself," Idris scoffed as he rinsed a pot. "I was cleaning his chamber when I saw a leather-bound diary sitting on his desk and managed to browse a page. Although I read some English, I couldn't follow all of it. There was something like: 'Even though I am the Officer-in-Chief, the Company pays me a pittance and I resent that. Twenty pounds a year might be a fortune for the lowly people here, but a joke for someone from England, someone of my caliber, someone who serves the Crown.'" Idris shook his head in disgust, picked up another pot, and began rinsing it.

"Haughty, isn't he?" Pratap, muscular and quick-moving, his skin like polished mahogany, sorted through a pile of fresh herbs. "He has a mean spirit that occasionally comes out. The other day he exploded when I was late bringing him his hookah. He was stumbling all over the room, drunk."

My fingers loosened their grip on the knife. I'd seen Job sahib's eyes fill with righteous anger at the priest on the cremation site. I'd detected arrogance in his manner and seen condescension in his gaze when speaking with people of my village. But to treat a servant poorly? I didn't expect that of him. The diary, however, interested me. I wasn't allowed in the sahib's chamber, only Idris and Tariq were. Although I didn't read English, I wanted to grasp what he wrote in his unguarded moments.

"Oh, maybe the sahib is feeling pressured," I said, trying to help figure out Job sahib and secure my position here.

"Of course he's feeling the pressure," Idris said. "This Factory is his life, but it's losing money, and he has to pay heavy taxes to the Nawab for trading rights."

"Job sahib is a bit aloof," Pratap said. "He dresses like us, not like the rest of his clan. He says he prefers lighter clothing because it keeps him cool. The other Factors respect him, but they don't identify with him. They think he's not as English as they are. I heard this from the keeper of a punch house."

"A punch house? What's that?"

"Curious, aren't we?" Pratap said, stacking a set of clean pots. "Punch—five. The drink they serve in a punch house is made of five ingredients: arrack or palm wine, lime juice, sugar, water, and nutmeg; strong, strong stuff. It has a mixture of tastes, sweet, sour, and bitter. After work the sahibs meet in the punch house by the river and take glass after glass of this drink. The keeper catches some of their drunken chatter. Job sahib doesn't go there too often. He says drinking parties don't interest him. The other sahibs play at cards, gab, and sometimes get into a fight."

Idris turned to me. "But they don't fight inside this compound. You're safe here."

"Are you sure I am safe here?" Trembling, I gave an account of the intruder in my room the night before.

"This should not happen," Idris said emphatically. "I'll ask Tariq to install a heavier door in your room. And we'll check to see which one of the—"

"Suppose we find out," Pratap interrupted, "what can we do? We're the servile class, we can't complain, we can't accuse anyone."

"Will you check this beef stew, Maria?" Idris pointed to a pot simmering on the hearth, a white veil of scented steam escaping into the air.

"I can't, I'm a Brahmin. We don't go near beef."

"Forget how you were raised," Idris said. "You'll have to leave those caste rules behind to work for the English."

I bent down and smelled the stew. It nauseated me; it also made me realize what I would have to sacrifice in order to survive. Once again, I wanted to leave, go someplace miles away from here.

"Well, the stew needs to be simmered longer." I tried hard not to wrinkle my nose in distaste. "I can tell by the color of the sauce and the raw smell."

In the next several hours, I stirred the pots, sped up and down the kitchen to pick up this spice and that, all morning and through the afternoon, feeling feverish from the pace. Then, after all the dishes had been prepared, I swept and mopped the floor till it gleamed. Despite the fear, fatigue, and even disgust that had crept inside me, I felt a certain sweetness swell inside, as though I was somewhat in control of my life.

The supper bell rang, but I didn't follow the sound. As a woman, I could do the menial tasks but wasn't considered fit to serve the sahibs. Frowning, I let my annoyance known to Idris.

"It's a custom of the Mughal Court; we must follow it." According to him, the regional Nawab employed ten male food servers, each one assigned to hover over a member of the royal family.

I thought the real cause lay elsewhere. Tariq, who saw me as a threat, didn't want me to be visible. Discomfort was a lump in my throat; I swallowed it.

The khansamas, dressed in white muslin uniforms and colorful head-dresses, arranged fully loaded silver platters on trays. Led by Idris, they entered the dining hall. I stole a peek from behind a curtain. About twenty sahibs streamed into the hall and arranged themselves around a large, rectangular table. The air throbbed with the aroma of spices.

I noticed a hazel-eyed man with auburn-hair, a round body, and a patch on his forehead. "Who is that sahib, with the patch?" I whispered to Bir who was on his way back to the kitchen.

"Francis sahib. He burned himself on the fumes of his hookah pipe last night."

"No! I believe he was burned when I threw hot lamp oil into his face last night."

Bir regarded me in surprise, but then his face changed. "Well, I guess we know how he spent his evening, don't we?" His laughter was sour.

How could a Factor get away with abusing a servant girl? The chair at the head of the table remained empty. Job sahib wasn't present. "Where's the Chief?" I asked Bir.

"Oh, he's still at the Nawab's Palace. But the Second and the Third

Factors are present. Notice how the sahibs sit—according to their rank and seniority. You can tell who's more important than whom. Francis sahib sits farthest from the head of the table; he's the least powerful."

And yet he could barge into my room at night with the intention of violating me. If he was the lowliest man at this table, I was lower still. He could hurt me and get away with it.

A moment later, I recovered myself. I might be the newest and the least experienced, the greenest guava, as we called such a person, but I was alive. I'd been saved by an Englishman and given a shelter of sorts here. Someday I'd be riper, rise higher, don a beautiful sari, and be allowed to serve, Tariq be damned! And on that day, I'd be offered safer accommodation by the same higher-up.

The sahibs guzzled glasses of liquor that had recently arrived by ship from England; they shouted rudely at the servers for extra helpings, as though they hadn't eaten in days. Idris translated for me. "*More rice, boy! Kala! You don't hear me? Have you already gone deaf? And what's that on your platter? Banana flower, you said?*"

In between serving, Idris came to the kitchen to refill the platters. His lips curled with annoyance and he tipped his head toward me, saying quietly, "I hate it when they call us *boy*. I hate it when they make fun of our food. I hate it worse when they call us *dark-skinned* in our own land."

With the meal finally over, I suggested to Idris that brass basins laden with scented water be sent for the sahibs to rinse their fingers. It was a custom from my village, usually extended to honored guests, and I was eager to introduce this new ritual, a chance to prove my worth. At first, Idris said no, but I insisted, and he finally gave in.

I watched from behind the curtain.

Arthur sahib smiled and said, "A little odd, but I'll try." As he dipped his finger into the basin, I felt a surge of power within.

Job sahib entered the hall with powerful strides. I felt a rush of adoration inside me upon seeing his kind and familiar face. The gleam of his long white coat added to his dignity. With Idris interpreting I learned that he'd already supped at the Royal Palace. All the Factors greeted him and he acknowledged the greetings.

A glance at the bowls of scented water and he asked in a light voice, "What's this new ritual?"

Idris explained. Job sahib listened without commenting. He sat down at the table and joined the small talk. According to Idris, it centered on various religious groups that existed side by side in this land and whether there was any discord among them. The sahibs argued in a boisterous manner, mocking, gesturing, and cutting each other off. The discussion took a turn that must not have pleased Job sahib, for a look of annoyance crossed his face. Head lowered, lips pursed, his face a mask, he sat quietly, as though not willing to reveal what brewed inside him. For an instant he looked alone, private, tortured. Then he raised his head and rejoined the group.

Here was my opportunity to convince Job sahib of my worth, the fact that I'd done much of the dinner preparation. I wanted to be visible and to be listened to. I stepped in through the doorway of the dining room, knowing full well I was breaking a taboo. Busy conversing with his subordinates, Job sahib didn't notice me. As I picked up a basin, I intentionally spilled a little murky water on the floor, creating a tiny black pool.

Job sahib turned. "Ah, Maria, are you the mastermind behind this? Did you also introduce the finger-bowl ritual?" He spoke to me in Bangla, his tone one of pride, his expression now neutral.

I nodded respectfully. Although I was oily, sweaty, and dusty, the compliment stirred deep feelings of both shyness and confidence in me.

"Perhaps you can join in our discussion and tell us whether or not Hindus and Muslims in your village treat each other well."

I so liked being invited by the sahib that a smile bloomed on my face. As I tried to formulate an answer, the lesson my father had once given me flashed in my mind. We Hindus made up the majority of the population in our village, but on occasion our Mughal rulers forced some to convert to Islam. Still harmony prevailed among us and the Muslims. We dressed differently, worshipped differently, ate different food, but shared a common tongue. I remembered how, when the drums announced a holiday, we all ran to the temple ground like we were brothers and sisters.

"I couldn't trust you that day," Job told me as we talked of the past one warm evening.

He had leaned toward her, but she remained silent, eyes downcast. Was the girl tongue-tied, he'd thought? She certainly didn't have much to say. How would she manage in the Factory? Had he made the right decision by employing her? And how would she protect herself from her husband's relatives who were believed to be in town? She went alone to bathe in the river in the morning. What if they got her then? He couldn't stop them; as a foreign trader, he had little power, not as powerful as she seemed to think. He would give her time to adjust.

I looked at him, eager to speak, but was overwhelmed by shyness and timidity. Words came to my lips, then they flew away, as it were, before my voice could give them color and life. As I stood there, flustered, feeling light on my feet, Tariq stepped in and engaged Job sahib on the subject, gesturing with a hand and speaking with an exaggerated air of authority.

How could I have missed such a splendid opportunity? I retreated to the kitchen and tidied up the place till it looked spotless. Well, perhaps another time. I imagined myself sitting alone with Job sahib and discussing the intricacies of my culture while a pleasant breeze cooled us. I badly wanted to influence him as Tariq did, for my survival, if nothing else.

Idris' whisper broke into my daydream. The sahibs were cooing over the evening's meal.

"A new hand in the kitchen? The sauce is smoother."

"For once the pulao hasn't been undercooked."

"The vegetable stew went down easily. I think I may survive after all."

I smiled a little. I had inherited a flair for using spices from my mother. I had also developed a sense of timing and a sense of smell under her tutelage, not to mention the special order in which ingredients must be added. Silently, I thanked her. Perhaps my cooking skills would save me after all.

"Now, listen to this." Idris smiled meaningfully and translated a remark from Francis sahib. "I can hardly eat this food. Send that ugly, skinny girl home."

I had finished washing the last vessel when Bir said, "I caught some gossip. The sahibs were talking. Your husband's brother is in town looking for you. He's asking everyone, but rest assured, he can't get in here."

The walls collapsed before my eyes. Where would I, a shabbily-clothed, rustic girl hide? How did Bipin figure out I was living in this town? Did he intercept the courier sent by me? Did he and his wretched family torment my parents following the courier's visit, darkening their days even more? Did my mother ever guess that I was still alive?

I stumbled out of the room.

FIVE

From that day on, my stomach lurched every time I remembered that my brother-in-law was near, but I pressed on, performing my duties as best as I could. One morning, I donned a plain yellow sari, the color of spring. Perhaps due to the golden praise I'd earned for my cooking and at Sal's urging Tariq had bought me this coarse cotton garb whose roughness I felt against my skin, the cheapest item he could have found. It could be my greed, but I wanted a finer sari, perhaps several, in a variety of colors. Still I couldn't complain. Tariq had also installed a bigger, heavier door for me.

For the first time since my arrival here a month or so ago, alone in my room, I picked up the ornate looking-glass, small and oval, with a handle made of animal horn and a frame encrusted with shiny stones. Sal had given me this expensive gift, perhaps borrowed money from a friend for it, because of my progress in English; he'd heard me practice the tongue throughout the day. As I looked into the glass, I couldn't recognize the reflection I saw in it. The dark eyes had grown bigger, deeper in their sadness. The face looked gaunt, the once-flawless, 'soft as muslin' complexion bereft of its sheen. Shorn of hair, my head appeared huge. Anger flared inside me as I visualized my husband's aunt pushing me down onto the floor prior to the sati ritual. I cringed at the cold metal touch of the sharp blade on my skin as she shaved my head, shearing my locks of shiny black hair. My glorious hair showered over me, falling dead to the floor. Tears sprung up in my eyes as I heard my mother's voice from a long-ago childhood day: "Your hair, your womanhood". The only consolation I now had were the signs of new growth, spiky on my scalp, like coarse grass.

My aunties used to call me lotus-faced, insisting I brought a calm grace to every place I went. That lotus bud had gone into hiding. My full lips, once described as a 'slice of ripe mango', looked chapped. I tried to smile, to bring the ripeness back to my lips, but to no avail. I, who had always been slender, looked pitifully emaciated. I'd lost a profound part of the woman I had been.

I stowed away the looking-glass.

In the kitchen, I felt glad to have an arduous task at hand: pounding the lentils in a large mortar and later cooking it with ghee, palm sugar, and water to prepare a sweetmeat to be served as part of the sahibs' mid-day meal. My arm muscles ached and hands throbbed as the lentil grounds gathered at the bottom of the mortar. The monotony gave me an opportunity to think back to my family days, the happy chatter, the warmth, the aroma as my mother cooked milk and palm sugar together, a less elaborate and more affordable dish. Much later, we'd eagerly reach for the tray laden with diamond-shaped, brown, luscious sweetmeats.

Idris shoved small pieces of wood inside the stove. "Well, the chulah is ready for you."

I picked up a pot, placed the ingredients in it, and drew near the stove. Seeing the yellow flames, listening to the crackling of logs, and feeling the heat on my face, I went back to the memories of another fire by the riverside not long ago.

I stood immobile.

"Are you all right?" Idris asked affectionately.

I nodded, touched by his concern, and placed the pot on the chulah with a thud. Head downcast, I dribbled ghee down the inside of the pot.

"It's hard for me to be in the kitchen and not think about my mother," I said. "It tears me apart. Do you have a family?"

"Yes, I have a wife and two sons," Idris replied, despair in his voice. "But how often do I see them? I seldom have enough money to pay for the boat passage. The sahibs do not know, nor would they care that I sit up half the night worrying about them. My only comfort is practising the flute, when time allows."

"Will you do a performance for us sometime?"

"I wish I could, but I am only allowed to play when we have honored guests."

I hid my disappointment. "How did you learn to play the flute?"

"Even though I'm a Muslim, when I was a young boy, I took up the flute. They say if you master that instrument, you could change the weather. Well, I'm not that good yet. I'm sure you're quite familiar with the stories of Lord Krishna playing the flute and attracting pretty maidens. Now that has worked for me. On a full moon night, in an empty field near my village, I was pouring out my feelings through my beloved flute when a beautiful young girl came by and sat down on the ground to listen.

"When I finished, she burst into tears. That's how I met my wife, Nazma. I call her my moonshine. You know, I haven't seen her in weeks." Idris backed out of the room, perhaps to hide his tears.

To the pot I added raisins and palm sugar as sweeteners, sliced almonds to lift the texture, and ground cardamom pods to inject flavor. I could see my mother instructing me to make slow circles with a spoon, so the mass didn't stick to the pot. I could hear her saying that these circular motions would infuse the dish with extra flavor. Once the preparation was complete, I scraped the sticky mass onto a platter, licking off a small lump that clung to my finger. Given that we weren't supposed to eat the food meant for the sahibs, I took wicked pleasure in its dense sweetness.

Later, as I began rinsing the soiled breakfast dishes, Bir said, a mischievous twinkle in his eyes, "That Arthur sahib, the Third Factor, he shouldn't be so critical."

"Why do you say that?"

"Well, you're very creative when it comes to greeting in English and that's been noticed. The sahib made fun of you. It's 'How are you?' not 'You are how?'"

"But . . . but . . . in Bangla, we say it like that," I tossed out, my face growing hot with embarrassment.

"Also it's 'Good Evening', not 'Evening Good'."

Bir laughed congenially. "Learn proper English, Maria. The sahibs think you're stupid every time you open your mouth."

I wanted to shout out to Arthur sahib: *I'm not stupid by any means. I don't know your customs or your language. Give me time.* In the afternoon, I took a short break from my kitchen work and went to the courtyard, the only free time I would have during the working hours. My legs ached from laboring for hours on end, and my eyes were teary from the smoke of the chulah. Every afternoon Sal and I sneaked away to this courtyard for my tutoring sessions. We'd sit on the earth, flicking off flies and shading our eyes against the sun's rays. Sal would teach me routine exchanges of English pleasantries and I would mouth the phrases. Some sounded stilted to Sal's ear, others were unintelligible. Still, I persisted. My body would bend from exhaustion, but I wouldn't let Sal leave until I'd mastered several new sentences. We laughed together at my tortured phrases and mangled pronunciation.

Sal had also taught me English manners. "An impatient bunch, they are, the English," he told me. "Even when you become proficient in

English, don't try to give them a long explanation. Answer a question in as few words as possible. Or greet them and move on."

As I loitered in the courtyard and waited impatiently for Sal, I wondered whether he had forgotten about our lessons. My English lessons mustn't be delayed. After a while, fatigued, I sat on the ground under a brown-barked sheesham tree flowering pink and fragrant. As I shut my eyes in the shade of the tree, images of home filled me with yearning for what I had left behind. The wavy green of the forest, the golden paddy, the wild elephants that stomped the valleys with their large gray feet, but, most of all, I hungered for my family, our mud-and-clay hut, sparsely furnished, but pulsating with light and warmth. Suppose I walked in through the door of our hut and stepped onto the cool clean floor this very minute and cried out, "Ma! Baba!" My bed-ridden father would attempt to rise, feeble, with a shrunken body, alert to the sound of my voice. His eyes would come alive. My mother would ask in her usual gentle tone from the kitchen, "Moorti?" Shouts and shrieks would fill the house as my little brothers would race to the door, calling, "Didi, didi."

Gazing up, I sent a prayer skyward. May the courier return and deliver me a dispatch from my family. May I join them soon. May we all smile again.

I felt the tug of a sudden gust of wind, opened my eyes, and saw Sal, accompanied by another man. The second man, taller, older, and heavier, sported a full beard. He carried a bamboo rod in his hand, closed at either end, the kind used for long distance delivery of important missives.

I jumped to my feet. "Afternoon good," I called out to Sal in English and realized, almost instantly, the silly mistake I'd made.

A shadow hung over Sal's face. "This is Abidur. He's returned from a visit with your mother."

My heart beat faster. Abidur raised his free hand to his forehead in the gesture of a greeting. Strange, he didn't wave a letter at me. Nor did he speak. He simply looked down at the ground.

"How's my mother?"

"She was lying in bed with the chills when I arrived. I talked with her, but she didn't believe a word I said. She thought I was trying to deceive her. 'What are you here for?' she asked. 'My daughter is dead. Her ashes have been sprinkled on the river. Please show her respect and stop making up stories.'"

My stomach tensed. "Did you show her the pendant?"

"I did. She looked at it, touched it, and screamed at me: 'You must have snatched it from her neck at the chita. She would never give it away.'" Abidur paused, as though words had frozen in his throat. "Then your mother began to weep. Your little brothers came bounding into the room, accompanied by a neighbor woman who seemed to be taking care of them. 'My sister is a sati,' the older of the two boys said. 'She's in heaven. She has everything there. We miss her, but our neighbors give us rice, fruit, and vegetables in her honor. We get to eat more.'

"I whispered to the neighbor woman that you were alive. She replied in a low voice, 'She's a fallen sati? Do you know what they do to such a woman? She would be spat on, cursed, shunned, violated. Better that she's dead.'"

"And my father?" I barely got the words out. "Did you see him? Did he ask for me? Is he well?"

"He, too, was lying in bed. He watched me and clearly wished to speak a few words, but he was too weak to make a sound. I saw him fighting his tears. At that point, I wished everyone peace and good health and left." Abidur paused. "On the way back to the ferry, I was approached by a man who demanded to know who I was and what I was doing there. I said I was a relative of your father and had just visited him, but he didn't believe me. He began to abuse me loudly. I ran away from there. He followed right behind, but couldn't keep up with me; after a while I lost sight of him."

That must have been Bipin. Blankly, I stared, as the landscape emptied before my eyes. What did I have left in life? I felt Sal's hand on my back.

"We must be going, behen." Sal made a half-turn. "I'll see you in the morning."

Abidur rummaged in his pocket and pressed the gold pendant on my palm.

"No, no, please, take it," I said. "This is all I can offer."

"Neither Sal nor I can accept it," Abidur replied softly. "It's yours. May the light of Allah shine on you."

With numb fingers, I clasped the pendant around my throat. My skin burned at its touch; I slipped it beneath my clothing.

A moment of reality burst open upon me. It would be nearly impossible for a stranger to convince my family of what had really happened. Although I wanted them to know I was all right, that I was being cared for, I couldn't go back. If I did, then my family would cease to receive gestures of kindness from our neighbors, so necessary for their survival.

What would happen to them then? I felt bereft. The very foundation of my life, that which had sustained me up to this point—family, tradition, and community—had slipped away from me. I wanted to cry out, vent my unhappiness, and unburden myself to whoever would pay heed. I had no one. I didn't deserve this cruel fate.

After spending a sleepless night, I returned to the kitchen in the morning. Alone in the room, I peeled and sliced a ripe, big pineapple, glancing frequently at the door. Sal usually tended the buffalos and milked them; then he stopped by the kitchen to drop off a bucket of rich, fresh milk and have a brief word with me. Today I wished to open my heart to him, I was sure he would understand. The doorway remained empty; not a soul peeked through it, and an odd sensation gnawed at my heart.

Idris drifted in, but he ignored me and crossed the room toward the chulahs, his mind elsewhere.

"Have you seen Sal?" I asked.

Idris gave me a sharp, quick glance. "Sal has been dismissed."

"But why?"

"Tariq found out he'd used the courier for personal services and showed him the door, even confiscated the half-month's salary due to him."

"Wait—it was I who—"

"Tariq wanted to get rid of you, too; you seem to vex him, but fortunately, Job sahib intervened. He'd returned from the Royal Palace last night when he heard the story. Sal was being escorted out of the gate. I could only have a brief word with him. Sahib wanted his tobacco pipe right away. I overheard him saying to Tariq that you were new here, didn't know the rules and shouldn't be sent away. He had no choice but to retain you, but he looked cross, as cross as I've ever seen. I wouldn't be surprised if . . ."

I considered my future and that of Sal. "Did you ask Sal what he'd do?"

"He said he'd be fine."

"But how? He has no money."

Idris turned away without answering. I stood numb by the chulah. The fire hissed as it struggled to assert itself. Coils of flame and billowing gray smoke rose. I felt as though I was back at the site where I had nearly died.

My attention elsewhere, I accidentally jabbed the tip of my finger with the knife. The sharp pain startled me; a drop of blood trickled out. Cringing, I hid my injured finger in the palm of my other hand.

Still, the rage inside me wouldn't die down. "Is it such a grave offense to send word to one's family?" I tried to keep my words respectful towards Idris; he had been kind to me, but I was furious with what had been done to Sal.

"Finish your job before Tariq catches you idling," Idris said curtly, without looking my way. "He's waiting for you to make another mistake."

My palm was crimson, the blood from my injured finger filling it and spilling over the sides of my hand.

"Oh, no, you've cut yourself."

Idris fetched a small strip of white cloth and pressed it to the wound. Instantly, the cloth turned scarlet.

"I am fine," I said.

I wasn't fine. I wanted to run out of this miserable place and go far away.

As though reading my misgivings, Idris cleared his throat. "You can't flee this Factory. Where will you go? You're young and pretty. You won't be safe alone on the streets. Much as it hurts you, this place isn't too bad."

There were two classes of people in this town, he explained—the laboring class and the aristocrats. The aristocrats used hired help—nurse-maids, butlers, butchers, and gardeners—but treated them harshly. "No matter where you go, you'll be of the laboring class. No matter where you go, you'll be treated cruelly. And besides, if you run away, if you try to hide from Tariq, he'll find you and punish you." He paused for a moment, scratched his chin, then continued, "The gate is shut every night at midnight when the temple bells ring. You can't slip away so easily."

Through the open window I could see the tall, robust, uniformed guard lounging at the entrance gate. Waving a peacock tail to drive away insects from his face, he kept watch over all entries and departures. Idris was right. I knew no one in this town. Nor could I sneak out of here without being caught.

I thought of Job sahib's benevolent face. "What if I speak to the Chief Factor and request that he bring Sal back? Explain my family situation? Why I needed to contact them? He'd seen my mother at the crematorium."

"The sahib left for the Palace early this morning." His tone was cheer-less. "He won't be back for a few days. If I were you, I wouldn't bother him with my personal problems. You see, Maria, you're a servant, a mere shadow. You have no past, no family ties, and no future. You are what you do for your master."

I stared at Idris's grieving face. We had a more urgent situation to handle. An innocent man had been wronged and that too due to a fault of mine. How would I compensate Sal? I slipped my fingers under my sari and touched the gold pendant, feeling the comforting weight on my skin, and unclasped it.

"Can you find a way to give this to Sal?" I held the gleaming pendant out to Idris. "He might be able to sell it and support himself for a while."

Idris mumbled his refusal and slipped out of the room. The slowness, the sadness in his movements tore through me.

For the rest of the day, I was visited by an unusual heaviness in my chest. How would I pass my days here without hearing the voice of my friend? I wanted to shout out about the injustice, but a woman wasn't allowed to express her feelings publicly. I left the utensils unwashed, burned the rice, and spilled cooking oil on the floor. The other cooks noticed, but no one said a word. Their silence pierced me more sharply than their words could have.

SIX

E arly that evening, the wailing began again. Like smoke curling up, darkening the atmosphere, suffocating me, Teema cried at the top of her voice from her room. "How could you do this to me? I loved you, loved you with everything I had, and I still love you. Come back to me, I'm waiting. I'll wait as long as I have to."

It was as though she were addressing wounded souls everywhere. I wished I could go knock at her door, offer her solace, and speak to her about my woes. We were the only two women employed here, both of us grieving. But my muscles ached and instead of comforting her, I curled up on my bed and succumbed to sleep, erasing her screams from my mind.

The following afternoon, I stole out of the kitchen for a short break to escape the oppressive heat. As I approached the sheesham tree, its dense foliage dappled with sunlight, I thought of Sal again. Guilt and sorrow drove me away from the place where we would sit for our lessons. I drifted instead onto the pillared verandah covered with a roof and bordered by rose bushes. The air was heady with the scent of the new blooms. In about an hour, the sahibs would be nestled here in comfortable padded chairs. Warming their spirits with tobacco, they'd talk about whatever was on their minds. At this moment, though, no one seemed to be about. The servants were taking their breaks somewhere, chewing betel leaves, a habit, which, according to Sal, "soothed their minds". The sahibs were indulging in a round of drinks in the meeting hall, local palm wine, "good for the gripes".

I stood a moment. There was a ripple of something in the atmosphere, something momentous, and it got hold of me. A group of pigeons had gathered on the pathway outside the verandah. Sal had told me a story once, of how Emperor Akbar kept a thousand pigeons so he could observe them frolic and make love. Now, I edged round a low table and sank down in a chair to do just that, observe them. Only a few minutes, I told myself, before someone drove me away. Dark clouds moved in and light rain began to fall, kind, soothing drops. 'Mango showers', our elders called it; showers that helped ripen the fruit to a richer yellow.

The frolicking stopped. As the pigeons took wing in a noisy cloud of gray, I saw Job sahib, the proud head, the white turban, the strong legs.

"Sahib!" I called out.

"Maria!"

Job sahib sauntered toward me and up to the verandah. His turban was wreathed with a chain of pearls, his eyes shone, his complexion glowed. In the week he had been away, he had rested well. A pearl-buttoned silk tunic, expensive beyond anything I could imagine, displayed his sculpted chest to good advantage. I smelled the fragrance of expensive attar. Perhaps he'd acquired the habit of wearing a floral scent during his stay at the Royal Palace.

I spoke in English. "It is my . . ." The rest of the words lodged in my throat. Again. *It is my pleasure to see you, sahib,* I'd wanted to say. I could feel my face turning red. I didn't want to squander my chance once more.

Job sahib grinned. "You're trying to speak English, I see that."

It pleased him at that time that the girl he had brought with him to this outpost of trade had overcome her initial shyness, somewhat. Last time, she couldn't even speak in Bangla with him. Her sadness, her loveliness, touched him.

"Quite right," I replied belatedly in English. Then I launched into an apology for coming onto the verandah, in a mixture of Bangla and English.

With a wave of his hand, Job sahib dismissed my apology. "Are you happy here?" He asked in Bangla.

I touched the necklace under my sari. "No, sahib, I'm not. Sal, the only friend I had, was asked to leave. My fault. I didn't know the rules, made a mistake by asking Sal to send a messenger to my mother. I'm sure she blames herself for my misfortune, considering herself cursed by the divine. She wonders if I've been given the evil eye at birth. What other reasons could there have been? She'll suffer forever for not having done enough to protect me. I wanted to save her the grief."

"You're missing your family terribly, I can see that."

"But there's more."

An opaque white blanket of rain fell around us. It was as if Job sahib and I were nestled in a soft liquid cocoon. "If I may speak my mind, sir," I blurted out in my mother tongue.

"Yes, you may."

"Do you know how long my work-day is? Fourteen hours. Yes, I have to slave most of the day for one meal and a place to sleep. Before I got married, I had to take care of a sick father and two little brothers—my mother was too frail—but that was nothing compared to this.

"At the end of the day, my back hurts, my knees buckle. Not only have I lost my family, but also the one friend I had. Now I have no one with whom I could share my misery." I paused, noticing the intensity with which the sahib leaned toward me. "I'm a Brahmin girl. I come from a family of honest people. My father isn't rich, but he's a scholar. He gave me lessons. I used to spend my days learning the ways of the world from him and how to conduct our lives. Here all I do is cook and clean."

Grief choked my throat; I stopped speaking. I knew I shouldn't have said so much, taken up the sahib's precious time, yet, I felt lighter, happier, and more hopeful.

"It concerns me that you're so unhappy, Maria," Job sahib said, his brows furrowed. "We tried to help you. I thought you would be thankful to be rescued and delighted to live here. Had I known my actions would cause you this much grief I might have. . .But no. No, I had no choice but to save you. I couldn't have done it any differently. To lose family, friends, and your place in the world, is devastating.

"You see, I went through a similar difficult period myself when I was your age. My father asked me to leave. And I . . ." His voice thickened and he paused a long moment. "But you must be grateful to be simply alive."

"Yes, sir, I am. I am happy to feel the rain, smell the shiuli, and see the pigeons fly. I appreciate your decision and actions, but I long to see my family. I want to be with them."

"Do you think you'll be safe going back?"

I knew the answer; I couldn't utter it.

"Just because your life is not to your liking right now doesn't mean it will always be that way. No one can foretell what the future will bring. I was raised on a small farm in England. I could never have imagined that I'd end up here, so many seas away and in such a different environment, in a position that allows me to serve my country." Job sahib paused.

"Tariq tells me the servants are content, they have what they need. I have to trust what he says. He's the supervisor and I am not completely fluent in Bangla. I, too, am trapped in my position."

"You're in a more pleasant trap, sir. We're miserable." My eyelids felt heavy, I stopped speaking.

Job sahib drew nearer. He pulled a frilly white handkerchief from his pocket and handed it to me. I dabbed my eyes with the soft cloth and stared at him. His tall body seemed to shield me from the lightning that streaked across the sky, from the sharp wind that blew past me. Only a short time ago, he'd snatched me from death's grip, a gift for which I'd never be able to express enough appreciation. And now, when I craved a strong shoulder to lean on, he'd reappeared. I stood up straight, savored the delight in having him all to myself, and smelled the fragrance of jasmine and the moist earth. The rain drowned all sound, making it seem as if we were the only ones in the world.

Tariq stepped onto the verandah, his sandals clattering, a plain white garb accentuating his grave expression. When he spotted Job sahib standing close beside me, he took a step back, then quickly collected himself. Our time alone was over.

"Won't you join us in the meeting room, sahib?" His voice was excessively deferential.

I mumbled a greeting, but Tariq paid no attention. He had spoiled our beautiful, private moment. I *wouldn't* leave.

Job sahib turned to Tariq. "You've been telling me the kitchen helpers are content, but I am hearing otherwise."

"Sir, you should see her," Tariq said emphatically. "She sneaks out, takes long breaks, and neglects her duties. I haven't punished her, even though we're short-handed."

"I take breaks to learn English," I said to Tariq. "Is that so bad?"

Tariq, his one good eye turning red and round, was about to lash out at me when Job sahib held out a hand. "Bass." He turned to me, hand stroking his chin. "The last few weeks I have been conducting important business with the Nawab. That's done now. I'll be spending more time here, looking after the Factory, improving the conditions here, although I must say my hands are tied." He paused. "And there's been a new development, a worrisome one. Your husband's relatives have filed a complaint with the Nawab's officials, stating that we've abducted you. They said you wanted to be cremated, but we stopped the ritual. They want me to be put under house arrest and take you away."

I lost touch with the cold stone floor. Had my parents heard about this? Or had the news not traveled yet? I lifted my head only to find Job sahib staring at me. "My husband's relatives have made up a story," I said. "You saved me from death. Never would I want to go back to them or be cremated. This might sound absurd, but is there any way I could help?"

"You have to file a petition at the Nawab's Court." Tariq said. "Do you even understand what a petition is?"

I shook my head.

"Every citizen," Job sahib said, "high or low, can present themselves to the Nawab on specific days to file complaints, place a request, or simply to be heard."

I, a woman, who had had no life experience outside a village, could actually petition the Honorable Nawab, also called the 'Protector of the Penniless', the 'Asylum of our land', and the 'Giver of Daily Bread'! That would be an once-in-a-lifetime event for almost anybody. Of all the stories I'd heard about the Royal Court, none had ever involved a servant girl. I looked up at Job sahib.

"I'm aware of the difficult situation in which I have put you. I have faith in you, Maria."

He'd made an exception that day, an exception to the commonly held belief to never trust a local.

"Yes, sahib, I'll do a petition on your behalf." Then, reflecting further, I said, "But I would need help. I don't know the Court etiquette. How does one address the Nawab? How does one behave?"

Job sahib looked at me, his gaze warm, concentrated. "Tell your story. That's most important. You showed me at the cremation ghat how strong you were. I want the Royal Court to see your spirit. Tariq can help you with the formalities. Can't you, Tariq?"

"Yes, sir." Turning to me, Tariq said. "The next petition day will be a week from now. Fortunately, you'll be able to speak Bangla there, formal Bangla, that is. Can you prepare yourself in such a short time? You mustn't waste the Nawab's valuable time."

"I'll do my best." I looked down at my wrinkled yellow sari stained with spices. I didn't have appropriate clothing to appear before the Nawab. I could tell from the impatient look on Tariq's face that he was keen to move on.

That gave me an opening. "Is there any way to bring Sal back?" I asked Job sahib. "Please. He's a good man, he taught me English. I'm the reason for his dismissal."

Tariq glared at me. "Servants are my responsibility. I fired Sal for a good reason. He didn't follow the Factory rules. You keep out of it."

I looked imploringly at Job sahib. He brushed aside a lock of golden hair peeking out from below his turban and asked Tariq, "Can we get Sal back?"

"No, sir, I don't know where he came from or where he's gone."

The empty socket of Tariq's left eye throbbed; he was lying. Job sahib seemed not to notice.

"Couldn't we at least try?" I asked Tariq.

Tariq's face flushed. "I'll spend weeks and get nowhere. Sal could have moved to another town. He's probably already found a job." Tariq's voice caught; he was lying . . . again Job sahib didn't notice. That bothered me, the trust he had in his subordinates.

"Are you eager to learn my language?" Job sahib asked me.

"Yes sir. I would like to be assigned a tutor."

"I can ask one of my chaps to give you lessons. His name is Charles, the Second Officer in our Factory, and he has just returned from England after a holiday."

I noticed Tariq's face brighten at the mention of the Second Officer.

Job sahib turned to Tariq. "Perhaps you can reduce Maria's work hours. Give her time to study."

"You can't be serious, sir." Tariq waved his hand impatiently. "We don't do such favors for servants; the work won't get done. Our budget is limited, and we can't hire more help."

I could see from the cloud of concern on Tariq's face: budget was an important consideration for him, conscientious employee that he was.

Still, I persisted. "If I speak English better, it will not only help me but also the Factory."

"Quite so," Job sahib said. "It will be most useful to have one more servant who speaks English fluently. I hope to expand our business in future. The more English-speaking staff we have, the better." His face shone, as though a bigger, more hopeful future dangled before him. He turned to Tariq. "Besides, she's motivated, unusually so. We've never seen that in the servants we hire. We ought to give her a chance."

"At all costs, sahib, we obey you." With that, Tariq turned to me, but the frown on his forehead only deepened. "I'll give you part of the morning off and make arrangements with Charles sahib for regularly scheduled tutoring."

"I will not disappoint you," I said to Job sahib, "even though English words do get stuck in my throat sometimes."

Job sahib broke into a good-natured laugh. This was for me, and I would nurture it in my heart. "If you only knew how difficult it is for us to correctly pronounce Bangla and Persian words." He held my gaze for the briefest moment. "I'll test your progress."

"I'll be so honored," I said breathlessly. "I will do all I can to pick up English faster." A small pain nudged me from inside. "But Sal?"

"Now, for the last time, Sal is not coming back," Tariq said.

"It hurts me to think that he's been punished so severely," I said to Job sahib.

"Reflecting back on the decision, I regret it. When I was young and worked on ship maintenance, I once stole an extra piece of bread during supper. I was caught and taunted cruelly for it; it was humiliating. They punished me by not serving me any food for a whole day." Job sahib looked far into space. A moment later, he blinked, recovered, and concluded, "If it's any consolation, Maria, you'll now learn English from a native speaker."

"That would surely help my pronunciation, sir. I am grateful for your generosity."

Tariq turned to Job sahib. "Shall we join the meeting now?" Glaring at me, he spat out the words, "Don't forget the petition at the Royal Court. I expect you to be ready."

Job sahib nodded at me. "I trust you will do well." I tucked away his kind expression in my heart. I had to succeed, so Job sahib could succeed. They walked away, their voices angry. Perhaps the sahib questioned his trust in Tariq, if only a little, a seed planted in unprepared soil.

It was time to report to the kitchen.

Job couldn't help but think about the Company, how he would like to see it grow, and how much that depended on the competence of his staff. If they were familiar with the language and the ways of the English, all the better, for the Company would need such people if it were to prosper in this often unfathomable land. Thus far, Tariq had been indispensable in the day-to-day running of the place, but could he really trust him? He would walk out the door tomorrow if his interests were better served elsewhere. But Maria—her eyes were full of admiration when she looked up at him. She was dedicated to her kitchen duties, and from all accounts, the quality of her cooking was consistently excellent. He could see that she had a strong desire, a spark in her to better herself. Just as he did. And she wanted to learn his tongue more than any of the other servants. Loyalty and motivation—yes, that was why he took the time to listen to her. He sensed that she would be an invaluable asset to him and the Company someday.

SEVEN

L ate that night, after twelve hours of toil, I retired, only to find myself unable to rest, my insides in tumult from both panic and excitement. Outside, a storm roared. I had to make a petition to the Nawab! In the dim light of the oil lamp, I conjured a mental picture of the Nawab's reception hall, the darbar, a space so big that it could accommodate a hundred elephants, so bright as to make it seem a part of the sun itself. Only if you accumulated a lifetime of good karma, my people said, could you dream of having an audience, a darshan, with the Nawab.

What if, surrounded by the pomp and splendor of the hall, I lost my voice before the crowd of petitioners, or worse yet, broke down? What if the Nawab laughed at me? What if my petition was rejected and Job sahib was in worse trouble than before? What if my in-laws were allowed to take me away?

I took a deep breath and stood up. I couldn't let any of that happen. I had to rehearse my talk in the quietness of my hovel, practise and practise until I got it right.

I covered my head with the sari train, only my eyes visible, as I would present myself in the darbar. "Your Lordship," I began in Bangla, my voice high but well-modulated. Although I listened to English much of the day, it was so much easier to weave sentences in Bangla. The sweet sounds were as much a part of me as my skin and muscles, as precious as my eyesight. I poured out the details: a brief marriage, my husband's sudden death, his relatives' plan to eliminate me, the arrival of Job sahib, the smoke and fights and confusion at the cremation site, and eventually, my rescue.

I heard a knock at the door. The door was sturdier than on that grim night of assault, but who could it be at this time of the night?

"Who's there?" I asked after a moment of hesitation, my voice guarded.

"Teema." Her tone sounded bright and eager. I could hardly believe my ears. Teema, the mysterious sweeper who never uttered a word of greeting, one who dressed in nothing but black, who wailed high enough at night to disturb my sleep, had come to visit me? She must have been listening to my outpouring through the thin mud wall between our rooms. I opened the door.

She stood at the door, commanding and erect, her black skirt billowing in the wind, her hair done up in a bun. Even at that late hour, her eyes glittered.

"What a surprise! Come in, do."

She slipped into the room, adjusting a sequined black scarf around her throat. "Please forgive me; I've been listening to you. Yours is an incredible story."

"I disturbed you."

"Can we talk?"

I nodded. We both sat on the floor mat, knees pulled up to our chests, the oil lamp flickering between us, quiet, not looking at each other. "I must tell you how much it pained me to hear you." Her gaze exuded warmth, her voice was mellifluous. "We're the same in many ways."

"I've heard you crying at night."

She was quiet for a while. When she spoke, her voice was soft, warm. "I was born not too far from here in the village of Kolapara where there was no talk of buying and selling and cheating. I lived with my family next to a pond. My father, a farmer, taught me how to plough when I could barely walk. We didn't have enough to eat because of the high revenue we had to pay the tax collector, but I could dance. As soon as I heard music, I would want to stand up, smile, and move. My legs twitched; my hands moved on their own free will. Dancing has always been in my veins. I am a nautch girl."

Dancing girl. One who practised the ancient art of nritya, performed for the public. Our community shut its door to such women. *It's not respectableto be out in public, to show your flesh to men and taunt them with suggestive movements,* the elders would say. Should I seek her company?

"Would you like to see me perform?"

"Why, yes, of course," I said, but I wasn't sure.

She removed the scarf from her throat, stood up, and began twirling, her legs loose, her spine flexible, her movements fluid. I almost wanted to stop her. The decorative gemstones on her skirt twinkled in the lamp light. A silver ring flashed on her third toe. She skittered into new positions, filling the space with her presence, compelling me to watch her. She whirled one arm round her head and loosened the coil of hair she had twisted into a bun. Lustrous black hair streamed down her back.

Although she could hardly be called a beauty, the light around her countenance made her seem like a celestial maiden, an apsara who, in ancient times, descended on earth to charm the mortals. The rhythm of her movements made my body tingle. I could almost hear rich instrumental music swelling around us. I felt an urge to get up and join her but shyness and a sense of propriety prevented me from doing so.

Teema stopped and bowed. She had transformed within minutes from the sweeper I was familiar with to one who stood on a high stage and charged the air with light and grace.

"Shabash! Shabash, Teema! How did you learn such intricate moves?"

She folded her legs beneath her as she settled onto the floor and caught her breath. "After my father's death, with three younger sisters to support, I had to earn a living for my family. That's when I came to town and wandered through the streets looking for a job. I hoped to become a dancer."

Her voice was thick with sorrow. "It must have been my destiny to perform. Soon enough, I got an opportunity to dance in a punch house filled with liquor, unruly crowds, bad manners, and fights. Still, many customers appreciated my dancing. It came easily to me—expressing my feelings, visions, and dreams through my body."

In the evenings, she dressed in a gold-embroidered muslin robe and gold bangles, sprinkled attar on her body, and chewed betel leaves to redden her lips. Ornaments dangled around her waist and she had a ring on each finger and toe. Silver bells on the chain around her ankles made tinkling sounds at every step she took. Brass lanterns shone on her. She smiled and flew onto the dance floor, her hands weaving images and emotions. All day long the beauty she saw, the love she felt, the fear that gripped her, would find expression in her nightly performance. The audience was made up of local merchants and foreign traders alike.

"And, oh, what an appreciative audience!" Teema said, her voice high pitched, delighted, yearning for that golden past. "When I finished my routine, they would rise from their seats, applaud, and shower me with gold coins."

Why did she stop dancing and work as a sweeper? Perhaps she sensed my curiosity; her face turned pale, but she didn't seem ready to confide in me.

"So what have you been doing with your spare time?" She asked in a light-hearted manner.

"Not much."

"Let me take you around the city. We'll start with a stroll through the market and you'll see the articles for sale, what brings traders from all over, the haggling that goes on, the liveliness."

"But Tariq?"

Teema laughed. "We're allowed to have free time, you know. That bojjat keeps it a secret. Let me tell you about him. His father was a petty criminal who is now in prison. Tariq is responsible for a large, extended family. He can't handle the pressure, so he takes it out on us. I'll speak with him. Day after tomorrow, at three in the grove. Achcha?"

"I'll be there," I said in a cheerful voice. She hadn't revealed why she'd stopped dancing, why she'd given up what she loved. She kept it bottled inside; I could see that from her sudden stiff gestures.

"That's settled, then," Teema said with a grin. "Rest well." On that note, she leapt to her feet and bent to pat my shoulder. Her skirt rustling, she dashed out.

EIGHT

I walked over to the verandah for my first English lesson the next morning, alert and hopeful, only to find my tutor wasn't there. I stood by the railing for some time, then, hearing footsteps, I turned. Charles sahib, the Second Officer, stepped onto the verandah. So far,

I'd only seen him from a distance. I smoothed the folds of my sari, bowed, and took a close look; this sahib was a foul-smelling man of substantial girth, with a high nose and florid face.

"Ah, there you be," he said in English, "on time. I didn't expect it."

I almost took a step back but met his eyes instead. "I always try to be on time, sir."

He stared at my bare feet and raised his eyebrows. "No shoes?"

In my village, inside our homes, we never wore footwear. "Our home is God Shiva's landing," my mother would say. "It's sacred. We mustn't bring in animal skin or dust from outside."

"It's our custom not to wear shoes at home," I said.

"Primitive, I should say." Lips curling, he gave out a laugh of derision. "All right, be seated." He sank into a chair and switched to thickly accented, broken Bangla. "I'm supposed to tutor you in English so you can follow our orders better."

Why did Job sahib assign this man as my tutor? My mother's voice floated out from my childhood. *Respect your elders, the monarch, and your teachers. Don't show the slightest dissatisfaction in their presence, keep your head down, and don't raise your voice.* Even if I dismissed Mother's words, the fact would remain that my employment here depended on the good graces of the sahibs. I must hide my annoyance and show only politeness.

"How did you learn to speak my mother tongue, sir?" I asked in a softer tone.

"It hasn't been easy," he said in halting Bangla, tilting his chin and giving me a cool stare. "I had no choice but to pick up some native phrases here and there. Only a few people understand English in this godforsaken place. But trust me, there will come a time when you'll hear our tongue spoken everywhere."

"I'm eager to take lessons, sir," I said, quivering with anger. "I'm thankful to Job sahib for making this arrangement." I wasn't thankful any longer, not if I had to take my lessons from this conceited man.

"Job asked me to find the time, as if I had nothing better to do. If only he wasn't performing his duties so poorly . . ."

Charles sahib let the sentence dangle. My gaze followed his to the walkway outside the verandah. Last night's storm had left a lot of devastation in its wake. Leaves, twigs, and broken branches littered the pathway.

The sahib scowled. "Why is that path cluttered with rubbish? It's an eyesore. Someone could trip."

Did Teema oversleep? Or did she walk past that pile of debris without even registering it? "Our sweeper will get to it soon," I said. "She's running late."

"Lazy people; no future." He paused. "You're ready for today's lesson, I take it? Can you describe this verandah in English?"

Hands on my lap, I tried to get my thoughts together in English.

He sighed heavily, shook his head, and said slowly, "Repeat after me, this is a chair. That's a table." He named at least ten more objects. "Come! Speak! Speak the great English language! And be quick!"

I repeated the sentences, misplacing a word here and a word there and biting my lips in frustration. Once corrected, I plunged in with renewed energy, my voice strong and steady. After a while, the sahib fell deeper into the chair, wiping perspiration from his forehead, as though I'd exhausted his store of energy.

"Please, sir, will you allow me to practise some more?" I asked eagerly. I was very much aware that he could drop me as a student, which would result in my forever remaining in the kitchen as a lowly cook. Nothing existed at that moment but Charles sahib, English, and I. On this verandah, the hard marble floor beneath my feet, I sat up straighter. Words and phrases rose and fell, stormed on my tongue, exhausted my breath, and muted the birdsong. At the end of the hour, I had acquired a new vocabulary, collected the prize of several new sentences, and felt famished, but I wasn't intimidated by the sahib. The sounds were now my own and belonged to my treasury of expressions.

Charles sahib stole a look at me. "It's passable, your English."

Mumbling a word of gratitude, I rose and bowed respectfully. As I was about to slip away, he said in halting Bangla, "Wait, Maria."

I was startled by his use of my name, the fact that he addressed me as a person and not as an ignorant help. "Yes, sahib?"

For a moment he was silent, as though attempting to choose the proper words. When he spoke, his voice was softer than it had been, more courteous.

"I didn't mean to be hard on you, but I've been unwell." He burped. "I get attacks of fever and can't seem to digest any food. They say drinking water from the Ganges will cure any disease, it's the "water of immortality", and I drink it. Why am I so sick then?"

I stood still and waited, smelling an opportunity for providing assistance.

"Do you think . . ." he asked, "do you think, you could prepare special meals for me, soups, some light dishes?"

I looked into his cloudy eyes, noted the exhausted slouch of his shoulders. Yes, I could see it; he was ailing. "It would be a pleasure, sir. I often cooked for my father. He always asked for mild fare when he had, what he called 'guts gripe.'"

"Good. Do that!" He suddenly seemed so pleased that I almost smiled. Then he asked, "Have you heard other servants passing remarks about me?"

I shook my head. His voice was still soft, as he said, "Well, if they ever do, report that to me right away, will you?"

So he wanted me to act as an informer. The concept was familiar and distasteful. The Royal Court was known to hire informers, people who lived risky lives and were often murdered. No, I had no intention of ever being an informer, which would put my kitchen mates and me in harm's way.

"Of course, sir." I bowed again, controlling the shaking that seemed to be affecting all my limbs.

I hurried away from the sahib, peering around the courtyard. Teema was nowhere in sight, so I peeked into her room. She wasn't there either. I picked up a spare broom and began sweeping the pathway.

Idris approached me. "You're covering for Teema? Do you have any idea the trouble you'll be in, if Tariq sees you?"

"I can't find Teema. I have to get this done or she'll be in trouble. You get back to the kitchen and start the meal preparation. I'll join you when I'm done here."

Half-an-hour later, I put the broom away, sprinkled water to beat the dust, and took comfort in the fact that Teema had been spared. Then I strolled back to the river ghat to wash up before heading to the kitchen.

I couldn't stop thinking about Charles sahib and this morning's English lesson, the way he'd treated me with contempt and then acted like a father, asking his daughter to help him with his meals, then turned around again and asked me to put my life in danger by being his informant. I couldn't avoid him now; he was my English teacher.

A terrible foreboding gripped my senses.

In the kitchen, I got hold of Idris. "What a nightmare, my first lesson with Charles sahib."

"You get English lessons?" Pratap asked, chopping carrots with angry strokes. "What about us?"

Jas, wiry, enterprising, and quiet, chimed in, as he measured spices: "I wouldn't want to take a lesson from that crotchety pink-face."

"That bully," Idris said. "Why did he have to come back? Do you know he once threatened me with a kitchen knife because the mutton hadn't been cooked according to his standards? We call him Mr. Earthquake. Wherever he goes, he shakes things up."

"He treats us like the dirt under his shoes," Bir said, squatting and pushing his mop across the floor. "He made me pay a fine, a half month's salary, claiming that I'd put a spider in his liquor cabinet, with the intention to harm him. And you know what? I never did any such thing. There are spiders everywhere in this compound. Crazy bastard. He has a talent for making you feel guilty. It gets even worse. He once invited me to his bedchamber at night. I refused."

"I overheard him saying to another sahib that you were extremely good-looking," Jas said. "Be careful. Charles sahib gets what he wants, when he wants it. He's a lusty man."

"He's a sick man," Bir replied.

"Exactly what he told me," I said. "He's sick. He can't take our food or water. I offered to serve him a special soup and—"

A chorus of laughter cut me off.

"That's his standard complaint, Maria," Jas said. "He doesn't feel good. The water isn't safe. No one understands him. He is downright wicked. Job sahib was forced to hire him because of his family's wealth in England. And you know what he's paying back with? He's spreading a rumor that Job sahib is failing in his duties. 'Job hasn't increased the Company's profit substantially.' I overheard Earthquake sahib hatching a conspiracy with two other sahibs when I served them their afternoon hookahs.

"He said he'd make a bigger profit and the Crown would support him. The other two pink faces agreed with him. I stood at the door until Mr. Earthquake yelled at me. 'Out! Don't you have anything else to do? Be off!'"

So that must be it, I reasoned. Charles sahib wanted to get rid of his superior and take over the Factory as the burra sahib, the Chief Factor. As I stirred a pot of legumes, my mind remained agitated. I pictured Charles sahib grasping me by the neck and shaking me, demanding to know if his wicked scheme had gotten out. A battle between him and Job sahib was in the air and I was caught in the middle of it. Dark patches of danger floated before my eyes.

"Charles sahib has his own pistol," Bir said.

"You mean the firing kind?" I asked.

Bir laughed. "Is there any other kind, Maria? I was cleaning his room when I noticed it under the bed. I shook all over, looked away, and recited God Vishnu's name. I also spotted a cartridge box in his cabinet. Everyone knows that rival English traders get in fights and shoot each other. Even Job sahib has several pistols in his drawer." He paused. "Did you know they found the body of an Englishman, an independent trader, near the entrance to the market a month ago?"

"No. But in-fighting among our superiors?" I said. "That's scarier."

Idris said, "Let us keep an eye on Job sahib, protect him at all costs."

"I am puzzled as to why he assigned Charles sahib as my tutor," I said. "He still trusts the man."

But he shouldn't. He should be suspicious. I distracted myself by shelling a pile of beans, but my attention kept drifting to the image of a bloody corpse in the market, the street stained, vultures flapping their wings overhead. My fingers shook.

I opened a trunk filled with dinnerware and got out an expensive porcelain set brought by ship from China. Originally meant for the royalty, this ware was supposed to break into pieces when in contact with poison. Only the sahibs could dine on them, not us, ever. I spat on a dinner plate, smearing it with my resentment.

Next I scrubbed the asanas, simple mats made of reed and meant for sitting on the floor. We serfs used these seats for our supper. There were no chairs or dining tables for us. We prepared three elaborate meals a day for the sahibs—four, if you considered the afternoon refreshments—but our food was rationed. We ate only one meal and that at night, a simple, unadorned supper of khichri, a medley of rice and lentils, accompanied by a pickled vegetable. Idris occasionally pilfered pieces of sweetmeat and popped them into his mouth; I did the same. Our humble evening meal was served on squares of freshly cut, disposable banana leaves.

NINE

The same night, after only an hour of sleep, again I dreamt of the burning pyre, the sparks, the smoke, the ashes, and towers of yellow flames. When I woke up, a scream seemed to be stuck in my throat. I lay awake for many hours, listening to the humming of insects, and finally fell back to sleep. As the day dawned, I hauled myself up from the bed, later than usual.

I entered the kitchen and noticed Idris hadn't yet fired up the chulahs. He, too, was late. Well, at least, I could do the harvesting. A straw basket in hand, I trotted out to the courtyard, under the canopy of trees. The morning was fresh, a light breeze blew away my gloom, and the insects murmuring among the leaves cheered me up. I had nearly filled the basket when I heard the swish of the broom.

Teema was sweeping the far corner of the courtyard, dressed in an all-black outfit, enveloped in a cloud of dust. I was about to call out a greeting when I saw Tariq rushing toward me, his eye glinting with anger.

Chin jutting out, voice oozing sarcasm, he said, "My, my, aren't we tardy?"

"Please give me a moment. A few more guavas and I'll be ready to serve breakfast."

Tariq wagged his index finger at me. "You've already delayed the sahibs. How many times do I have to tell you their time is precious? You could be terminated on the spot, do you know that?"

The basket fell from my hand and struck the ground. The soft guavas spilled out, their skins bursting, white flesh smeared with dust. A bird rustled through a tree, making a mocking chuck-chuck sound.

Teema stepped forward, placed the broom on the ground, and planted herself defiantly in front of Tariq. "Look, give her a few minutes," she said. "She's not well. I cared for her last night. Poor thing—she was shaking. She had chills."

"You're indisposed?" Tariq asked me, incredulous.

I held my tongue.

Teema said, "Can't you see how pale her face is?"

Tariq's gaze flitted over Teema's proud posture; her face sparkled with a new light, as though she was performing on a raised platform while he sat on the ground, a spectator. It remained unclear as to whether he believed her story, whether he'd run out of the will to contradict her, or whether her reputation as a fine dancer had put her in a better position to bargain.

"All right," Tariq growled. "I'll explain it to the sahibs this time, but don't let me catch either of you tardy again, ever. Understand?"

He turned on his heel and departed. I caught Teema's eyes and grabbed the basket. She picked up her skirt and stepped over the wet splatter of fruit on the ground.

Mid-afternoon, we walked through a mud flat on our way to the market. The sun's rays on this cloudy day were weak. I thanked Teema. Not only had she stood up for me this morning, but she'd also gotten Tariq's permission for a longer break.

"Why you look so gloomy then?" Teema asked.

I couldn't bring myself to confide in her my little act of theft. Only minutes ago, my fingers turning cold and lifeless, I'd lifted a little money for this trip from a jar tucked away in a corner of the kitchen yet still in plain sight. Only Idris was allowed to use this money to pay for groceries, and the thought of betraying his trust had nauseated me, made it harder for me to breathe. How I'd hoped that no one would notice. I listened to the gentle murmuring of a nearby stream, glanced at Teema's bright face, and said, "Oh, it's nothing."

"I know, I know. You have to deal with Tariq and Charles sahib. Let me tell you. Those two are fragile and easily threatened."

I didn't understand her words, but I felt better. We reached a wide acacia-lined road leading to the town center. Swarms of shoppers, mostly men in cotton and accompanied by goats, bullocks, and mules, chattered animatedly. All seemed to be headed in the same direction. As we meandered through the crowd, I heard discussions around gold, silk, grains, and opium.

Teema pointed to an orchard on the right and said lightly, "See those mulberry trees? Silkworms feed on their leaves." She adjusted her odhni, a silver-embroidered, pearl-fringed, silky, chiffon head-covering that framed her oval face beautifully.

If I felt jealous scrutinizing Teema's accessory, I didn't show it. "I love silk, but it'd take me years to save up for even a single piece like your odhni," I said, complimenting her on her possession.

Teema adjusted the scarf. "It's the only silk piece I own, a gift from a friend."

Who could have given her such an expensive present? The man who had left her? I wanted to hear more about her love life, even though that might make me more jealous. She was older, more experienced, and had gone through a lot, yet she seemed to carry a childish joy within her.

Teema parted her veil with a delicate hand, exposing at her throat a gleaming gold necklace worked with emeralds. "My mother gave it to me when I left home." Her voice broke. "It was a wedding gift from her mother. It's been so long since I have seen . . ."

She left the sentence dangling. An Englishman in a high-crowned hat towered over all the pedestrians swirling around us. As he passed us, he gave Teema a brief sideways glance. Her eyes filled with pain and she quickly pulled the veil lower down on her forehead.

"I didn't like the way he looked at us," I said.

"He's a hustler in his spare hours."

"A hustler?"

"You're so innocent." She laughed. "A hustler is someone who arranges sexual services. Oh, the characters you meet in this town—hustlers, thieves, predators, and other criminals, as well as the devout."

A bigger, messier world had just opened up before me.

A floral arch supported by four pillars loomed before us. We swept through it and plunged into the main section of the market in the midst of a sea of people. It was similar to our village market, only much bigger. On either side of us, hawkers sold all kinds of goods: jewelry, clothes, dried fruit, toys, and clay idols. The crowd and the market sounds made me feel cheerful. Skeins of silk, along with velvet, satin, and taffeta, in yellow, red, blue, and purple, dazzled my eyes. Trades people bought and haggled; a cacophony of jokes, friendly banter, and hard bargaining infused the air. Children pranced by. From inside a tent, a male voice recited the Holy Koran. In the midst of it all, a handsome man whirled like a dervish. At that time, I couldn't make much of the activities around us; on looking back, each stands out clearly, my first experience of the wider world, a world more colorful, more exciting, more promising, and more mysterious.

I left my ignorance and misgivings behind and soaked in the noise, smells, colors, shapes, and movements around me. My steps became lighter. With the stolen coin, I bought two servings of freshly harvested molasses from a vendor and shared them with Teema.

A short distance away there stood a performance stage, a mandapa. Pillared on four corners, it was marked by a crimson canopy so stunning that I simply stood and stared at it.

"Wait till you listen to the music, my favorite part of the market."

As we approached, a band of musicians stepped up to the stage; soon they began to tune their instruments. The tuneful drone of a tanpura filled the air around us.

We left the area and browsed the long rows of tents dedicated to toys. A pair of miniature clay elephants, beautifully painted in brown and white, caught my attention. I could imagine my brothers Nitya and

Nupur squealing in joy at the sight of those toys. I couldn't afford them. I'd already spent the little money I had stolen by indulging in that sweetmeat, and Nupur and Nitya weren't with me to enjoy these things. I had no idea when I'd see them again.

A brick stucco building stood a short distance away, its door painted red. "Shall we have a look?" I asked.

Teema shook her head. "There are plenty of stalls to browse right around here."

"Only a peek?"

"All right." She seemed to hesitate.

Through the open door, I beheld a dark chamber with a white floor. A few shadowy figures huddled inside even so early in the day. This must be a punch house. I heard snatches of drunken conversation, the smashing of a glass, someone bellowing. As we were about to turn, an Englishman emerged, his face framed by a floppy hat. His cheeks were flushed and he clutched a glass in his fist. Tall and broad like a banyan tree, he filled the doorway.

He locked eyes with Teema. "My darling! Queen of the Night! What a happy occasion!" On unsteady feet, speaking broken Bangla, he stumbled nearer. "I had no idea you missed me so much."

Teema's eyes displayed a flicker of loathing and dread. "We're here for the music, John."

Was this the place where Teema had once performed?

"Do you know how long it has been, my Jasmine?" John's reddened eyes brazenly took Teema in, his gaze moved up her body, openly admiring the curve of her hips, the swell of her breasts, and he said with a grin, "I see you're still as ravishing as ever, my sweetness."

Standing in front of this punch house crammed with drunks and listening to a drunken man's lecherous words, I wanted to flee. I tried to catch Teema's eye, but she was giving John a fierce, withering look.

"Why in the name of Shiva, why do you pursue me, John?" She said. "I tell you many times, I, I not want to see you again."

John winked at me. "And who's this beauty?" Meeting Teema's silence, he said to me, "Allow me to present myself. John Richardson."

I barely nodded. John Richardson made me uncomfortable and his brazen manner had disturbed my friend greatly.

"Do you know Edward is getting married to an English woman?" John Richardson said to Teema.

Teema wilted into silence. Sensing her shame, that strangling feeling of wanting to disappear, I said, "Let's go, Teema," and stepped away, taking hold of her hand, encouraging her to follow.

She stirred and half-turned toward me, but John Richardson touched her shoulder, leaned in close, his lips almost brushing her ear, and whispered in a husky voice, "Not so fast, my love, let us get together soon, shall we? I've missed your charm, the feel of your soft skin, the way you moved and moaned under me. I promise to put back the smile on your face again."

Teema, clearly mortified, shrank away from him, but he blocked her path and threw his arms around her shoulders with a confident laugh. "Come on, love," he said playfully.

I saw the revulsion on her anguished face as she struggled to free herself from his embrace. I could tolerate it no longer. I edged forward, rammed both hands into John Richardson's chest, and shoved him back. Taken by surprise, the brute wobbled back, and steadied himself against the wall of the punch house.

Before he could straighten up again, I shouted at Teema. "Let's get out of here."

We broke into a run. Behind us, John Richardson called out with a careless laugh. "I'll have you yet, my flower! You wait and see."

In a few minutes, we came to a dead-end and stopped. Still panting, I craned my neck but, thanks to Goddess Durga, there was no sign of John Richardson. We waited for our breathing to return to normal. The sun blazed mercilessly overhead; my throat felt dry.

"My savior," Teema said.

Chest heaving, I stood there, my mind churning with questions. *Who's John Richardson? What was that about? Who's Teema, really?*

"Where can we go? What if he finds us?" I didn't realize until this moment how frightened I was, how stiff in every limb.

Teema looked up sharply, studying my face. "It's all right, Maria. Do not fear. He didn't look like he was in any condition to chase anyone. And I know a route where he's not allowed to go."

We entered a maze of narrow alleyways with grass huts on either side. As in my village, these huts had been built close together to provide shade to one another in the scorching heat. At this time of the day, with the sun nearly overhead, any cover would be welcome. Entering an alley wide enough for only one person, we slowed our pace and began walking single file. A pair of curious eyes peeked at us from behind a door. It belonged to a young mother nursing her baby inside a low-ceilinged hut decorated only with mats. In the adjoining residence, a woman swept the packed earth floor with a broom. We came across a small garden, lush with vegetables, where a woman harvested small shiny cucumbers.

"This is the women's quarters," Teema whispered.

Now I understood. At this time of the day, when the men were away to earn their wages, the area belonged to women only. No man would ever step in here to disturb the women's daily chores or their time with their children, an unspoken social agreement. Teema had chosen the perfect escape route for us, I thought thankfully, as I took in the quietness all around me.

We emerged from the women's quarters into a lane not far from the market but with fewer pedestrians. "Let us stop here for a minute," Teema suggested.

We sat cross-legged on the ground and viewed the sun-drenched lane. A bullock cart, carrying cattle fodder, hustled past us. Teema's cheeks seemed to gain color; a certain confidence lit up her face. Still, questions about her and my new surroundings plagued me. How, in the long run, would she be able to avoid the clutches of John Richardson? Who was Edward? What was this town really like? I'd only just touched its surface, as well as that of Teema's existence.

We could hear the sound of conch-shells followed by drum beats not too far away. Ah, finally, the music was about to begin. Teema lifted her gaze. I could tell she longed to clap and cheer at the performance; so did I. We exchanged a glance and both of us sighed. It wouldn't be safe for us to attend the event.

I rose and asked, "You won't come back here again, will you?"

"This market belongs to all of us," Teema replied. "But see how John acted. Like they're the lords here. Like we must do what they ask us to do, or else . . ."

The day had lost its luster for me. I saw how vulnerable we were in our own town. In the back of my mind, an uneasy question about my own safety was taking shape.

Teema stood up, straightened her back, shoved out her chest.

"John Richardson means it when he says he wants you back," I said, looking up at her. "You should stay away from him and this market."

"We will see," Teema replied.

Her pride had been hurt, although she wouldn't weep or display her weakness. She would trot back here another time for the music, whose

sounds and rhythms were woven into her being. Exhausted, we trudged
back to the Factory.

TEN

T he next morning, my kitchen friends told me the story of how
the Nawab's family had commemorated his birthday with a huge
ceremony, part of which involved weighing the Nawab against
gold. Not only was the scale made of gold, but it was also suspended
by gold chains. The Nawab sat on one scale while the other was loaded
with gold coins – mohurs – which he would donate to the petitioners
the next day. Those getting such a gift would be lucky indeed.

Still uncertain about my appearance at the Royal Court the next day,
I decided that I must somehow speak with Job sahib.

He'd finished his supper and was on his way to his bedchamber; I
stood at the foot of the stairs, a dust rag in my hand.

Job sahib's face softened when he saw me, his long beige coat illu-
minating the space. "Tomorrow is your big day, isn't it?"

I forgot the day's fatigue and my own apprehensions. "Yes, sir," I said.
What if my words stuck in my throat? What if tears formed at the
corners of my eyes? What if my knees became weak?

"The Nawab's officers will, no doubt, inundate you with questions,
try to confuse you to test your morals and your honesty, but I have
utmost confidence in you, Maria."

He looked at me brightly, while making me aware of the obstacles I
had on my way. Not many women appeared at the Court, much less a
widow. In the blue depth of Job sahib's eyes, I read his thoughts: *You've
gone through the fire test once and survived. You'll go through it again and come
forth victorious.* Perhaps the thoughts were mine, but it gave me the
encouragement I needed to think they were his.

"But . . . sir . . . I hardly know anything about the functioning of our
government. Maybe I don't need to know that much. But, but I am
curious, always."

"I am glad to hear of your interest. Indeed, I find it fascinating."

He went on to describe, in a tone of authority, how the Nawab, our
regional ruler, followed orders from Emperor Aurangzeb, who was

already being called the 'Last Great Mughal' by the English. The Emperor ruled much of Hindustan from his perch in Delhi. I couldn't picture such a big domain, which existed side by side with a slew of independent kingdoms, although not always peacefully. Nor did I find it easy to accept the fact that the greedy Emperor was not satisfied with the wealth he had accumulated, the vaults he had filled with gold, silver, and rubies. He wished to annex independent principalities so as to own a larger territory and act as the sole ruler of the land; Job sahib doubted he'd succeed.

"It's quite a spectacle, the petition at our regional Nawab's Court, a hundred people gathering in a magnificent hall," he said. "I hope it will prove to be pleasant for you."

He'd cared enough to explain this much. Still feeling apprehensive, I said, "I've never traveled that far away from the Factory."

As though understanding my need for support, Job sahib gave a hint of a smile. "I will accompany you. Tariq might join us too."

Was he lying to make me feel comfortable? Would he actually accompany a lowly servant, a cook who had no clothes worthy of the Nawab's Court?

My boldness dissipated. Why did he have to invite the irascible Tariq? Didn't he trust me enough?

Although I had many more questions, I didn't wish to delay the sahib any further, so I stepped aside and bowed. "God be with ye," he said and went up the stairs.

I walked to the courtyard, extended my arms toward the night sky and inhaled deeply, taking is as much air as I could, thanking the gods for their beneficence. Then I made my way back to the kitchen, humming a merry tune, and tackled the cleaning chores with new-found energy.

The following morning, four well-muscled porters, carrying my palanquin on their shoulders, marched along on a road that led to the Nawab's palace. Having never ridden a palanquin before, I was sick with anxiety. I couldn't trust my eyes. To be taking this trip to the Royal Palace in this elaborate conveyance bedecked with tapestry, studded with colorful glass, and suspended between silver-plated poles. Nor could I believe that I'd actually be received by the Nawab to present my case before him.

I inspected myself in the mirror affixed to the wall of the palanquin. Teema had loaned me her gold-bordered indigo sari and a set of four rose-gold bangles embossed with tiny white shells. She taught me how

to bow before the Nawab. "Bend from the waist," she said. "Lower a
hand, take the dust off the ground, touch your forehead, and rise with
a slight smile. Let your bangles make pleasant music. Let your gestures
be soft and speak of your humility. Let your expression be one of glowing
gratefulness."

Sitting in the palanquin, I tried to picture myself at the Nawab's
reception hall. I had hoped that Job sahib would stand next to me in
the ornate hall as I made my petition to the Nawab, but he had cancelled
at the last minute due to an 'emergency meeting', Tariq informed me.
I was on my own. The pebbled road snaked in and out of sprawling,
pastel-washed brick homes with columned entrances. Soon we passed
a paddy field, a stone temple, and a three-domed terracotta mosque
with a large courtyard. Streams of pedestrians, mostly men clad in light
cotton clothes and colorful head-dresses, looked at the palanquin in
awe.

Much later, a red sandstone structure crowning a hill, its bulbous
domes gleaming pink in the sun, its façade decorated by colorful tiles,
loomed before us; it was surrounded by a high fort wall. We arrived at
the arched gateway ornamented by black and white marble work. The
porters laid the palanquin down. "You can walk from here; we'll wait
for you," one of them said.

Scores of pedestrians poured through the Palace gateway. Some arrived
on hooded bullock-drawn carriages and others on horseback, stirring
up dust clouds as they trotted along. The sound of hooves matched the
pace of my fast-beating heart. I lingered for a moment, unsure of which
direction I should go. My cheap sandals clattered on packed dirt as I
trailed after a group of petitioners dressed in their finery. We strolled
through the courtyard past a pool in the shape of a lotus petal, a lavish
formal garden with pavilions on either side, and headed toward a public-
audience hall taller than our Factory.

"I hope the Nawab is in a good mood today," said a rotund man ahead
of me to his friend. "I hope he'll not only grant my request but also
give me a mohur. Just one coin will feed my family for months."

"I'll be content to be one of the earlier ones to be called," his
companion replied. "The public hour lasts a short time. After that, the
Nawab leaves, and his courtiers take over. They're not as kind, nor do
they distribute gold. In fact, they try to get rid of the petitioners as fast
as they can."

A mohur would be a nice surprise, but I could hardly imagine the

Nawab slipping one in my hand. Instead, I worried about how he might receive my story. Would he show me a wrinkled brow, a flushed face, a stiff posture as he pointed to the door and shouted at me in commands I couldn't follow?

As we filed through the carved brass door, an attendant sprinkled rose perfume on our hands. Inside, the walls of the large hall were covered with a gold-leaf design that sparkled in the daylight. The ceiling was decorated in an intricate pattern with mirrors and semi-precious gems; the floor, paved with stonework, was enchanting in its beauty and symmetry. A lush carpet in crimson and black, woven in elephant images, covered most of the floor. Taking the cue from other petitioners, I dropped down and arranged myself in a lotus position in the second row. A hundred people shared the carpet with me, all smelling of rose-water. Sitting there in the heat, perspiring profusely, my mind went blank. Drumbeats announced the Nawab's arrival, trumpets blared. The sounds reverberated in my stomach. The Nawab entered through a side door, surrounded by officers and generals. When he stepped onto a marble platform, I heard the sound of footsteps marching along the floor, their sharp report bouncing off the walls.

The whole assembly stood up and bowed. The man ahead of me bowed and touched his right palm to his forehead; I did likewise. Did I bow deeply enough? Did I rise too clumsily?

Decked in a golden satin robe, the Nawab, a man of middle years with clove-colored eyes, mounted a high dais. Diamonds sparkled around his neck. A sword encased in a crimson sheath dangled from his waist-sash. He ascended the throne, a dome-roofed, octagonal silver chair fitted with pearls and rubies and facing the East. The painted panel behind him depicted a garden. As a young boy, it was said, he had fought off an angry elephant that had tried to pummel his horse with its trunk. He was supposed to have subdued the elephant's fearsome head and menacing tusks with his bare hands.

The Nawab exchanged a few niceties with those who surrounded him: ministers, bejeweled noblemen, members of the imperial house-hold, and principal officers of the army. Two servants fanned him with jade-handled bamboo fans. His bodyguards, dressed in yellow, stood alert nearby. They all acted so important and so sure of their position that I felt small and insignificant in comparison. As the Nawab surveyed the crowd, our eyes met for an instant. Finally, he asked everyone to be seated.

"Joy and peace to you," the Nawab said in a deep, guttural voice.

"Joy and peace to you," the audience muttered.

Several petitioners stood up and voluntarily stepped forward with nazranas—ritual gifts of pearls, silver bullions, and also the finest of mangoes, a favorite fruit of the Nawab, the town's speciality. A smiling courtier, pushing a cart, collected the items on a platter. The imperial scribe, a man attired in a waistcoat with an embroidered cap on his head, eased onto a stool in one corner of the room. A pen, a porcelain ink-pot, and a ledger were at his disposal. Now, at last, the Nawab was ready to receive claims, complaints, and reports from his subjects, and to dispense justice as necessary. An imperial officer marched forward, his gaze searching the crowd. In what appeared to be a random selection, the officer pointed to an elderly man with a sun-beaten face and haunted eyes.

Dressed in home-spun cotton, the man stepped forward and stood about fifty paces from the Nawab. A cane under his arm, he gave his name and the village he was from and described his problem. His farmland, his only means of support, had been flooded by the recent downpour. Despite this calamity and the expenses he'd incurred, he'd been required to pay a substantial tax to the revenue officer on crops he hadn't been able to grow. He spoke haltingly, his thin voice wavering often. Judging by the somber mood of the room, others were also favorably disposed toward him.

"O, Lord of the Earth," the farmer said in conclusion, placing the palm of his right hand on his forehead and bending at the waist. "In the name of the merciful Allah, I prevail upon you to settle this dispute. I am a humble peasant. I live or die with my land."

The Nawab consulted with his council for a long moment. The conclusions were communicated to the scribe.

"We understand and take note of the situation," an officer said to the farmer. "Your petition will receive further attention. If warranted, we'll reimburse you for the revenue you've been required to pay."

"A thousand salaams to you," the farmer said, his voice thick with emotion as an officer took him aside for further questioning.

Another courtier scanned the room slowly; his gaze eventually came to rest on me. My cheeks grew warm as he signaled to me and said in a booming voice, "You! Next."

I stepped forward, faced the Nawab, and bowed the way I'd been taught by Teema. Then I stood motionless, unable to summon a word of the speech I had practised for days. After taking a few deep, panicked breaths, I tried to slow the hammering of my heart.

"Your Honor," I said eventually, my voice cracking. "I salute you with reverence. I am here to beg your pardon of a man who has saved me from an attempted human sacrifice by fighting off an entire community. He courted the wrath of a priest, risked the danger of causing harm to himself, carried me off to a boat, and gave me a new life in a new environment. Job Charnock."

The Nawab smiled, perhaps in recognition of Job sahib's name and the heroic praise awarded to him. His head tilted toward me; his officials exchanged glances among themselves.

"I wouldn't be standing here if it weren't for that Englishman." I let the words flow from my tongue in a forceful but gentle manner. "What might seem like an abduction was in fact a generous act. I beg that Job Charnock be cleared of all the charges and commended for his act of generosity and courage."

While the Nawab consulted with his Court, a uniformed official of lower rank bustled forward. "Where do you live?" He asked, looking suspiciously at me. "What kind of work do you do? Why are you alone?"

Had I been a man, would he have spoken to me this harshly? The injustice prickled, but I decided to take the opportunity to further reveal my situation. "I work in the Factory and live under strict rules, but I have a life only because of the Englishman. Job Charnock has saved me from being a sati. The charges against him are false and should be dropped."

"Why should we believe you?' The official asked. "Why isn't Job Charnock with you?"

I couldn't come up with an answer.

"Why weren't you a sati?"

"I don't believe in that custom."

"Are you a prostitute?"

"No! I'm a cook."

The official kept questioning me, his angry glare surely meant to unnerve me. I wasn't deterred. Job sahib had prepared me for such questions, and now his faith in me encouraged me to answer with courage and humility. In the end, there was deep silence for a moment. Perhaps the official heard the truth in my voice. Finally, he relayed the information to the Nawab who turned toward me.

"It will be so," the Nawab said. "The case against Job Charnock is hereby dismissed."

I bowed deeply and thanked the Nawab.

No more troubles for Job sahib. Time for me to take my seat, feel relief and gratitude, yet, swept away by this victory, I forgot propriety. "Your Honor," I rushed ahead in a high voice, as though addressing a friend alone.

The Nawab looked amused. He watched me closely; his eyes grew darker.

"I am here also to speak about Hindu widows, especially Brahmin widows. Few people are aware of the fate they suffer. I got away from the village before I could be burned alive. Many widows are not so fortunate."

The Nawab's initial amusement over my lack of propriety was lost. His expression grew grave. "Continue," he said gently.

"People pity a widow as they pity an animal. She's scarred for the rest of her life. Although a widower often remarries, a widow, even if she's young, isn't allowed to remarry."

The Nawab tapped the toe of his shoe on the marble dais. He rubbed his cheek and gazed up at the ceiling as if in deep thought. After a few moments he beckoned the officers to join him. Together, they slipped out to an adjoining chamber.

I turned to take in the reaction of the audience. There were Brahmins, Hindus from other castes, and Muslims among the people gathered in the hall. A young girl sat stunned, as though she'd seen a horrible sight and was now trying to erase it from her memory. A tender-eyed elderly woman wrapped in a gray shawl muttered a few kind words to me, but her husband looked indignantly at me. I looked away.

A man seated in the front row leapt to his feet; his eyes rained fire on me. "How dare you speak lies, you, shameless widow? Our pundits say, 'Your mere shadow brings misfortune to those it falls upon. Woe to those who encounter a widow in the morning, for their day shall not end well.'" He addressed the entire crowd of petitioners. "I say she should be expelled from this room. She should be cast back into the funeral pyre. Do you all agree?"

"Yes, back into the fire!" A man yelled from somewhere behind me.

"Stop speaking to her like that," another man shouted out from the third row. "All women belong to the tribe of mothers. We should respect them."

"Back into the fire," the first man said.

I clutched my sari tightly around my chest, checked the distance between where I stood and the doors through which I'd entered the hall. Guards stood at the doors; some of the petitioners appeared doubtful, others hostile, and then there were those who cast kindly glances at me. In the end, I resolved not to run away like a coward.

"No!" I shouted. "The Vedas say women lead men. They should be pampered and respected, all women, including widows."

"She's correct," said a young Hindu priest from a far corner, wrapped in a saffron shawl, his forehead smeared with sanctified beige paste. "Listen also to this sloka, which extols the virtues of a woman."

Together we began reciting in Sanskrit from opposite corners of the room, his voice calm and cultured.

An irate man in a red tunic interrupted us. "I'll thrash both of you if you don't stop your false slokas."

"Leave her alone." The priest dropped his shawl on the floor, displaying his bare muscled chest. "Come hit me then."

"Don't you dare hit our priest," said another man dressed in a yellow waistcoat. "Let me have the joy of striking at you instead."

Clenching his fist, the defender of the priest wove through the audience and lunged at his opponent, pushing him away from the priest. Many in the immediate area hurried to their feet to avoid being injured.

As the two kicked and punched each other, people all around me yelled. I heard someone's plaintive voice cry out, "Calm down. In the name of Shiva, calm down." Another man joined in the fight. The crowd watched, their eyes enlarged, their mouths open in shock.

I could take it no more. I lifted my voice and shouted, "Stop! With due respect to the Nawab, stop!"

The Nawab had returned. The echo of my voice bounced around the hall as he approached his throne. He frowned at the crowd, raised a hand, and commanded, "Take your seats. Stop yelling. Those of you who have caused chaos will be punished."

A group of uniformed guards rushed in, seized the fighting party, and whisked them out of the door. I assumed they would be locked up.

"Pay no attention to their misbehavior," the Nawab said to me in a deep, pleasant, yet forceful voice. He paused and addressed the entire assembly. "A generation ago, Emperor Jahangir had passed a law to abolish sati, but his law is not being obeyed. There are social forces against it, which makes the job of enforcing it difficult. I am personally opposed to sati. I will not allow such a practice to continue. I would also like to reenact the Widow Remarriage Provision of the law."

A woman applauded. "We sing your praise for delivering justice."

The Nawab nodded in her direction. "The law might take time to enforce, but my men will counsel the elders of each village. We will let the people know that those who violate the law will be punished."

"Our Lord's commands shall be obeyed," said a man in the crowd.

A courtier came forth and spoke to me on behalf of the Nawab: "We will have a talk with your in-laws. They will be punished for performing sati, and we will compensate you with a mohur, even though we realize that this is not enough to repay you for the pain inflicted on you." He handed me a large shiny gold coin. "You may now be seated."

I bowed as I received the generous gift, cupping my hands around it. My throat felt tight. The heavy coin was made of pure gold and inscribed in flowing calligraphy. I looked up from it and almost saw the God of Good Fortune, a celestial figure, bluish and ethereal, appearing before me and smiling.

At that moment, I examined my heart's longings in a new light. Much as I wanted to return to the loving embrace of my family, my destiny no longer lay with them. I thrived on the bustle of business in our Factory, in this town. But what talents did I, a humble servant, have that allowed me to dream of a better future in the Factory? Well, at least I was eager to learn and not completely lacking in intelligence. I could pick up the intricacies of the trading business; I surely could. Then I would be able to act for the benefit of my downtrodden people. By extending a helping hand to them, I would also perhaps heal my own wounds. A feeling of glorious possibilities swept over me.

The doors to the hall were flung open. An imperial messenger burst into the room, his white loin cloth and vest filthy with soot. He stood before the Nawab. Gasping, his chest heaving, he laid his hand on his breast and bowed low.

"A thousand pardons, Your Lord." He said, catching his breath. "I am sorry to interrupt, but I have a critical matter to report."

"Continue," the Nawab said.

"A fire has broken out in the market. It has already destroyed at least five tents and several bamboo huts and, unless brought under control, it will reach the nearby houses."

"My shop! Is it still there?" A man in the audience jumped to his feet and ran through the door.

The room buzzed with questions and shouts of dismay. My insides knotted as I thought of the poor merchants and their wives and children out on the streets with no shelter.

"No one has ever seen a blaze of this size," the messenger continued. "Shopkeepers are rushing to the river with their pails, but the process is too slow. We need help to extinguish the fire quickly. We need to move the women and children to safer quarters. Your attention to this matter is urgently requested."

Did Teema go to the market this morning? Might she be in danger? I stood up and began to rush from the room after the others, but the Nawab's voice stopped me.

"Order, order," the Nawab called out. Turning to his officers, the Nawab said, "Dispatch help immediately on horseback." Rising from his seat, he faced the audience. "Will you all be willing to aid your fellow citizens in containing the fire?"

"Yes, Your Lord," a chorus of voices roared.

"Go forth then," the Nawab announced. "This meeting is adjourned. Peace be upon you."

"But I want to present my petition," a woman cried out. "I came all the way from the village of—"

Her plea was drowned by a hundred voices showering over the Nawab. "And on you also be peace."

The whole assembly streamed out of the door. Horsemen galloped out.

"Can we go to the market quickly?" I asked a palanquin bearer. "I want to find a friend and help others."

"No," a porter said. "We're taking you back to the Factory—Job sahib's order."

"You see, I must—"

"That will not be wise," the porter interrupted me. "There is looting in progress, pandemonium. We will be punished if we don't take you back safely. Please get in."

As we passed by the market, we could see people running back and forth with buckets of water. Columns of dense black smoke curled upward, and the stench of burning thatch pervaded the air. Timber-framed houses creaked as they crashed to the ground. A child howled. Distressed voices of people rose in the distance. Wild dogs barked. I listened for Teema's voice. Was she there or was she safe in the Factory?

Red-coated horseback riders wearing helmets leapt through the smoke. Birds screeched from treetops. Flames coiled up—crimson and gold, with a dark center— like in another deadly fire scene not long ago.

I shut my eyes.

ELEVEN

"**D**o you know what started the market fire?" Idris asked everyone in the kitchen the next morning. "A hookah! A careless smoker not minding his hookah. A hundred stalls and two hundred houses gone."

He also informed me that Teema had been seen consoling a group of women whose husbands had lost their shops.

With the news still ringing in my ears, I walked over to the verandah for my twice-a-week English lesson. Charles sahib appeared wearing a high-crowned black hat, white doublet with shell buttons, and white breeches reaching to his knees. My cooking must have helped him. His face had regained its pinkish hue, but it was still a trifle blotchy. His sparse, flat, straw-colored hair peeked from under his hat, combed for a change.

"Describe the bazaar fire in English," he said casually. His piercing eyes seemed to be indulging in their usual pastime of searching for a mistake, an opportunity to ridicule, or to identify a victim. I'd gotten Job sahib cleared at the Nawab's Court; it must have surely angered him.

"I didn't see much of it, sahib."

"You've seen other fires."

Sweat gathered in my armpits. I liked English words and phrases. They came from a distant island, sounds that were hard, precise, and dripping with confidence. But on this occasion, the words, phrases, and sentences describing a fire scoured my throat and I felt the heat they discharged. "A fire rises, destroys," I began.

"Don't you call it the fire god?" the sahib barked out with typical impatience, "or is it a goddess? Doesn't your fire goddess only destroy?"

"No, sir, our fire goddess also brings new life, new hope. Some wild flowers grow well near ashes."

"For simple folk like you, hope is important," he said, waving his hand dismissively. My eyes must have asked a question, for he added, "A simple folk is one who does simple tasks. Tell me what you do all day."

"I get up, I bathe, I cook, I clean, but I'd like to take on more important tasks, sahib, if I were allowed to."

"A cook and a servant, that's your fate. We, the sahibs, do the important tasks."

"What are they, sir?"

"You want to know?" He unleashed phrases commonly used by the Factors: taking inventory, receiving a shipment, meeting with local merchants, making payments and recording them in ledger books. Although I didn't fully follow the significance of each and every task, I welcomed the new vision that opened up before me: the daily life of a Factor.

"That will be all for today," he said.

I stood, thanked the sahib, and bowed out. The next three lessons went similarly, my struggles with English pronunciation non-ending, but I hung on. Several afternoons later, as we finished and I was ready to step away, Charles sahib glanced up at me and barked out in Bangla, "Wait." He paused. "Your soups are good, I feel much better, and I also might add that you've made a bit of progress in your English conversation. I didn't expect it."

I bowed my head and allowed the flattery to slide over me, then realized he'd given me a chance to express myself. "I study whenever I have a spare moment, sahib." Seeing that he was listening to me, his head cocked, I spilled out more in a mixture of Bangla and English. "I practise English with whoever I can find."

Charles sahib gestured with a short pudgy hand. "I'd wager that you can't find too many people. How many locals speak English fluently? They ask us why we don't pick up their beautiful mother tongue. Well, we try. Most of us can speak some Bangla or Persian, beautiful or not, but they don't seem to understand our accents. And, Lord help us, there are so many dialects. Of course, we have Tariq to do the interpreting, but he has other tasks to perform."

Interpreter. I imagined myself seated amidst traders and brokers, voices soaring, mingling, and crashing as I discovered the nuances and helped them reach an agreement, switching between languages efficiently.

"I would like to know more about the duties of an interpreter, sir."

"It's a tough job. Your people don't seem to make good interpreters."

"Why so, sir?"

"Two fellows we hired left because neither could handle the pressure of negotiating for hours on end. One didn't like the rough behavior of the traders. Of course, we have to be careful who we hire. One chap added in things we didn't say. Later, he admitted he did it for laughs, and since that time, we've been picky about who does this important work for us. Without an interpreter no negotiations can happen."

While Charles sahib went on, I envisioned a different kind of life opening out before me, if I could ever find a way to be placed in such a position. Tending the kitchen, inspecting the food supplies, and scrubbing the floors consumed my hours, but I could do so much more. I'd garner a better wage too as an interpreter. I'd be closer to Job sahib and function in the universe in which he operated. It warmed me, the thought of proximity to the man whom I admired but rarely saw. I smiled, imagining myself doing translation work for the Company, English words bubbling in my throat.

Hearing the sound of footsteps and a familiar greeting, I reined in my fantasies and looked up. Charles sahib stopped speaking and followed my gaze. Job sahib was coming toward us, wearing a loose-fitting red waistcoat buttoned with rubies and a pair of ivory trousers. A silver sword rested in a scabbard at his waist. I felt shy and awkward. Why? Was it the magnetic pull of his masculinity?

Job sahib looked as though he had something on his mind. His shoulders were stiff, and a kind of heaviness seemed to have settled around his eyes. I smiled spontaneously, drawing nearer to him out of a natural inclination, deeming his arrival here to be a most fortunate occurrence. Then I berated myself and took a step back. Should I be studying him so minutely?

I saw a frown cross Charles sahib's forehead at the appearance of his superior, but quicker than a sparrow hopping to another perch, he got hold of himself. His expression became welcoming as he returned his superior's greeting.

Job sahib shifted his attention to me and folded his hands in namaskar, the local gesture of respect. I did likewise, pleased at being treated with deference.

"I must praise you for clearing the charges against me at the Royal Court," he said in Bangla. "It helped to have the Nawab hear your story firsthand."

"It was an honor, sir." I blushed.

"And I hear you're picking up English much faster than we're learning Bangla," he said with a faint smile, his voice ringing with a note of sincerity. He glanced at Charles sahib and nodded politely, acknowledging the other man's contribution to my learning.

I accepted the compliment, looked up into Job sahib's eyes, and mumbled, "Well, I still can't say everything I want to say."

Eyes twinkling, Job sahib smiled at me a little more broadly. "And what is it that you haven't said to me that you'd like to say?" His face had softened. His eyes drank me in as though I was the only person standing there, as though Charles sahib had disappeared.

I bit my lower lip and felt the color rushing to my cheeks. Could he read my mind?

At this point, I considered taking leave to hide my embarrassment, but I remained rooted to the spot. Silly as it might sound, I felt responsible for Job sahib's physical safety. No one trusted Charles sahib, none of us from the servile class. He could change at a moment's notice, turn into a tyrant. Even though he tutored me and we'd established a rapport of some sort, I, too, regarded him with deep suspicion.

The moment passed. Charles sahib was watching us, his face pinched, an artificial smile on his lips.

"I went over to the bazaar this morning," Job sahib said, addressing us both in Bangla. "The fire has all but burned itself out, but there was so much ash and debris that I almost didn't recognize the place." He shook his head and his eyes clouded over with pain.

"That'll affect our commercial interests," Charles sahib said.

"I'm worried that many hawkers have lost their livelihood," Job sahib said. "It's our duty to help them get reestablished."

"We don't owe them anything," Charles sahib said sharply.

How callous of the man! I spoke before I could hold back the words. "I believe it will be necessary to help the merchants get back on their feet," I said in Bangla, wishing I could have spoken in English. "They supply our daily needs. Already we're short of provisions."

Charles sahib looked at me unkindly and began to correct me for my disrespect, but Job sahib cut him off.

"I have a plan to give them aid," Job sahib said. "But the Company can only spend so much money. We can't cover it all."

It bothered Job that one of his major competitors, the formidable Dutch East India Company, whom he called the 'Dutch menace', planned to give bigger aid. They would, of course. They'd arrived in Hindustan earlier than the British East India Company, thus gaining a head start, and successfully built up an intra-Asian trade network in the last half-century, extending as far as Japan. They traded raw silk, saltpeter, spices, opium, and indigo dye, just like the Company, but with the experience they had acquired in Asia, they far surpassed it in magnitude. Not only did they have bigger warehouses, but had also adapted well to the nuances of conducting business here, established a number of trading stations, and developed an extensive network of trading relationships. The closest Dutch trading post was in Chinsura, a town adjacent to Hooghly, a little too close for his comfort. Their goal would obviously be to eliminate the English as a competitor as they'd done with the Portuguese earlier.

He didn't say all this that day, keeping his thoughts to himself, to shelter the frail but determined girl before him.

I wasn't aware of his thoughts or the facts at that time, but I was ready with my response, as though I were an important player in this enterprise. My English lessons had helped in an unexpected way. The hard consonants and their implosive sounds as well as the demanding vowels had made me feel confident, even when I wasn't speaking the language.

"To start with, we could buy quantities of grain to feed people," I said in a voice rising high with enthusiasm.

"Yes, and a citizen's council could be formed," Job sahib said. "It could decide how to distribute the food and find housing for the homeless."

"In the long run, in my humble observation, this type of aid can only help the Company," I replied. "We, the people of Hindustan, melt when kindness is extended to us. We remain indebted forever. And we repay many times over."

I was still shaking with excitement from expressing so much when Arthur sahib, the Third Factor, appeared. Big-cheeked and ruddy, he took Charles sahib aside, conferred with him for a moment, and they departed. Job sahib and I were once again alone together in this ornate, marble-floored verandah lined with rose bushes and jasmine climbers.

"If it's not too audacious of me to ask this, may I discuss another matter of importance with you?" I asked.

I was violating yet another unspoken custom. Household servants and their masters didn't discuss matters of importance as equals. An iron screen stood between us, layers of propriety certainly, but also differences of skin colors.

The sahib looked startled but pleased. Smiling, he extended an arm toward a chair and nodded. "What do you wish to speak about?"

"I know I still have a long way to go," I said, making it sound like a normal request. "I...I'd like to have a better position. I'm capable of it, working toward it, Job sahib." I switched to English and said, "I want to be an interpreter."

Job sahib sat back a little, an indulgent smile on his face. "An interpreter!"

I drew in a big gulp of air and spoke in Bangla, more assertively. "I understand local customs and manners, what people really mean when they are negotiating. I could be very useful to the Company."

On that day so long ago, I didn't know my abilities well enough to be able to say: *If you would allow me, I could sit between the Factors and the local traders and help bring two sides together.*

"I can see that you wish to be advanced."

I studied him. He represented hope, like the rising sun, this dignified man, fair in his dealings, more so than the other Factors. Basking in his radiance, I imagined my future: a jumble of luminous days filled with the thrill of helping to negotiate important business deals.

"But do you think you're ready? You're speaking Bangla with me."

My throat went dry, though a strange force within me wouldn't let me cower. "But it won't be long before . . ."

"We're starting a new set of trade dealings in a matter of days. Tariq has helped me hire an interpreter. We'll have to see how he works out, but that's not really the problem. Most merchants are men, so are our Factors. You, as the only woman present, might feel out of place."

I registered his unspoken message; men might not be comfortable in my company. Oh, that silly woman, they'd think. What's she doing here? Yet I wasn't ready to give up. A story Sal had told me about an independent kingdom, Virganj, leapt to my mind. Situated only miles from Cossimbazar, it was run by a queen. Like all such noble women, the queen dressed in silks and jewels and was known to lavishly entertain her important guests. She ran her kingdom with kindness and cleverness, and determination, bringing riches and honor to her people.

"If I may be so bold as to ask this, sir, do you ever have the occasion to deal with a queen, a landowner's wife, or a merchant's mother? If so, I could be of help there. In wealthy households, women control the money. A good man would think twice before going against his mother's commands or his wife's wishes."

Job sahib leaned back in his chair and regarded me thoughtfully. Then he smiled, a slow, lazy smile, but one of recognition, of acknowledgment.

"You're clever indeed, he said."

To me he said just that, words of immense comfort and encouragement to my parched heart. But there had been more on his mind. Much
more.

The girl, a simple cook, had actually offered him a valuable idea at a
time when he worried that the Company's business expansion was beginning to stall in the face of stiff competition from the Dutch. That wasn't
all. At the time rumors were rife about a group of rival Englishman
planning to petition the Crown for a licence to trade with Hindustan,
to stop the Company monopoly. His business would surely suffer if they
succeeded. And if he didn't show a profit within three years, he would
lose his charter and cease to exist; the English Parliament wanted it that
way to foster competition.

The girl had a bold look in her eyes, bolder than it had been before,
wistful, too. Perhaps she thought she hadn't been advancing fast enough.
Yet he had gotten good reports on her. Charles had commented on her
rapid progress in English. Arthur had heard her practising English with
her kitchen mates and been pleasantly surprised. Only Tariq still found
faults with her.

"She's too assertive," Tariq had said to him the other day. "She doesn't
know her place, that village girl. Always sniffing around for more."

Now Job chuckled. If only Tariq understood the background of most
of the Factors on his staff. However arrogantly they might speak and
act, they had traveled this far, practically gambling their life in the process,
simply because they hadn't been able to make it in England. Each was
a cast-away, desperate for a break. It would simply be a matter of time.
That ambitious village girl, with her drive and her obstinacy, would fit
in well with that bunch.

"I get your point," he said. "Although we haven't had any occasions
like that so far, a woman interpreter would surely help us to form
connections with prominent local women. Some tribal leaders have
powerful wives we ought to get to know as well. You're correct in saying
that we've neglected an important segment of the Hindustani society.
Unfortunately, this is how the Council prefers it to be, at least at this
point."

At least he thought my idea was sound. I smiled.

"I think I can trust you. There are rules and regulations the Council
imposes on us that I don't necessarily agree with, although I abide by
them and I am always honored to serve the Crown. Someday, however,

I'd like to have my own trading company, one that would encompass a much larger geographical area as its base." His face glowing, he added, "At that point, my vision would take wing."

I'd never seen so much excitement in the sahib. I felt a similar spark inside me until I heard him saying, "But getting back to your request, we have another requirement, a most important one. You have to be able to read and write English, record the details of the transaction, such as the parties involved, the discussions that take place, the resolution. How are your writing skills?"

I couldn't answer. I could scribble the English alphabet, a few words, and a sentence or two. I looked down at my hands.

"I am sorry, Maria," Job sahib said, gently. "We can't hire you as an interpreter, but keep studying."

I couldn't look at him just then, but I nodded.

He stood up in one swift move. "Now I must be off."

I murmured my thanks. Did I go too far? I replayed the brief encounter in my mind. My hands were empty, but by sharing his secret vision with me, Job sahib had made me feel as though I mattered.

TWELVE

A few days later, I strolled to the ghat to take a sacred dip in the river. Fresh from the bath and the sweet, pleasant morning air, I headed out toward the Factory. On the way, I noticed two men, both with graying hair and knives hanging from their waist-belts, staring at me from a short distance. I stared back at them.

"Isn't she the widow who caused trouble at the Royal Court?" One of them said loudly.

"Yes, that's her," the other man replied. "She got away, that whore."

I gave them a hard look, covered my head with the ghomta, and quickened my pace.

"Shall we show her how a whore should be treated?"

Both men hurried toward me, their sandals flopping. A burning sensation constricted my throat. *Run!* Just then a herdsman with a long procession of wild-eyed goats burst onto the road. Accustomed to these animals, I wove in and out of their knots, listening to their plaintive bleating, quick on my feet. Soon the goats wandered away from me. The two men didn't have it so easy. Perhaps sensing their aggressiveness, several goats charged at them as a group, pushing with their thick horns. I turned to see an argument ensuing between the herdsman and my would-be attackers. While they battled with the animals and their care-taker, I strode quickly to the other side of the road and eventually reached the Factory. Once inside, I collapsed in relief. Once again, the Factory had saved me.

In the kitchen, I related the story to Idris, pouring out my hurt and frustration.

Idris stopped slicing a slab of partridge meat. "Stay away from the ghat for a few days, Maria. Those are goondas. You'll do well not to leave this compound. Don't go roaming the streets." Idris leaned toward me. "It won't be for long, Maria. Rumor has it that the Nawab will soon abolish the cruel rite of sati and reinforce the Widow Remarriage Act. Your petition has had an effect. If it is enforced, the two goondas will be punishable under the law for their intended action against a widow."

"But, Idris, I must go to the water. I can't forgo my river bath."

"Remember to keep yourself well covered."

His warning rang in my head as I stirred the porridge. Just then our grocer, bazaar boy as the sahibs called him, appeared at the door. A pair of cymbals hung at his waist; these clattered and announced his presence. Pratap and I came out of the kitchen. The large bamboo basket on the grocer's head was filled to the brim with fresh produce: potatoes, squashes, leafy greens, and bunches of herbs.

Grave-faced, the grocer set his basket down on the ground. "Our beloved Nawab, Protector of the Poor and the Needy, left the table in the middle of a meal last night. He isn't feeling well today."

I forgot my usual practice of peering into his basket and selecting the best produce.

"The grand banquet he was supposed to have given has been cancelled," the grocer continued. "So the Royal Kitchen, which demands the best produce, did not buy from me. Since I had to pay a top price for these vegetables, I will have to pass the cost on to you. The price will be double today."

"What an excuse for charging more!" Pratap said. "How do we know you're telling us the truth?"

"You don't trust me?" the grocer said. "You don't honor our Nawab? Then I am leaving."

"I do respect the Nawab," I said to the grocer. "But we can't pay more. Our budget is strictly controlled by the sahibs. Look, your produce will be spoiled. Why don't we buy double our usual amount at the same rate you usually give us? Your profit will not be as much as you expect, but at least you will not suffer a loss."

The grocer thought for a moment then grudgingly agreed. As we conducted our negotiations, Arthur-sahib, who was passing by, asked what the matter was. I explained as best as I could.

"May God protect our Nawab," the grocer said as he left, seemingly happier now that his basket was less full. "May God protect us all."

Arthur sahib smiled faintly and continued on his way.

At the end of my working hours, with moonlight as my guide, I traversed the long courtyard, skirted the swaying bamboos, and reached the back of the compound. I couldn't let go of my concerns. As an unaccompanied woman, I wasn't safe in this compound, either. Already Francis sahib had tried to molest me in my room.

Alone in my room, I lit a tiny oil lamp. It was time for my studies. I hunched over a stack of rough creamy paper, a quill pen, and a stone inkwell, atop a plank of wood, all items bought at the Company's expense and donated to me by Charles sahib. I paid little attention to the annoying sounds of a wild dog yelping and a mosquito whining as I scribbled the English alphabet and the words I had learned thus far. I took delight in drawing the loops and curls, placing the dots, slashing the T's. It was slow-moving as I wrote a word and then waited for the ink to dry before attempting to write another.

My eyelids were heavy hoods, but I stayed bent over the paper, my hand sweeping across the page as I imitated Charles sahib's handwriting. The words grew tiny as the night stretched on, the ink started to bleed. Still, with each mark, I discovered a new purpose in me.

Someone pounded at the door. The wind? A wild dog? An intruder? Who could it be at this hour? I leapt to my feet, a prickling at the back of my neck. "Who's there?" I called, my voice quivering.

"Teema."

I could barely contain my surprise. I jerked open the door. She stood there, a sheer black scarf about her head, her chin lowered, as though she was embarrassed to call on me.

"Where have you been?" I asked, clasping her hand and drawing her into the room.

"Shall we take a stroll?" Carrying the wick-lamp, I stepped outside.

We walked toward the far end of the compound. The sahibs never came to this part of the compound, mostly uncared for, where vegetation grew wild. Still, I could hear the voice of my kitchen friends saying, "They don't take it well when they see us walking all over." I stayed alert for signs of wild animals, intruders, and molesters.

"No one will be able to hear us out here," Teema whispered.

On this dark night, in the flickering light of the lamp, Teema appeared quite unlike her usual self, smaller somehow. Her movements were more angular, as though a hidden turmoil inside had stolen her grace.

"Bir has a little joke, you know," I said lightly to cover my concerns for her. "We have a ghost sweeper. You never see her around, but she keeps the place spotlessly clean."

For a second, Teema didn't speak. Then, her voice rough with emotion, she replied, "The ghost is about to disappear."

"What?"

"I'm leaving this place for good."

"Oh, for heaven's sake! Is it due to John Richardson?"

"Quite," Teema said. "Since I didn't jump into his arms, the scoundrel is taking revenge. He's complained to Tariq, I heard from the other servants. 'That fallen woman. Why do you keep her on your staff?' John has also circulated false stories about me in the town: I'm seen in the market too often. Even at night. There are other men. Earlier this evening, Tariq told me he wanted to have a talk with me tomorrow morning. I could tell from the tone of his voice how terribly displeased he was with me. He'd surely send me on my way. I want to save myself the humiliation of a dismissal."

"What nonsense! John speaks a bunch of lies. Tariq shouldn't listen to him. What proof is there? Stand up for yourself. Don't let lies win."

"Shall we sit?" Teema pointed to a grassy spot barely visible in the lamp light. I sat across from her, tucking my feet under me.

"Lies do win sometimes, Maria. Tariq is protective of the Company's reputation. You see, John works for a rival English trading post. If he can drag English East India Company's name through mud, he will, and the Company's commerce will suffer. The local tradesmen have choices. They can make deals with whoever they like, not necessarily the Company."

I couldn't let her go away so easily. "But it sounds ridiculous that you alone can bring disrepute to an enterprise of this size," I said to Teema. "Let me speak with the other cooks."

"There's more to it," Teema said. "You saw the punch house where I used to dance; it was my temple, my home, the reason for my existence. John, that rough, big man, became my first lover. Then, he introduced me to Edward, an acquaintance from England who had joined the Company and dropped by for a drink, and everything changed. Edward was tall, had strong arms, and a thick accent. I couldn't understand a word he said, but my blood rushed in his presence. Right away, I felt certain he was the one for me."

So deep was Teema's voice, so firm were her words, so intense the light in her eyes even in the semi-darkness, that she broke open a similar longing in me for Job sahib.

"All day long, my heart would hammer with the secret of my love," Teema said. "I would stop to consider how my elders would speak behind my back, ruin my character, if they knew of the desire I kept hidden. Then one day Edward found me alone in the dark alley behind the punch house. His eyes flooded with longing. He whispered that I was beautiful, that he wanted me. I shook all objections from my mind, followed my fantasy, and leapt into his arms.

"That night I danced better than I ever had. Afterwards, Edward and I met in the same dark alley. I was still seeing John, but before long, I gave up all contact with him; but he wouldn't let go of me so easily. 'Edward will leave you, crush you, that boor,' John said. 'Take it from me. It's only a matter of time.' Drunk on happiness, I smiled at John and turned away."

In my amazement, in the flickering yellow lamp light, I watched Teema, a spirited woman, only a few years older than me, with a spark of determination in her eyes. At times I envied her the freedom she had, doing exactly what she wanted.

"One evening, John found us together in that alley, kissing," Teema said, her voice quavering. "He and Edward got into a fist fight right in front of me—kicking and punching and swearing and hitting. At one point John lost his balance and tumbled on the ground. He scraped his knee, which made him even madder. A Dutch man heard them from inside the punch house, rushed out, and separated them, but John was wild with anger and wouldn't leave the scene easily. He threatened to hire an assassin and murder both of us. I no longer felt safe going to the punch house after dark, dancing there, or spending my spare hours with Edward in the alley."

Fear for one's life. Threats. I understood those so well. "It seems to me that Edward should have protected you more."

"Well, he at least helped me get a job in this Factory, a lowly job as a sweeper, but that was sufficient. To be near Edward, that was all I could dream about. We would sneak a look at each other on the verandah, across the courtyard, outside the meeting hall. I'd wait all day to see him for a few hours late at night in his bedchamber when everyone was asleep. I gave up dancing for him, what thrilled me the most, and yet I didn't regret it."

Teema paused. Job sahib loomed large before me, the yearning that Teema felt strong in my heart.

The scarf dropped from Teema's head. "Before long, the other sahibs caught on. They resented our affair, all except Job sahib. He considered it a private matter between us and left us alone. Shortly afterwards, Edward changed. We were together, snuggling in his bed, moonlight outside his window, when he began to call me names. I was a mere sweeper, he said. I could be bought by anybody. Not true, not true at all, I told him." Tears strangled Teema's words. "I couldn't figure out the reason behind Edward's sudden change in attitude toward me. Within days, he'd snapped up a job in another Factory in the South and left, without saying goodbye to me. I was shattered; I couldn't even get up from bed for a few days. Then I heard Job sahib had found him the position and gotten him transferred. Take it from me, Maria, the English are two-faced."

Cold, invisible fingers swept my back.

"Let this be a lesson for you," Teema said. "The sahibs don't see us as we are, if they see us at all. They have their noses up in the air. Their blood is as cold as that of a snake. I want to tell them: I am not just a woman, not just a sweeper; I have a heart and a soul, I have principles. I know how to love, how to sacrifice for love, how to embrace the dark side of love. I tell you, never get involved with an Englishman. I've seen you looking worshipfully at Job sahib. He'll split your heart open, steal your tenderness, and then drop you. No good will come of it. Rumor has it he's waiting for the 'Fishing Fleet.'"

I stared at Teema's tear-stained face. "Perhaps not all Englishmen are the same."

"You're fooling yourself, Maria. In Job sahib's eyes, you're only a woman, to be used and cast aside. Haven't you noticed there's a color bar? In the eyes of your own people, you're a widow, and you know very well that widows aren't entitled to a happy life or any life, much less a love life with a foreigner. Don't, Maria, don't. Don't stay here."

"Perhaps you're right, perhaps not. There's a different path for me."

"You'll have to carve that new path for yourself. How easy do you think that will be?" Teema looked lovingly at me. "I have to leave now. I came to see you one last time, my dearest friend."

"You can't be serious. Where are you going?"

"I'll hide out somewhere for a few weeks, until I can line up a ferry passage to Hooghly. It's a big town, a major port. I want to dress up and dance. I want to get back to what I love to do." She looked at me imploringly. "Will you join me?"

"Join you?"

"Here you slave for twelve hours a day, for what?" Teema said. "A meal? A bed? Some fantasies? Pack up your things, girl. Be smart. Let us slip out of this compound tonight. The watchman has gone to bed. We'll travel together, like sisters. I'll look after you, and I'll teach you how to dance."

"I? Dance?"

"Just so. You're not a complete woman until you release your feelings through dance." She paused. "You have fine features and the grace of a dancer and I'll wager you will pick up the movements rather quickly. You'll feel free, possibly freer than you've ever felt. Standing before an audience, silently communicating with them, you'll be happy in a way you've never been."

Temptation dangled before my eyes. My father had taught me about *Natya Shashtra*, the classical Indian treatise on performing arts, in which the dance-form was considered a key element. At home we worshipped Shiva, the Lord of Dance. My father had explained how using body movements and hand gestures you could give expression to any emotion stored inside. A dancer could be released from her sins. Or the dancer could simply enjoy herself.

A dancing woman, however, was considered shameful and not allowed in most homes. What would my mother say if I took up such an activity? Her face would turn purple with shame. Besides, I had other options, a different vision. Urged on by Job sahib's encouragement, his faith in me, I saw myself not as a dancer but as a capable woman, one who labored alongside the English in a world of commerce. My elders too might not like that, but that was the direction I would take.

"Look at what happened to you." I paused. "No, dear friend, I love you as a sister, but if I follow you, the same will happen to me. I sense my future lies on a different path."

"Future?" Teema broke into laughter. "What a dreamer! Stop aiming at the stars. You'll lose what you hold precious to a heartless Englishman. He'll use you, toss you out, and take another woman. Best if you left this place now. Look, I have it all planned. We'll take a detour and stop by your village so you can visit your family. Don't you want to see them again?"

I vacillated, memories of home crowded in on my mind. How long had it been? How desolate a corner of my heart remained.

"We'll also spend a few days in my village," Teema resumed. "It's filled with ponds, trees, flowers, and peacocks. I'll breathe the air, kiss the soil, drink the water. Then I'll touch my mother's feet, pay my respects to her, and we'll move on. Once we reach Hooghly, I'll locate a punch house and get hired as a dancer. Soon you'll be dancing, too." Her voice crackled with cheer. "In our spare time, we'll browse the shops and walk the river banks."

"No, I have another agenda. The Nawab has promised to intervene on my behalf and that of other widows. He wants to safeguard us. I have to make sure his promise is carried out."

"You *are* a dreamer, Maria. Come down to the ground, girl. You won't change the future of widows. You won't even change your own future. Look at the sari you're wearing. Cheap. Cotton. Ugly. Too ugly for someone as pretty as you are," she finished with a grating laugh.

The wick-lamp trembled. "These things mean little to me."

We sat in silence, each weighing her decisions. "I see that you, too, have a passion you want to pursue," Teema said. "I'll leave you with it." She rose to her feet.

I stood and faced her, desperate to find a way to stop her from vanishing into the darkness. Yet I could see from the distress in her posture that she needed to flee to another town, for John Richardson would surely follow her every move and try to harass her. There were other complications. Edward's unseen presence, his kisses, his embraces, his broken promises would haunt her at every corner she turned. Tariq would make her days miserable by picking at her faults. She had nothing to keep her here.

"Will you be safe, traveling alone at night?" I asked. "Robbers might be lying in wait. Tigers might be roaming around. Snakes could come out of hiding and who knows what other animals?"

"Don't trouble yourself over me." Teema seized me, her chest heaving. Something in her was broken. As we disengaged, she uncoiled her shimmering scarf, fastened it around my neck, and studied my face with loving eyes. "You're so pure, so pretty, and this scarf makes you glow even more."

"But I can't take it. It's your favorite piece, a gift from your beloved."

Playfully, she examined my forehead. "I see an inscription that it belongs to you now." She laughed, a hollow sound, more tearful than gay. "When you wear it, think about me."

I wiped my eyes and gazed at her. "Do contact me when you can."

"Farewell, my friend." She turned, waved, and hastened out toward the gate, leaving rain clouds inside me.

THIRTEEN

The next morning I woke to the siren-like blasts of the kokil bird. My gaze flew to Teema's scarf, the shiny black chiffon cloth hanging on a wooden peg. How much I already missed my friend. I could see her gyrating in this very room, her fancy footwork, twirling hands, eyes like stars. We wage laborers were as permanent as a gust of wind, I thought.

In the kitchen, as I measured, fumbled for this and that, scoured and cleaned the pots, I found myself being haunted by Teema and her confession. Idris, standing nearby, stoked the fire in the chulah. Bir, Jas, and Pratap worked at the far end of the room. Spoon in hand, I stood before a pot of porridge, talking about my worries.

I must have become distracted, for the porridge boiled over, creating a sticky mess that spilled down the front of the stove and onto the floor, accompanied by a burning smell. How could I have done that? I stared at the mess for a moment, then fell on my knees, scrubbing and mopping.

Tariq came charging into the kitchen. He surveyed the scene, rolled one eye, and clucked his tongue. "Goodness! What happened?"

Before I could make up an explanation, Idris said, "It's not Maria's fault. The chulah was burning hotter than usual."

Tariq's gaze skimmed the room. Any moment now, he would yell at me for the mess on the floor, but his face puckered with enthusiasm. "I have an important announcement to make. I know it is short notice, but we have to arrange a feast for this evening. It'll be our 'Grand Feast' of the year, Job sahib's order. He should have informed me sooner, but he forgot. We've never entertained on this scale before. At least fifteen courses will be served, along with wine and imported liquor. We'll also have to decorate the dining room and the meeting hall. Job sahib wants it that way."

All of us stood in uneasy silence. Given that our hours were already filled, nobody jumped in elation at the prospect of having to do extra chopping and mixing and simmering and cleaning for this grand feast. I clenched my hands. Couldn't the sahib have given us more notice?

Idris flitted forward. "Who is it for, if I may ask?" He had a way of being polite and demanding at the same time.

"It's for a group of English memsahibs who have arrived here by a boat from England," Tariq said in a softened voice. "Haven't you heard of the 'Fishing Fleet'?"

"To be sure!" Jas said lightly.

"These lovely ladies, twenty of them, all suitably unmarried, are passing through our town, hoping to attract the eyes of the sahibs and get married," Tariq said. "The sahibs are eager to meet them, too. And so we're throwing a banquet, a big Hindustani-style welcome. We must make sure the ladies have a 'jolly good' time."

He paused for a while, and then continued, "Among them is a widow named Anne, who's supposed to be quite a beauty. She's from Lancashire, where Job sahib is also from. They'll meet for the first time. The sahib's eager, as you might expect."

Although I'd heard the rumor before, I braced myself. A stranger from a far-off land, a widow for that matter, would float in here to meet the man I dreamed about. Since our last conversation, I'd often wished we could spend more time together. Now the thought of losing him made my knees weak. But then how could I, a penniless woman, a mere cook, only seventeen years of age, of a skin tone darker than the sahib's, dare to nurse such a monumental dream? Teema's warning rang in my ears.

"Are you listening?" Tariq's voice pierced through my thoughts. "Will you be so good as to take over the cooking? The sahibs can't praise your table enough. Tonight you'll have to show the ladies the kind of feast Hindustan is famous for. I want to see only empty platters returned to the kitchen. You follow?"

Tariq wanted to see me make a blunder in front of Job sahib. That must be it. "Yes, of course, I'll be happy to be in charge."

"What do you think we should serve?"

My mother had enormous skills in the kitchen. Whenever there was a feast in our village or another one nearby, she'd be asked to prepare an elaborate meal, which included goat meat but never beef. She'd come up with recipes we could never afford at home. Now I rattled off the names of a few popular regional dishes—biryani, a malai dish, koftas, and kormas—and invented a few more in a hurry. Fish, game, mutton, vegetables, fritters, sweetmeats, pickles, I included them all.

"But that's only eleven," Tariq said. "We need four more. The number of dishes provides a measure of our means and hospitality."

"A jhol."

"Three more."

Perspiration formed on my forehead. If I was lucky, the preparation of those twelve elaborate dishes would take up the remaining hours of the day. "Please give me a minute." I counted off the dishes in my head again, trying to imagine what more I could bring to the table.

Fortunately, Idris, ever the quick thinker, hurled a question about shopping for necessities, which distracted Tariq. Since the market had been ravaged by fire, buying fruits, vegetables, meats, and spices had been next to impossible.

"We're short on time." Idris remarked. He cocked his head to one side. "We can't spend hours shopping."

Tariq, distracted from me for the time being, answered Idris. "I'll ask the grocers to deliver all the necessary ingredients to our doorstep. They'll each get a substantial gratuity for that."

Pratap, usually reserved, badgered Tariq with an additional request, his voice ringing with obedience. "Will you make sure we get golden raisins?"

Jas chimed in: "Oh, and nothing but the kamini bhog variety of rice, please."

Bir: "Don't forget we must have the freshest of molasses."

"That's enough," Tariq said. "I'll get you what you need. There'll be a ball after the dinner. We'll have to get the meeting hall ready for that. Needless to say, you'll not take any breaks today. You'll also clear and clean up after the meal, however late that might be. I'll be around to check your progress." As he backed away, he cast a glance at me. "No more spilling and no more wasting food."

I gritted my teeth.

"Is it always like this here?" I asked.

"Yes, servants are like slaves," Idris said. "We're thought to be liars, cheats, thieves, complainers, and lazy people. Unless treated harshly, we don't get any work done. They also think we'll get into mischief if we're idle even for a moment."

"Don't you think we should protest?" Bir said.

"Forget that," Idris said. "We'll lose our jobs and worse. They'll go after our families."

"And we can't go back to our villages," Pratap said. "There are no jobs there. Here in this town, I've checked out a few possibilities, such as the job of a boatman. It's back-breaking labor; as a porter in the shipping yard, na, not easy. The money you make, you spend in buying food. At least we get one meal a day here."

In the brief silence that followed, I considered what other better jobs I could possibly get, but came up with none. "Shall we work as a team then?" I asked the other cooks.

"Yes," a chorus of voices said. "You're our leader."

"Chalo," I said, mimicking Tariq.

Everyone laughed.

As the sun reached higher and higher in the sky, we struggled with the chores, stewing the meat, kneading the dough, grinding the black pepper, shelling the cardamom pods, washing the rice and the pulses, straining the molasses, and cracking the mace. Casually, I introduced the subject of the visiting English maidens.

"They're staying in a bungalow by the river near the Dutch quarters," Bir said. "From the rumors I hear, if they can't catch a sahib this evening, they'll move on to other towns where the English have trading stations, Hooghly, Madras, Patna, Dhaka, Ahmedabad or Surat. They'll try their charms on another set of Factors."

I kept listening to the back-and-forth as I sprinkled mustard seeds into a pot and watched them spurt rebelliously in the hot oil. Fragrant vapors spiked with cinnamon rose from another pot. Being distracted, I over-fried a batch of vegetable fritters and hid them in a bowl. I hoped Idris hadn't noticed.

He glanced at me. "The sahibs are lonesome, but they can be choosy. Many of them want a fair-complexioned wife. But give these women a month or so under our sun and they'll turn a light brown. A year and they'll be like us."

"Wait till they dance together." Bir dropped his knife on the table for a moment and whirled around with an imaginary partner. "Wait till they whisper to each other. Oh, the silver coin of the moon. Oh, the perfume of a hundred jasmines. Oh, such silky footsteps you have."

"Let us leave this dancing cheek-to-cheek for now and wash this pot," I said jokingly, concealing my feelings. Would Job sahib dance with any of the ladies?

I passed the next several hours cooking and stirring, bending low to smell the aroma of the dishes, my kitchen mates giving me a hand at every step and sharing their knowledge of the English. Outside the window, dusk had fallen and the sky looked about ready to close down upon us. I wanted to freshen up for the evening. After all day in the hot kitchen, the sari stuck to my sweat-soaked body. My shoulders felt heavy from lifting pots, my arms inflamed. Hunger made my stomach churn. My curiosity, mixed with envy, about Anne-memsahib was at its peak. I had to see her and measure her with my own eyes.

"My work is done," I announced to Jas, the only person left in the room. "I am in need of a bath. I'll go to the ghat, if that is all right with you."

I was about to slip out of the kitchen when I heard high feminine voices outside.

Idris swept in. Clad in a white vest, white trousers, a white headdress with fringes, and silver shoes, he appeared tall and proud, ready to serve. "The ladies have arrived," he announced with a smile, as though catching the mood of the evening.

I'd have to do without a bath. I shuffled over to the window to catch sight of the new arrivals. Covered in long robes, which I'd later know were called gowns, made of linen and satin, the women alighted from horse-drawn carriages like scores of butterflies freed into the air. The watchman flung open the heavy front gate with a rattle. He bowed, hands cupped before his face. The women clattered up the front steps of our stone mansion. A gigantic wreath of fresh marigold, exuding a yellow-orange light, festooned the entrance doors. Arthur sahib, dressed in a linen doublet and tall boots, stepped forward and ushered the guests in, saying, "Welcome, ladies, welcome." The women returned the greeting. Even though I was now somewhat fluent in English, I didn't understand many of the accents, which I guessed changed from place to place in that faraway island. I admired the poise of these women, dressed elegantly and adorned with hats. How easily they mingled with men.

As they were escorted to the dining room, I, too, moved in that direction. Since the distance from the kitchen was short, it would be easy for me to go back and forth. With Idris keeping me company, I watched through a gap in the curtains. The long rectangular table gleamed with silver settings and bowls of fresh roses. Oil lamps laid on golden trays were lit and gigantic flower bouquets arranged in baskets stood in every corner. The sahibs were resplendent in their dinner jackets. Job sahib gleamed in tunic and trousers made of the finest satin and intricate laces and shoes with ribbon roses. Precious stones glistened from the hems of his sleeves and added to his radiance. Light-footed, he appeared even taller than usual, towering over the crowd, resembling an Indian prince.

My heart skipped a beat. "You're blushing, Maria," Idris teased.

Face glowing, Job sahib proposed a toast. "By the Grace of God, King of Entire Britain, Defender of Faith." He raised his glass.

"The King!" chorused the soaring voices.

They drank to each other's health as well. My mood rose, as though I was part of the crowd. I watched Job sahib as he picked his way through the room in which men and women eyed each other over their wine goblets. When I peered more closely, I observed that a few ladies were ill-at-ease. One sallow-complexioned woman wearing a lace-lined hat spilled her drink on the floor. Another woman wearing red velvet shoes kept her eyes downcast, as though not feeling equal to this grand occasion. Such beautiful shoes and still unhappy? A third, with a gold clasp at her throat, constantly stroked the folds of her pale blue taffeta gown. The fourth woman, tall and regal with petal-white skin, light blue eyes, and pert nose, stole the show. Dressed in a shiny pink gown and shoes to match, she drew glances from all the men as she floated across the room, causing some to pause in mid-sentence. A pearl necklace shining at her throat, a flowery hat enhancing her silhouette, she took delicate steps. Ruffles fell over her wrist as she accepted a drink, a patch of lamp light frolicking on her cheek.

Close behind me, Idris whispered, "That's Anne memsahib. Gorgeous, I must say, absolutely gorgeous."

I looked down at my spice-streaked sari and felt the sweat under my arms. In the room, Job sahib stood face-to-face with Anne memsahib. As he smiled and chatted with her, he seemed to change visibly. His gaze was fixed on the woman in front of him. For a moment he'd tossed aside the mantle of his official duties. However beguiling the Chief Factor was this evening, Anne memsahib was more enticing. Even as she responded to Job sahib's queries, her blue gaze flitted to other prospects in the room flush with laughter and conversation.

One of the servers consulted with Job sahib after which he requested that everyone be seated. The seats had been allocated according to rank, recent accomplishments, and seniority. Anne memsahib eased herself into a chair on Job sahib's right, the most coveted seat at the table that evening. Her face pink with pride, Anne memsahib looked as though she'd earned the seat by being the most beautiful woman in the room.

The aroma of food throbbed in the air and heads turned as four servers paraded in, bearing silver trays stacked with bronze platters. There were gasps of admiration, as each person was served the first course: a meat soup.

"Let us steal the cook!" one of the women chirped; the company laughed.

"We might as well be at a soirée in the Royal Court," said another woman. "Shabash!"

"Who made the soup?" a third woman asked Bir.

"Maria, our chief cook," Bir replied.

Job sahib's face flushed, momentarily, or perhaps it was my desperate imagination.

Anne memsahib took a small portion of the soup, pushed the bowl aside, turned away from her host to her other neighbor, the one on her right, Arthur sahib. Above the clattering of silverware, they conversed. She laughed coquettishly, whispering into his ears and leaning in closer to him, her earrings swaying. He seemed to sparkle from her attention, while Job sahib looked away.

All eyes were raised as the servers circled the table, offering the next course, a fragrant chicken biryani. The air was charged with the fragrance of clove, cardamom, and black pepper. There wouldn't be any left for us, those who had slaved away in the heat to prepare these dishes.

The guests ate with gusto and the smiling servers kept their wine glasses filled. The stream of conversation flowed from the effects of smallpox in England, to that of a plague epidemic, to the growing popularity of tea as a beverage. Some women attested that tea houses were springing up in London, serving a strong dark beverage called tea, so loved by Queen Catherine.

Yet another course arrived in a white oval platter: mutton korma, with cubes of tender meat drenched in deep brown gravy. Bir uncorked another bottle of fine wine.

Anne memsahib's roving eyes caught the gaze of Charles sahib, dressed in a brown doublet and a cape trimmed with green taffeta, sitting across from her. Although I could only see his back, I imagined him scratching his chin and responding with a deep seductive look, his lips pursed and pale, beady eyes burning. Job sahib leaned back against the gold velvet of his chair. More than one woman in the room glanced at Anne memsahib suspiciously, tension palpable in the room. The conversation slowed. It was as though everyone either contemplated or dreaded who would pair up with whom. Anne memsahib with Charles sahib, I thought, smiling to myself, a perfect match.

Standing next to me, Idris shook his head. "She's cheeky, she'll ruin the evening. Ah, let me go serve the next round of dishes."

I too retreated to the kitchen where I kept filling the serving platters, making sure that each was garnished with herbs, nuts, and dried fruit. The food vanished in no time and the servers returned. "They're having the time of their lives," Bir said. "One lady said it was worth taking a long voyage from England if only to taste our roasted brinjal dish. The idea of roasting brinjal is exotic to her."

"You can't please them all," blurted Pratap. "I saw one lady crinkling her nose. She's not used to our style of food. Bread, cheese, onions, and boiled cabbage, that's what she eats at home."

Tariq swept in through the door, dressed in a light green vest and a white muslin headdress adorned with silver threads. "Good work, everyone," Tariq said. "Everything has gone without a hitch, although I think the korma could have been garnished better. They're going to relax in the courtyard for a few minutes before the dance begins. The meeting hall has been cleared for that."

I sighed with relief, but Tariq's gaze was on me. "Now it's your turn to use your English skills, Maria. Job sahib and Anne memsahib have retired to the verandah to have a private moment. Go ask them if they'd like more wine."

I stared down at my soiled sari. "But—"

Tariq cut me off with a sneering laugh. "Do you think Job sahib will look at what you have on? With that beauty on his arm? The ladies are curious about the genius cook who has prepared this banquet. They're full of praise, although I noticed that not everyone has polished the last course off their plates. You must have rushed too much. Well, next time, make sure. Now, hurry! Go tell Anne memsahib you planned this whole meal. She's our guest of honor and you should respectfully present yourself to her."

How would I greet an English lady? Who would help me? Idris came to my rescue. He had previously worked in a French household and showed me how to curtsy. I practiced by bending one knee, placing one foot in front of the other, and sinking, whileholding a hint of a smile.

"Oh, you're a natural at this," Idris said after a few rounds and rushed off to play the flute to our honored guests.

I covered my head with the sari train and bearing a tray of wine, I walked, feeling hungry, weary, and lost amidst so much pomp.

I paused at the verandah bedecked with lanterns and roses, with incense smoldering on an ivory burner. The sweet strain of flute music, an invocation of courtship, flowed from a not-too-distant spot in the courtyard. It filled the space to overflowing, silencing the mosquitoes, speaking as though to the longing in my heart.

A strong wind blew. Drops of rain began to fall as I stepped onto the verandah. Job sahib and Anne memsahib idled on wicker chairs. Job sahib leant forward, smiling and trying to make a joke.

She gave me a cold stare and a long-drawn-out, "Yes?"

I put the tray down on a low table and sank into a curtsy. "I have not yet had the honor of presenting myself to you, memsahib. I am Maria, the cook. May I offer you a glass of wine?"

She shrugged, gave me a disdainful look, and turned to Job sahib. I stood there, holding my breath, and waited for recognition from him. He'd always greeted me in the past, joining his hands in namaskar, eyes twinkling with welcome. Now, in a secret chamber of my heart, I hoped for a similar greeting.

Job was enamored by Anne's gorgeous appeal. He couldn't take his eyes off her. All evening he had been admiring her satin complexion, her elegant carriage, flirtatious hand gestures that spoke as much as her azure eyes. She aroused feelings in him that he had not felt since he was a much younger man. It wouldn't be easy to win her favor. He'd already seen her catch the attention of both Arthur and Charles. Yet he trusted in his own virility as never before, and he welcomed the challenge. He would simply draw her into his arms and kiss her passionately, erasing any thoughts of other men from her mind. She would be happy that he had done so.

Only in passing did he notice me. He was about to look up when Anne memsahib leaned closer to him and squeezed his hand. That touch made Job sahib forget his cook. Anne memsahib was trying to take him away from me, I thought. The lights blurred in the rain. The music faded.

The jasmine fragrance cloyed. Job sahib looked deep into Anne mem-sahib's eyes. Standing forlorn with a tray of wine, I wished I could make myself invisible.

"I wish you a safe return journey, memsahib."

I bowed gracefully and hurried toward the servants' quarters; rain-drops pelted my forehead. The revelry continued all around me; a roar of laughter emanated from the meeting hall as I passed by it. For the sahibs and the ladies, the night was still young, still full of promises. I was alone, hungry, exhausted, humiliated. In my mind, I glimpsed Job sahib and Anne memsahib whirling, taking intricate steps, inhaling each other's scent, laughing, mumbling sweet words, kissing. I nearly screamed.

"Maria!"

I heard Job sahib's voice and swiveled around.

He stood on the verandah, Anne memsahib was nowhere in sight. I walked back toward him in the misty rain. "A splendid job, Maria, far beyond what I'd expected. I must extend my compliments to you person-ally. You and the other kitchen workers have impressed our guests."

I drank in the compliment, my voice catching, and bowed. "That's most kind of you to say, sir."

"And please do not take anyone's manners as being directed toward you."

He was about to turn away when I inquired, "Why did the ladies come so far, sahib? Couldn't they find suitable mates in England?"

"No, not if they want to marry in station."

He sighed and continued, "Even though some of the women have perfected their French and know how to dance, not all are highborn, but then neither am I. Some are plain looking, middleclass, and corpu-lent, as you can very well see. Others are daughters of farmers and laborers. Still others work as milliners and tailors. But all of them dream of living in the Orient, of having jewels, domestic help, estates, ballroom dances, and meat dishes at every meal, none of which they can afford in England. They're also seeing this as an adventure. We English are a seafaring people born to adventure, you see."

I was grateful for the apologetic gift of an explanation. How I would have liked to dress like an English lady: the feel of a smooth cool velvet gown against my skin, the clinking of bracelets, and the rustle of silk petticoats under my skirt. How I'd have liked to twirl and laugh and jostle and fritter the evening away; to be surrounded by candles, flowers, incense, music . . . the warmth of a man.

"I must return to my guests." He bade me good night, turned, and walked away, leaving me feeling empty, weary, and convinced that his heart was elsewhere, despite that lost look in his eyes.

I was drenched. I rushed to my room, the thunder in my ears, and discovered that this night of misery wasn't over yet. The wind had forced open the door of my room, and the rain had drenched my only quilt. I would have to sleep on the cool hard floor, but I had to first return to the kitchen to help clean up.

FOURTEEN

The next day at dawn, I marched down the walkway that led from the servants' quarters to the main wing. A flight of crows cawed as they wheeled overhead. I halted in surprise when I saw Charles sahib and Anne memsahib speeding down the front steps of the mansion. Hand-in-hand, laughing and murmuring, they lurched toward a waiting carriage. Her loose brown hair streamed behind her, her creased gown swept the steps.

Smiling to myself, I went to the kitchen. As Idris fanned the fire and I skinned a ripe pineapple, Bir said in a low voice, "Can you make a guess which sahib's room was the messiest this morning?"

To my relief, several names were floated around, but not that of Job sahib. In the pink promise of morning, I saw us together in the verandah, in the courtyard, in his bedchamber. The tug at my heart was as real as the knife I held, as constant as the smoky air from the chulah I inhaled. How did Job sahib really feel about me? Did I appear in his dreams in the depths of the night when all that was untrue dropped away? Or was he simply being kind to a girl he'd saved from death's clutches?

Bir looked up from rinsing a pan in a bucket of water. "Guess who could be crass enough to leave his door ajar in the early morning hours, even if it was much hotter outside?"

Idris laughed. "Couldn't be Mr Earthquake, could it? A man or a woman?"

"I saw him abed with Anne memsahib, naked and tossing in the sheets," Bir said. "The door was ajar when I passed by, so I got a full view of them kissing and had an earful of vulgar words."

"Are you joking?" Pratap said, pounding spices. "Mr Charles sweeping a princess off her feet? In my mind, he's the last person."

"Oh, you, the wrestler," Bir said, interrupting. "You think looks and strength are all that matter. Charles Jones, though not of royal blood, has money, a whole mint of it, and he can turn on his charm when he wants to. He's perfect for Anne memsahib; she craves money and status, I think. I also think Charles sahib is trying to knock Job sahib down so he can get the position of the Chief Factor. He likes to be on top, and he'll do his best to get there, that vicious man. Shiva, Shiva! Had he noticed me peeking, I wouldn't be alive."

I arranged the pineapple slices in a flowery pattern on a platter. All the while I imagined Charles sahib on the verandah, heard his ominous barks, the threats I'd received from him insisting he'd punish me if I didn't report kitchen gossip to him. What if he found out how we had discussed him in the kitchen this morning? I had no time to seek answers to my doubts and worries.

Judging by the amount of sunlight streaming through the window, I could tell it would soon be time to serve breakfast. Cloth bag in hand, I slipped out the door to pick some plums.

My bag was only half-filled when I glimpsed Job sahib waiting by the stable, his lean form in sharp profile in the light from the rising sun. He seemed to be waiting for his favorite stallion Sudarshan to be saddled. I plucked a dozen more plums and stowed them in my bag, all the while stealing glances at him, hoping to catch his attention, but he seemed preoccupied.

"Late again, aren't you?" I heard him bark at Pratap who was tending the stable. "You get your meals and a place to stay, but no work? Next time I'll have you expelled."

Seeing Pratap shrink and feeling his shame, I bowed my head. I had not expected Job sahib to speak in such a rough tone to another person, to a worker. The sahib turned, noticed me, and strode toward me. His eyes were a sleepless red. Even though the sun shone on him, his complexion looked dull. I could tell from the stiffness in his posture that all was not well. I wondered if it concerned Anne memsahib. Did he know about her and Charles sahib?

"Good day to you, Maria," he said in a pleasant tone. He complimented me once again on the night's feast, but he had bad news. Our beloved Nawab had collapsed last night in the middle of a meal, and his condition was deemed to be serious. "I'm off to the Palace to visit him."

To maintain law and order, the Nawab employed 200 war elephants, huge beasts said to be as unmovable as mountains and as aggressive as lions. He also had several thousand armored horsemen. His army, which had already subdued many Portuguese pirates, would fight to protect our traders from the hands of bandits and insurgents. Those security measures were likely to be revoked if another Nawab ascended the throne.

However, I wanted to speak about another matter of more immediate concern. "I am a humble servant, sahib. All of us who work here are lower in status than you and the other sahibs. Pratap is a hard-working man, sahib, and he deserves . . .

"Of course," Job replied. "I didn't mean to . . . I shouldn't have . . ."

His harsh treatment of Pratap had had to do with how miserable he felt. The sense of being rejected was strong in him. It also revived bitter old memories of which Job would speak at length another day. For the time being, he had failed to win Anne; she had taken to Charles instead. Wasn't he handsome and desirable? Hadn't he told her she was beautiful?

Yet another blow to Job had been the news Anne had brought from England.

He didn't know whether he could confide in the girl standing in front of him, accusing him of rudeness, of insensitivity. She was a stranger still. He wasn't used to revealing his feelings to any woman other than his mother. It was easier to discuss personal matters with the Nawab and Arthur, also with Tariq, at times. But Maria? Well, for some reason, she made him feel relaxed, safe.

"You see, Maria, after I left home as a young man, I had to take many small jobs. Away from my family, amid many difficulties, I haven't forgotten what it was like to be ill-treated. Yes, I am upset, but not with Pratap. Last night I got news from Anne that my mother is seriously ill. I wonder if I might be indirectly responsible for her illness, if my being away for so long . . ."

A blend of emotions deepened the etchings around his mouth. "She's the only member of my family I still correspond with, but I haven't written to her in a while. I haven't been a good son."

He turned back at some movement and found Pratap waving from the stables. He nodded to Pratap in a friendly manner, walked up to his horse, swung himself up onto the saddle, and galloped off, a pale sun shining on his back.

I could imagine the empty space inside him, its crying need to be recognized and healed. Was he even aware of it? Did self-blame really cause his occasional angry outbursts? I didn't fully forgive him at that instant, but I was less angry, more willing to understand.

Before returning to the kitchen, I looked in on Pratap. He went back inside the stable, his shoulders sagging. How long would it be before his day brightened again?

For the next several hours, despite the company of the kitchen staff and the rigid details of meal preparation, I felt distracted. Why did these people from a far-off land treat us so poorly? Why didn't they consider us their equals? How could we ever change the situation?

What if I, a woman of humble origin, could attain a position which would offer me a broader perspective than that provided by my current cramped reality of cooking and cleaning? What if I could then reach out to those less fortunate among us?

FIFTEEN

Three days later, Idris reported the Nawab's death. "May God protect us all. He's the only Nawab in our memory that we respect."

I stopped sorting through the rice. What would happen to the custom of Sati? Idris said the late Nawab had declared it illegal and put an end to it before his death, giving widows the right to remarry. "How long do you suppose the Nawab's decree will last?" I asked.

"His officers began enforcing it even before he died," Idris said. "The new Nawab will have to go along with that for now."

"Someone must set a precedent for widows to remarry," Jas said with a sly glance at me. "I have a friend who's looking for a bride."

Idris stood dead still. I followed his gaze to the tray of limeade resting on a table, each tumbler garnished with a sliver of lime, the only bright spot in the room.

"Why don't I take over the serving?" I suggested, wanting to take a break from the stifling atmosphere of the kitchen. I could slip into the expansive meeting hall and find out how the news of the Nawab's death had affected the Factors. Job sahib had called an emergency meeting, though it was rather early in the day for the sahibs to convene. Still, it was understandable as this news affected the Factors as much as the rest of us.

"But, but . . ." Idris broke off, reminding me, once again, of the unspoken custom that women weren't fit to serve food or beverage to men in public.

I was stung by the sense of inferiority that was imposed on me. You, the country girl, everyone seemed to say, you're not as yet fully conversant with the rules and manners of this grand mansion, and you hope to serve at a formal meeting?

"So I'll break another rule," I said aloud. "And for all I know, the sahibs might not even notice."

"What if Tariq finds out? We'll both be in trouble."

"I'll explain to him that I speak English much better now, and it's an altogether silly custom. I'll also tell him that I am responsible for this, not you."

Idris was uneasy, but I picked up the silver tray. Balancing it in my hands, I entered through the curtained door of the high-ceilinged meeting hall. The walls were a polished ivory hung with colorful brocades, the windows draped with gilt-edged sheer cotton. For a brief moment, I stood in a corner, an invisible fly on the wall, and trained my eyes on Job sahib. He was settled in a padded yellow chair at the head of a large oval mahogany table. His eyes were sunken, cheeks dark with stubble. He was still recovering from a recent bout of fever, and now, seeing his flushed forehead, I feared that the fever had returned.

At least twenty equally somber subordinates were seated around the table. On this overcast morning, shadows clung to the corners of the room, deepening the saffron-and-blue tapestries on the wall. The atmosphere felt heavy, suffocating; the sour aroma of stale wine from the previous night permeated the air.

"Gentlemen, I've asked you to join me on this day of mourning," Job sahib said in a heavy voice. "The Nawab's death is a big loss for us all, but especially for me. He was a friend, a most generous person, who helped me adjust to this land. I would not have survived without him, nor would I have remained here as long as I have. I had the privilege of access to much inside information from his Court. For that and all the other courtesies extended to me and the Company, I'll remain forever grateful to him."

In the pause that ensued, I came forward and began serving the limeade, placing the tumblers to the left of each man. No one seemed to notice me. Charles sahib took off his high-crowned hat, slapped it down on the table, and said in a condescending tone, "Let's keep our sentiments separate from our Charter. Did we double our profits because of the late Nawab? No, even though we should have. Did we have to pay illegal levies to his officers? Yes, even though we shouldn't have. Our policies have been sadly misguided."

I kept serving and hoped that Charles sahib in his annoyance wouldn't notice me. How could he speak so casually and disrespectfully to his superior? His eyes seemed to gleam with a naked lust for power.

"You're in unusually good spirits, Charles." Gordon sahib put his tumbler down on the table. Occupying the position of a recorder, otherwise known as the Writer, he kept account of all commercial activities, but he was believed to compose poems in his spare time. "At least your personal profit must have soared overnight, in spite of our sadly misguided policies."

At this reference to the amorous night he'd spent with Anne memsahib. Charles sahib leaned back with a smug smile and glanced at Job sahib.

His forehead creased, Job sahib pressed his lips together tightly, dignified even under pressure.

"I'll tell you what the fuss is about, Charles," Arthur sahib said. "Last month in Surat, a school chum of mine and his bodyguard, walking down the street at night, were impaled with spears and died on the spot. Who committed such a heinous crime? No one knows. It's all hush-hush. But one thing is clear; my friends didn't get protection from their rulers like we do."

The remark remained suspended in the air. I placed a tumbler before Job sahib, taking an extra moment to do so. He darted a glance at me, caught my eye, and his face brightened. I felt as though he'd pulled out a chair for me at the table.

In the next moment, Francis sahib spoke up, and I cringed in revulsion at the sound of his voice. "I hear Emperor Aurangzeb in Delhi, who calls himself 'Conqueror of the Universe', is also ill. When he goes, his Hindustan will crumble like a dry leaf. There will not be a functioning government and that should open up opportunities for us to expand our influence."

"Right now, we must concern ourselves only with trade," Job sahib replied. "That is our Charter."

Charles sahib brought his palm down on the table forcefully. "But we have the Crown behind us. I've noticed there isn't much unity among the independent kings, the citizens, or the tribal groups. Many of them want freedom from Mughal rule. We could get them to fight each other. Let's also look for every weakness we can find in the next Nawab's administration and try to exploit it. All this will begin to tie Hindustan's destiny to that of England's. We're not here for trade alone."

I took a step back. So, if the opportunity arose, they'd take over, like other foreign powers in the past?

"We have to proceed cautiously and not cause chaos, always keeping the citizens in mind," Job sahib said. "We want expansion, not exploitation. We're as yet few in number, isolated, and lacking in administrative experience. If we're to sustain our position, we must have at least the tacit consent of the population. If we're seen as yet another occupation, they will rise up against us and all will be lost. We must be patient."

"Patient?" Charles sahib stared mockingly at Job sahib. "Your patience seems to have brought you little."

At this veiled reference to Anne memsahib, Job sahib's eyes flashed with fury and the veins on his temple stood out. He rose and walked over to the window, his back turned to Charles sahib. His face was even more flushed than when I'd entered the room and I wished that he would sit down.

"Let's cease all this nonsense, Charles, and get down to business," Arthur sahib said. "Our Chief Officer is correct. We really are in trouble. With the Nawab's death, it's not clear who's in charge of his army and who's maintaining order, if anybody. This morning, I saw a group of hooligans loitering by the river."

My people. "Carry a pistol!" Charles sahib roared. "That's the only way to deal with people you don't trust."

I slipped out of the room and reached the courtyard. The English weren't our guests; they intended to stay, not merely as traders, but as rulers. Our attitude of "Guests are God" had indirectly paved the way to this. Slowly, they would seek to reign over our beloved land like so many foreign powers had done in the past—looting, burning, seizing properties, and subjugating the citizens. Who then would grant the common people their food, shelter, and dignity?

SIXTEEN

Two days later, on my way to the river ghat in the morning, I looked out over the shore. In the blue mist, the harbor was lined with vessels. Fresh-faced children frolicked in knee-deep water. From a boat moored nearby, a boatman delivered a song, his lyrics praising the river, the notes blending with the sound of the flowing water. After finishing my bath and changing clothes, I was about to step away from the water when a commotion on the north end of the shore caught my attention. A babble of voices, vultures flying overhead . . . I pushed through the muttering crowd. About fifteen people had gathered around a man lying on the ground, his left cheek flat against the earth.

Bir!

Unmoving, his wet tunic clinging to his frame, to his muscular shoulders, arms, and thighs, his hair dripping water, Bir lay on the ground, one cheek against the wet earth.

I knelt on the ground and touched his arm. Lifeless. A ghastly circular hole showed through his bloody torn shirt, and, to my horror, I saw into his chest.

I buried my face in my hands, my mind churning with questions, stomach lurching.

A fisherman spun out from the gathering. Gesturing wildly with his hands, he said to me, "I found his body floating on the river, caught him with my net, and dragged him to the shore. Do you know him?"

"Yes," I said, nearly out of breath. "His name is Bir. Is he alive?"

"Allow me to check," said another man standing near me. "I am a doctor." He lowered himself and put an ear to Bir's chest, only to stand up again and pronounce him dead.

A hush fell over the spectators.

In the chill that ensued, my gaze returned to Bir. None of it made any sense. I could see the shock on his face as he was silenced by death. It was abrupt and final, this dark decision on someone's part to do away with him. I knew Bir. As a bachelor, all he cared about was this river, his friends, his card games, and his job. Then he met with an assassin who snatched it all away from him. Did he whistle as he drew his last breath, as he did in life?

I couldn't feel my legs as I turned and sped toward the Factory. Within minutes, I burst into the kitchen, panting. "In the name of Shiva," I said, my voice turning feeble. "How could this happen?"

Standing by the stove, Idris looked up at me. So did Jas and Pratap.

Haltingly, I described the tragedy on the river bank. All activities in the room ceased. His head cocked to one side, Idris asked, his voice full of disbelief, "Are you sure it was Bir?"

I stood there trembling. Jas poured me a glass of water from a large earthen pitcher kept in a corner. I gulped it down and replied, "Yes, yes, I am. In the name of Goddess Laxmi, he'd been shot and thrown into the river."

Idris slapped his forehead with a hand. "Oh, God, why didn't I go with him? We'd played cards last night in a shop by the river. Bir wanted to take a stroll by the river, catch some fresh air, and see the new moon. But I declined. He'd walked away, whistling."

I rinsed a washcloth with water and pressed it to my forehead. "I don't suppose you were near the punch house by any chance?"

"Well, it was next door." Idris paused briefly. "What are you saying? Just because the sahibs carry pistol doesn't mean . . ."

I saw evasion in Idris's eyes as he looked away. How could this have happened to Bir? Was it an accident or a murder? If murder, why? Who? Charles sahib? A person of power, easy to suspect but hard to pin down, the man who had once invited Bir to his bedchamber and had failed to have his way with him. I could see him pulling his drawer open, picking up his pistol . . .

Tariq marched into the room. "Why is no one working?"

"Do you know where Bir is?" I asked.

"I am responsible for him, not you. I'll look for him. Go back to work. The sahibs' breakfast must be on time." He strode out of the room.

"If we hurry, we might be able to pay our last respects to Bir before they take his body away," I said to everyone present.

We scrambled out of the room and through the entrance gate toward the riverbank. Sahibs' breakfast would be late but for once no one expressed any concern. Bir was only a few years older than me. I simply couldn't believe that he would no longer be part of my life, that we would never see him again in the kitchen. *He'll be back*, I kept saying to myself. *He'll be back*. In another life, with a new name and guise, he'll be there.

I pushed my way through the crowd. Had Bir recognized his assailant? He must have. This couldn't have been a random accident. At the final moment, with the assailant pulling the trigger, he must have fallen back a few steps, first in recognition, then in revulsion, and finally in regret.

Idris stumbled forward. He dropped on his knees and stooped over Bir's body. Face tear-stained, his shoulders shaking, Idris wailed: "Please forgive me, Bir, please forgive me."

"Oh, dear God," mumbled Jas, tears sliding down his cheeks.

A priest in orange robes materialized from somewhere. He chanted a short prayer and offered to lead the assembly in a collective prayer of peace. We folded our hands. Under the dense blue of the still silent sky, we prayed: May the soul of the departed soar above in tranquility. We raised our hands, pointing them to the sky, and ended the ritual by chanting: Haribol. With the ancient sounds throbbing in my ears, I could almost see Bir's spirit merging with the white clouds above and ascending to heaven, leaving behind all that was impure.

Several pallbearers approached with a bamboo trellis, lowered it to the ground, arranged the corpse on it respectfully, and bore our friend away.

We retraced our steps to the Factory and the kitchen. None of us could speak, not even to console one another. My mind swirled with questions, doubts, and deep sorrow.

Jas broke the silence. "If what they say is true—that a victim knows his attacker—then we should be able to make a guess as to who it is."

"Best not to gossip," Idris said.

"But Idris," I began.

"No, Maria, no," Idris said quickly and glanced back at the kitchen entrance, as though expecting Tariq to return. "We must be about our work. Breakfast is already late and if it gets delayed any further we will find ourselves without jobs. Come now." He clapped his hands together and we all knew that a discussion on suspects would have to wait.

I had just finished arranging mango slices on a dish when I noticed Idris slipping out of the room. I was already suspicious. I waited only a brief moment, and without alerting the others, I followed him silently at a distance.

At the far end of the courtyard, I saw Charles sahib on his way to his chamber. He gave Idris a sidelong glance. Standing behind the bamboo hedges, I watched both men.

The sahib signaled to Idris, his arm raised in an imperious gesture. "Boy!"

His gaze to the ground, Idris said, "Yes, sir."

"Not a word to any one—you follow?"

"As you like, sir."

Charles sahib glared at Idris, then departed on quick feet.

I tried to make sense of the conversation. The possible implications struck me so hard in the stomach that I had to hold onto a bamboo branch. I returned to the kitchen and finished preparing the breakfast.

Half-an-hour later, still in a flustered state, I went to the verandah for my English lesson. This would give me a chance to find out about Charles sahib's involvement in Bir's murder. I took a chair and stared vacantly at the shoots of a nearby jasmine bush creeping around a pillar. My kitchen friends were like family to me, the only family I had. An assailant, possibly a Factor, had taken away part of my family. Yesterday, at the meeting, I'd learned that the British had more than trade in mind. This loss had struck closer home. Who had really committed the crime? Idris who might have been privy to the murder, seemed to be reluctant to speak. Like the blazing sky above, I burned with rage.

The familiar flock of pigeons walked nervously down the walkway, their heads bobbing. A sparrow took flight, leaving me alone with my sense of injustice. An ailing rose, shorn of most of its petals, hung limply at the end of a stem on a rose bush. Where was Charles sahib? This was the first time he'd failed to turn up for a lesson. I must see him up close, look closely into his eyes. At the door of Charles sahib's bedchamber I hesitated. The emotions brewing inside me had pushed my heart to my throat. My limbs were alert, as though ready to respond to an emergency; my mind was incapable of thinking too far ahead. Drawing the curtain aside, I tapped on his door and stepped aside. What was I doing? An unspoken law forbade a servant from infringing on a sahib's privacy. In my present mood, I was beyond propriety, the compulsion inside me to address a heinous crime too strong.

Charles sahib emerged, clutching a crystal decanter filled with a pale liquid, his face drawn and gray. A frown creased his forehead. "Maria . . ."

"My pardons, sir, sorry to interrupt. I waited for you, for . . . for my lesson and thought I would check with you."

"It slipped my mind." He sounded far away.

"If you ask me, I too am not in a mood to study. It will suit me to postpone our lesson till tomorrow morning."

"Time has come for me to give up my tutorial duties."

"Oh, I'm so sorry; the lessons have meant so much to me."

He gave out a small meaningful smile. "Anne is still in town. We are getting married."

The mention of Anne memsahib's name stung me. I could almost see her complaining to Charles sahib that he was spending too much time on a servant girl. I swallowed and peeked past him to see if she was there. She wasn't.

"Congratulations, sahib. I am sure you'll be very happy together."

Gazing into the distance, looking forlorn, he seemed to think out loud. "She loves money, and I have lots of it. That's a good match." Then, perhaps becoming aware of my presence, he said, "I must rest now," and turned away.

"Please, wait," I called out, wringing my hands. "Have you heard about Bir?"

The sahib faced me, his face suddenly florid and the red-rimmed eyes filled with fury. "Do you know what happens to a servant girl who is persistent, nosy, ill-mannered, and . . . pretty?"

Controlling my voice, I replied in a servile tone, "I beg pardon."

I had half-turned when, eyes gleaming, he drew near, so quickly that I couldn't take another step. With one hand he grabbed me by the waist, with the other, he caressed my breast. His lips almost met mine, one finger working through the folds of my sari. I drew back my hand and slapped him hard on the cheek. The force of that vibrated up my arm to my shoulder and made him wince. A hand hardened and made strong by kitchen work. He stepped back, gave me a baleful glare, then stepped away from me and slammed the door.

I retired to the kitchen and stood by the window until I could breathe normally again. The room was quiet, the air still. Jas and Pratap had abandoned their tasks and gone off somewhere. Idris squatted on the floor, lost in sorrow. Had he been an accomplice or was he blaming himself afresh for the tragedy? After a moment, he raised his eyes to me.

"What's wrong, Maria?"

I poured out the details of my ugly encounter with Charles sahib. Testing to see how Idris would react, I said, "The sahib acted strangely, in a vulgar way, as though he was under severe pressure."

Idris pulled himself upright. "Oh, but that's normal behavior on the sahibs' part, in case you haven't noticed. We servants are the scapegoats.

The masters vent their frustrations on us. Why would Charles sahib be any different?"

"Still I must say not everything is falling in place for me, like there are secrets—"

Idris cut in. "Look, we all have things to hide. You think I don't know that you stole money for your trip to the market? Well, I do, but I didn't tell anybody." He paused. "We'll never know for sure what happened with Bir."

"Doesn't the Royal Palace have an official to whom we can report the murder?"

"Yes, but the officer will turn a blind eye. I'm only a servant. If I make waves, I'll cause trouble for myself and, worse yet, for my family. The official will likely ask me for a rose, a bribe. I don't have any money to pay him."

"I wonder if Job sahib might be able to help us."

"No, being a foreigner, he doesn't have the legal rights. Besides, I'm told he came down with a fever last night and has locked himself in his room. He's not to be disturbed."

"We can't let the murder of one of our dear ones drop."

"You're very young, Maria. You'll soon learn that sometimes it's better to keep your mouth shut and bear the grief and injustice. I'll advise you not to go anywhere near the sahibs' quarters. Don't roam the streets, either. I'll ask the other servants to keep an eye on you. Anytime you need help, if someone comes at you, shout."

I saw resignation in the lines of his face. Despite all the wisdom he'd acquired, he accepted whatever life handed to him; I found that difficult to accept.

I walked out of the kitchen and wandered around the courtyard. I looked up with awe at the exquisitely decorated exterior walls of this mansion. How much I'd grown to appreciate the beauty all around me. A perceived threat from Charles sahib couldn't drive me out of here. I would continue to make this Factory my home, with its usual round of duties, however dreary, disordered, and dangerous. I wouldn't let Charles sahib get away so easily for trying to touch me, or for murdering Bir, if indeed he was the culprit.

And yet on that day long ago, a hint of a breeze stirring and the sweet scent of bokul flowers floating about me, I found a tiny doubt about Job sahib creeping inside me. How much could I really depend on him, if he was always so unavailable?

SEVENTEEN

On my way to the kitchen a few days later, I came across Tariq. I hadn't seen much of him lately and I was happy about it. Quietly, in a friendlier tone, he told me the details of Bir's cremation ceremony, which he had been allowed to attend as the official representative of the Factory. With a crime possibly having been committed, the cremation had been conducted in secrecy on strict orders from the new Nawab.

"So a new Nawab is already in place?" I asked.

"Yes. Rafi Khan has been given the position by Emperor Aurangzeb."

Nawab Khan was as tough and belligerent as the Emperor. A man with a foul temper, he was also known to dislike foreigners. "He might impose stricter rules on the Company's trading practices. He might even send his army if we don't comply." His head bent, Tariq walked away.

I envisioned horsemen, guns, spears, and blood.

In the kitchen, I found pots and pans, several burning chulahs, and ingredients for the day's meals. Only Pratap was present. The other cooks had apparently abandoned their posts. I picked up a pot, then put it back in its place. "Work is worship," so went a local saying, but with Bir's spirit, his easy laughter, his goodness, his vitality, hovering over this space, I couldn't worship.

Suppose I stole out of here to visit Teema, to commiserate in our grief? I had learned from Idris a few days ago that she was hiding out in the women's quarters. With Tariq in a gentler mood, this was the perfect opportunity. I asked Pratap if he could handle breakfast.

I withdrew to my room, opened a tin can that hid my few treasures, and fished out the gold mohur. There it was, the gift from the late Nawab, with its brilliance and the flowing calligraphy, the heavy weight signifying its monetary value. I wanted to give this to Teema; it was my only savings, but Teema needed it more. Besides, I owed her. Not long ago, she'd saved me from being discharged by Tariq when I was late for work. I stared at the glorious coin then gathered the ends of my sari train, tucked the coin in its folds, and held the bundle to my bosom. For eons we women have carried money safely this way, without arousing any suspicion. I pictured the surprise on Teema's face as she received the mohur. She'd raise her shining eyes at me and smile. The coin would be enough to pay for her boat passage and get her started in a new town.

As my last act, I wrapped the chiffon odhni around my face with only my eyes peeking out. Wearing it gave me a sudden delight, a lightness of spirit, permission to be frivolous, what Teema had often wished for me.

As I stepped out the door, Idris's warning echoed in my ears. *Don't go roaming the streets.* For now, I blew my caution away, slipped through the gate, and headed for the women's quarters. The flow of traffic, pedestrians, wooden oxcarts, and palanquins, was light. My face and body were well hidden, head-cover arranged above my eyes, and a sense of daring propelling me forward. I passed by a watchtower, several ponds, and brick edifices. Occasionally, I turned back to see if anyone was pursuing me, but saw no one.

Taking a right turn, I followed a road that offered a view of the market. Many of the shops were charred. Left behind were piles of gray-black ash, scaffolds, animal carcasses, and debris. The sights slowed me down; I walked as if in a haze. The air carried the nauseating odor of rotten flesh. Sorrowful and sickened, I wound my way farther to the east into a narrow alley to avoid the odor.

"Is that you, my darling?" a man's voice called from behind me.

I swung around to see John Richardson. Cheeks sunken, the corners of his eyes reddish, his doublet soiled and wrinkled, he stared at me with an intensity that sent a tingling sensation throughout my body. I wanted to run, but my feet were unsteady, and this man would catch me in a second.

"Oh, you're not Teema," he said, with a laugh and a sneer, reekingof alcohol. "But you're wearing her scarf? You're her chum, right?"

"Yes, my name is Maria," I said in a level voice.

"Where's Teema?" His face withered, John Richardson looked bereft. "I haven't seen her in days. Suppose you take me to her?"

I stood to my full height. My voice rose high, angry, and confrontational, as though I was speaking with someone my equal. "No, it would be best not to try to do that."

"But . . . but she must know how . . . how much I adore her, how much I want to get her back."

"That won't happen, I am afraid."

John Richardson's eyes brimmed with repentance. He attempted to speak, but words didn't form. I could have taken the opportunity to run away; in his distressed state, he wouldn't have been able to catch me. But I lingered there, offering him an opportunity to collect his thoughts, and giving myself time to formulate a suitable remark. This would be my only chance to speak with him, to get my point across before we parted. If he understood how futile were his search for Teema, he would give her up.

"Can you imagine having no money, being afraid to go out and be seen in public, and not being able to get a job?" I asked.

He took a long moment to recover. His fingers curled as he rummaged in his breeches' pocket. He withdrew some coins and pressed them into my hand.

Head bowed, I thanked him.

He turned and walked away, the scorned man. I stood for a moment then secured the coins in the bundle of my sari train.

This exchange had left me flustered, but I'd stood up to a man, an Englishman for that matter. I resumed walking, my legs stronger than I had expected them to be. The sight of a meadow lush with weeds, wildflowers, and sunshine lifted my spirits. Up ahead, a farmer in a ragged loin cloth sowed seeds in a rice field. The scene reminded me of my village; the mango trees, the jungles, the planting season, and my family. I recalled the faces of my family members—my parents, little brothers. It had been so long since I'd seen them. I halted, wiped away the moistness in my eyes and resumed walking.

Within minutes, the clean pleasant grass huts of the women's quarters came into view. In a corner of the field that fronted the huts, wide-eyed, chubby-cheeked children flew hither and thither. A group of young women gyrated in a circle to the rhythms of a folk dance, their tresses sparkling in the morning light. They were dressed in matching, high-waist, long-sleeved bodices in various colors and prints with a flared skirt that fell above their ankles. They had designed their own clothing, I presumed. Miming motions of planting and harvesting, the women kicked, skipped, bent, and exclaimed in joyous outbursts, rattling their bracelets. Occasionally, they'd leap up and down, as though drawing heaven closer to earth. I stood under the shadow of a banyan tree and watched with fascination: women bubbling with happiness, enjoying their leisure time together to the hilt. As they twirled around, they seemed to look alike, and then a familiar face swung into view.

Teema.

Arms upraised, she whirled in frenzy at the center of the circle. Clad in a skirt sequined with silver and flaring around her, she spun currents of red, purple, and blue, her toe rings sparkling. She sported a spangle on her forehead, her hair was arranged into plaits secured with ribbons, and her hands were decorated with henna.

She spotted me, halted, and frowned. "Maria! Tariq didn't send you, did he?"

"No, I came on my own."

"Come! Join us!"

After a moment of hesitation—the footwork appeared dizzyingly complicated—I slid into the circle. The other dancers welcomed me in. I began imitating the movement of their legs and hands, and was soon caught up by the rhythm of the dance. I waved my hands and lifted my feet; I felt free, open, and powerful, as though I could gather up all the sunlight in my arms.

None of us, however, could keep up with Teema. So light were her steps, so nimble her feet that she seemed to float among the clouds. In a few minutes, she came lightly to a stop and so did we, catching our breaths, panting, smiling, and clapping. Teema sashayed toward me and pointed to a grassy spot under the banyan tree. "Shall we sit over there?"

We squatted on the ground, our backs resting against the thick tree trunk. I gave her an account of Bir's death and sat in silence, our eyes moist. As though to cut through the somberness, she said, "You look lovely in that scarf."

I told her about my encounter with John Richardson.

"That bastard! He never gives up. Fortunately, my friends have given me a temporary refuge where he can't find me. I still have the hope of gathering funds, quietly moving to Hooghly, and finding a punch house where I can be hired." She sighed. "It's only a dream."

"Your dream might come true." I untied the bundle of my sari train and held the shining mohur and the coins before her, telling her how the former was the Nawab's gift to me and the latter were from John Richardson.

Teema leaned back. "I can't take your mohur. You must save it for a rainy day."

For a moment, I was tempted to withdraw my hand and take the lustrous coin back. Then, examining the pained expression on Teema's face and assessing her circumstances, I said, "Please, this is a gift from me."

I expected a word of thanks. Instead Teema shot back with: "Are you getting chummy with John?"

"No. And believe me, I am not taking his side either, although I had the chance to see the mental state he's in. He's broken. Take his money in good faith and spend it on necessities. That'll give him some peace, if anything will."

Teema sat still, the light in her eyes dimming. "Maybe I ruined him. Maybe that's why he drinks so heavily. Maybe the stars intended it to be different and I didn't follow their guiding light." With a stiff hand, she scooped the coins from my palm.

"Send word when you settle down in Hooghly."

Teema stood up decisively, her eyes glowing with quiet determination. "We shall meet again, dear friend."

I rose and stepped out from the shadow of the tree. As I veered toward the path leading to the town, I looked over my shoulder and waved at Teema.

Smiling, her cheeks shining, she said, "Maybe, just maybe, wearing that scarf, you'll get lucky enough to find the happiness that escaped me."

EIGHTEEN

Alone in the kitchen, I stood stirring a large pot of rice pudding when Tariq glided into the room.

I nodded at him, but not without apprehension, then noticed the changes in him: a long face, a less confident walk, hunched shoulders. Was he still mourning Bir? Had he suddenly discovered the possibility that his life could end as abruptly? None of us had been the same since Bir's death.

"This is only an hour's notice, but Job sahib wants me to find an interpreter who can speak the dialect of Dhaka."

His words sounded as divinely sweet as the rice pudding before me. Although my English lessons with Charles sahib had stopped, I still practised speaking English and nurtured the hope of becoming an interpreter. Silently, I thanked Goddess Durga.

"Oh, I speak that dialect fluently," I said.

"Have you heard of a tiny kingdom named Virganj?"

I hadn't forgotten Sal's stories about Virganj. Literally the place of the brave, it was a tiny principality located east of here, barely more than a patch of villages governed by a queen known for her courage and governance.

"For sure," I replied. "A famous queen governs it."

Tariq stroked the tip of his handlebar moustache, his usual gesture before he launched into a long explanation. "Indeed she's famous. Everyone calls her Rani Mata, Queen Mother. She's one of the few independent monarchs in our province, not under the Mughal rule. Years ago, she was the chief advisor to her husband, the king. Our Nawab, not the one you met, but his predecessor, sent his army to take over the kingdom. The Nawab's army beheaded the king and captured several members of his army.

"Although grief-stricken, Rani Mata, who was watching from the roof of her fort, took over from one of the remaining commanders. The amazing woman had studied the art of battle in her spare time. She wielded the sword, fought, defended her territory, and once again declared her independence. The mighty Mughal army retreated fast. She became the ruler of her kingdom.

"Rani Mata is called the 'bravest man alive,'" Tariq added. "The spirit of her strength is equal to any man's." Although she was only queen until her son turned eighteen, two more years, she held much power and always would. She had a fortress and bighas of prosperous agricultural land around it and her people produced fine quality goods. Virganj was miles away from here. To keep Job sahib from having to travel such a long distance on hazardous roads, she had come up with a strategy. She had disguised herself as a man and set off on a horse to the house of a wealthy landowner who lived only a few hours from here. She wanted to meet with Job sahib secretly in that house. Her intention was to arrange trade with the Company.

Tariq's words ruffled me. We would defy the Nawab's wishes by clandestinely meeting with the queen. As a girl of humble origin, I didn't like to play such a dangerous, possibly unethical, game. It had been drilled into me since childhood to revere our ruler, the Agent of God on Earth, yet, here was an opportunity for me to prove my abilities by serving as an interpreter.

Silently, I wondered if I was up to this important mission. I had never seen a queen, nor had I ever expected to meet one.

I noted the hesitation in Tariq's eyes; he didn't trust my abilities and, indeed, I spoke limited English. I stirred the pudding vigorously once more. "I would be honored to accompany you and Job sahib and do the necessary interpretation."

"Except for the dialect, I would have done it," Tariq said. "But then my accent might betray me. I'm a Muslim; Rani Mata might see me as aligning with the Nawab."

"So you believe that since the queen's people worship Hindu gods, she would trust me more."

Tariq nodded. "Also you're a . . ."

"She might find it easy to speak with me as a woman. Since my writing skills are not up to standard, you might want to act as the scribe."

If only for a moment, Tariq's eye glinted in the flattery and with pleasure at my quick understanding. "But I must alert you to the perils of the road journey," he said. "We'll travel for several hours in a slow-moving palanquin, keeping ourselves well hidden. Tigers could attack us. Also the new Nawab's horsemen have been patrolling the roads. They're armed with bows and arrows. They keep watch on who goes where and for what purpose. If they suspect the Company has aligned with the queen, they'll harass us.

"Worse still, the Nawab could revoke our trading concessions. It's especially risky for Job sahib. As a foreigner, he could arouse suspicion of conspiracy against the Mughal throne. In the event we're stopped, Job sahib could lose his head and so could we." Tariq paused. "The sahib is unwell, but he doesn't want to miss this opportunity. He'll try to rest on the way."

"Is he well enough to travel?"

"Nothing could stop Job sahib," Tariq replied.

This occasion, my very first assignment as an interpreter, sounded risky. Still, I didn't want to miss it. I had been at death's door before. And it could very well be that the wheel of fortune was turning in my favor.

"I have never met a queen before," I said. "How do I present myself?"

"Speak formally, as you did at the Royal Court. You might do well to lavish praise. Listen, watch, act carefully—you'll be the eyes and ears of the Company." According to Tariq, since her battle with the Mughals, Rani Mata had gone into *purdah*. She spoke with men, with the exception of her attendants and servants, from behind a curtain or from another room. So far the seclusion hadn't stood in the way of her accomplishing her objectives. Before leaving, Tariq said, "You might wish to dress in your finest."

My wardrobe consisted of three cheap saris, two of them made of cotton and one of jute, all of which I kept clean and pressed. My sole jewelry consisted of a gold filigreed necklace with a pendant, my grand-mother's gift.

"The palanquins will be ready in an hour," Tariq said. "You'll have one for yourself. And, oh, be sure not to peek out through the curtains. Let no one see your face. You follow?"

I nodded. Tariq slipped out of the room, mumbling, "May Allah, Most Merciful, protect us all."

I finished preparing the rice pudding, scrubbed the kitchen floor, drew water from the well, and retreated to my room to examine my meager wardrobe. The henna-green sari was too faded and the blue jute one too coarse. The saffron-yellow in cotton would do. It had a deep purple border with a mango design on the aanchal. After draping the sari, I made sure that my necklace was visible. I combed my hair, which now reached my ears, then prepared a thick white sandalwood paste. I dipped my ring finger into the paste and placed a large dot on my forehead with several tiny ones along the outer curve of my eyebrows. In the looking-glass, each dot glimmered like a jewel. I smiled. This decoration would add a festive touch, even if my clothing and jewelry were not extravagant enough for an audience with the queen.

Soon I found myself riding a palanquin inlaid with silver and carried by four white-cloaked, well-muscled porters. The roads were so poor that wheeled carts couldn't travel on them. Another four or so men, armed bodyguards, marched along with us, daggers stuck in their waist belts winking in the sunlight. A separate palanquin in which Job sahib and Tariq were riding followed closely behind mine. That too was accom-panied by armed guards. Disregarding Tariq's advice, I peeked out through the curtains. Thatch-roofed houses, herds of cattle, and a laborer hefting a bundle of grain on to his head came to my view. We passed by vast meadows covered with thick short grass and ponds shimmering with reflections of the sky and trees. An owl hooted.

My palanquin plodded along sunbaked country roads. We traveled through a desolate area, mainly grassy fields shaded by trees, with no sign of humans anywhere. An occasional pillar indicated the presence of a well, meant for the benefit of thirsty wayfarers. Before long, lulled b the sameness of the scenery and the swinging motion of the palanquin, I dozed off.

The thundering beat of horses' hooves startled me. I opened my eyes and peered out. A small procession of red-coated horsemen galloped out of a side road toward us, kicking up swirls of brown dust. There were at least eight of them, one carrying a banner that identified them as the Nawab's soldiers. The horses were decorated with gold chains. We must have drawn attention, for they were slowing. I needed to consult with Job sahib and Tariq, but how? My body stiffened.

"Stop!" the lead soldier yelled out to the palanquin porters and they began to slow down. Swiftly, the soldier reined in his horse and dismounted from the saddle, his shoes caked with mud. An iron sword shone ominously from a sash tied to his waist. As he drew his sword, with its curved and tapered blade, the sound and gesture numbed my muscles. He halted only a few feet from us. He had a large nose and ferocious eyes; a helmet covered his head. "By the order of Nawab Rafi Khan, Shadow of God, stop at once!"

The bearers set the palanquin down on the ground so jerkily that I bumped my head against its ceiling. I shrank into my seat. O Shiva. What should we do? We were helpless against such a force. A gust of wind blew, the palanquin curtains shifted, and I came in full view of the soldiers. They stared curiously at me, at my bright yellow clothing and the festive dots on my forehead. My heart shuddered, Tariq's words of caution leapt into my mind.

A second soldier, possibly the commander, slid from his horse and stood guard. Behind them, the entire line of horses and riders halted and waited a short distance away. My legs cramped, my stomach knotted, I couldn't breathe.

The first soldier directed his gaze at a bearer and asked, "Where are you going?"

The bearer, bathed in perspiration, sank down on his knees and did his salutation, but seemed to have lost his tongue. Waiting for a reply, the soldier frowned.

I poked my head out and said in a voice loud enough for Job sahib and Tariq to hear, "To a wedding, huzur."

The soldier stepped in closer and crouched to the ground to be at eye level with me. "A wedding, huh? Whose wedding?"

"My cousin Amrita's." I said, with a smile. Fortunately, palanquins were in common use for nuptial occasions and my tilak was a mandatory wedding feature among Hindus. "She's the oldest of my cousins, very dear to me."

He pulled at his wide moustache, which flared out over his lips, and regarded me with mild suspicion. "Which village?"

Quickly, I made up a name. "Palasparah. It's small. You might not have heard of it."

"Who's in the other palanquin?"

"My mother. She's in purdah." Another lie. Far worse. If caught, I could be beheaded in an instant. But what did I have to lose?

"Ask her to speak."

"I can't. She's unwell, resting." Looking at the army official steadily, I added, "Please don't cause us delay. We're running behind. Our relatives are waiting for us."

"Do you have roses with you?"

Rose. Bribe. If only I had a few coins to offer. I felt the touch of the pendant against my skin, the precious memento, the only item of any value in my possession. I unfastened the sweat-drenched necklace, took it from my neck, and held it before him. "Take this, but please keep it with care," I said, with deep sadness. "It belonged to my grandmother."

The soldier snatched the necklace from my hand, his eyes dazzled by the intricately designed pendant.

"What's taking so long?" asked the second soldier who had been standing behind and watching the road.

"She's giving us her grandmother's jewelry." Clasping my necklace tightly in his fist, the first soldier studied the inside of the palanquin as well as my clothing. "I don't see anything else hidden there. And see how she's dressed. Cheap, old clothes. She doesn't have any money. She's probably a servant."

For an instant, I was glad to be a domestic. The second soldier stepped closer, examined my face, and tightened his lips in a long moment of contemplation. Perhaps he had a daughter of my age at home; perhaps he saw through my answers and was playing a more sinister game.

"Don't take it," he said to his friend. "Don't mess with grandmothers. A neighbor boy stole the ring my grandmother had given me. She cursed him so bad that he fell from a tree and died instantly. Give her jewelry back and let us be on our way."

The first soldier handed my necklace back, turned, and waved at the bearers. "Proceed!" His gaze descended on me. They saddled up and raced off in the opposite direction. I exhaled a sigh of deeply felt relief; from the other palanquin, there was complete silence. The bearers rolled their eyes to the sky and chorused a respectful prayer: "O Ganesh, we'll sing your praise forever for saving our party."

They hoisted the palanquins on their shoulders and resumed marching. Their legs shook, making for a bumpier ride. The sound of hooves died down and the road ahead appeared safe. I fidgeted, my throat was parched, and sweat trickled down from my armpits. What if the soldiers turned round, followed us, and found out there was no wedding?

I also wondered about Job sahib's health. There was no way to check with him or Tariq. Did they approve of my lying? Or did their silence mean they didn't? By now, the bearers had increased their pace and stopping even for an instant was out of the question.

After another fearful hour, we approached a walled compound. Inside, there stood a massive, stone-and-brick house fronted by a lawn and surrounded by a grove of pomegranate trees blooming with red flowers. The windows were shaded by muslin curtains decorated with floral embroidery. A male servant sprinkled water from a bucket onto the lawn. As soon as he spotted us, he stood upright, placed a hand on his chest in the local gesture of respect, and hurried inside.

So this was our destination. The bearers slowed down and set both the palanquins down at a short distance from the arched entranceway.

Tariq and Job sahib got down from their palanquin and rushed toward me, their faces etched with weariness and relief.

"You truly are courageous, Maria." Job sahib folded his hands in a greeting. He was decked in a long off-white waistcoat that reached to his knees, its color contrasting with his feverishly red complexion, and a matching round turban decorated with a gold feather. "You stood up to the soldiers all by yourself. We'd surely be lying by the wayside, if it weren't for you." He leaned toward me, eyes steady. "Is it common to travel such a long, potentially dangerous distance for a cousin's wedding?"

"Yes, sir. It is believed that gods arrange a wedding, so one must attend, to both give and receive blessings." In an attempt to lighten everyone's mood, I added, "I do have a cousin named Amrita."

In the light of the day, far away from the Factory and our respective duties, we stared at each other; in his gaze I saw what I felt in my heart. I found myself smiling, already forgetting the trials of the journey.

"But, sir," Tariq broke in, his voice high and cracked, "we could run into the same soldiers on the way back."

"Perhaps we could tell them we're returning from the wedding?" Job sahib said.

"They wouldn't believe us, sir," a bearer said. "Hindu weddings last for days and relatives usually stay for the entire ceremony."

I might have gotten us out of trouble temporarily, but I had created a new problem. "We must find another route," I said.

A young male aide, dressed in velvet trousers and a brocade jacket, emerged at the entrance of the house and walked toward us. We exchanged salutations.

"Allow me to welcome you on Rani Mata's behalf." He bowed with a hand at his chest. "She's ready to receive you. I trust you had a pleasant journey?"

He spoke the Dhaka dialect, which only I understood. I interpreted for Job sahib and Tariq.

"It wasn't as pleasant a journey as we had hoped for," I replied. "We were stopped on the way. Please be sure to have someone keep an eye on the road. And please interrupt us if you hear the soldiers approaching." I relayed this in a mixture of English and Bangla, as though giving birth to a third language, so Job sahib and Tariq would be better prepared.

"Very well," intoned the aide. He shepherded us through two court-yards to an annex. He offered seats to Job sahib and Tariq on the verandah in the front. Then he opened the door and showed me into a lofty room, its floor spread with fine woven cane mats on the periphery and a rich colorful carpet, illustrated with the scene of a battle, at the center. Plush velvet cushions were scattered on the carpet. This was the inner quarter, andarmahal, the aide explained, from where Rani Mata, who was in purdah, would address the Company Agents. Even though the room was bright and airy, several lamps gleamed, creating a festive atmosphere. I studied the layout of the room. If I positioned myself near the curtained window and translated loudly enough, I could make myself understood to Job sahib and Tariq.

An inside door creaked open. A graceful woman, much of her face hidden under a veil, glided through the door. She looked dignified, alert, confident, sure of her position and its importance. Stepping into the room, she adjusted her ghomta, revealing her sharp regal features and searching eyes. Her pink-and-saffron sari, lavishly worked with beads, shone like a hundred moons under the lamp light. Adding to the dazzle was a pair of coral-set bracelets encircling her wrists and displaying exquisite gold filigree work. In my plain saffron cotton sari, I was dressed worse than her aide. But at least both Rani Mata and I had chosen similar colors. Then I noticed the ugly brown scar slashing the left side of Rani Mata's forehead and going down to her right cheek. She must have acquired this horrible disfigurement during the battle with the Mughal troops. Now it became clear to me why she had chosen to be in purdah. Our society expected a woman to always project beauty, poise, and perfection. The disfigured women in my village never left their houses, always fearful of being ridiculed. It moved me to imagine the strain Rani Mata must go through to maintain her seclusion, to safe-keep her secret.

The aide bowed to her. "We salute you and praise your glory, Rani Mata. And may I present to you our honored guests?"

"Of course, you may," Rani Mata said in a low refined voice in Dhaka dialect.

As Job sahib and Tariq identified themselves from the verandah, Rani Mata acknowledged them with grace and ease. It didn't seem to matter to her that she couldn't see their faces or that they couldn't catch even a glimpse of her.

Rani Mata studied me, her gaze turning gentle. I lowered myself and touched her feet with my right hand; she placed her palm on my head.

"Revered Queen," I said. "It is a great honor to be in your presence. I have heard of your many brave acts."

We took our seats on the colorful cushions. Sitting close to her, I couldn't help but think that here was a woman who had fought in a battle with a sword, who had annihilated the enemy, one who could be both a mother and a warrior. She seemed to be a bit on edge, trying to listen to every sound, as though expecting trouble.

"How do you prefer to be addressed?" she asked.

"Maria, Excellency."

"Strange name for someone whose mother tongue is Bangla."

"Once I was called Moorti, but when I came to work for the English, I was given a new name."

She smiled knowingly and rested a gentle hand on my shoulder. "You're not much older than my son."

The question on her mind shone in her eyes. This young, inexperienced, plainly dressed woman would serve as my interpreter? Through a gap in the window curtains, I watched a bird make an arc across the sky. How tiny a creature, yet how big the arc it made. The aide set down two brass tumblers of sweetened limeade on a low table. The limes, he explained, belonged to a special rare variety grown only in this region.

He returned in a moment with a silver platter of almonds, raisins, pistachios, and mango slices.

Palm upraised, her bracelet sliding down her arm, Rani Mata said to the aide, "Do not disturb us for the next two hours."

"Very well. I will not be too far away, should you need my assistance."

Rani Mata turned toward me with an elegant sweep of her head. "Let us proceed then. You may begin translating for the Company representatives, but not everything, my dear girl. When I lower my voice slightly, I am sharing my private thoughts with you alone."

"As you wish, Revered Queen."

"As you very well know, mine is a small kingdom located on the plains of the Ganges River," Rani Mata began. "We have maintained our independence for as long as anyone can remember. The Bengal region, of which we are a tiny part, is called the Granary of the Gods, and not without reason. My land is fertile; it yields three bountiful crops a year. Our farmers are the most productive in all of Bengal, and we grow more crops than we can ever use. All my subjects are well fed and sheltered. I patronize music, painting, dancing, and other art forms. Our doctors, kaviraj, are extremely knowledgeable in planetary positions and they can cure most ailments by prescribing proper herbs. People come from far and wide, Dhaka, Chittagong, and Hooghly, and bring their sick to be treated by our doctors."

I interpreted her as best I could in English interspersed with words of my native tongue, hoping that I'd made myself understood to Job sahib and Tariq. Rani Mata watched me closely, as though trying to intuit if I was translating accurately.

"That's all well and good, but what do you have to trade with us?" Job sahib asked. I translated.

A flicker of annoyance passed across Rani Mata's face. "Tell the Englishman we will get to that in due time."

"These matters cannot be rushed in our culture, sir," I told Job sahib. "It is not in our interest to offend the queen, I must add."

Rani Mata, her expression alert, seemed to be trying to absorb as much as she could. I embraced this lull in conversation to pick up the topic with her. "It is marvelous that you can provide such excellent medical facilities to the citizenry."

"Oh, but that's not all," she said, casting a glance at my attire, then at hers. "I also have the best textile workers. You will have to see the silks and cottons we weave, many with gold and silver thread embroidered on them. But with all of that, we have no peace, no security. Much of what we produce lies idle. We can't openly trade with other independent kingdoms for fear of being harassed by the Mughals."

Her forehead was creased, her voice strained, eyes anguished.

"Nawab Rafi Khan's soldiers could breach the walls of my fortress any day, depose me, destroy my army, enslave my people, and take over my territory," Rani Mata continued. "They covet our riches and our fertile land, which is why I maintain a small but highly efficient army."

I relayed her thoughts to Job sahib and Tariq. Even when I couldn't come up with the proper English phrase, I used my voice to full advantage to express the nuances and the emotions, the effort both exhilarating and draining. Under my sari's edge, my hands trembled.

Job sahib nodded and replied from the verandah, mixing languages as I did: "I agree. It would be most unwise to make an enemy out of the Nawab under any circumstances."

"You aren't asking me to surrender my Virganj, are you?" Rani Mata asked, her voice tense but firm. "I'll fight again, if necessary." Then, eyes narrowing, she whispered. "This Englishman throws in many words and phrases from our native tongue, rare indeed. Clearly, he's immersed himself in our culture. But is it because he wants to establish a mutually beneficial business partnership or to get the best of our merchants?"

"The latter might be the motive of some Englishmen, but our sahib—

Job sahib's voice interrupted my explanation. "Even a temporary truce with the Nawab might be a better solution."

There was truth in his suggestion, but Rani Mata's face turned red.

"Truce? They murdered my husband." Her eyes flashing, she went on to provide details of the slaughter, destruction, and looting at the fort by the Nawab's troops.

Both sides now began to reason with each other, like swords flashing and clanging but inflicting no visible wounds. Someday, I thought, I'd like to be as astute, to speak with as much confidence, to have as much awareness of the world around me as Rani Mata.

"Can we trust this woman?" I overheard Job sahib saying to Tariq. "Could an alliance with her prompt the Mughals to come after us, too?"

"It's a possibility," Tariq replied. "We have to find a way to cool her down."

"Ask Rani Mata if she would consent to paying land taxes to the government." Job sahib said.

"Land tax? Don't you know that the Mughal revenue system is exploitative?"

"It is so," Job sahib said, his voice somewhat agitated, "but it might benefit you in the long run." And indirectly benefit the Company, I thought, pleased to see how the sahib's mind worked, the strategy he had of influencing Rani Mata to ally with the Mughals, before doing trade with her.

They went back and forth for a while on that topic. As I helped interpret each party's argument, I made mental notes of the information being shared, in case it came handy in the future. Although tempted by the ripe crescents of mango on the platter, I decided not to indulge in food or drink in front of a sovereign, particularly when the room was thick with apprehension.

"And do you think that paying land tax to the local Nawab will be sufficient in the end?" Rani Mata asked. "My informers say Emperor Aurangzeb in Delhi, the Nawab of Nawabs, the biggest fish in the pond, is the one pulling the strings. He wants to win over the Marathas in Deccan and take over the independent kingdoms in the East, which is why the regional ruler is hostile to me."

Job sahib listened to my translation and replied to Rani Mata, "Then it seems you may want to appease the Emperor as well."

Rani Mata's eyes blazed. "The Emperor is old, sick, and cruel, not to mention stupid. His doctors haven't been able to cure him so far. Why, when he has carbuncle, does he have to let his horses trample other people's crop lands? Is he too sick to care?"

"It is true that Aurangzeb doesn't have popular support," Job sahib said. "His court is corrupt, his army is poorly led. He is, as they say, the 'last flicker of a dying flame'. I think he'll be around a few more years, though he's already chosen a successor. However, in the meantime . . ."

As I translated, I was stunned at the prediction for the Great Mughal Empire. Who could imagine it crumbling?

"What would you do if your trading outpost was invaded by the Mughal army?" Rani Mata questioned. "Do you have a defensive force? It is a possibility, you know. Before they go, the Mughals will inflict whatever damage they can."

I communicated Rani Mata's remark and waited breathlessly to hear and interpret Job sahib's reply. "We have a limited number of Company troops," he said. For my benefit, he sprinkled his views with Bangla words as often as he could. "But the Crown will provide me with troops and weaponry. A powerful fleet from England will arrive soon, the Bengal Fleet, with ample weapons and ammunition. We'll have more than sufficient strength to counteract the Nawab."

So we expected a war at our doorstep?

A deep silence ensued as both parties pondered possible strategies to ward off a Mughal invasion. "You might wish to make a gift to the Emperor," Job sahib said. "To keep him in good humor, as they say."

"What gift? He, the King of Kings, sits on the Peacock Throne. Doesn't he have all he needs?"

"Not really." Job sahib gave a list of nazrana regularly brought by English ships for delivery to the Emperor, luxury goods that pleased him: knives, mirrors, wine, and English horses.

"I don't have any foreign goods to offer him," Rani Mata said.

"We can be of help," Job sahib said.

As I translated that statement, a piece of information exchanged earlier in the conversation flashed across my mind. Here was a chance to leap beyond the limits of my job. I would make a daring suggestion, one that might aid Rani Mata in her ability to change the attitude of the Emperor more effectively than a mere exchange of gifts.

"You've said the Emperor is ailing," I said eagerly to Rani Mata. "And you have the best physicians in the region. Might you be able to send a team of physicians to Delhi to treat the Emperor's carbuncle?"

"What a wise plan!" Job sahib exclaimed from the verandah. I turned to the queen and interpreted his remark. "Suppose the Emperor regained his health," Job sahib continued, "that would certainly win him over." Not getting any response from Rani Mata, Job sahib began to recount the story of the early English envoy, Sir Thomas Roe, who had ingratiated himself with Emperor Jahangir by supplying him with, among other things, medicine from England. Upon regaining health, the Emperor offered the envoy a permanent position in his court. He became the first ambassador from England. "When a man is ailing, even if he is a monarch, his first thought, his only thought, is about getting well, wouldn't you say? Possibly the biggest gift you could make him."

"Treat him?" Rani Mata said. "I despise him. Do you know what he did to a group of innocent Hindu pilgrims who were protesting against the jizia tax that had been imposed on them? A train of elephants were allowed to run wild, to destroy any and all that crossed their paths. Hundreds of protesters were strewn on the ground like crushed insects, their cries splitting the sky, their blood soaking the earth."

"Aren't you placing your personal feelings over the well-being of your people?" Job sahib asked.

"Job sahib suggests it would be beneficial to consider what the Emperor would do to your own people now if you defy him. There's nothing you can do for those poor souls the Emperor treated so cruelly earlier, but you can do something to spare your own subjects a similar fate."

Even though Rani Mata nodded, she didn't seem convinced. They continued their arguments about priorities for a considerable period of time. As often as I could, I interpreted their dialogue creatively to reduce the distance between them and strove to draw them together into a compromise. Eventually, Rani Mata softened her stand. I saw her body relaxing into the cushion. I breathed a sigh of relief.

Rani Mata turned to me, her face catching the yellow rays of the afternoon. "How clever you are, my dear girl. Yes, I'll take your suggestion and send my best physicians to Delhi. Let them examine the Emperor and suggest some herbal cure. To my knowledge, one such cure does exist."

Tariq, who'd been quiet until now, said, "Suppose the Emperor doesn't trust your physicians and . . ."

"My physicians are known for their code of ethics." Rani Mata cut him off sharply. "They'll never harm a patient, regardless of who he is. Besides, don't you know that the Emperor has a set of plates and glasses specially made to test for poison? Any poisonous ingredient falling into them, be it food or medicine, will instantly discolor them."

"I've seen such a custom being employed at our local Nawab's Palace as well," Job sahib said.

"I'll get the physicians ready for the long journey." Rani Mata paused. "Then I'll do my pratikkha," she said. Although I translated the word as "period of waiting", I was well aware that 'pratikkha' implied much more. It spoke of humility, reverence, and prayerfulness while one waited, a whole concept rolled into a word which had no equivalent in English, not to my limited knowledge that day.

Rani Mata rewarded me with a warm smile. "Now, can we talk about trade?"

I began to translate, this time adding my own opinion about the quality of Rani Mata's clothes and jewelry and the lush décor of her room. Eagerly, Job sahib replied that the Company would consider purchasing fine silk fabric from Rani Mata, as well as elaborate wall hangings to be sold in the London market.

Rani Mata leaned toward me and murmured: "Should I trust the Company? Should I trust this Englishman? And his assistant?"

"Please allow me to speak confidentially." I whispered to her an account of my earlier history, of having to face cremation, of escaping with a group of strangers, and eventually landing on my feet. "I can't say it has been a perfect life for me, my pillow is wet at night from my tears, but . . ."

"You're still a servant though," Rani Mata said to me in a low voice. "I don't trust the English. They come from afar, they're aliens. Like the Dutch, the French, and the Portuguese who arrived before them, they want to grab what they can. Right now they're weak. The Mughals are stronger. For now, who knows who will be more dangerous in the future? I might have exchanged one enemy for another. Regardless, I'll work with both until the situation becomes clearer. Tell the Englishman, my broker will visit his Factory soon."

My heart felt as though it was being split into two. I remained loyal to the Company for giving me employment and indebted to Job sahib for rescuing me from death. In fact, I swelled with affection for him, but Rani Mata's words struck deep within me, making me aware of what I didn't want to admit to myself: a possible British takeover of our land. On that day so far in the past, sitting on a velvet cushion, in a quiet village far from the seat of trade and government, I trembled as I envisioned the future.

Once I recovered, I broke the good news to Job sahib. His voice soaring with elation, he laid out the subsequent steps: check out textile samples, negotiate the prices, and firm up a delivery schedule. At sahib's request, I asked Rani Mata how we could set up a trading session in our Factory in the near future.

I'd barely finished the sentence when I noticed the aide hovering at the door, his eyes filled with dread. At Rani Mata's nod, he flew in, one hand extended in a gesture of protection.

"Your pardon, Gracious Queen," he said in a hoarse voice. "I've received the news that soldiers on the road are inquiring about a wedding party. They're not very far away. They've been misdirected to another village. But we must take you to a secluded location at once. This meeting will have to be adjourned."

"Where are the DOJJats?" Rani Mata asked. "How much time do we have?"

"A few minutes, only."

Both Rani Mata and I hurried to our feet. I relayed the aide's warning to Job sahib and Tariq. Rani Mata pulled her veil back over her head. "I'll send a broker to your trading lodge soon and we'll continue the negotiation process." She wrapped me in a momentary embrace and whispered, "Should you ever need a job or a place of refuge, please don't hesitate to call on me. You'll be most welcome in my fortress."

"That's most kind of you, Your Excellency." I touched her feet, she wished me a safe journey, and I slipped out the door.

At the gate, Job sahib and Tariq conferred with the bearers. Job sahib turned to me, "Thanks to you, Maria, we've forged a solid contact." His gaze held mine longer than usual.

"My pleasure, sir."

"Your translation was a tad peculiar at times," Tariq said to me, with a dismissive laugh.

My face grew warm with embarrassment. "Next time an interpreter is needed, perhaps you'd be a better fit, although you'll have to learn different Bangla dialects. You might even have to disguise yourself as a woman, should we visit a queen."

Tariq's face became dark. "You need to watch your bearing, Maria, or you'll find yourself in a bad way."

"You mean like the Company has found itself now?"

Tariq looked angrier. Job sahib stepped in closer and smiled at me. I turned to a bearer and asked, "Is there another route?"

"Yes," he replied. "While you were at the meeting, we asked around. There is another route through a jungle. The soldiers don't attempt to go through there, but it is hardly desirable because of poisonous snakes."

"And mosquitoes," announced a second bearer. "The most blood-thirsty ones."

"Don't forget the tigers," said the third. "They're even more blood-thirsty. These villagers have a proverb for this last one: 'It gets dark about the time you arrive at the spot where there are tigers.'"

For a moment all of us stood in silence.

"Excuse me, sahib," a fourth bearer called out in an unnaturally high voice. "I can hear the soldiers coming."

"Let us be off." Job sahib's eyes fleeted over my face in concern. Was there affection in them too? "God help us."

NINETEEN

On the return journey in the palanquin, we passed through a field flecked with wild flowers, then forced our way through a dense forest. The ride was cooler, pleasanter than on the open road, but I was worried, frightened. What if the soldiers traced us? I looked out the window and almost screamed. A large snake, with an olive-green body, was draped over a tree branch ahead of my palanquin. My heart leapt. We passed under the branch and the snake disappeared from view. A second later, its hood brushed the roof of the conveyance and the snake became visible again. I had little time to worry about it making its way inside before a swarm of mosquitoes invaded us. Although I covered myself as best as I could with my sari, there was no escaping their bites. Every so often I would picture Rani Mata's luminous face and a light of inspiration would burn inside me.

A bearer began to wail. "Help! I can't take it anymore."

From inside the palanquin, I peered at him. His shoes were torn, feet bloodied and blistered, face swollen from mosquito bites; he was barely marching. One of the spare bearers took over his duties while he, sweating profusely, crawled into my palanquin and fell asleep on the floor. I squeezed to one side of the bench and covered my nose with the sari train, almost immediately chiding myself for my attitude.

Toward dusk, a storm caught us and caused further delay. It was almost night by the time we got off the palanquin and trudged through the Factory gate, wet, hungry, and fatigued, but delighted to be alive.

Eyelids heavy but his face holding the warmth of appreciation—or was it affection?—Job sahib approached me. "Do you suppose Rani Mata will back up her words with appropriate actions?"

A sweet thrill bubbled inside me. The Chief Factor was seeking my opinion! "Yes, sir, I do. You should have seen how eager she was to make a deal with us. She's shrewd, and she looks to the future."

"It's a first for us, to trade with a queen, and the results far exceeded my expectation. Thanks to the interpretation you did, it has opened a new avenue for us." He chuckled. "And we didn't get killed on the road, either."

Turning to Tariq, he said, "Please see to it that Maria is amply rewarded. Also pay a substantial bakshish to the porters and the guards."

The sahib met my gaze and held it for an instant. How this remarkable day had changed everything between us.

In the morning, fatigued but happy, I was on my way to the kitchen when I noticed Tariq's tall figure emerging from the stable.

"Maria!"

From the keen look in his one good eye I could tell that he had an urgent matter to discuss. Instead of blurting it out, he stared down at me and indulged in unexpected niceties. Did I sleep well last night? Wasn't the morning pleasant? Wouldn't more rain be welcome?

"Were you going to ask me something?" I asked.

"Job sahib has asked that you be assigned better accommodation; I have one available. Come, let me show you."

I suppressed the joyous shriek that rose to my throat. He hustled me to the back of the mansion's main wing, in the same facility as the sahibs' residential quarters and a long stroll from the servants' hovels. He opened the door to a room and waved me in, saying, "This was intended for guests, but rarely used."

I stepped into a tiny, bright, airy chamber sporting a high ceiling and a tiled floor that could use a bit of cleaning. I'd have to wait till the afternoon to sweep and dust the floor to remove the insects, dry leaves, and flower petals that had floated in through the open window. A low charpoy, a cot of strong thick ropes knotted and stretched across a wooden frame, stood next to a wall. In the opposite corner, there rested a stool and a stand for hanging clothes. A lattice window offered a view of the Eastern sky, an inverted bowl of blue streaked with gold. My people considered a view of the rising sun a blessing for the day ahead. I pressed the palms of my hands together at my chest and gazed upward at the sun.

Tariq stared at me. "I presume this will suit you?"

I could only nod. I was grateful to Job sahib. Although he didn't employ me as an interpreter, he'd offered me better lodging. Then, it dawned on me; I'd be closer to the sahibs' bedchambers. My mind floated back to two separate unpleasant incidents with Francis sahib and Charles sahib. I felt a stirring at the back of my neck.

"You can move in any time you like. I'll also give you a little extra pay to buy better clothes."

I looked down at the coarse jute sari I was wearing. I'd get new clothes!

At the servants' quarters, I collected my meager belongings and looked back one last time at the hovel from where I'd started my journey in this Factory. I'd come some way since then.

In my new room, after I'd arranged my few personal effects, I picked up the looking-glass. The shine hadn't fully returned to my dark eyes, my complexion didn't quite have the bloom of my village days, and my hair, in the past luxuriously black and abundant, was barely long enough to caress my shoulders.

During my afternoon break, I took a broom from the storage room and humming a happy tune, I headed to my new abode. Charcoal clouds gathered in the sky. A red-beaked bird scampered ahead of me.

Rain began to fall. Like all girls, I'd been taught folk songs in my childhood; lyrics praising the harvest, the river, and the rain, or simply describing the toils of a villager, but I had never considered myself to be a songstress. I couldn't carry a tune, yet, my voice, after yesterday's perilous journey, felt free, as though my throat had opened wider and I'd snatched a perfect melody floating in the air. Now I sang a farmers' simple rhyme: Come, come, gentle rain.

I pranced past the meeting hall that, on certain days of the month, was occupied by the sahibs for business debates. Usually, we were informed about a scheduled meeting far ahead of time, so we would be prepared to serve a beverage. The sahibs had their choice of limeade, ghol, tisane, or on rare occasions, the China drink, a cup of precious black tea made from expensive leaves. After serving, one of the menservants would squat outside the hall, ready to carry out further errands. At the conclusion of the proceedings, the sahibs would continue to chit-chat. Some would demand hookah for smoking, tobacco flavored with country sugar and burning brightly on charcoal, to while away the time. Later, alone in his chamber, a sahib might indulge in a pill of opium to cope with the strains of the day.

Today, however, wasn't a meeting day, and most of the sahibs had retreated to the punch house by the river, so when I caught Job sahib's angry voice coming out of the meeting room, I halted in surprise. The door, hung with an orange curtain, was slightly ajar.

"Rubbish!" Job sahib bellowed. "Pure rubbish!"

Not since the incident with Pratap had I heard him speak with such wrath.

"Damn it!" said another voice.

Charles sahib! His spiteful tone piqued my curiosity. I stood still.

"You're a blackguard, you are, Job! Take the next boat back to England! I'll run this Factory better than you!"

Were the two rivals merely angry, or was this more serious? I peered through a gap in the curtains. The two sahibs sat across from each other at the curved end of the oval table at the far end of the room. His opponent was about to hurl more threats when Job sahib stood up hastily. Gaunt-faced, the corners of his eyes crinkled, a reddish cast to his complexion, worn out, he stepped over to the window and rubbed his forehead. His fever was still apparent in his face, made worse by the arduous mission to visit Rani Mata. I didn't trust Charles sahib. He rose to his feet; he was wearing boots, and stood like a pillar. There was something in his movement, stealth mixed with malice; it sent a shiver through my body. The vengeful expression on his face was like that of a tiger about to leap at its prey.

Charles sahib dropped his cloak and from his waist-belt he drew a pistol. From where I stood he seemed drunk, unsteady on his feet.

At the sight of the firearm, I began to tremble, but I wasn't willing to only stand and watch as Job sahib was shot down. The brief time with Rani Mata had helped bring out the warrior in me. I tiptoed into the room, fast but like a shadow, holding the broom upside down in my hand. The carpet muffled my footsteps. Job sahib still lingered at the window, slightly stooped.

Charles sahib's fingers began to tighten on the trigger. I lunged at Charles sahib from behind and with all my bodily strength I struck him on the head with the broom. My humble weapon, consisting solely of sticks and twigs, made hardly any noise, but the blow was so sudden that Charles sahib became disoriented. He rubbed his eyes with his free hand, blinking at the dust that had been shocked from the bristles.

Before he could turn around, I hit him on his neck with the side of my hand, a hand strengthened by kneading and scrubbing and stirring in the kitchen. Almost simultaneously, I struck Charles sahib's right hand with a sweep of my broom. The sahib loosened his grip on the pistol. As he began to fall, I grabbed an empty brass tumbler from the table and hit him in the back with it; the force of the blow sent me staggering back for a moment.

Charles sahib collapsed to the floor. The pistol slid from his hand and landed on the carpet. Flailing, he pushed the pistol further away with his feet. Panting, trying to catch my breath, I stood ready for the next move.

Job sahib turned away from the window. He glanced at me with incredulous eyes, then at Charles sahib, and darted toward the fallen pistol even as Charles sahib struggled to get up.

As Job sahib advanced toward me, Charles sahib, still on the floor, kicked him, but Job sahib managed to push the pistol away with his other foot.

Charles sahib staggered to his feet. Again, I was ready with my tumbler, but he struck me in the stomach with a sharp elbow. Severe pain shot through my belly, followed by a wave of nausea. Charles sahib reached for the pistol. I too leaned toward it, but he got hold of the weapon before I did.

Turning toward the door, I let out a shout, hoping that one of the servants would hear me.

As Charles sahib aimed the barrel towards me, Job sahib lurched forward and shouted: "For heaven's sake, Charles, no, no."

Job sahib's arm moved out. He shielded me, facing the barrel himself. I pressed my face into the warmth of his back. O, Shiva, please come to our aid.

Eyes bright with malevolence, unsteady on his feet, Charles sahib faced his rival and me. "You blackguard! You heathen! I'm going to . . ."

"No, you won't." Job sahib made a sudden move and struck out with a well-aimed kick at Charles sahib's wobbly legs. He drew back a powerful fist and struck his opponent squarely on the jaw, knocking him down to the floor. The pistol glistened on the carpet.

"Maria!"

Idris's loud voice was followed by the sound of footsteps racing down the corridor. Accompanied by Pratap, the wrestler, Idris rushed into the room. Charles sahib began to writhe in discomfort, occasionally opening an eye and shooting hostile glances at those who surrounded him, but he had no strength left. Job sahib had grabbed the pistol and now pointed it at his rival, his other arm wrapped around my shoulders. Charles, the Factor hated by everyone present, was outnumbered.

Job sahib stood guard, his expression one of quiet determination. He seemed to be deliberating his rival's fate. Pratap kept his eyes on the captive as well. If Charles sahib made the slightest move, both men would be ready to tackle him.

All the help—some ten of them, the cooks, the gardener, the laundrymen, the valet, the watchmen—now streamed into the room. Idris recounted the episode, whatever he'd seen of it.

"Look who's on the floor for a change," the watchman said. "You should be ashamed of yourself, planning to assault our chief!"

Charles sahib, with his limited vocabulary of Bangla and squirming on the floor, must have understood some of this, for he muttered, "You'll be sent to narak."

"We'll feed you to the crows first!" said Pratap.

"The filthiest swine," snarled Idris. "We'll have you put in chains!"

"No," said Job sahib. "Tie him up with ropes." As he shoved the pistol in his trousers' pocket, I gave it a quick look. It had an octagonal-shaped muzzle and a barrel etched with a foliage pattern. However handsomely designed, the weapon made me shudder.

Idris fetched coils of thick strong jute ropes, and as the servants bound his hands and feet, Charles sahib began to kick, scream, and curse, all at once.

In this perversely sweet moment, while everyone's attention was centered on Charles sahib, Job sahib seized me in his arms, brought his face down to mine, and planted a kiss on my lips, a warm whispery delight. I opened my eyes, unaware of how much time had elapsed, and looked up at him.

Idris looked over his shoulder at Job sahib and cleared his throat. "We're ready to escort the sahib to his room, sir."

At the sound of Idris's voice, I disengaged, took a few paces back, my heart clenched. I was sure Idris had noticed the joy radiating from my face. The frown on his forehead was unmistakable.

Job sahib struggled to collect himself. "Lock Charles up in his room overnight, keep him in seclusion, but give him food and drink and have a guardsman watch him closely at all times."

Pratap wagged a finger at Charles sahib. "You're lucky to be alive."

Tariq entered at the very moment that everybody else erupted in mocking laughter. He nearly screamed at the sight that met his eyes— Charles sahib rolling back and forth on the floor, hands bound at the wrist, legs tied at the ankles. After he had heard the story, his face darkened with hostility toward us. Disheveled, his face blotchy, Charles sahib was dragged unceremoniously to his feet. As he was being carried out of the room, he cast a malevolent glance at me.

I blinked and shook off my misgivings, glad that the ordeal was over.

"What will happen to him?" Idris asked Job sahib.

"Charles will be immediately sent away from this Factory. Tomorrow he'll go to Hooghly, accompanied by Tariq. From there he'll be packed off to Surat where the Council, a body of Factors which administers all the British factories, and of which I am a member, will decide on a suitable course of action. I will dispatch an express note to the Council. Charles will be charged with attempted assassination."

"You will not notify the Nawab's police at all?" Tariq asked.

"No. I'd like to use our own judicial system."

Tariq stood uneasily, displeased. "As you wish, sir."

All around the room, there were smiles and exclamations of relief. "We'll protect you with our lives," Pratap said to Job sahib.

Job sahib nodded and acknowledged the remark, his face ashen.

My voice low, lips still warm from his kiss, mind anxious because of it, I said, "You're pale. Shouldn't you be resting?"

The sahib's lips twitched. "I ache all over. I suppose I could go to my bedchamber and rest for a bit. Will you attend me this evening?"

His tone was intimate; still warm from his embrace, I couldn't have asked for more. As Job sahib slipped out of the room, I saw pain and relief in his eyes, and delight, too. I asked Pratap to call on the best herbal doctor in town. Then I made for the kitchen and quickly prepared some vegetable broth, what my mother served me in my childhood whenever I had fever.

Idris came by and stood silently, looking decidedly troubled.

"What's the matter?" I asked.

"I must now confess what I've hidden from you and everyone else all this time." His voice was thick with grief. "It has to do with Bir's murder."

I felt a knot in my stomach. "Are you admitting that Charles sahib . . .?"

Idris nodded. "Yes. I could have prevented it, perhaps, but I didn't." He folded his hands, as though to calm himself, as though uttering a silent prayer.

"Please tell me the details if doing so will help relieve your burden. It'll certainly relieve mine."

Idris squinted. "You might recall that the sahib had an eye for Bir. On that night, after playing cards at a shop by the river, Bir and I parted company. He went toward the water for the cooling breeze and moonlight and I . . . I hate myself for it, I headed for the Factory. My eyes were nearly closing from the fatigue, even though I had a feeling . . . You see, Maria, the shop was situated right next door to the punch house and I saw Charles sahib coming out. The whole area was poorly lit and no one else was about. From a distance, I saw the sahib call out to Bir. Oh, Shiva! I knew it then. The sahib rushed toward Bir and they exchanged a few words. It was obvious what the sahib had in mind from the way he leaned toward Bir and tried to embrace him. Bir pushed him away. The sahib staggered back a step. My insides screamed to me; something terrible was about to happen. Coward that I was, I began to run in the opposite direction; I knew well the consequences Bir would suffer for refusing the sahib's advances. I'd gone only a short distance when I heard a gunshot from behind. I went numb, stumbled, got up, and ran faster, without ever looking back."

"And you stayed silent the next day and the next day," I cried out. "You never accused the sahib!"

Idris paled. "How could I take action when I am well aware I'd never get justice and might even lose my job? I have a family to consider. Our lives don't mean much to either our Mughal rulers or the sahibs, and we can do nothing to change that." He turned, his voice broken. "Forgive me, if you ever can, Maria." I stood rigid for a moment, thinking: We must try to change all this, we must.

Then, with a steaming bowl in my hand and my mind reeling with this new revelation, I mounted the staircase to Job sahib's private quarters.

TWENTY

The door was half-open. Inside the room, Job sahib rested on his back under a canopy and a quilted white silk cover. I had never been to this chamber, accessible only with permission. Job sahib appeared to be asleep, his chest rising and falling, slowly and deeply. I lingered in the doorway for a moment and took in his well-chiseled profile in repose. Quietly, I slipped in, put the soup bowl gently on a side table, and was about to tiptoe out when Job sahib opened his eyes.

"Maria!" he cried out, trying to prop himself up on the pillows.

I flushed from the excitement of hearing him say my name, worried at the same time about how weak he appeared.

"Please, don't try to get up. I've sent for a doctor. He should be here shortly."

He fell back, eyes misty and swollen, and expelled a breath. "Sit by me," he said; his tone was affectionate. I was almost afraid to linger. My reputation could suffer from being alone in the sahib's quarters.

"Perhaps I shouldn't."

"Don't worry; I won't let anyone harm you."

Seeing him vulnerable and longing for my company, I let go my worries and sat on the edge of the bed.

How satisfying that I could be so near him when he needed me. What a thrill to experience his feverish warmth, to be able to help ease his discomfort. He pulled the blanket tightly around him. "Oh, God, what a time it has been! I'd be a dead man by now, if it weren't for your quick response."

I closed my eyes for a brief instant, recalling what I had heard from Idris about Bir's murder only minutes ago. Wishing not to overburden Job sahib, I simply said, "We cooks had suspicions about Charles sahib all along."

"It was my fault, given everyone's misgivings about his character and actions." Job sahib rubbed his forehead. "But his family is influential in England and they can cause great damage to me and the Company. Only the future will tell if I've made the right decision."

"Many eyes will be watching, many ears will be listening for indications of anyone trying to harm you or us, sahib."

"You were there when I needed help. That means a lot to me. And, please, don't call me sahib again."

My heart swelled, bringing with it long-suppressed feelings. I turned my attention to the soup. I needed to rein in my feelings for the time being, pay attention to the caution that reared its head in my mind. "You must have nourishment," I said. "Here's some vegetable broth, specially prepared for you."

His eyes softened with gratitude. "Oh, my sweet, capable girl!"

He raised himself up into a sitting posture; I spooned a little soup into his mouth, and he slid back down onto the bed.

"Stay a little longer, will you?" he asked. "Your presence soothes me." He rolled onto his side and took my arm. For a moment he seemed to struggle with an inner battle, and then his eyes cleared. He reached out slowly, took my hand, and gently kissed it. Speechless, I didn't resist as he reached for my face and drew me closer to his chest.

"We're entering a dangerous zone, Maria, but I can no longer contain how I feel about you. I've always wanted to be a successful trader in this beautiful land, doing the work I love. And now I have a bigger dream; to have you by my side."

I lifted my head in wonder and gazed into his eyes; he pulled me closer and smothered me with kisses. A wave of warmth surged through my body, but I drew back momentarily and managed to whisper, "I have been yours since the moment we met. But all this time, I had no idea that . . ."

"I am shy. I should have expressed myself sooner, but I might as well confide in you now. I was sixteen, still living at home, and fancied a neighbor girl, also sixteen. Her name was Rose, a pretty thing, aptly named. I would stare at her in the field, at the shop, on the street; whenever I ran into her, whenever I heard the rustle of her skirt, the day would turn into a song for me. Then one day, I gathered enough courage to approach her. She looked at me with her expressive, violet eyes. My heart thumped so terribly that I almost choked. I managed to tell her how I felt about her, how I dreamt all night about her. She screamed at me. 'Stupid boy! I don't like you. Don't ever bother me again, or else,' and she ran away. I . . . I was crushed. I remember how I simply sat down on the ground and cried. Since then, I always thought I'd never again fall in love. I thought that part of me had died. But then, many years later, I met you."

Job paused, his eyes caressing my face, and I sat with the gift of that which he had confided in me. He enfolded me in his arms; the remnants of my resistance crumbled in his embrace. For the first time, in a very long time, I experienced a deep sense of security.

"I am so happy, Job." I saw myself through his eyes: a woman more capable, confident, loving, and worthy than I had ever deemed myself to be. No, fate never intended me to be a mere servant. How eagerly my mother had listened to the astrologer's prediction that I would one day sit on a throne, dressed in silk and jewels.

I allowed myself to dream again of marriage, a home, the bliss of conjugal love, and children. Even in that exultant moment, a part of me wondered how long it would be before the doctor arrived.

Face contorted with pain, Job mumbled, "Oh, my shoulders are burning. And my head is in a fog."

His voice slowly faded, and he fell asleep. Our hands still clasped, I remained seated beside him, listening to his raspy breathing, praying for the doctor's arrival.

I looked around the room. I can vividly recall how I was struck by its size and opulence: a high four-poster bed, brocade pillows, a mahogany cabinet, two chairs whose gilded legs were carved in a vine pattern, a mirror almost as tall as me, a trunk, and a teakwood desk. In this room lit by scented oil lamps, the walls were draped with multi-colored tapestries and the windows hung with delicate bamboo shutters. Even though the marble floor made the space cooler than the rest of the building, a swinging pankhah was suspended from the ceiling. Two side tables, their top decorated with mother-of-pearl, flanked the bed. A window afforded a vista of the flowering shrubs below. Having grown up in humble surroundings, I was intimidated by the opulence of this space; at the same time, I also felt drawn to it and not simply because of Job. I found myself attracted to the prospect of wealth and the comforts that accompanied it.

Hearing a knock at the door, I scrambled to my feet and went to open it. A stranger, clad in a white dhoti and white turban, clean-shaven, clutching a wooden box, stood at the door. He identified himself as the herbal doctor, the kaviraj.

The doctor placed his hand upon Job's head, asked his age. Then he examined Job's tongue, pulse, chest, lips, and eyes. He asked Job about the particulars of his fever and questioned him about his daily habits.

I left the room and waited in the hallway to allow them privacy, as well as to calm the agitation inside me. Would they bleed Job? I couldn't bear the thought. All too often they bled the patient to reduce swelling. I feared the accompanying risk of death.

The doctor came out of the room, his face dark.

"What will ease his fever?"

"The sahib drives himself too hard. When a man's body isn't recharged with adequate rest and recreation, it breaks down. You must advise him to lighten his workload. He must do so if he wishes to live a long happy life."

"Will you prescribe any medicine?"

"Yes, I'll have it sent shortly. It's a brew of cobra venom, minerals, and herbs—the only way to treat such a high, obstinate fever. The sahib will have to take it three times a day. He might have trouble swallowing it. I also recommend foot and forehead massage, a light diet of vegetables, reduction of alcohol consumption, and complete bed rest." He paused and caught my gaze. "I have one more diagnosis. There's a Bangla word for it. Can you make a guess?"

"Ashukh?"

"Precisely. Absence of happiness. Lack of harmony. Keep him happy—I can prescribe no better medicine. The sahib is particularly susceptible to imbalances in his environment, although in the end, it's all in God's hands."

Ashukh.

I vowed, then and there, to lavish on Job the best personal care possible.

"The doctor ordered me full rest," Job said, eyes half-open. "But the Factory . . ."

"Arthur sahib should be able to make sure it runs smoothly."

"Will you check on him?" Job closed his eyes and sunk into deep slumber.

I kissed his burning forehead and tiptoed out of the room, intensely aware of my responsibility. Lantern in hand, I descended the staircase and encountered none other than Arthur sahib in the corridor. Dressed in a beige linen doublet, he was incongruously carrying an umbrella. His eyes were scarlet; he'd returned from another bout of drinking at the punch house. He glanced at me suspiciously from under his broad-brimmed hat. Women weren't allowed in a Factor's chamber.

I lifted my chin and locked eyes with him. He looked straight ahead, ignoring my presence, but I stood resolute. At that moment it didn't matter to me what he or anyone else thought of us. Job and I loved one another. I had to relay his message to Arthur sahib.

"Sir!" I called out.

A servant had dared to address a sahib. Arthur sahib swiveled around and faced me, his visage stern, forbidding. I was in no mood to waste time for the sake of propriety. "Job sahib has fevered." As I reported the details of the doctor's diagnosis, Arthur sahib's expression softened a little.

"This is indeed a grave matter." His eyes took on a vague, uncertain quality; his voice faltered. "We must, of course, do whatever is in our power to get him well."

I reached deep inside myself to put strength into my voice. "I have experience of nursing the sick. My father was frequently ill when I was growing up. I'll tend to Job sahib, do all I can, but I'll need help from others." I also conveyed to him that during this period of Job's incapacity, the Factory must continue to operate without any interruption. That was Job's wish.

Arthur sahib looked me full in the face. "None of us can match Job's dedication to the Crown, although I must say, he doesn't delegate enough. We'll do our best and for now, I'll give you permission and authority to call on whomever you deem is appropriate. And I will be available whenever you need me. God keep thee."

He disappeared down the corridor. I couldn't help but smile at the change in the sahib's attitude, like a storm wind whirling and howling but ultimately dissolving.

As I began walking back to my room, I imagined a happy outcome from this exchange. So much had happened in this one day. Job and I had finally come together. I could still feel his warm embrace, his kisses, his loving words. How I yearned to snatch more such intimate moments with him. We had so much to share. I wanted to hear about how he grew up, about his family, whether he missed his parents. Did he ever think about me during the day? What sorts of things did he like? Of course I would like to take Job to my village to meet my parents. I could only imagine the days of celebration that would follow.

The night's darkness seemed to dissipate for me. A bulbul bird sang full-throated somewhere, a joyous accompaniment to the elation I felt.

TWENTY-ONE

The rooms and hallways of the Factory were smeared with rumors, ugly as monsoon mud, rumors not about Charles sahib, the man who had attempted to assassinate Job only weeks ago and consequently been dismissed from this Factory, but about Job and me. The sahibs gossiped about us as they supped, lounged on the verandah, or smoked their hookah pipes in a cloud of rose water-scented fumes. Their words were later whispered into my ears by ever vigilant servants. Gordon sahib had insisted that Job and I were spending wild nights together, complete with drunken laughter, sweet moaning, and rhythmic creaking of the bed.

If only Job and I were married and the gossip were true. The fever kept him confined to his bed. I brought him specially prepared meals, caressed his hands, massaged his forehead and feet, fanned him when the temperature outside soared, and spoke with him gently when he felt up to talking. I let him know that he was cherished in every way.

I longed for the feel of his shoulders, the rough warmth of his skin, but I kept my desire well hidden. Only occasionally did he feel strong enough to sit up, hold my hand, and smell my hair. Then he'd fall back on the bed, as though drained of all strength, and toss about in restless sleep. I kept his red slippers by the bed in case he wished to get up, which he rarely did. Despite that, Francis sahib had added frills to the gossip by suggesting that Job was feigning illness as a means of spending time with me. When Idris told me that, I couldn't help but laugh.

One night during supper, as I helped the servers, I overheard snippets of conversation between two Factors. "She's not our class or color," one of them insisted as he sipped from the soup bowl. "What does he see in her?"

My heart beat fast. I wanted to respond, to snap back at him for the vulgarity he had shown someone who was not his class or color.

"Job's in love with Hindustan," said the second sahib, taking a bite from the roast fowl. "See how he dresses. Notice what he likes to eat. He is rather Brahmanized. Do you suppose he was born here?"

"He could very well have been. Still, their affair could get scandalous. Remember how we got rid of the sweeper girl?"

My jaw tightened. I would certainly fight back if they tried to send me away.

With Teema gone, I could only grieve in private. Fortunately, Job wasn't aware of any of this gossip. He didn't care to receive any visitors, so he had no idea what those around were saying about us.

One morning, when I swept into Job's room, he stirred, opened his eyes, blinked to steady his gaze, and wished me a pleasant morning. Swaddled in a robe of white brocade, he slid to the edge of the bed. I rinsed his head in a bowl of water from the river and massaged his scalp with my fingertips.

"What a marvelous cure," Job said. "How pure the water feels. I don't mind having a fever, just so I can feel the cool water and your touch on my head."

"I'd like to see you up and about, as would everyone else in this Factory."

"I have never been away from work this long," After drying his hair in a towel, I gave him the medicinal broth, which he had a hard time swallowing and served him a light meal of greens and squash. I handed him an express letter from his family that had been delivered by a messenger. Stained and crumpled, the letter had been sent via a shorter shipping route through Egypt, but it had still taken months to arrive.

Reclining on his back, his face translucent in the lamp light, Job scanned the pages. "It's from my mother," he said softly. He set the pages aside. I was curious and also aware of the sense of loss and regret in that action, but I decided to withhold my queries.

"I've never told you about my family, have I?"

Moving closer to the bedside, I replied, "No, I'd love to hear."

"I had a most miserable childhood, no other way to describe it. My family owned a tiny farm in Lancashire that provided barely enough for us to subsist. My parents didn't get along. The house was full of the sounds of their quarrels. I had three older brothers and two younger sisters, and we fought constantly. I didn't look like any of them and realized early on that my father didn't care for me. Do you know what it's like for a child to feel that way? My father was always angry because he could never rise above his circumstances. Only my mother loved me. She loved me dearly.

"One day when we were working in the field, my father turned on me and told me of his suspicion that I wasn't his son. 'A bastard, that's what you are, the grocer's boy. I can't abide your ugly face.' He kicked me a few times. I cringed in fear and humiliation; I whimpered, then I tried to run away, but he grabbed me by the arm, his nails pierced my skin as he dragged me home. My whole body ached for days afterwards. I was in such distress that I wanted to die, but I didn't tell anyone about it."

Job's face looked stricken. What if the fever spiked? He rarely expressed this much emotion. To allow him a few private moments, I began dusting the furniture.

Job began again, his voice trembling. "Then when I was seventeen, my father ordered me to leave home. 'I never want to see your ugly face again,' he said in a cold, dark voice. I looked up at him and saw he meant it. Proud that I am, I didn't beg. My mother pleaded and pleaded, but he wouldn't relent. I walked out of the house with my meager possessions in a worn sack. I had always nursed a desire to go far away, to see what was out there in the world, but when that day finally came, I stood by the roadside and cried." I put the dusting rag away and began arranging the furniture, but kept my ears open. I wanted to hold him tight, help mend the broken parts, but I could see he needed to speak more. All I asked that day was, "Did you stay in touch with your mother?"

"Oh, yes. I wrote to her often, and she replied. Years later, when the pain didn't keep me up all night, I got the news about my father's death from her letter. By then, I had arrived here. Much as I hated my father, his dark shadow stayed with me. I am not as good a person as I'd like to be. Oftentimes, I mistreat people the way my father did me." After a few moments, he picked up the letter again and his fingers caressed the rough pages. "My mother wants to know why I am still here and what my plans are for returning. She'd asked me to go home right after my father's death and I did consider that, but ultimately decided not to. Going back would only add to my suffering."

Still I wondered about the call of his family and of the land where he was born, the shared rituals and beliefs that bound people together. "What made you decide to stay here?"

"Actually, I had no choice," he said, speaking as though from a feverish depth. "At first, I didn't like it here. This land was far too strange. I wanted to go back. Then, over time, the rivers, the mountains, the bustle, the religious fervor, the rich soil, and the people stole my heart. I can neither fully understand the bond, nor deny it. You might say it is fate.

"Now that my father is long gone, I could easily go back home, where I'd find meadows, my people, my mother's kind face, as well as hearty loaves of bread. But the desire never lasts long. Hindustan beckons me, her arms wide open, her heart brimming with warmth and wisdom. She demands that I serve her, and I fall at her feet."

I listened to this extraordinary confession that mirrored my own sentiments.

"The other Factors complain about the filth and the chaos they see in this town, about people being untrustworthy, but I am well familiar with clean homes, hospitality, and loyal, good-natured folks, the vivid colors that add to their lives. I've seen their delight in celebrations, the love that binds them with their family, their willingness to make solid friendships, far more than what I've ever experienced.

"You know, I never thought I'd live in a place where crops are so abundant that farmers can be idle part of the year, where trees are loaded with fruit, and where the rivers teem with fish. Quite a contrast to our household in England. We seldom had enough food at mealtime, which caused my brothers and me to squabble over who would get the biggest slice of bread. Of course, I always won."

Even as he spoke so glowingly, there were aspects of life here that had failed to please him: the oppressive heat and humidity, for example, which often made him lethargic; on occasion, he failed to understand the people or their motives, as polite as they might appear. He wondered if the gulf between the two cultures was simply too great to overcome.

I turned and drew closer to him. Despite a different language, upbringing, and manners, and a distance measured in months at sea, the English were like us in many ways, I thought with pleasure. I had secured a foothold of my own in this foreign habitat, which the sahibs called their 'Little England'.

Young as I was on that day, I was blissfully ignorant of the painful differences that would arise between us.

"I, too, had fights with my two brothers over my mother's dishes," I said to Job. "I usually lost."

We laughed together. I asked Job what the English countryside was like. His eyes shone as he took me to the gentle hills dotted with ponies, grazing sheep, and fields of golden wheat. "I don't miss the long dreary winter months—snow, fog, cloudy skies, and winds sharp as a 'witch's curse'. The more we stayed at home, the more my brothers and sisters and I found it impossible to get along. We shared a room. Even though it was large, it felt crowded. I always wanted a room of my own, land of my own."

His gaze was fixed at a distance, reminding me of the day we'd met. Then he had peered far out toward the horizon, as though wishing to lay claim to the territory that his vision encompassed. More than a mere longing, I believed, it was a solid goal that he carried with him, one of owning Hindustan, even if he wasn't fully aware of it. Foreign powers had always wanted to occupy my motherland, a desire whose legitimacy I rejected. But in that moment, bursting with love for Job, I allowed my doubts to slip away. "Looking back, I see that the darkest day of my life, one that took me away from my loved ones, has been a blessing." I clung to his hand. "I wouldn't have met you otherwise."

"It changed my life too. Now that you are by my side, I could admit to my allegiance to this land."

Job shut his eyes, his face calm. Only moments ago he'd acknowledged what he'd perhaps suspected for a long time: this land, not a far-off misty island, was his home. A burst of hope rose in me, a strong sense that he would get well. He would ride his stallion once more, return to the meeting hall to address the Factors, and make his appearance at lavish meals in the dining room. Our love would flourish, as naturally as the river swelling in the monsoon rain.

TWENTY-TWO

After leaving Job's room, I climbed down the stairs and came across Arthur sahib, draped in a purple cloak, a white scarf around his throat and a black umbrella under his arm. I stood in his path, blurted out the status of Job's health, and inquired if any message needed to be given to him from the other Factors.

Without the steady gaze typical of him, Arthur sahib seemed lost in the uncertainty facing him. "Well, I wouldn't bother Job with this, but I am in need of an interpreter."

Rani Mata, decisive as always, had approached the Company via a broker named Chand with a detailed proposal for textile trading. The broker was due to arrive at the Factory that very morning to display samples and negotiate prices. "And Tariq is no longer here to negotiate for us."

I kept my elation to myself, not realizing that I hadn't seen the last of Tariq.

"When Charles was expelled from here, Tariq decided to leave also. He will relocate to Hooghly, that's all he's told me." He paused. "I have no choice but to ask you to be our interpreter, an offer I am sure you'll accept eagerly. But be aware that you will also have to be a shrewd negotiator, one who will look after our interests, in short, top quality goods at the lowest possible price."

I swallowed. I wasn't as eager as the sahib might have expected. I visualized Job lying in bed, tossing and turning due to his fever. How could I spend two long hours away from him? What if his condition worsened? Moreover, would I be able to handle such an important assignment? I'd done a credible interpretation for Rani Mata, but that had taken place in a pleasant home setting in the presence of only three people, and Job was already somewhat conversant with the native tongue. This was an entirely different matter, an adversarial encounter where I would be expected to outmaneuver an experienced negotiator. It was as though I was staring at a high wall, too high for me to scale.

"You're the only one who is familiar with the broker's dialect," Arthur sahib said. "Although your English is, shall we say, less than adequate at this point, you seem to make yourself understood."

My heart beat wildly in both eagerness and apprehension. If I failed to bargain effectively on behalf of the Company, I could be dismissed. No, I couldn't accept this offer. Then I went back to the day when, sitting on a bamboo mat with my father and my husband-to-be in our mud hut, I'd done the dowry negotiation. I had won that day; my father did not have to pay any dowry.

"Yes, sir, I would like to try my hand at this new task."

"We'll see how well you do. Don't deceive yourself that it's as simple as cooking."

"I am at your service, sir. But would you kindly ease my kitchen duties so I can fully dedicate myself to this new endeavor?"

"No, that is out of the question. See you at the meeting." Arthur sahib turned away.

Within an hour, I found myself sitting at the end of an oval table in the meeting hall where only a short time ago, I could enter only to serve a beverage. The ivory wall facing me flushed with the sunshine pouring in through a window. My eyes scanned the familiar space. This was the location where I had, only weeks ago, thwarted an attempt by Charles sahib to assassinate Job.

The Factors, twenty in number, distinguished in their doublets and hats and occupying padded velvet chairs around the table, chatted amongst themselves. I looked down at my attire of a forest green sari in fine cotton, plain but presentable.

Chand, Rani Mata's emissary, burst into the meeting hall. He hefted a large well-stuffed cloth bag and had a ceremonial dagger at his waist. He didn't look like someone who could be trifled with; that was clear the very moment he stepped in through the door, his sharp eyes taking in the room and the occupants at a glance. Several distrustful eyes appraised him coolly. He noticed me and smiled faintly. Although intimidated by my role, by the responsibility I'd taken on, by the people who surrounded me in this room, I tried hard not to show it.

Chand pulled a chair up next to mine. Since the sahibs were busy chatting among themselves, he turned to me. "I hear you're new at this, Maria, and I have been at my job less than a decade, but I am already considered one of the best brokers in the district. I go far beyond my immediate duties. I have helped set up a district-wide network of artisans and intermediaries who will sell their products through me. If I don't have what you want, I can get it for you. We brokers have a network that stretches across the region and beyond. Rani Mata's profits have gone up handsomely since she hired me."

I looked at Chand again. Young, slender, and of medium height, with a prominent nose and mahogany complexion, he sported a neatly trimmed beard that would measure four finger-breadths, as had been specified by Emperor Aurangzeb in Delhi. A white turban decorated with an opal set in gold made Chand a dashing figure. Still, I wondered if this brashly confident man would be able to work effectively with the sahibs or even me.

"So how did you figure out all the intricacies of your profession?" I asked.

"From my father. He was a weaver, a most dedicated one, and made the finest cloths in the district. My mother says that when I was born, he took only a few hours off, then went back to work. She maintained all his weaving tools. My mother still has a renowned design he did, a life-size scene from *Mahabharata* in red-and-purple brocade worked in gold thread. It shows trees, houses, animals, and stylized human figures. But, even with that much expertize, he couldn't make a decent living. When he died nine years ago, he was deep in debt. Merchants and brokers always paid him less than he was worth. I promised myself that I would become a broker some day and correct the situation for the artisans I dealt with."

Arthur sahib cleared his throat. In his role as the facilitator, he addressed the assembly, introduced the agenda, and then signaled Chand to speak a few words, adding that I would interpret for everyone present.

"I come here to offer my greetings and services," Chand began. It might have been his dagger, his probing eyes, his attitude, or the fact that the sahibs didn't fully trust me, whatever the reason, an uneasy silence cloaked the room.

"It is my utmost pleasure to represent Rani Mata, the Great Queen of Virganj," Chand announced, speaking theatrically in his native dialect. The others looked toward me after he had finished.

After I had translated his salutation to the Factors, Chand spoke. "We wish to form an alliance with the Company, but would prefer that the Nawab's revenue officers remain unaware of our relationship. Our textile products are the finest in the region, but not known beyond our borders, a situation we would like to remedy."

I translated as well as I could in my broken English, pronouncing every English syllable with equal care, sounding a trifle slow to my own ears, yet trying to make myself understood to the sahibs, staying true to the spirit of what was being said.

Reactions from the sahibs were not long in coming. Gordon sahib, a would-be poet in his spare time, often given to exaggeration, said, "Isn't Rani Mata also known as the 'Queen of Nowhere'?"

I pictured the spirited queen blazing in her pink-and-saffron sari, gesturing with a graceful arm adorned with coral-set bracelets, her voice gentle but strong, and wished the sahibs wouldn't dismiss her so easily. Job's face, too, swam before my eyes. It was as though this room was brightened by his invisible presence. If he wasn't still recuperating, he'd have presided over this meeting, and supported Rani Mata.

I interpreted Gordon sahib's words briefly for the benefit of Chand but without mentioning the insult. "The queen is, of course, a popular figure."

"Let me show you our swatches, sir, some of which have been personally selected by the queen." Chand bent down, opened the sack resting on the floor, and retrieved a single rectangular piece of dress material. So this was the tactic he would employ. I had seen it in my own village when retail cloth merchants came to sell their wares. Initially, Chand would show only one sample, although he had hundreds, and watch the reaction of the Factors. If the first sample didn't engender enough interest, he would show another, and then another. Little by little, he would wear down the resistance. Eventually, they would be ready to buy, and on terms favorable to him.

With a flourish, his eyes circling the room, Chand laid out the first sample on the table, explaining that it was sold by the bolt in the market. It was a breathtaking article, this mustard-and-maroon brocade, lavishly decorated with gold threads and woven with beads and precious stones. "Straight from our master weaver," Chand said, caressing the length of the fabric.

The colors were dazzling. The quality of the weave was exquisite enough to pass for tapestry work. I had an intense desire to reach out and stroke the cloth, but I resisted the impulse.

"A woman able to adorn her body with such fabric is fortunate indeed," I said, translating from the heart.

Arthur sahib reached out, picked up the swatch, studied it, and passed it around the room. "And the price?"

I posed the question to Chand. He threw a number in the air, an exorbitant sum, but did so with the flair of a snake charmer.

Words sometimes got stuck, but I made the necessary interpretations; when I scanned the faces of the sahibs, I found only suspicion and condescension.

"He's a cheeky little bugger," Gordon sahib said, slouching in his chair, "but shrewd as the devil."

William sahib smelled the fabric. "Quite out of his mind," he said. "It's a ridiculously high price. Does he take us for fools?"

"No, sir." I gulped, realizing the delicacy of the situation. "I don't believe that is his intent."

"And why do they have to embroider a fabric in such gaudy colors?" William sahib burst out haughtily. "It's in bad taste. They're living in a prehistoric age, I suppose." He erupted in contemptuous laughter, his fleshy cheeks becoming even fuller, but he quickly retreated into silence when no one joined him.

I asked Chand to explain the purpose of the story woven into the fabric. His reply was drowned out by Arthur sahib's voice: "We'll pay only half that much."

Now I understood the strategy. The sahibs, too, were playing a game, trying to outwit Chand by downgrading the quality of his merchandise. I explained Arthur sahib's response to Chand, but he seemed to have already sniffed the general feeling of discontent in the room. He glowered.

"Obviously they don't understand our love for nature," Chand said to me. "We take colors from indigo plants, marigold flowers, pomegranate rind, henna, you name it. We take stories from our scriptures. The English are the crude ones."

He began folding the piece of fabric. If he walked out of here, that would be it for me. I couldn't let that happen.

"No doubt what we've seen is impressive," I said to Chand. "But suppose you showed us more ordinary weavings, bhai?" In our region, we treated each other as relatives, addressing even a stranger as 'brother', 'uncle', or 'cousin'. I hoped to soften Chand's attitude. I wanted him to understand we could end up together on the losing side of the table.

Chand laid out a larger piece of cloth: fine cotton muslin, gossamer white, smooth, delicate, and nearly weightless. He held it up to the lamp light. "Captured air," he said. Then he folded it, slid his gold ring off his left middle finger, and before our incredulous eyes, using a long dramatic sweep of his hand, he drew the entire length of the fabric through the ring. He declared the price to be slightly below that of the first sample fabric.

Gordon sahib yawned, Arthur sahib stared into space, and the rest of the sahibs bantered among themselves about how this time would be better spent in the punch house.

I began to interpret the responses for Chand. As before I stayed away from a literal translation, but he had gauged the sahibs' mood and attitude.

"Why do you work for these barbarians, Maria-behen?" Chand asked.

"Please ignore their behavior, bhai. You're here to trade goods."

"In Rani Mata's land, we're free," Chand said. "We trade with whom-ever we please. The French have a nose for fine things. Even the Portuguese, those reprehensible pirates, are easier to negotiate with. Crude bunch, these English." Again, he made a move to stand up.

"Please wait," I said to Chand, raising a hand to stop him. "The English East India Company is a venture already more powerful than you can imagine. They have traders who cross many treacherous seas, islands you have never heard of, countries as far away as China. They return to our shores with goods we've never seen, tea, porcelain, lacquer ware. Wouldn't it be wise to make a partnership with them, even if you have to go through a tough negotiation, even if you have to lose money at the outset?"

"You're asking me to give my choicest selections away?"

"Less profit in the short run, but more profit in the long run. The Company will be here a long time."

Chand roared. "Do you believe only Rani Mata is in danger of being annexed by the new Nawab? You should hear about the military prepara-tions that are going on. Unlike his predecessor, our new ruler has no love for the English traders. I predict the Nawab will send his forces to this Factory, loot the money and the valuable goods, and return it to dust. What'll happen to you then, behen?"

I trembled and struggled to keep my voice calm. "Do you have any basis for making such a prediction?"

"Indeed, I do. Rani Mata has informers who scrutinize the Nawab and the state of his army. Recently he has added more elephants to his cavalry." Chand paused. "There is discontent in the Nawab's Court that may have slowed the war preparation a little, but I suspect it will happen."

"Why is it taking so long?" Arthur sahib interrupted angrily, fixing me with a hard stare. "What kind of rubbish is that blockhead talking now? Dispense with this idle chit-chat, Maria!"

Every eye in the room was fixed on me. I couldn't take it anymore, the verbal skirmishing, the lack of manners on either side. I stood up and addressed the assembly. "Let us please all work together, shall we?"

"The interpreter is upset," Gordon sahib said in jest. "Shall we adjourn the meeting?"

"No," I replied in a resolute voice. "It is in everybody's interest to reach a price compromise. Our alliance with Rani Mata will extend far beyond this particular transaction, or so I hope."

I decided not to disclose the grave news about the Mughal army; what if it took the attention away from the transaction at hand? A deep uneasy silence seized the room. Before everyone's stunned gaze, Chand propelled himself to his feet, drew his dagger out of its wooden sheath in a ceremonial fashion and placed it on the table with a thud. It was a double-edged stabbing knife, with a gold-inlaid handle, which now glittered in the lamp light. Such a knife was usually intended to complement a sword in combat.

"I salute you, behen, by placing my weapon at your disposal," Chand said to me, dropping to his knees. "You've quieted this ill-mannered bunch. You represent the spirit of the Company better than these fools."

Arthur sahib's eyes bulged at the sight of the weapon glistening on the table. "Why did he have to get that knife out?" he asked. "What kind of trickery does he have in mind? Tell him to remove it at once."

Although shaken, I replied, "A dagger is only an accessory, sir. Chand doesn't mean any harm. In our culture, to bow down and present one's dagger means to honor, to obey."

"Remove it!" Gordon sahib said.

I conveyed Gordon sahib's request to Chand. "The dagger stays," Chand said, "until we reach an agreement."

"The dagger helps clear everyone's thinking," I interpreted.

As though to break the impasse, Arthur sahib said in half-jest to his colleagues, "I suggest we 'obey.'" His eyes betrayed a hint of unease as he turned to me, "Shall we proceed?"

I regained my seat and motioned to Chand. "Show us lesser grade, more substantial material."

He laid out a series of heavier weight swatches next to the dagger: a floral aqua fabric threaded with silver; a second in a green-purple color painted with lotus leaves, symbolic of Hindu mythology; and a third in indigo, soft, glossy, and fringed with gold-worked lace.

"Well, finally!" Arthur sahib burst in approvingly. "Looks like we'll be able to sell these in London. They can be used for any number of home furnishing items—wall hangings, tablecloths, curtains, even bed spreads."

"Not to forget gowns for English ladies," I suggested.

"Right, right," Arthur sahib said.

Chand quoted individual prices for the fabrics, adding, "Take it or leave it. I will not go any lower." He mumbled a few words about the plight of independent craftsmen.

"He will not compromise any further, sir, nor would I," I said to Arthur sahib. "I have known artisans in my village, spinners, weavers, embroiderers, and dyers, who work from dawn till dusk, live from season to season, and still don't make enough. They have to put rice in their family's mouths, marry their daughters, take care of their elderly parents. Let's not be unfair to them."

"Bloody Hell!" Gordon sahib said. "Another joyless story."

"How do we know both you and this glib man aren't telling us lies?" Francis sahib said.

Several heads nodded. I unclasped the gold chain around my neck and displayed the pendant which shone brilliantly. "If he proves false, you can have my pendant."

The room was silent. Trembling, I shut my eyes.

Then I heard the triumphant voice of Arthur sahib consenting to the quoted prices. I opened my eyes and leaned forward, eagerly.

We went on to discuss the details—thread count, quantity, the procedure for checking quality, a cash advance for buying raw materials, and the date of delivery. As we eventually reached an agreement satisfactory to both sides, the sound of enthusiastic applause greeted my ears. I rose, stepped to the door, and signaled to Idris who was waiting outside, his body lost in a voluminous white tunic.

"After all the shouting, sneering, bargaining, and dagger-watching," he whispered, "everyone must be thirsty."

Bearing a round of beverages, he served each of us, then winking at me once in support, he departed on nimble feet.

Gordon sahib rose from his seat and excused himself. Before leaving the room, he doffed his hat at Chand, a mischievous smile on his lips.

Chand gathered his samples and turned to me. "Should you ever wish to secure another employment," he whispered, "Rani Mata would be most happy to accommodate you. And you might consider her offer seriously, behen. It's only a matter of time before the Nawab—"

"Will you be kind enough to inform me if you hear of an imminent attack?"

Chand nodded, put the dagger back into its sheath, and retied it to a loop in his waist belt. "My thousand apologies for any difficulty I've caused you," he said to me. "These cunning people want to make a profit and so do we. They're proud and so are we. They're clever, but we're no less."

I nodded. Chand bowed to everyone, saying, "Long life and health to thee." In his native dialect, he said that he would come and visit me again, and indeed, in the next several months I would have the chance to speak with him further.

Chand slipped out the door, the white gem in his headgear shining brighter than before. Arthur sahib thanked me, but the other Englishmen avoided my eyes. My negotiations weren't over yet. With the sahibs still seated and sipping from their glasses, I dangled another idea before them.

"Why limit ourselves to silk?" I asked. "Rani Mata has excess food-grains in her warehouse, rice, wheat, and barley, which can very well be exported."

"We grow or we die," Francis sahib said to the men. "I've heard of beautiful furniture arriving in our port from eastern islands. What if we exported a shipment of grains to those islands in exchange? Bartered with the native fools?"

My body tightened. *Stay calm, Maria. Don't lose your temper. This isn't about you.*

"An opportunity, indeed," Arthur sahib said. "Let us meet again next week. Perhaps we'll call this contractor back. Without his dagger, of course!"

As we filed out of the meeting hall, Arthur sahib took me aside. "Splendid!" he said, smiling broadly. "You negotiated well in male company. A woman! A Hindustani woman at that! A two-tongued one!"

"Sir, would you consider promoting me?"

"You're not ready yet. By the way, I must point out you didn't pronounce the word cheap right. It's not pronounced like ship." He explained the difference, with a laugh. My face hot, I repeated after him until I got it right.

"My only regret is that with you being absent from the kitchen, our meals have fallen in quality. We're back to watery lentils and under-cooked rice. Can't you teach your cooking magic to those lazy sods in the kitchen?"

How I wish I could tell him that those 'lazy sods'—Idris, Jas, and Pratap—toiled twelve hours a day.

Arthur sahib hadn't agreed on retaining me as an interpreter, but one victory a day was sufficient. I decided to give a helping hand to the kitchen crew but not get caught up in a hundred tasks there.

I would miss their company and bantering in my mother tongue, but the river was widening before me. Maria, the Interpreter. Maria, the Negotiator. Would it be possible, one day, to become Maria, the Factor?

TWENTY-THREE

S tanding at the landing, brimming with happiness, I watched Job come down the stairs; my heart quickened at the very sight of him. His high-necked indigo satin tunic and matching vest stood out in startling contrast to the pallor of his face. Although his cheeks were still gaunt, his legs seemed sturdy as he prepared to resume his normal activities for the first time in nearly three months.

"Dearest love," he whispered tenderly as he reached the landing, taking my hand and squeezing it. "I will devote the rest of the day to a long list of pressing duties. I can hardly wait to get back. But I shall wait for you in my chamber this evening."

So far, with him being unwell, I hadn't shared his bed. Each evening, I would feed him, massage his forehead, watch him fall asleep, and slip out of the chamber.

I hesitated. Voices echoed in my head, Teema's voice of experience. *He'll split your heart open, steal your tenderness, then leave.* The voices of my elders: *A girl from a good family shouldn't go to a man's chamber at night.*

"Yes, I'll be there." I responded happily.

Job walked toward the meeting hall. Dreamy-eyed, I watched him and then strolled toward the kitchen. Idris stirred the fire in the chulah, wisps of smoke rose in the air. I greeted him enthusiastically.

"I am at a loss," Idris said in a subdued manner. "I have to quickly come up with dishes to prepare for Anne memsahib's visit. Any suggestions?"

"She's still in town?"

"Oh, didn't you know? She's been staying in the Dutch quarters farther down the river, a regular at their nightly parties, and from what I hear, a popular figure."

"But why on earth is she visiting us?" I asked. "Last I heard she was engaged to Charles sahib. He's been sent to Surat and will be tried there for attempted assassination of his superior. Their engagement is supposed to be over."

"May Allah help her," Idris said. "She has had a change of heart; women from England are entitled to that. She's decided she wants Job sahib. She insists she would have visited him sooner, but Arthur sahib had asked her to wait, given Job sahib's frail condition. She'll be here this afternoon to take refreshments with the sahib."

For an instant the air was still. "I look after Job day and night."

"I have been informed that the lady wants to reignite the flame of passion in Job sahib. She thinks she can win him back with her beauty and charm, and surely, other tricks she knows."

"Why didn't anyone tell me?"

"My dear Maria, it pains me to say this. A servant is told only what she is required to know to carry on her duties. And, also, the others were advised to keep their mouths shut. Arthur sahib has had a hand in this matter, if you haven't guessed it already. He's a crafty man, haven't you noticed? He needs you as an interpreter and praises you accordingly, but rumor has it that he'd eventually like to dismiss you. He prefers Job sahib to marry an Englishwoman, racial purity and all that. Arthur sahib is playing the match-maker. I overheard him say so during last night's supper. 'Anne fits the bill. She'll make a lovely hostess for this Factory. I'd take her myself, but I think she wants Job.'"

I stood numb, shattered, remembering Job's kisses, the cocoon of love we'd created in his bedchamber, our shared memories, and how much we both love this land.

"You've gone through more than most of us, Maria. I wish you well and I always will, but you've chosen the wrong course of action. Your dream will never be fulfilled. It is not the path of a poor Brahmin girl from Kadampur."

"And Job?" I asked. "What does he have to say?"

"I'm told Job sahib has agreed to spend the afternoon with Anne memsahib."

I couldn't utter a word. As I took a step toward the door, Idris called out. "Wait, Maria. Will you be able to do the serving? I've been asked to play the flute. The other cooks are busy with various chores."

I nodded.

"The sky is for the rich," Idris said, his voice gentle, kind. "We only have the earth to fall down on. Let me warn you that you could ruin Job sahib's life and your own."

You're wrong, I wanted to say, *you don't understand what I feel about Job.* Such a discussion would go nowhere.

I walked out of the kitchen, stepped into the courtyard, and headed to my room. The roses lining the outer walls of the main building had lost their blush. The squirrels which ran about freely near the palash tree ahead of me couldn't bring a smile to my face. The sun did not lighten my heart. I sat on the floor of my room and sobbed soundlessly.

I spent the next several hours in the kitchen, helping Idris prepare a host of delicacies. As the afternoon rolled past, I made up my mind. When our work was over, I returned to my room. I had to dress properly, show myself in the brightest possible light.

I wore a sky-blue cotton sari with an indigo trim, the best from my meager collection of clothing. I was too thin and lacking in the curves that would have made me a beauty, but I didn't let that thought ruin this moment. I combed my shoulder length hair, tied it into a bun, and wore a necklace of fresh shiuli flowers. I checked myself in the looking-glass and banished the sad look from my eyes in favor of a pleasant smile.

As I reentered the kitchen, Idris looked at me, smiled, and then looked again. "How pretty you look, Maria! I have never seen you dressed so well."

"Has the lady arrived?"

"Yes, they're sitting on the verandah. She will pale before you. Be warned, however, not to incur her wrath. A maidservant mustn't outshine her mistress."

I picked up a silver tray arrayed with a variety of colorful tidbits placed on white platters. Idris headed out the door first, turning once and saying, "Allah, the Sacred, is the only judge of our hearts."

If my legs felt a bit wobbly on the way to the verandah, I didn't show it.

The verandah appeared festive, bedecked with oil lamps, the pillars entwined with chains of marigold. Idris had already positioned himself in the far corner of the courtyard, playing the flute. I stood for a moment, soaking up the music, hearing in my mind what Idris had always said, "Allah breathes through the flute and creates the sounds that dance in our hearts."

Job and Anne memsahib sat across from each other on wicker chairs. His posture perfect, the gold ring on his hand sparkling, Job wore an expression of thoughtfulness, as though churning over a grim matter in his mind. As I stepped closer, Anne memsahib, a pearl necklace around her slender neck, straightened her spine. She avoided facing me and I took the opportunity to turn my curious gaze on her. Although she had on a lace-collared, high-waist violet gown worked with floral sprays, her face had lost some of its vibrancy. In the few months she'd spent under Cossimbazar's merciless sun, her complexion had darkened. A pair of elaborate pearl-drop earrings and a hat trimmed with rosebuds only partially augmented her appearance. With deep shadows under her eyes, surely the result of keeping too many late hours, she seemed weary and desperate. And yet, she had the perfect poise of an Englishwoman.

After taking a deep breath, I set the tray down on the table and bobbed a curtsy. "I am Maria, the cook," I said easily. It thrilled me to realize how much my English had improved since her last visit. "It is my great honor to serve you again."

No response came from the lady; Job sahib gave me an admiring look, a smile on his lips. He eyed the platters, saying, "What a lovely meal you've prepared, Maria."

He asked for the names of the dishes and I reeled off the list. Encouraged by the eagerness in his voice, I lingered.

Her eyes flaring, Anne memsahib bit out the words. "You may go."

"I do beg pardon, memsahib." Quickly, I turned and slipped out of the verandah.

"Too impertinent, that serving girl." Her words followed me. "She acts like she's one of us."

"She's indeed one of us," Job said in a definitive manner.

I cherished Job's remark. With the instinct of a server, I sat on the ground beside the ever prolific jasmine bush trellised high and lining the entire length of the verandah, a mini-jungle of green and white. I waited, in case they wanted more food or beverage. The afternoon sun caressed me, the vines tangled playfully over my head, and the blossoms teased me with their scent. Even Idris's somber flute music didn't dampen my mood. I could observe both Job and Anne memsahib from here. Job sat facing me, but I could only see Anne memsahib's profile as she sat fanning herself with a hand-fan made of palm leaves.

Her voice took on a dreamy quality. "Ah, Job, what a pleasure. I have missed you all these months."

"Truly?" Job had a bemused smile on his lips. "I thought Charles . . ."

"That rogue, that nightmare who would take anyone to bed? Oh, dear, what a time it has been. He actually tried to shoot you? And you, brave soul, fought him off? The story has circulated all over town. I am proud of your valor. Indeed, I am very proud."

"I must correct you, Anne. It was Maria who thwarted the assassination attempt. It was she who saved my life and possibly prevented other disasters. She's the one who should be commended, not I."

"Her skin is dark, her English pitiful, and she's not our class; you mustn't dwell on her. Perhaps you were lonely, too lonely for too long a period. From now on, I'll be happy to fill your free time."

"Why would you seek my company, with so many handsome Dutch traders around?"

"Oh, Job, please do not put your trust in idle gossip. Lies! Ugly lies! Mean jealous people slandering me. Let us turn back to the evening of the grand feast when we first met." She leaned closer to him, her voice grew deeper. "What a marvelous occasion that was. We sat together right here, drinking wine, listening to the flute—"

"Please listen to me, Anne. It will not work between us. It couldn't be any clearer to me and I am trying to make it clear to you."

Anne memsahib's long, pearl-drop earrings brushed her neck. "But why, Job? Is it because of Charles? Don't fret. I have put him out of my mind. I didn't love him. I simply couldn't return to England without a husband. You know what people would say? 'Poor thing, she returned empty-handed.' They'd look at me pitifully. I've received plenty of pity for being a widow."

She covered her face with a hand and ceased speaking. Job held out a gauzy white handkerchief. She snatched it from him and wiped her eyes. I shifted my position. I had been watching her and listening to her confession with a certain vengeance, but now my jealousy melted into momentary sympathy.

"I am ready to start a new life with you, Job," the widow from England said.

"You didn't hear me correctly, Anne."

His words sounded sweet to my ears and thrilled me. It was doubly thrilling because I wasn't present in the scene and Job was confiding in my rival.

"Oh, let me break one other piece of good news," Anne memsahib said. "I have grown used to this town. I never thought I would. The food here is magnificent. And what a great market—all the silk, satin, brocade, and pearls you could possibly want to buy."

"Anne . . ."

"I can see myself living in this beautiful mansion. I'm an expert hostess and I'll help you get important business leads by throwing lavish balls and suppers. By now I know how corrupt the Dutch businessmen are, the tricks they use to gain an upper hand in the trading circles. I'll share them all with you, which will help you enormously in your trade negotiations. But first, you must get rid of that annoying cook."

Job made a move to rise. "I need to return to my duties, Anne."

"You're thought to be a gentleman, Job. We both come from the same part of England; I've met your mother. You owe me an explanation. You couldn't possibly be in love with . . ."

"What if I said I was?"

Shiva! Let me sing your glory! Dizzyingly happy with Job's admission, I wanted to jump out with open arms, hold him tight, and burst into tears. I clasped my hands over my mouth to keep from singing out loud.

"For God's sake, you don't intend to wed her, do you?" Anne memsahib gasped. "You're an Englishman, a Christian, the Chief Factor, and she is nothing but a dark-skinned, idol worshipper."

The mellow, soothing sounds of Idris's flute soared and dipped.

"The greatest moment of my life was when I saved her from burning," Job said. "If she was born anew on that day, so was I. I who have always hated myself for being poor, unworthy, and outcast, saw myself differently through her eyes. I, who had thought I could never love again, felt the stirring of . . ."

"Stop it!" Anne memsahib's voice was thick with disgust. "She's not of our race. How could you have descended so low? Not only do you wear native clothes, but you have taken this heathen into your bed! How can a proper Englishwoman like me have anything further to do with you?"

"You've never really had any use for me, did you, Anne? What am I to you?"

"Please don't make such a serious mistake, Job. As Chief of the Factory, in the name of the Crown, for your loyalty to England, please reconsider."

Job rose from his chair. "I'll escort you to your carriage now," he said gently but firmly.

Job had maintained his dignity, choosing his words carefully, keeping his voice well-modulated.

Anne memsahib sat rigidly, her face paling. "Should you change your mind . . . I plan to stay in this town indefinitely."

"It would be better for you to return to England."

"I will not," she said, her body shaking. "I will stay here and make your life quite difficult. As for your reputation, there are powerful traders who would love to see you disgraced and your whole enterprise turned to ashes. And, hear me well, I'll tell Arthur you have taken advantage of me on this verandah, with no one in sight, and now refuse to marry me."

Job chuckled. "Arthur, who has invited you here, has been listening to our conversation and watching us from that room over there." He pointed to an adjacent parlor with a blue-painted window open to the verandah. "Arthur and I met earlier in the day. He fully understands my position and volunteered to monitor our time together."

So Idris had misunderstood Arthur sahib's intention! Anne memsahib looked about her, her face contorted. "Arthur?" she cried out. "Are you there?"

Arthur sahib cleared his throat from his hidden nook.

"Arthur will know exactly what to do with you," Job said. "You've managed to give the English residents in this town a bad reputation. We can ill afford that, given the predisposition of our religiously inclined Emperor and local merchants against licentious behavior. We could lose our trading privileges. On top of that, you've made threats to me and the Company; this will not be tolerated. I will consult with the Company management in England. Should you ever return, I will let them decide the course of action to be taken against you."

Abruptly, Anne memsahib stood up. "You can't mean any of this! You once saw me as a beautiful woman. Have you forgotten?"

"As Indian sages say, a woman's beauty is an illusion, *maya*. It fades. What really persists is a woman's inner nature."

"So you've become Hinduized?" Anne memsahib's laugh was shrill and sarcastic, her face dense with some kind of madness. "What could possibly be more degrading for an Englishman?" She shoved the tray; it landed on the floor, shattering the fine porcelain dishes and scattering bits of food all over the ground, squandering all that Idris and I had done to prepare the lavish spread. Yet, I smiled.

Job glanced at the mess. "Say what you will, Anne, but I cherish my life here. I have finally found a place to settle down, to do the work I enjoy. And I've met a woman who I can truly love, not just for how she can advance my business interests. I'll accompany you to the gate now. Arthur will escort you home."

Slowly, reluctantly, Anne memsahib turned. I got a full view of her face, blank as a piece of paper, her eyes motionless. As they stepped away from the verandah, I jumped up and scampered victoriously toward the kitchen, absorbing the happy tune Idris was now playing on his flute.

TWENTY-FOUR

That evening, standing at the doorway of Job's bedchamber, happy to see him up and about, I smiled. Under the light of an oil lamp, he pored over a stack of papers, a few ledger books scattered nearby, his face a picture of intense concentration. Attired in his night robe, he seemed agitated, the lines around his mouth tight. Whether that state of mind was due to trading concerns or a trying encounter with Anne memsahib, or both, I couldn't tell.

Hearing my footsteps, Job turned. "Maria!" Standing up, he gathered me in his arms and kissed my lips. The fatigue of the day evaporated from my body. I shut the door behind me.

"You look worried," I said.

"I have a new set of problems to deal with that have to do with Charles. He's free. Can you believe it? Even though the Council has strict disciplinarians, they let him go on account of the wealth and status he enjoys in England. Now he's taken to conspiring with the new Nawab against our Factory, or so I have been advised. Last week our regular shipment was confiscated by the Nawab's customs officials. Only after paying a huge bribe did we get it back."

"I have been talking with Chand periodically and getting updates about what goes on in the Royal Court. Perhaps we need to form alliances with Court officials to get advance knowledge of such schemes in future."

"Who can help us do that?"

"Although I, a woman, would not be able to handle such an assignment, Idris might. He can start befriending the Court's kitchen staff. Chand has told me there is discontent in the Palace and some well-placed officers might also be amenable to bribe. 'From ear to ear', we say in our village, 'from small fish to big fish.' With your permission, I'll speak with Idris."

"Good idea, Maria," Job said. "I have some good news too. Arthur and I had a long discussion. He happened to have watched you negotiate produce prices with the grocer, and was duly impressed with the results. You've also demonstrated your competency in dealing with both Rani Mata and Chand. Both transactions have benefited us tremendously. With Tariq gone, we need an employee who can speak and write English. So it seems an appropriate time to announce that we have decided to promote you to the position of Apprentice Factor."

I put a hand to my mouth. "Oh! Job, I really want the job, but am I ready? Will I be able to handle the work?"

"I will personally see to it that you get the necessary training."

The doctor's warning played in my head. "It would really please me if I could reduce your workload."

"I'll give you a chance." Job studied my face for a while, then, in an intimate tone, he said, "I've been waiting for you for hours. What took you so long?"

I felt the color creep to my cheeks. "The kitchen crew still needs help, so I have to be there."

Job smiled. "Except when you stand behind flower bushes, I suppose."

He had seen me! I laughed. "Please forgive me. I couldn't help but listen."

"Actually, I am glad you were in the vicinity. I meant every word I said." Job peered into my eyes and spoke, his voice deep, resonant, "I love you, Maria, love you with all that I am. Will you marry me, my darling?"

I clenched my jaw to fight off tears, smiling at the same time, trying to stand up straight, and not allowing my knees to buckle. "Without the slightest doubt." I couldn't trust myself to speak further.

He lowered his lips to mine and kissed me tenderly all over my face. I tried to stand as tall as I could, but felt a little unsteady. He pulled two chairs close together and motioned me to sit. "If it meets your approval, I will start the wedding preparations immediately."

I registered the tone of urgency. Did it have to do with the condition of his health? Was he marrying me for trade advantages? I could be useful to him.

"My illness has afforded me time to ponder," Job said. "Although my health needed mending, my mind was clear. Lying in bed for hours, I decided to pursue what's most important in my life, what's most precious; you, and our life together."

"But who will marry us, dear love?" I said. "First, we're of different faith. Second, I am a Brahmin widow. We aren't allowed to remarry. Third, we're of different color."

"No matter." He clasped my hand. "I would like a big traditional Hindu wedding, complete with music, dancing, and a big feast. With the late Nawab Haider Ali's sanction of the Hindu Widow Remarriage Provision, I don't envision any difficulty. Many young Hindu priests desire to be part of the reform and will gladly conduct our wedding ceremony. I've heard of at least one such priest in town. A devout Brahmin, he's married many Portuguese men who have taken local wives. Color is a consideration for the others, and they may try to belittle you for your association with me, but it isn't a consideration for the priest or for me. I look beyond skin tone, to a person's nature, to inner beauty." He paused, his face dreamy. "So, put your mind at rest, darling."

I tried to smile, but my breath caught in my throat. *Where are the two families?* The guests would ask at the wedding. Marriage not only joins a man and his wife, but two families together. 'Two blessings are stronger than one', so went a common saying. Usually, the bride's family welcomes the guests as they arrive while the groom's family invokes god's blessings. Neither Job's mother nor my family would be present to carry out their respective obligations.

"Nothing will give me more pleasure than to go back to my village with you, pay respect to my parents, and seek their blessings," I said. "Even though I can't be sure how the neighbors will react to my presence, whether it'll be safe enough for me to go back, I have to go there."

"We'll visit your family as soon as I can arrange a private boat." Job's pale eyes held an intense light. "What an excursion that will be. I want to breathe the air you breathed when you were growing up, see the scenery that sustained you. If you have worries about your neighbors, I'll be there to shield you."

"What would it be like if we traveled on a big ship and went to England? Would I have to wear a long gown, a big hat? Would they understand my English?"

"I'll be happy to take you there, my love, but you don't have to wear a gown. The colorful clothing you wear looks lovely on you, and you mustn't hide your beautiful face and hair under a hat. Your English has improved remarkably in less than two years, far beyond what I'd expected. But going back to England . . . Let me think about that."

In the gray shadows, I could see the torment inside him. He couldn't go back to England, not yet, if he ever could. "I've never shared this with anyone, dear love. There is a battle going on inside me. One part of me stays loyal to the Crown. I am grateful for being born in England and having the chance to be of service to the mightiest nation on earth. My eyes fill when I see our flag fluttering in the wind. I'd love to see our old farmhouse again. But there is another side of me that has embraced Hindustan and feels like it belongs here. Mostly, I think Hindustan is winning, although there are times when I see my mother's face, and I wonder if . . ."

"Your mother, what's she like?"

"I remember her wearing her favorite dress. It was of a natural color, with a high bodice, round neckline, long loose sleeves. She looked loving, beautiful. I can still see her kind eyes smiling." Job's voice mellowed when he talked about his mother; it became poignant, nostalgic. His words brought her alive for me as he remembered her. A kerchief tied about her neck, her hair arranged in a cap, she cured the meat, baked the bread, and sliced the cheese. Occasionally, she would look out the window with troubled eyes, searching for the middle son whom she so sorely missed. An everyday woman, she was like me, only dressed differently, only speaking a tongue foreign to me.

I sighed. "Surely you would want her to bless our marriage?"

"I do. I'll write to her immediately."

"Oh, I can almost hear the shehnai in the background. I can see and smell the fragrant accessories for the ritual—turmeric, coconut, sandalwood, and marigold flowers—which we'll bring into our room after the wedding."

"I suppose you'd like a house for us?" Job asked.

Job had acquired some wealth through a little illegal trading every now and then. Not as much as the other Factors, but enough to buy a house for his bride-to-be. He hid it at the moment, but, he had hoped desperately at the time that the girl standing before him, soon to be married to him, wouldn't ask about his finances.

I envisaged my present abode—the residences, the garden, the court-yard, the annex and the warehouse. Once a fearful newcomer, I had made every inch of this place my own. With soft rain falling outside like a gauzy curtain and the heavy scent of jasmine drifting through the window, I said, "Actually, I am happy here. Where could I find more beautiful surroundings? Where could I find as much camaraderie as I do in the kitchen, even if I don't cook any longer?"

"If you prefer to stay here, it will be so. It'll be our kingdom."

Yet I could see in that frown on his face that he had been slightly displeased at my refusal, but he shrugged and seemed to shake it off.

"Do you expect ill feelings from the other Factors?" I asked.

"I won't deny that I do, and at times it worries me. But you're known for your talents in the kitchen and they've seen you learn English fast and perform superbly as a negotiator. It is my hope they will gradually accept you as one among us."

Smiling into each other's eyes, our hands gripped tightly, we rose in unison. Job put a strong arm around my waist. In the next moment, we were abed, and I became lost in a field of warmth. His kisses crushed my lips, then made them whole again. "My queen," he whispered. "My guiding light, my ruby."

Ruby red, the color of celebration. I pictured the color suffusing me and reminding me of all I wanted: a husband, a family, an opportunity to serve others. I felt complete in a way I'd never had. Did I fret about what my parents might say? Yes, for a bit, intensely, then I let it go. Would it hurt? I blocked that thought too. I loved this man. Did the sound of feet shuffling outside the door steal my breath? Yes, but I didn't dwell on it. And what if the other servants found out? What if they did? All concerns were secondary. We lay entwined on the bed, cozy and nurturing, murmuring sweet words to each other. There was more air in the room than there had been before. The flower bushes outside the window released their evening fragrance. The night lengthened, and even with insects buzzing, I slept more soundly than I had in a long time.

TWENTY-FIVE

A stiff breeze blew as our boat edged away from the quay at Cossimbazar; the blue-purple morning sky was streaked with silver. The river, flowing between banks overgrown with lush tropical forest, blazed with morning light. We were on our way to my village, Kadampur, nearly half a day's journey to the south. The wooden vessel, which could both sail with the wind and be rowed, was festooned with colorful flags ruffled by the breeze. The boatmen, clad in waistcloths and skullcaps, began pulling hard at the oars, cutting a line on the river, the rhythmic splashing making a sort of music. What a privilege to be alone with Job; what a thrill to be away from the Factory for the first time since my arrival. But then, what if my parents rejected me? What if the villagers victimized me for not being a sati, refused to speak with me, or worse, pelted us with stones and attempted to drive us out?

As we glided leisurely along, the jungles on the riverbanks came alive before us. I pointed out to Job a peacock strutting out from under a tree spreading its tail. I showed him the cranes and pelicans that grazed the treetops. The sharp cry of a jackal echoed eerily. The sounds and sights of my childhood, of the life I had left behind. Job seemed to absorb all that he saw and heard, taking delight in everything.

As the boat progressed, the speed of the current increased, the river broadened, and the banks receded. "Ma. Baba," I said. "That's what I call my parents."

"That's easy," Job said, pronouncing correctly after me.

"Noo-poor and Neet-yah, are my two brothers."

I noticed the childlike delight in Job as he mastered the pronunciations. He missed his mother at that moment; in sharing my joy in my family, he sought his own.

How would my parents react when they heard my new name? How would they receive Job? Would they regard him with mistrust, or welcome him as a soon-to-be son-in-law? Wait till they hear him speak Bangla, I thought.

Kadampur at last. Back at last where I belonged.

The moment my feet touched the soil of my village, I felt light and dreamy, my heart beat rapidly in anticipation. Despite being surrounded by the luxury of the Factory, I hadn't lost my contact with the soil and simplicity of my birthplace.

I had dressed in my best sari made of silk, purple shot with gold. My grandmother's pendant whose priceless, comforting weight I always felt glittered above the sari folds.

Although I'd gained a little weight and my hair was not quite as long as before, the neighbors should recognize me. They've seen me wearing this pendant.

A woman walked past, clay pot on her head, bangles tinkling.

"She has quite a bit of fine gold jewelry on," Job said. "Where does so much gold come from?"

My mother had explained it to me. "Poor as we are, we still have a collection of gold jewelry passed on to us by our older relatives. We always carry it with us."

"So if the relatives take money and land away from a woman, she would at least have her jewelry?" Job asked.

"Correct. It's all the independence most women have, although widows are treated differently, as you know."

"You, dear, will have a better fate than that," Job said. How he made me smile with his words, his love, his ability to reassure me at every step. Sometimes promises are not kept. Life would change.

We reached a mango grove with a profusion of dark shiny leaves and swarms of bees buzzing among its young blossoms. Beyond that, plantain trees vibrated with color, their plump buds covered with purple sheaves. At a distance, ten or so women were planting in a rice field and singing in unison. Time seemed to have been rolled back, and I was reentering the past.

We turned onto a dirt road lined with bamboo-and-thatch houses. Cotton-clothed laborers walked about, some casting curious glances at Job. He stood out. Tall and fair, he was magnificent in his chintz tunic with flowing sleeves, an emerald-encrusted turban on his head, a pearl-embroidered silk sash at his waist, and his feet shod in golden satin shoes. An older bearded laborer glared at Job. Charmed by the scenery, he seemed unaware of everyone.

As we passed by a neighbor's grass hut, I caught sight of a young girl, about seven years of age, loitering in the yard, surrounded by several pheasants. Recognizing the girl, whose name was Priya, I halted. She too stopped.

Eyes shining in disbelief, she headed for the hut, running, leaping, scattering the pheasants. "Ma, Ma, come, look! The Goddess has returned from heaven!"

Goddess? How had I acquired such a title?

We walked past a cow shed and listened to the gentle mooing of the animals. Before long, we reached my family's mud-and-thatch cottage bordered by an acacia tree and a palm grove. A woman stood before me, her eyes bulging with shock. Hema Mashima. Aunt-Mother. I wanted to rush to her, but she stood like a statue on the threshold, her vivid orange sari a stark contrast to the brown mud walls. My mother's age, she had always been a source of comfort to my family.

"Mashi," I said, my voice cracking.

"In the name of God Shiva! Is it really you, Moorti?"

She folded her hands and bowed her head before me, as though I was really a deity. I felt the flush spread over my face. Then she began sobbing and couldn't say another word. Her veil slipped off, showing her graying, disheveled hair.

I stood numb. In a moment, Mashi stepped back inside and returned with her husband, Romen Mesho. Round-faced, clad in a white lungi, this man of middle years had an ash-gray stole wrapped around his shoulders. He looked down at the ground, as though needing time to collect himself. I introduced Job and noticed the stiffness with which Romen Mesho exchanged pleasantries with him.

"Where are my parents, Mesho?" I asked.

His black eyes glistened with tears. "Your father died—most unfortunate—it's been nearly a year."

I felt like somebody had knocked me down, choked me. "He was a good man, a learned man, respected by everyone," Romen Mesho continued. "He had been suffering from a stomach ailment, but his condition worsened when a man pretending to be a messenger from you arrived. Your parents didn't believe a word he said. They didn't believe you were alive. The messenger's words only aggravated their grief.

"Conflicting news also came from your late husband's neighbors. Some said you weren't a sati. That you'd been abducted by strangers and forced to take off on a boat."

Romen Mesho glanced at Job. "The priest who performed the sati ceremony insisted that people were simply fantasizing when they saw you, in your white sari, being carried off in a white-sailed boat by an Englishman. We believed the priest."

I stared unseeing at Romen Mesho. So long ago I'd sent a courier to contact my parents. That well-intentioned effort on my part had been misunderstood. That it would lead to my father's demise stunned me and filled me with guilt.

"We heard a young girl call her the Goddess," Job said to Romen Mesho, glancing at me. "What did she mean by this?"

"Agni-Devika," Romen Mesho said to me. "The force of a goddess. That was how we honored you, our goddess, in the fire ceremony we did. We thought you were dead."

At that moment Hema Mashima returned with a few low stools, which she placed on the ground in the shade of the acacia tree. Her eyes were red. "Please be seated."

I took my seat stiffly, as did Job. A young boy from a neighbor's hut stood by, gawking at us. We stared at Romen Mesho, waiting for him to tell us more about the ceremony that had taken place.

A wan smile came over Mesho's face. "On the anniversary of that unfortunate date, we neighbors dug a pit in the ground, filled it with sandalwood, and built a fragrant fire. A monkey watched from a tree branch; where it came from no one knew. Children danced around the fire, your brothers leading, and made offerings of flowers. Adults sat in a circle, sang your praises, and spun stories about your courage." Mesho fell silent for a moment; then he continued, "Your father couldn't attend the ceremony, but your mother was seated in an honored place. She sobbed the whole time." Bitterness showed in the glance Mesho shot at me. "All those present took a little ash home and placed it in special urns."

Job's gaze met mine and held it.

Mesho clucked a noise of dissatisfaction. "Although most families took part in the event, a few shunned it. They didn't believe the priest." He glanced at Job. "They started ugly rumors about you being stolen and possibly sold. The very next day, bickering and fighting started between factions. We have never had such disharmony in our community. A few people even gathered outside your parents' door—right here, as a matter of fact—and called your father names, blaming him for raising such a bad daughter.

"His stomach ailment worsened, but he refused to take medicine. Eventually, he stopped eating."

I felt my insides tearing to pieces.

"The day he died, the whole village came together and repented at his feet. His body was carried down to the river by a long procession of neighbors and cremated. Everyone sang sacred hymns in his honor."

My lips barely came together as I asked, "And Ma?"

Mesho hunched over, looking wooden and tired; no sound issued from his mouth. He seemed to be having trouble breathing. He left me, rigid and staring, to assume the worst. Mashi came to sit next to me, took my hand, and began speaking haltingly. "I admired your mother. She was strong and pliable like this acacia tree. Even the day after your father's funeral, she cooked and cleaned and fetched water from the well. I would have been too devastated to get out of bed. I'd probably have howled like a mad woman. She was different. She comforted me instead. She asked us to move into this hut. 'My boys are your boys,' she said. 'Let's raise them together.' We agreed.

"That evening, she went alone to the river. 'I want a good bath,' she said, 'I won't be long.' I should have gone with her. It was dusk, it had been raining, and she skidded on a wet step. Her head hit the edge of a rock. It cracked open."

A cry froze in my throat. In the stillness, I saw the light of truth. Ma! Baba! Did my actions cause them to make a pact with death? Did they sacrifice their lives so I could have mine? I was scarred forever because of their sacrifice.

For a moment I heard nothing but the thumping of my heart. I could never repent enough for not dying by my husband's body that fateful day so long back.

"Your loss is our loss too." Mashi's voice rose slightly. "We barely exist. I am still trying to make my peace with my god."

I sat staring at a fallen branch of the acacia tree until I heard Job's voice saying, "Where are the boys?"

There was a long pause, too long for my comfort.

I wanted to rise and shake Mesho's shoulders.

"Another misfortune befell us, as if there hadn't been enough already. The boys were staying with us. They hardly took any food. They stopped going to the pathsala. They simply roamed around the village, but they always returned in the evening. We told them stories while they picked at their supper, we tried to get them to play games, but it was like playing with ghosts. We treated them like our own and wanted to see them reach manhood, but the gods didn't intend it that way."

Somehow I managed to push the words out of my mouth. "What happened?"

"They were taken away by a Dutch merchant who had come here by boat to shop at our Saturday market. He was tall, fair, and heavy, wore a long dark coat and a hat, a wealthy man. His interpreter told the shopkeepers that he lived in a mansion in Hooghly. Your brothers were lingering near the indigo stalls where the Dutch man was shopping. He took immediate interest in the boys and talked to them through the interpreter.

"'See that big boat with white sails lying at anchor over there? Would you like to take a look inside?' The Dutch merchant asked the boys. 'Come with us, we have sweetmeats to share with you.' The indigo shop-owner warned the boys not to go with strangers, worse yet, foreigners. 'Go home,' he said to the boys. 'Run. These people have evil intentions. They'll harm you.'

"The boys turned round and started walking. The Dutch man followed them and kept up his sweet talk. The shopkeeper couldn't leave his stall to intervene. His customers were waiting. He heard Nupur saying. 'Why not? We've never boarded a big boat.' And Nitya said, 'I love sweetmeats. No one buys me any.' The Dutch man and the boys trotted toward the river and that's the last anyone ever saw of them.

"When the boys didn't return home that evening, we went searching for them. The shopkeepers gathered around us, told us what they'd seen and heard. They regretted that they couldn't stop the abduction. 'We're simple folks,' they said. 'We were fooled, as were the boys.'"

I stared ahead, saw nothing. I heard Job's voice, "It's a grave crime to lure young boys and take them away. Did anyone contact the Nawab's police?"

"No, sahib, we're poor people," Mesho said. "We don't want any trouble. You don't understand that, do you? The police would harass us. They'd accuse us of wrong-doing and extort money from us, but we care about our own and so our village council decided to act. Three of our elders scraped up enough money, bought a passage to Hooghly, and went searching for the boys.

"It wasn't easy. As you know, Hooghly is a big trading town where many languages are spoken, and at first the elders were simply lost. After a few days, they located the Dutch section of the town. They knocked at many doors, but no one would give out any information. Many times they were asked to leave and even threatened with violence.

"The elders persisted despite the threats. Finally, they located a weaving workshop, a karkhana, run by the Dutch. That workshop employed young boys, mostly orphans and runaways. They're put to work for long hours in a large crowded room, given little food, and almost no money. The elders tried to walk into the workshop, but one of them got beaten up by a guard. The other two fled. All three returned home. The elder who was assaulted still hasn't recovered from his wounds."

I cupped my face in my hands, but a moment later, emboldened by the anger I felt, I raised my head and said, "We won't give up. We'll look for the boys in Hooghly." I turned to Job; he looked unsure about my declaration.

Neighbors, about ten of them, streamed into the yard and gathered around us, their faces drawn. Maya Mashima carried a plate loaded with rounds of sweetmeats—cooked rice mixed with honey—a gesture of formal welcome extended to honored guests. With a blessing on her lips, she placed a round in my mouth and another in Job's. The honey tasted bitter on my palate. I gazed unseeing at nothing in particular.

Word seemed to have gotten around. More neighbors poured in. Among them was Priya, the girl I had met earlier. She came closer and asked, "You'll still be my goddess?"

I'd come back from the dead. I tried to smile at her but couldn't.

"Goddess or not, you're back and we're happy to see you," Neera Mashi, another neighbor, said. "You're the first person in anyone's memory who had the power to refuse being a sati. I wish your parents were here to see you return."

I looked up as a frowning elderly woman, Nandini Mashi, dressed in a white sari, arrived. Before I could stand up and greet her, she screamed at me, "You have the nerve to return, you wretch! You killed your parents? And you've brought a beef-eater with you?"

I stared at the ground, choked by a lump of sorrow in my throat. A yellow-beaked myna walked around me. Only vaguely I remembered how we considered cows sacred and never ate beef.

"You have no right to speak to our guest like that," Hema Mashi told the elderly neighbor.

"Go! Leave, at once." Nandini Mashi spat on me and cried out, "You, the killer, you'll go to narak." She was whisked away by two other women.

Platters of mangoes, guavas, and lychees appeared; I barely looked at them. Along with that came a large bowl of freshly harvested palm syrup. My neighbors reminded me how much I used to like the syrup, how I could drink tumblers of it, how my eyes would sparkle in pleasure; I had no appetite for it now. My legs wobbly, I stood up. "I hate to break up the celebration, but our boat is waiting. We must go."

"Please, Moorti,' Hema Mashi said. "Please don't pay attention to what Nandini said. She's old. She went crazy after your parents died. Please stay here tonight. We'll be so honored."

I shook my head. That neighbor's accusations, harsh as they were, had stirred a realization in me. I had added to the suffering of my parents by foolishly sending a messenger, thereby worsening their aggrieved state of mind.

Hema Mashi mumbled a prayer for our safe journey. "Do come visit us again. You'll always be welcome here."

My parents had given me life; I'd taken theirs. The thorn would bleed me forever.

"Let's go home," Job said.

TWENTY-SIX

After a three-day journey, Idris and I arrived at Hooghly, a large port town situated on the banks of the sacred Hooghly River, settled long ago by the Portuguese, and known as 'River Mouth.' The river was of prime importance to this bustling town. Not only did it supply water to the residents, but also made the town the chief port of the province, the 'Key to Golden Bengal'. Ships from England, France, and Holland regularly anchored on the river to exchange foreign goods with those produced locally. A struggle for power was palpable in the air of this town awash in gold, silver, and a competitive spirit. The streets were crowded with rival fortune seekers—the Portuguese, Dutch, French, English, Afghans. We walked past a grand church, where the rich tones of a choral hymn could be heard through an ornate window. I observed horses, oxcarts, palanquins, hawkers, and warehouses, as well as walled homes with elaborate columns. It seemed as though every thoroughfare here, even the narrowest lane, was as busy and frenetic as the Cossimbazar market. The aroma of milk and molasses drifted in from some corner, signaling the presence of sweet shops that Hooghly was famous for.

Nupur and Nitya's faces crept into my mind; Nupur with his wavy black hair, and exuberant voice; Nitya with his big soulful eyes and tender expression. Both loved sweets. With the rest of my family gone, the thought of a reunion with them was the only solace I had, one that would make this long journey worthwhile.

Idris waved me into a spacious, river-front, brick house, painted a golden yellow, with the name Sonar Kuthi written on a plaque over the door. House of Gold. Although Job had not been enthusiastic about this trip, he had made arrangements so we could stay in this house owned by the Company and intended for the use of the Factors.

One bright spot for me was the fact that Teema lived in this town, not far from the harbor, or so I'd been told.

While Idris got the house ready, I stepped outside; only my eyes showed from beneath the cover I'd drawn over my head. Once on the main road, I nudged through crowds of people of various sizes, shapes, and complexions, their movements sharp and purposeful. Feeling lost and out of step with the others, I hugged the shawl tightly around my chest and increased my speed. Turning right, I saw a herbal doctor's tent, a jewelry room, and a street-side tailor mending a tunic. A column of smoke rose from a chulah somewhere.

A sweet shop came into view, a tiny one-room affair from which emanated the fragrance of cardamom, rose water, and country molasses, and packed to the brim with shoppers. I lingered in its shadow for awhile, checking the departing customers. Once the store emptied, I poked my head through the door. Platters of yellow and white sweet-meats, syrupy and luscious, in square and diamond shapes, reposed on a table. How my brothers would covet these treats. My presence must have alerted the scrawny owner for he craned his neck around a corner and cast a quizzical glance at me. I gave him a description of my brothers and asked whether he'd seen them around. "They love sweets, could have come here," I said hopefully.

The shop-owner shook his head. I turned away, walked for a while, and reached a street studded with kathal trees. Soon I located the cottage surrounded by oleander bushes and knocked at the door. No answer. I was about to turn away when I spotted Teema a short distance away, sitting on a mat under the shade of a tree, doing embroidery work. In an ankle-length blue-printed cotton skirt, a matching bodice, and a voluminous bone-white veil, street-wear for a woman of modest means, she didn't appear at all like a popular dancing girl. Her face showed stillness, resignation even. Grim-faced, she continued her work, her nimble fingers rising and falling above a piece of fine cotton fabric.

"Teema!" I called out.

Teema's eyes shot up, searching for the person who had called her. As soon as she caught sight of me, she dropped the needlework on the mat and bounded toward me, arms extended. "Maria!"

For a moment, we held each other in a silent embrace.

"What a pleasant surprise to see you here," she said. "Shall we sit?"

"I see you've picked up needlework," I said.

Her expression turned dense, gloomy. "Only because I had to give up dancing."

"But that wasn't what you had planned."

"Well, the stars must have wanted it that way, or else why would such misfortune befall me?" She shifted her position, refolded her legs, and grimaced. "My left leg hurts. Practically, the moment I arrived here, I got work in a punch house, one of the most popular in town. Oh, you should have seen me, Maria! I was so happy dancing, didn't want my evenings to end. Soon I was studying with an ustad to pick up advanced classical techniques. Word got around. My new improved dance routine packed in even bigger audiences.

"Dutch, Arabs, Afghans, Portuguese, English, all crowded the punch house. They adored me, gave me bakshish like I'd never received before. I rented the lovely cottage over there, bought fancy clothes, and even indulged in a few pieces of jewelry." She extended a hand to show me her pearl ring and touched her coral earrings. "Then it all crumbled."

I peered at her, wondering if she'd fallen and injured herself too badly to keep dancing.

"Why did the person I least expected to see show up at the most inopportune time?"

"Edward?"

"Yes, my one and true love, the man who hurt me before and who would do so again." A plaintive note crept into Teema's voice. "As you might remember, he'd abandoned me and gone to England to get married. On learning that a trader could strike it rich quickly in Hooghly, he returned to try his luck exporting goods on his own. On that fateful evening, I had the biggest audience I'd ever had. I was in the middle of an intricate series of foot movements when I noticed a familiar figure entering. A handsome face, one I still dreamed about nightly, one as close to me as my skin. He wore a green taffeta cloak.

"At first I thought it was nothing but a dream. Then we exchanged a glance. The blue-gray eyes, the fire that flew from them, the lips that I loved to nibble, distracted me at the most difficult point in my routine. I lost my balance and tumbled off the stage. As I landed, I hit a table, slipped, and heard something snap. Later it turned out I'd broken a bone in my leg. I have been convalescing for the last five months. Only in the last few days have I emerged from my cottage."

I placed my hand on her arm. "Do you have anyone to look after you?"

"No, even though I must have made Edward feel guilty," she said in a sarcastic tone. "He bribed the owner of the punch house to find out where I lived and came to visit me, pity in his eyes, acting very contrite. After a few minutes of talking he dropped some coins on the table, wished me a quick recovery, and walked out, never to return. The English are treacherous, Maria."

I decided to withhold the news of my impending marriage to Job.

"My dancing days are over. However, Edward shared some important news with me. It's still not common knowledge that he and his associates in England have petitioned the Crown for a license to trade here. They've complained about the Company's monopolistic practices and he thinks they have a chance of winning."

More competition? Already our profits were meager. Charles sahib too might be stirring up trouble for us.

Teema must have grasped what I was thinking. "This is a small town, as far as the Europeans are concerned. They all know one another. My Dutch patron says that the English are their most formidable opponent, not the French or the Portuguese."

"You have a Dutch patron?"

"Yes, why do you ask?"

I told her about Nupur and Nitya, of the suspicion that they were employed in some dingy workshop set up by the Dutch merchants who were widely known to exploit child labor. "They're all that remains of my family, and I'll do anything to find them, but I don't have a single lead."

"I might be able to help you," Teema said. "I know there's a carpet weaving center in town. Rumor has it that it's mostly young boys who work there. They pick up the skills to weave rugs quickly, but the owners pay them next to nothing and hold them like prisoners. Let me speak with my patron. He works for a Factory run by the Dutch East India Company, what they call the 'Company of Far Lands.' He was posted in Batavia before. He has plenty of influence in his station there."

I hesitated. "Why would he help me, a competitor?"

"Egon will do anything I ask," Teema said with a knowing smile. "Yes, he's my new flame. I tried to erase every trace of Edward from my mind, but couldn't. Then Egon stepped in. Not much to look at, not smooth like Edward, but what a wild beast he is! He does his best to please me in and out of bed. We have nights where the stars never stop twinkling."

"Well, perhaps the next time you see Egon . . ."

"Of course. As soon as I have some leads for you, I'll send a messenger. I must go back home now and rest."

Three days later, a courier wearing a huge white headdress rapped at my door. "Teema has located your brothers," the courier said cheerfully. "Tomorrow she'll arrive here in an oxcart and take you to where they can be found."

While doing my chores that evening, I dreamt about meeting my brothers. I dreamt of how they would leap in joy when I approached them in the karkhana, their joyful outbursts of "Didi, Didi!" as they ran to meet me. "Come, let's get out of here," I would say. Then I would execute the most important part of my plan: stealing them away from their workplace, escorting them to the waiting oxcart, and riding back with them to my temporary residence here. I hadn't been this happy in a long time. My brothers would no longer be slaves. What more could I ask for? "We'll follow you to Cossimbazar and live in a mansion," Nupur would say, sitting at the table and helping himself to big portions of sweetmeats. "We'll fly kites there. I haven't flown a kite in a very long time." Between bites, Nitya would giggle. Seated across from them, I would look lovingly at them. Finally, we would be together, a family once again.

Someone knocked at the door and I came back to reality.

The next day, Teema and I rode a hooded oxcart to a far corner of the city. I carried a bamboo-leaf box stuffed with colorful sweetmeats for my brothers. According to Teema's Dutch patron, two boys answering to my brothers' names were, indeed, working in a carpet-weaving center. I could hardly wait. Before long, we left the shiny waterfront area with latticed windows and lavish gardens to enter a more congested section

of town where the roads were uncared for and the ride bumpy. Soon
we reached a dilapidated neighborhood with broken doors and the odor
of fetid garbage. A limbless beggar sat on a corner and moaned. Not far
from him, a crow menaced a lone child. A man in tattered clothes,
sitting nearby, swatted at a fly, oblivious to the child's discomfort. A
wild beast I couldn't recognize bellowed loudly nearby. As the cart
approached a cramped lane, the driver suddenly pulled the oxen to a
stop. "I can't go any further," he said, turning his worried gaze toward
us. "You have to walk from here. Please be careful, this neighborhood
is full of hoodlums."

We descended from the cart and entered the dirty narrow lane,
walking single file, repulsed by the stench of urine. Looking down at
my silver brocade sari, I felt out of place. Teema walked ahead of me.

A large, windowless, thatch-roofed building loomed before us. "That's
the carpet-weaving center," Teema said. "It fits the description Egon gave
me. A prison, he called it."

It did indeed look like a prison, and to complete the picture, a doorkeeper, holding a bamboo baton, was posted at the entrance.

"Oh, heavens," I said, marching toward the building. "How do we get
in?"

"We've timed our arrival perfectly," Teema whispered. "The main
guardsman is on a break. His assistant, the young man standing there,
has been bribed to let us in."

The doorkeeper made a sharp turn on his heels and faced us. He had
a narrow face and an expression that grew even more wary as we
approached him. Teema flashed him a smile and mentioned Egon's name.

His eyes lit up; he said, with a slight bow, "Salaam, salaam." After a
brief hesitation, he unlocked the door. "I am not supposed to let anybody
in. That's a strict order from the authorities, so please, only a few
minutes."

"We'll be quick," I said, slipping through the door, Teema behind me.

In the long semi-dark room, under the yellow-brown glow of lamps,
at least twenty boys, all between the ages of nine and fifteen, huddled
in small groups. Squatting, they wove carpets in silence, deftly tying
every knot by hand. Scattered about them were various equipment for
weaving. We walked the length of the room, the air heavy and damp
and smelling of unwashed boys. A black centipede made its way across
the room. I cast my glance in every direction but didn't spot my
brothers.

"Nupur! Nitya!" I finally called out. "Are you here?"

A few boys stared at me, their eyes reflecting fear at the intrusion. A cold silence hung over the room. We weren't wanted here.

Finally, I spotted Nupur and Nitya. They were positioned at the far corner of the room, their backs toward me. I recognized them from the shape of their heads, from their sitting postures, and hastened toward them.

Nupur's eyes were focused on a vertical loom, a complex of bamboo sticks suspended by strong jute ropes displaying a nearly finished rug. He started and looked up at me, eyes deep in their sockets, his once-glowing complexion now muddy, his ribs protruding from underneath a flimsy tunic. It was obvious that he'd been working long hours and was not being fed well. Seated on a mat next to him, Nitya hunched over a horizontal loom, tightening a finished row of knots with a small comb. He glanced up from the loom with frightened eyes. He was much thinner than when I'd last seen him.

To my surprise, neither of them scrambled to their feet. Their aloofness was like a punch to the stomach. I had practically raised them until the day of my first wedding, and here they sat, staring at me as at a stranger.

I heard a commotion at the entrance and turned. A guard dressed in a long coat of white cotton marched in. A moment or two passed before I recognized the familiar tall familiar figure.

Tariq!

"Why is this door open?" Tariq barked at the doorkeeper. "Who are these women? Why did you let them in?"

The doorkeeper mumbled a few words of apology. Tariq strode in my direction. His one good eye blinked in surprise, even as his face hardened.

"Maria! What do you want here?"

"My brothers," I said, pointing. "I've finally found them, Nupur and Nitya. This is no place for children of their age. I'll take them home. They're eager to go with me."

Nitya shrank against the wall. On glancing at me a second time, however, he began to waver. I knew from the forlorn look in his eyes that he wanted to spring into my arms.

Standing across from Nupur, Tariq asked him in a menacing voice, "Do you know this woman? Is she really your sister?"

Nupur stared at the floor. Perhaps afraid of being punished, a beating with a baton, or worse, perhaps having been imprisoned for so long, he had begun to see these walls as stability and felt safer in here. "No," he eventually mumbled. "My sister is a goddess."

Tariq laughed out loud, a big, ugly laugh. In a mocking tone, he said to me, "Maria, why don't you fly before us with your invisible wings, so we can see your divine powers?"

Her face contorted, Teema commanded from behind me, "You mustn't insult her like that."

Tariq gave both of us a stern look. "You must be mistaken. These two boys come from a poor family. Their parents have willingly given them to us. They're well cared for here. You're causing far too much trouble. They have to finish their work by a certain hour or they won't get their meals."

"How can you have such a rule for young children?" Teema asked, eyes burning with rage.

"I didn't make the rule," Tariq said.

"Nupur, Nitya, I am really your sister—Moorti." My own name sounded strange to my ears: another life, another designation swept away by a fiery wind. "They haven't seen me in a while and they're feeling shy," I said to Tariq. "Nupur, Nitya, please, come with me." Nupur froze in his seat. Nitya wept, making small shrieking sounds. The other boys fidgeted and looked away.

Tariq turned fiercely toward me and bellowed: "You must leave at once."

"Please, Tariq, for all the work I did for you at the Factory, and for the sake of these two young boys who've been abducted . . ."

For a moment, Tariq seemed to consider, his one good eye fixed in space. Then fear flitted across his face.

Casting one last teary look at my brothers, I placed the box of sweet-meats at their feet. Neither of them met my eyes.

"Do you realize the owners might punish them for receiving gifts from you?" Tariq said.

"You mustn't say a word about this to the owner," Teema said. "Look, I know a friend of the owner. I can make a complaint about you."

A shadow passed over Tariq's face.

"Suppose I came here once in a while and visited them?" I asked Tariq.

"No! Bhago! We will remove you if we see you anywhere near this building."

My heart a deep wound, I slipped out the door. The return journey seemed bumpier, the roads more dusty, the frenzy of the crowd more incessant. Teema clasped my hand as we rode in silence.

During the following week, I went back several times to the miserable workshop and pleaded with Tariq, but in vain. He barred me from the vicinity and threatened me with violence if I persisted. My heart ached when I considered the treatment Nupur and Nitya might be receiving from Tariq because of my actions.

With Teema's help, I bribed the doorkeeper to deliver a message to my brothers. They were to secretly meet me after dark at a specified spot, a short distance away from the karkhana. The doorkeeper said my brothers were overjoyed at the prospect.

That evening Teema and I waited with our ox cart driver for hours. Nupur and Nitya did not show up. We scoured the area; they were nowhere to be found. I went back to the house, feeling empty and dejected, wondering what might have gone wrong. I got to know the next day. The bloody, naked bodies of my brothers had been found in an alley in the most crime-ridden section of the town. They'd been sexually molested and bludgeoned to death.

I lost sleep, appetite, and the ability to think. I couldn't face anyone and constantly blamed myself. Would they have lived had I not intervened? Although we were rebuffed several times, Teema and I finally managed to contact the Dutch management of the karkhana. A representative told us that the boys had run away on the day of the incident and had likely fallen prey to hoodlums who infested that area.

I didn't believe the story. Could it be that Tariq had gotten wind of their planned escape and decided to make an example of them, lest other boys followed in their footsteps? I would never know the truth.

Their tragic end made me doubly aware of the lack of workers' rights. Hire them, use them, offer them no protection, and throw them out or murder them when they cause trouble. I vowed to rectify that.

TWENTY-SEVEN

B ack in Cossimbazar, hunched over a ledger book one morning, quill and ink before me, I began transcribing necessary trading details in a curly flowing script. Job had assigned me the task of maintaining these books. Yet, as I worked, the sad pale faces of my family would often rise in my memory. It had been three long months since my trip to Hooghly. Gradually, with Job's help, his insistence that this mansion was my home, I'd come to terms with my loss. I promised myself not to let sadness tear away at my insides, adopting a happier expression whenever I saw myself in the mirror or went out to the market.

I was free of the past. Now it remained for me to weave my future in whichever pattern I liked.

I recorded texts, charts, and numerical data, which formed the backbone of the Company's operation. As goods were purchased from local vendors—silk, cotton, black pepper, mace, indigo dye, and salt-peter—I filled in the pages with the details of the contract: names of the goods and their dimensions, when appropriate; their quantities and prices paid; and details about their sources. Today's first item: forty bales of the finest silk, with a thread count as high as 2100, bought at a price of four thousand rupees from the best local silk vendor. I paused momentarily. I could barely imagine seeing so much expensive fabric or so much money in one place. Once I came back to mysenses, I resumed my work, allowing the ink on each page to air-dry before flipping to the next.

The ways of commerce were amazing. There were a few written rules, but many were merely whispered, conveyed by a wink, or generally understood. A handsome bribe to a particularly corrupt Mughal official would stop any bulk package from being inspected too closely. An armed guard must be dispatched with the drivers of oxcarts bearing merchandize to fight off robbers on the overland routes, killing them, if necessary. No matter what, the commission payment to the King of England had to be delivered on time.

I shut the ledger and pushed it away, picked up another one, and flipped through its pages. This book kept track of 'homeward' voyages, the commodities being shipped to England and other corners of Europe. Only much later, when I was older, would I be able to fully imagine an entire ship destined for a distant shore, its cargo consisting of nothing but black pepper, its pungent aroma permeating the vessel. I would be able to visualize the well-heeled merchants in London, in their doublets and breeches, peering out from beneath their wigs, jostling each other and haggling over the price of a few ounces of this exotic spice.

I transcribed the details slowly and legibly, in a curly flowing script.

Decades later, these ledger books would be archived as important historical documents.

On that day however, at the appointed hour, I rose and walked over
to the meeting hall where Job presided, grim-faced. There, in the soft
light of the afternoon, sitting in a padded chair, I had to negotiate with
a broker, Manu, a stocky man with a surly mien. He traded saltpeter, a
crystalline solid used to make explosives. Gordon sahib was the only
other Factor present.

"I can sell this damned material to any number of clients, maybe even
at a higher price," Manu said to me, a glass of limeade in front of him.
"Why should I sell it to you?"

His reference of course was to our competitor, the Dutch; I was
sure of that. I thought for a moment and decided to appeal to his
sense of compassion. "Because the English need it to protect their
homeland and their families. There are wars going on in Europe and
England is constantly being threatened with invasion by larger enemies.
Without gunpowder, they'll be defenseless. And be aware also that
saltpeter isn't used over there just for war. The English use it to
preserve foods called cheese and sausage, two of their staple items.
Do you now see?"

What I didn't disclose to him was that the Company could sell saltpeter by the ton and make a handsome profit. From England it could
be exported all over Europe because of huge demand for manufacturing
gun powder.

Manu grumbled a bit and we talked more. Eventually he and I settled
on an attractive, mutually acceptable rate for this vital commodity. As
the session drew to a close, Manu gave me a slight nod. "Hooray," Gordon
broke in, raising his limeade glass to me and the 'Saltpeter Man'.

Job's face remained clouded for reasons I didn't understand. He had
been silent during the meeting. Once outside the meeting hall, I took
him aside and asked what he thought of the negotiations.

Job fixed a warm gaze on me. "A bloody good session, I must say.
The Dutch are trying to get a monopoly on saltpeter, but you've pried
that broker away from them."

"Was I too assertive?"

"I don't think so. Better for us to develop our connections now. Even
the Nawab has decided to go into the saltpeter business, which could
mean serious competition for us." He paused and his voice became
somber. "Perhaps even trouble."

Why hadn't he shared this important information with me sooner? Hadn't he noticed I was intelligent and capable of understanding such matters? I would have explored this situation with other brokers, kept myself up-to-date on the Nawab's commercial interests. Little did I know that in future this habit of Job, keeping things from me, would put us in harm's way.

For the time being, I simply asked, "But why?"

"Guns are like a lifeline to him, if he wants to hold on to his territory. And he can sell saltpeter to neighboring countries quite easily. But we'll keep him away from the darn stuff, as best as we can. It's a symbol of our power, British power, dear love."

I looked into Job's eyes. He'd always have my full support, the negotiations about this particular commodity being the least of it. But at this reference to the Nawab, I felt knotted inside. "Won't we alienate our ruler in the worst way?"

"If we haven't already done so." Job's eyes strayed to the distant horizon for a moment. He squinted, as though trying to see through the hazy light into the future. "The Nawab is sulking because he has to lower his prices. But it's business, and we must run a profitable operation. Our shareholders in England demand that, so does the Crown. If we don't show a profit for three years, our Charter will cease to exist, and we'll have to shut down the Factory."

I shifted on my feet. We were accustomed to obeying our provincial ruler. We sang his glory. Locally, we'd often say goodbyes to each other with an expression such as, "Long live our Nawab, our Protector." I had never considered competing with him. At the very least, we considered the grave consequence of any form of dissent, given the Nawab's military might and rumors of his ruthlessness.

"So, this morning, I've negotiated a deal against the Nawab?"

"Yes, my dear, and which is why you're considered a rising young Factor. You're a natural at this."

I stole away from him then, the self-satisfaction of moments ago dissipating within me. On the way back to my chamber, I looked skyward, the blazing sun on my face. As I passed by the shiuli bushes and took in their fragrance, I considered the reality of the trading life—cold, cruel, greedy and all-consuming; nonetheless, it had brought out my hidden potential as a tenacious shrewd competitor getting ready to rise and score more wins for the Company.

Under the scorching sun, the realization thrilled and frightened me.

Still, I couldn't have predicted that only months from now, our lives would be in turmoil because of this morning's business deal, conducted successfully by me, over nothing more than decayed organic matter known as saltpeter.

TWENTY-EIGHT

Our wedding day.

I awoke in Job's chamber, rubbed my eyes, and yawned in a leisurely fashion. No ledger books, no meetings, no concerns about alienating the Nawab—this day was special. I, a widow, was to be remarried in a gorgeous ceremony to a kind and loving man. How many people had heard of a formal union between an Englishman and a Bengali woman?

We considered spring to be the best season for marriage and this day had been chosen by an astrologer for an unusually auspicious alignment of stars and planets. I stared out the window to see the scorching sun and hear the gentle cries of a kokil bird. I focused my attention on the lively trumpet-like sounds of shehnai being played by a hired musician in the courtyard below.

I opened my wardrobe. Only a few weeks ago, I had received a visit from a cloth merchant commissioned by Job. "Tell me what you want," the merchant had said, "and I'll deliver it to you."

I had taken him to the garden to show the colors and designs I preferred. Sure enough, he'd kept his word. My wedding trousseau consisted of bright-colored silks, appliquéd cottons, and brocades in petal and floral creeper motifs, embroidered with gold and silver threads. My wedding sari was in auspicious red, threaded with gold, the hues equally intense on both sides. I took a step and peered at the sari from another angle. A shifting volume of light deepened the red, made it brighter. I placed a hand over the fabric, luxuriated in its fluid touch, absorbed its brightness.

It was time. I anointed my body with sandalwood and draped the red silk. My hair had grown long; I brushed it out, watching the gleaming blackness as it fell like satin to my waist. Then I coiled it up on my head in a bun and looked into the tall mirror—a happy bride, too skinny, not a beauty, but happy. What a contrast to my first wedding day when I'd sobbed for hours.

My grandmother's pendant peeked from underneath the beautiful red sari, again reminding me of my family. I would wear other ornaments, but this one remained the most precious of all. I slid open a cabinet drawer. Next to Job's pistols, which I preferred not to look at, there rested a jewelry box. The goldsmith Job had dispatched weeks earlier had appeared with a box of sample designs and produced custom-made ornaments to suit my taste. I pulled out the box. Bangles, anklets, earrings, and an elaborate wedding necklace glittered in the daylight.

Finished with dressing, I chewed a triangular-shaped paan of betel leaves to dye my lips red and sweeten my breath. A woman servant named Lila, hired by Idris, braided shiuli blossoms into my hair and stained my palms a vivid yellow with turmeric.

As she left, I heard footsteps outside my door. Idris appeared, distinguished in a formal purple robe, his elaborate headdress encircled with gold chains. He, of Muslim faith, had offered to do the kanyadan, the giving away of the bride in this Hindu ceremony, insisting that he considered me his daughter. I didn't fail to observe the trace of worry clouding Idris's eyes. What worried him so much? That I would not be accepted by the other Englishmen, for I had not converted to Christianity? That I'd be persecuted by the Brahmins for reentering matrimony?

He recovered in a moment. "How beautiful you look, Maria! Let me be the first to wish you a long and happy married life, with truth and righteousness as your guide."

"I wish our families were here. I wish Job heard from his mother."

Idris hesitated. "A letter from Job sahib's mother did arrive this morning. She wanted him to cancel the wedding."

I couldn't breathe.

"Much as he loves his mother, Job sahib said he would not obey her."

My eyes became misty as I considered how much agony Job must have gone through to come to this decision, how deep he considered our bond.

"It's been quite a morning for Job sahib," Idris said. "Another bit of news has devastated him. As you already know, the Council didn't punish Charles sahib, given his status in England; in fact, they freed him. Now he's back in town for a conference with the Nawab."

"I wonder what kind of trouble he'll stir up for us."

"We have sufficient security for this event, so I don't expect any trouble today, but in the long run, only Allah knows." Idris tossed a glance toward the window, motioned with his hand, and adopted a light voice. "They're pouring in, practically the whole town. It's the biggest wedding of the year. Shall we go?"

With Idris escorting me, I stepped lightly down the stairs and through the hallway to the courtyard. The blowing of conch shells announced my arrival. I gazed in wonder at the crimson-and-purple velvet mandap, situated in the center of the courtyard, embroidered inside and out, specially built for this occasion. The canopy glowed with the light of a hundred lamps. Amidst the sound of drums beating, I entered. A small open fire flickered at the center and the fragrant smell of burning sandalwood permeated the air. Agni-dev, the fire deity, messenger between heaven and earth, would witness our wedding.

Job beamed at me. My prince. Resplendent in a golden satin coat fitted close to his body and buttoned in front, he wore a white muslin turban on his head, held together by a ruby brooch. An emerald-worked silver sash was wound around his waist. A glimmering beige dab of sandalwood paste shone between his eyebrows. Eyes glowing, he cast an admiring look at me. I found myself smiling in return, my heart over-flowing with emotions bigger than I could measure. In that moment, I released my concerns over Charles' presence in town and Job's mother's disapproval of our union, anything that sought to dampen this wonderful day, and looked into the eyes of my beloved.

Arthur who had dressed for the first time in Mughal style, a long maroon tunic extending to his ankles and a headdress adorned with a cream-colored feather, stood next to Job. Arthur didn't have his umbrella with him. He greeted me, eyes wide in merriment. Never before had I seen him in such a jolly mood. A young Hindu priest, dressed in white, welcomed us in a solemn manner. Guests, adorned with silks, pearls, and diamonds and conversing among themselves in low voices, sat in a semi-circle on plush rugs placed around the canopy. There were many familiar faces—Jas, Pratap, and the other Factors—as well as Job's busi-ness associates. Children, dressed in festive and colorful clothes began singing a folk song and dancing in my honor. I was the focal point of all this! Even among such a huge gathering, I spotted Chand, the bearded broker. He acknowledged me with a nod, his face betraying a puzzle-ment that I didn't understand. Possibly he had some news to share.

The shehnai player paused and the whole courtyard became still. At the priest's request, Job and I took seats next to each other on decorative wood planks, our heads bowed. Idris and Arthur sat nearby.

The priest began the ceremony by speaking about our respective duties in a shared domestic life, frequently punctuating his talk with a sprinkling of water from the Ganges on our heads. The air turned more somber when the priest asked us to join our hands; it was time to take our marriage vows. Voices merging, Job and I took pledges of love, loyalty, and fidelity, the Sanskrit words creating a kind of blissful music. Despite the unfamiliar nature of the ceremony and the strangeness of Sanskrit, Job seemed steadfast. We ended our vows with: "Your heart and mine are one; it belongs to us both."

I trembled with joy. Using a ladle, the priest poured more ghee into the nuptial fire. Huge tongues of golden flame leapt up, almost as high as those of my first husband's funeral pyre. Smoke engulfed me and I drew back in a sudden panic.

"Time for the saptapadi ritual around the nuptial fire," the priest announced.

The bride and the groom would circle the fire seven times, each step symbolizing a different aspect of their journey of life, the most beautiful part of a Hindu marriage ceremony.

Perhaps noticing the momentary terror in my eyes, Job smiled reassuringly at me. He understood my fear, but his smile also told me that I had to let go. It was time.

The priest asked us to stand and tied the edge of Job's robe with the end of my sari to symbolize the marriage knot. He reminded us that the wife would be the ruler of the household, the husband, the follower, and as such I must lead this walk.

"Begin your steps and repeat after me," the priest said. "With the first, we join together for partaking of water, the sustainer of life."

I recited along with Job, summoning courage as I took each step around the glittering flames and grey smoke.

At the end of the seventh and most important step, we recited: "With this step, we become friends and companions, so that we may bask in the warmth of each other." As I listened to Job's richly resonant voice, my heart swelled. I didn't doubt for a moment then that he'd accept me as his full partner.

How was I to know on that occasion of pure joy that our happiness wouldn't last long?

Job and I stood facing each other. At the priest's signal, we exchanged necklaces of yellow-orange marigold flowers, an emblem of the circular nature of our love. For a fleeting moment, I felt my parents' blessings, their presence with me.

Amidst the sound of conch shells blowing and logs crackling in red-orange flames, the priest announced, "You are now married. May God bless the duties you will be asked to perform."

A messenger sent by Teema walked over and handed me her gift of a lovely brooch studded with amethyst.

Chand, attired in a white muslin robe, offered his blessings and conveyed Rani Mata's regrets for her inability to attend the wedding. With a flourish, he opened a purple velvet box and held it out for me. Inside, there rested the coral-set, filigree-worked bracelet I had so admired on the brave queen's wrist. I stared at the ornate piece made of solid yellow gold. Power seemed to emanate from it. I looked up at Chand, my mouth open, my hand at my throat.

"Rani Mata wants you to wear it," Chand said. "She wishes you both a peaceful life."

With the shehnai playing a wistful tune, I slipped the bracelet on my wrist and stared at it. Yet I couldn't help but register the slight tremor in Chand's body.

"Any news?" I asked Chand.

He lowered his face and withdrew.

"Please," I said to his back.

But he was gone. Fireworks erupted over the moonlit sky, whistling a tune and shooting out silver stars, then fluttering down with an explosion.

TWENTY-NINE

Four months since our wedding.

Heavy monsoon winds and torrential rain had replaced the stifling heat of spring. Job and I toiled day and night to keep the Company afloat; we were happy, contented.

"How have you managed to expand your business so much in such a short time?" A visiting merchant from Hooghly had asked Job the other day in my presence.

Job had looked at me, his eyes twinkling, urging me to reply.

"The credit belongs to our workers," I said.

Indirectly, through the brokers, I employed craftsmen and laborers, promising that if they did their best, they would be properly compensated. Even when we sacrificed some profits, I made sure the workers were paid a decent salary, which in turn inspired them to produce goods of higher quality.

A few English Factors were also present at that meeting. The next day, I overheard William whisper in the dining hall: "I say, the bloody little heathen actually seems to think she's going to take over."

I had no such ambition; I simply took pride in the products of my land and in helping the Company realize its potential in the European market.

Besides my regular duties, I conferred with the local and regional tradesmen and went on-site for inspections. I had learned how to choose among thirty-three varieties of silk and one hundred-fifty varieties of cotton, where the best saltpeter deposits were to be found, the silk dyer with the best reputation in the region.

Job was my inspiration, my temple of support, in all I undertook. Our days were rich and fresh; our eyes sought each other no matter where we were. Only last night, my body molded against his, I found the day's trials dissipating from my mind. Although my English had improved to the point where I could converse easily, I couldn't always give adequate expression to my feelings. But in the intimacy of the night, snuggling against Job, in the afterglow of our pleasure, I felt that language was superfluous. That we were meant to have been together, always; it was all that mattered.

The next morning, I stood by the window and talked with Job as he finished dressing. He looked elegant and vibrant in a white tunic decorated with pearls. He drew close and put his arms around my shoulders.

A pleasant shiver ran through my body. "My darling," I whispered softly.

"You look so beautiful in the morning," he said, cupping my face in his hands. "I don't want to leave you, ever. Throughout the day, whenever I have a trying moment, I picture your face. The pressures vanish, and I can handle anything."

He hadn't mentioned any recent pressing business problems. I worried about that for a moment then let it go.

"You wouldn't believe how petrified I was when I first came here," I said. "Now, with your love surrounding me, I find myself acting smarter, cleverer, and braver. Even speaking English has become pleasanter."

"I never thought life could be so good, so full for me, either." He kissed me gently and pointed to the side table where a letter lay open. "That letter is from my mother. She has finally given us her blessing. She says she has come to understand what you mean to me and that is all she cares about."

My voice rose in excitement. "Shall we go to England to visit her?"

"She may have written this letter from her deathbed," Job said, his voice heavy with certainty. "The handwriting. The sentiments. The lengthy farewell. I have lost a part of my life; it's prudent that I accept it, my love."

He looked long and lovingly at me. He kissed me and drew me closer into his arms. "I shall always miss her, but I am happy with you, happy for the first time in my life, ready to face whatever challenge the day brings."

And then the story changed.

I was too naïve yet, too happy in my newly expanding world to understand its impact. That evening is fresh in my memory. A storm thundered outside and rain pelted the roof. Dressed in a delicate pink-tinged yellow sari patterned with leaves, my hair knotted at the back of my head with a chain of white flowers, my body perfumed with shiuli essence, I entered our well-illuminated bed room and smiled at Job.

Clad in white nightclothes and red slippers, Job paced the room absent-mindedly, his lips compressed, a sure sign he was perturbed. He raised his eyes but didn't seem to notice me. I drew near, smelling the warm familiarity of his skin.

In a voice both rough and desperate, he broached an important matter—the new levy the Nawab had imposed on us. "Surely you've noticed the dictate from our governor."

"Yes, I have."

A wax-sealed document from the ruler demanding extra tariff from us: the letters inscribed on silk paper in black against an ivory background, the language both formal and severe. It had appeared without notice a few days ago. "We can't pay such a large sum unless we reduce our expenses by a fair amount," I said.

"The levy is both exorbitant and unfair," Job said. "I won't submit to a demand like that."

His tone had an alarming finality to it.

Although the rain had subsided, the heat and humidity still pressed down. A feeling of stuffiness had settled over the room; I picked up a palm-leaf fan from the table and dropped down on a chair.

"We should stay in the Nawab's good books," I said, "that is, if we want to continue to do business in his territory."

"I will not pay," Job insisted, his tone calm. His ambition, the momentum to push forward to expand the Company's business, had collided with a stone barrier. After all, his loyalty was to his trade and to his monarch. "It's an insult. I want to teach him a lesson."

In the reddish glow of the lamp light, I studied my proud husband, his furrowed brow, the arms held rigidly close to his body. "Didn't the document say no leniency would be shown if the levy wasn't paid? Have you considered the consequences?"

He nodded.

Once challenged, the ruthless Nawab would stop at nothing. Our very existence might be under threat. *We're no more significant than the dust on the Nawab's feet*, so went a common complaint. Any warning from the authorities dangled before most citizens like an executioner's sword. Fanning myself, I sat firm in my belief that we shouldn't take this course of action. The big impressive gold royal seal on the Nawab's letter clearly indicated that it was an order, not to be taken lightly. Would Job be willing to pay the price for dissent?

"It'd be well to recall how your close social contacts with our previous governor, the late Haider Ali, proved beneficial for the Company," I said. "Will it be wise to alienate our new ruler?"

"Unfortunately," Job said tightly, "there is bad blood between the new Nawab and me, and not merely on a personal level. He's a puppet of Emperor Aurangzeb, who's corrupt, ineffective, tyrannical, and a poor administrator.

As I listened, Job spun out other details about the Emperor.

Emperor Aurangzeb had hundreds of vaults filled with gold, silver, and rubies. Besides the enormous sums of money he received as revenues, he took nearly three-quarters of all crops that were raised, but what did he do for his subjects? With the exception of a small wealthy class, most citizens barely got by. Beggars roamed the streets in this land of plenty. Hindus, the majority population, were especially vulnerable. They weren't entitled to work as Court appointees and were restricted to certain professions only. The Mughal rulers failed to realize that their base of support had grown dangerously weak. Marathas in the West had already begun to revolt. Protest, bloodshed, and instability would result in other parts, Job suspected. There was endless in-fighting in the Royal Court. Some local chiefs were beginning to defy imperial authority by operating independently. The roads were being taken over by caravan robbers, the seas by pirates.

"If things continue the way they are, there will be an uprising which will be bad for trade," Job said. "Now do you see why I am for resistance?"

"But isn't this the opposite of what you had suggested to Rani Mata?"

"Circumstances have changed. So have I."

"If you're depending on the Factory workers to provide the resistance, let me remind you they're untrained," I said. "They'll be slaughtered. When the Nawab is finished with them, he'll come for us."

Job laughed derisively. "Of course, we will need defensive forces to achieve our goal, but we will not depend on untrained people. Our fleet from England, our military force of several ships, will arrive here any day. Not only are we over five hundred strong, but we have better weapons, better trained soldiers, and better tactics."

My throat became constricted. "Won't you alienate Emperor Aurangzeb as well?"

"We're English. We don't like to lose." Job's booming voice bounced off the walls. "We bow before no sovereign other than our own. The Royal Charter allows us to wage war, if necessary. Aurangzeb is not satisfied with the wealth he has accumulated. I hear that rascal is ready to go on a campaign to conquer and eventually rule all of Deccan. Foolish of him. Indeed. He'll never win there, never. He and his army will retreat or die in the heat, but that actually might be to our advantage. With him absent from the Court for a period of time, we'll defeat the Nawab's army, negotiate a better trade treaty, expand and grow our business base. I'd like to have the powers of a state in whatever territory we occupy—executive, judicial, and military. Like the local zamindars, but with more authority."

He looked closely at me, sensing my doubts. "We'll surely administer better than the corrupt Nawab, not to mention the equally corrupt local landowners."

Against the sound of chirping crickets coming through the window, I said, "Didn't we decide our goal was to serve Hindustan and its people? Wouldn't a war take us away from our goal? Do we have the necessary experience to administer?"

"Once I was kicked out of the house by my father; that was unfair. Do you think I ever forgot that? I was helpless then. I'm not helpless now. The Council will help us. The Crown is behind us. We won't lack necessary personnel."

The air in the room felt stale. "But Job . . ."

"I don't wish to discuss this matter any further."

We went to bed without touching or kissing. In the darkness, I watched Job's chest rise and fall. For the remainder of the night I barely managed to sleep.

The next morning, I rose early and took a stroll through the white muslin mist to the river to cleanse myself of the gloominess I felt. The sun barely peeked out, dew still glistened on the grass, and a light wind teased the surface of the river. I walked down the broad steps to the water's edge. For days now, I had been noticing and feeling subtle changes in my body. Now, still fully dressed and submerged in the supporting embrace of the water, I sensed those changes even more keenly. A new life was sprouting inside me. To be a mother—the highest fulfillment for a woman. What a strong current of affection I experienced for Job and our baby. The next moment, I reflected on the previous night's argument with Job. Apprehension mixed with jubilation as I scooped water to wash my face.

After a while, I came up out of the water, dried myself, rubbed aromatic clove oil on my face and neck, dressed again, and returned to the Factory. By now, the mist had evaporated. As I entered through the gate the guardsman dropped to his knees; I was the wife of the Factory Chief.

"Please," I said, holding out my hand. "There is no need to bow."

Once inside the huge compound, I spotted the gardener weeding the flower beds, a riotous mélange of red, white, and purple blossoms. Workmen transferred a pile of jute bags loaded with saltpeter into the warehouse. I lingered for a moment, watching the familiar scene in this lovely residence, home to Job and me. What a perfect place this would be to raise our first-born.

In our chamber, Job, still in his dressing gown, paced the floor, an air of seriousness about him. At my approach, he stepped toward me. Perhaps he wished to utter a few words of apology, but I couldn't hold it any longer.

"Darling, I am with child," I said.

Instantly, the glow returned to his cheeks. He gasped: "Are you sure?"

I nodded. He enfolded me in his arms and traced his finger around my face. "Oh, I couldn't be happier, my love," he said in a thick voice. "It's been my greatest hope to have a child, our baby. I had a dream about it last night."

We held each other in a tight embrace. I moaned in anticipation of the feel of Job's skin next to my body. I could hear his quickening heartbeat.

Then he said in a serious tone of voice, "You must stop working immediately and take rest."

I envisioned a blessed life with a baby, suffused with affection, and surrounded by a faithful staff in a town where we had set down roots. "Are you trying to spoil me?" I laughed. "I could never be that indolent."

"But no walking around in town. I'll have a palanquin ready to take you wherever you wish to go. Any food you have a craving for, I'll make sure the kitchen gets it ready. We'll, of course, hire an ayah when the baby is born."

His bright mood, his protectiveness, further elevated my own. I kissed him and laughed again. "We'll have plenty of time to plan for the baby."

It was time for Job to get dressed and head for an important early meeting. He struggled into his favorite high-necked, beige waist-coat, which fit him snugly, now that he'd regained the weight lost during his convalescence. We chatted while he slipped his feet into embroidered white shoes, but neither of us brought up the subject of the levy. On this extraordinary day, with the sky donning its best blue, I banished that unpleasant subject to the back of my mind.

THIRTY

A month later, before leaving the bedchamber in the morning, Job mentioned that Chand had sent word. He hoped to visit the Factory this morning. "Do you care to receive him?"

"Oh, yes," I said, hiding my apprehension. "He's due to report the progress of his artisans. Their initial batch of piece goods is expected to be delivered soon."

After Job departed, a chill gripped my bones; I dressed myself in a lustrous pink sari with a band of silver at its border. As I entered the kitchen, I could smell the grain-like aroma of the porridge stew simmering on the stove; I felt at home. While Idris and Pratap brought me up-to-date on the latest gossip, lighthearted and trivial, I consumed a large bowl of the porridge, my insatiable appetite a reminder of my pregnancy.

"You're wearing pink today," Idris said to me jokingly. "I hear that's the color most used by our Nawab in the Royal Palace."

At the mention of the Nawab's name, I lost my appetite. It had been weeks and I could still picture the cursed document and Job's burst of fury that had resulted from its arrival. The levy hadn't been paid. Nor had our fleet from England arrived. I pushed the bowl away.

Sitting on the verandah with my bulky ledger, with pigeons milling about on the path below, I thumbed through the rough off-white pages. I tried to determine where our expenses could be slashed, so we could gather the necessary sum for the new tariff, should Job agree to pay it.

I looked up at the sound of footsteps. Chand, his eyes watchful. He wore a silver-colored tunic and his bearded face looked wan. He had no sooner finished stammering a salutation than Idris materialized, bearing tumblers of ghol and a platter of almonds and dried plums. He arranged the dishes and the elegant silverware beautifully on the table; then, as Idris withdrew, Chand slumped back in the chair, his face puckered.

"Have you come bearing news for me?" I asked.

"Yes, I am afraid so. Rani Mata has it on good authority that the Nawab is preparing his army for combat. Lately he's been going hunting. That's a clue that he's getting ready for an expedition."

"An attack on Rani Mata's fort?"

"No, the Nawab plans to leave us alone for awhile. Our spies are sure about that." Chand cleared his throat. "The Nawab is planning to storm this Factory. It's imminent. You can almost hear the horses' hooves."

"What? This must be a mistake."

Silently, I reviewed our finances. How could we respond to the Nawab's demands before he sent his troops our way? How best could we negotiate the terms of our obligation?

"What reason does the Nawab have to attack us?"

Chand looked back over his shoulder and lowered his voice further. "According to Rani Mata, the Nawab is highly offended by the manners of the English. He considers them arrogant. Even worse, they're out-competing him in the saltpeter trade, a situation he intends to remedy. Rumor has it that he'll order those blasted people to cease all trading activities in his territory. When they naturally refuse, Job sahib will be put under house arrest and his saltpeter supply confiscated. If any of the staff offers resistance, he'll be put to the sword."

"The English are ferocious, highly disciplined fighters," I said. "They'll be no easy target for the Nawab. In addition, the English fleet will arrive any day with troops and the most modern weapons. The Nawab will pay a heavy price and may well lose in the end."

Chand shrugged. "The Nawab's army has guns too. The English fleet isn't here yet. The Nawab's forces vastly outnumber that of the English here in the Factory. If he mounts an attack before the fleet arrives, this building will be reduced to rubble and most of its residents will be slain." He paused. "You must leave this place at once and come with me, Maria. Rani Mata is most concerned about your welfare and offers you shelter. I have a palanquin ready. Come now, while there's still time."

"You're asking a wife to leave her husband and . . ."

His eyebrows raised, Chand interrupted me in a bleak tone. "By defying the Nawab, without being in a position to back it up, Job sahib has placed not only his life in danger, but yours as well. It is said that the Nawab intends to publicly torture him as an example to all those who would resist his rule."

Consumed with both rage and fear, I could only glare at Chand. Finally, I managed to say, "Both you and the Nawab are underestimating the English."

"Why do you put so much faith in the English, if I may ask?" Chand's voice registered disgust. "Why did you marry one of them? They're only here to exploit us, to fill the coffers of their country with goods made by our back-breaking labor."

"This Factory is my beloved home, as it is Job's. With his help, I was reborn, and so I've bound my fate with his and that of the Company. The Nawab can't keep us down for long. We'll soon be back in business. The Company has been generous with the local artisans and they'll support us."

Chand sighed as he rose to leave. "Very well then. Your loyalty is praiseworthy, as is your toughness. You have a genuine concern for the artisans, but let me warn you once again. You've chosen the wrong path, the wrong side."

I watched Chand vanish down the pathway. I sat for several moments to steady myself then went looking for Job. Entering the meeting hall, I found him in conference with Arthur and a few other subordinates. A dark shadow seemed to hover over the stately room. Job spoke rapidly in a hushed tone, his eyes burning with intensity. The faces of the others in attendance expressed alarm. Were they hatching a plot of some sort? Quietly, I listened.

"But I love this land," Job said, his voice strained. "I love the people."

"Your loyalty to the Crown comes above it all," Arthur said.

"Still," Job said, "just to think I'll have my sword bathed by the blood of—

He flinched as he heard my footsteps, left his sentence half-finished, rose, took me by the arm, and excused himself. Noticing the distress on my face, he escorted me to a secluded part of the courtyard where we stood facing each other.

"What's the matter, love?" he said.

I relayed to him what I had learned from Chand.

"Lord have mercy," he said in a trembling voice. "I should have told you that I was advised of this possibility two days ago. Then, yesterday, our boat carrying saltpeter was detained by the Nawab's deputies. We were discussing this very topic at our meeting just now. What you have passed on to me only confirms our worst fear."

"And yet you chose not to tell me? Am I not your wife and partner? Do we not have a child to consider? How could you?"

"Your insights are always helpful, darling, but, as the Chief of the Factory, I have the responsibility to protect everyone. I didn't want to cause any undue alarm, especially when you're with child."

I locked away any thought of personal well being into a corner of my mind, along with the temptation to be outraged. "What about our fleet?"

"Unfortunately, the fleet has been delayed due to a severe storm." A note of desperation crept into Job's tone. "We have little time. I've already made arrangements to send you at once to our Hooghly house. Idris will accompany you."

"And you? Won't you join me?"

"I'll remain here to defend our property."

I pushed a lock of hair away from my face. "But I won't go without you. It is my fate to suffer what you must undergo. And I'll fight along with you."

Job leaned toward me. "I do not question your ability to fight, my dear love, but you must leave for the sake of our child, if nothing else. This is the only reasonable course. You've been to the Company's Hooghly residence. I trust it will again be comfortable for you."

"Why Hooghly when I can go to Rani Mata's?"

"It will not be safe for you to visit Rani Mata, given how the Nawab feels about her. Pack your belongings, darling. Now! You'll leave in less than an hour. Idris will travel with you and help you settle down there. I'll send for you as soon as the situation improves and it is safe for you to return."

"Please, dear, reconsider your position. You're hopelessly outnumbered. There is no doubt this will end badly for you. Think of the innocent people who will die for a lost cause, because of your stubbornness."

"It is warfare. I didn't start it, but I am rather good with guns, as are most of the Factors. I am also an expert swordsman. I can cause damage to the Nawab's men far worse than he imagines. Our fleet might still arrive."

For the first time, I derived no assurance from Job's words. "Why not try to negotiate a truce and stall for time?"

"I hope to win. The Nawab's army is poorly trained and incompetently led. We will prevail and before you know it, everything will be back to normal."

All I could do was shake my head in frustration. "Why, we might even gain some ground as far as our trading privileges go," Job continued. "I'll have the customs rules rewritten for our benefit and the levy overthrown." He looked into my eyes tenderly, but his voice betrayed him. "You must hurry, dear love. We don't have a moment to spare. I'll send a courier to you with updates, as soon as I can."

"How long do you expect this war to go on?"

Job Charnock, the Chief Factor, was not sure of his actions that day. He confessed to it too late, after great upheaval, after they had almost lost each other to his pride, but that day he only pulled his wife closer; his lips lingered on her brow. He studied her face intensely; it was his desire to carry an image of her with him. His heart was crying silently for her, already missing her. What had he gotten them into? Then he walked away.

My hand flew to my mouth; I stifled a sob born of a futile desire to pull him back even as I watched him move away from me.

Who could have foreseen this dangerous turn of events? When did it all start to go wrong? How could it have been prevented? I touched my eyes with the train of my sari and looked around the mansion, the silence and defiance of the outer walls, the gentle lace of the bamboo leaves hugging them, the silvery sunlight flirting with the orange-and-blue tiles of the courtyard. A white heron flew overhead. I could no longer share the tranquility of this beautiful, opulent mansion, the grounds that surrounded it, the river that gurgled past it. Here I had been reborn into a glorious new life of limitless possibilities, known deep love for a man for the first time, and even now carried the natural fruit of that consummation in my womb. Now I seethed with a sense of impending loss as the ramifications of Job's intemperate decision and my misplaced faith in him began to sink in.

Where now did my future and that of my unborn child lie?

THIRTY-ONE

A lthough our Hooghly house, Sonar Kuthi, had a generous balcony, colonnades, and a garden, I trudged through the rooms in a detached manner. My mind still rebelled at having to leave Job alone in Cossimbazar. I could picture the desperation in his eyes, the rash of fury on his cheeks, the halting sadness in his steps as he walked away from me for the last time.

The only consolation was that several of the rooms and a balcony looked out onto the sparkling waters of the Hooghly River and its palm-fringed shoreline. To us Hindus a river represented serenity and blessing, so I assumed that this temporary residence would have healing properties.

Hours passed, many a boat anchored, temple bells boomed, but no courier came to my door. Idris proposed that he would go to the dock and see if any arriving passenger had any news of our Factory.

Grave-faced, Idris returned late. "A boat has returned from Cossimbazar," he said. "As we feared, the army has surrounded the Factory. Job sahib is under house arrest. A small army sent by the Council on an emergency mission couldn't get far. They were captured by the Nawab's soldiers."

I stared ahead; all sounds were meaningless. My restless, proud husband must be pacing in his room, seething with rage. I pictured his guns in the chest drawer. What if he reached for them? Wouldn't the situation worsen if he drew the trigger?

A notion bubbled up inside me. "Do you think we might be able to help Job flee, by making a deal with the guards?"

Idris thought for a moment. "That's possible. I am a Muslim and the guards are my brothers. I'll appeal to their sense of mercy and compassion, which Allah commands all Muslims to show toward others. I'll tell them that Job sahib is newly married and his wife is pregnant. Also, he's a foreigner, a guest in our land. We must never harm a guest. Furthermore, the sahib, our lion-hearted leader, donated money to the victims of the market fire. That saved lives. Now we must save his."

"I'll come with you."

"No, Maria, you stay here. I must go alone. I'll sneak Job sahib out of the Factory and put him on a boat."

Listening to Idris's unwavering voice and seeing the light of sincerity in his eyes, I knew he'd do his best. Under a sky darkened by rain clouds, I made a silent resolve. While Idris was away, I'd send a messenger to Surat, at least a ten-day ride to the west, to the Council of Directors. I, an Agent of the company and Job's wife, would seek the Council's help. Surely, they wouldn't want their most loyal Factor to be hurt and one of their major factories reduced to rubble. Yet, watching the waves crash on the river bank and shrivel into foam, I couldn't be sure of any assistance from that office.

"I've already hired a maid-servant for you," Idris said. "Her name is Sahira. She's related to a cousin of mine. She'll report for duty tomorrow. In my absence, she'll take good care of you."

"How long do you think you'll be gone?"

"It might be days," Idris said. "We'll have to take a longer route to get back here. But I promise I'll return with Job sahib. May Allah, the infinitely compassionate, protect you."

THIRTY-TWO

Two weeks since Idris's departure. No word from him or from anybody else from Cossimbazar.

The silence oppressed me, especially since I grew tired easily due to my pregnancy. I had sent several messengers to Cossimbazar, but each time the ferryboat failed to land there. Still, at the slightest sound, I would run to the door, hoping for news.

Remembering the schedule of ferryboats arriving from nearby villages, I left the house mid-morning and hurried up the river bank. "Do you have any news of Cossimbazar?" I asked the every sailor and fisher boy I met, but to no avail. Finally, exhausted, desperate, I ran up to a newly arrived boat and began to question two passengers who had disembarked.

"You want to hear what's going on in Cossimbazar?" asked a young male passenger. "I live only a few miles west of there." He reported that boats to and from there had been stopped by the order of the Nawab. His officials had put heavy metal chains across the river to keep any boat from entering or leaving the town. "Fortunately, my village has been spared, and our ferry is running."

"Oh, it's much worse," said his older companion. "Rumor says bodies are lying at the gate of the English Factory. At least two people have been beheaded. Many are injured. Their blood is washing the ground."

After they left, I sat down on a boulder, unable to think or act.

When I eventually reached home, Sahira, my new maid-servant, greeted me at the door. A graceful woman in her thirties, she was dressed in soft pink and had covered her head.

She served up a plate heaped with big-grained rice and a tangle of greens. "You don't look well. You haven't had any food in hours. You must eat regularly, if not for yourself, for your child."

During the meal, as I spoke to her about my plight, she listened with respectful attention. "Your husband will return soon," she said. "Not only has he a will to win, but also, with a wife and a baby on the way, he has reasons of the heart, a much stronger pull, if you ask me."

I took solace in Sahira's simple but powerful belief. Still, the hours hung long and tense, too dark to bear. I perched on a chair in the balcony and listened to the murmur of the river.

In the afternoon, I heard a knock at the door.

Teema! She stood with a bouquet of rare water lilies. The air took on a sudden verve, as though a nightingale was about to break out singing.

She handed me the flowers, saying she'd plucked them from a pond and they were meant to cheer me. As I pressed the bouquet against my chest and inhaled its fragrance, I was transported back to the Factory, the sunlit marble verandah, the frolicking pigeons, and the rhythm of life with Job.

In the balcony, as we sat down, Teema placed a leaf box on the table. Inside, there rested square-shaped sweetmeats made of milk, in white, yellow, and orange.

"I came to say goodbye," she said solemnly. "I need to run away once more."

I couldn't believe my ears. "Where are you going?"

"Back to my family. You see I came to the big city to dance. Now that I can't perform anymore, I've decided to leave. Two nights ago, Egon left for the Netherlands. He cried on my shoulder and said I'd given him more than any other woman ever had. He is in love with me, but we have no future together."

We watched the water, the cluster of sails and fishing nets; a sense of emptiness engulfed me. "I hope you have carefully considered what you're about to do," I said.

"Yes, I have. My decision might seem strange to you, but here's the truth. My journey is in many ways the reverse of yours. You were like a tight bud when I first met you. Now you're beautifully open. For me, things haven't gone the way I had hoped for. This town has used me and tossed me aside. It is time for me to go back to the place I came from and restore myself." She paused. "But will you send word when your baby is born?"

"It'll be only a matter of months," I said. "Why don't you come and stay with me for a while when the baby is born? Otherwise we might never see each other again."

"I'd like that." She paused, a flicker of envy in her eyes. "I always wanted a child, but I don't think I'll ever be blessed with one."

"Suppose you became my daughter's godmother?"

"Oh, Maria, nothing would make me happier."

I reached for a piece of sweetmeat, tasting its softness against my palate, and finished it in no time. Our conversation drifted to my concerns regarding Job, our shared memories of the Factory: the lavish grounds, long hours of toil, rationed food, Tariq's frequent rebukes. These things had strengthened our bond. Together, we let our hurt go. From behind the clouds, the setting sun blazed a deep purple over the western sky.

Teema rose to her feet. "I won't see this sunset in a while, or you."

I stood up slowly. My lips quivered as I bade her farewell. "Hope it won't be too long before we meet again."

THIRTY-THREE

The following weeks were painted a deep blue-black. Though the sun shone, without Job beside me, everything seemed dark, fruitless.

And then one day, there was a knock at the door.

Factors, about ten strong, including Arthur, Gordon, William, and Francis, stood in torn and soiled doublets, fatigue etched on their faces, each with a large sack slung over their shoulders.

I greeted them and beckoned them in. "Where's Job?"

"The Lord only knows," Arthur replied. "The four of us fled soon after you left on Job's orders. The rest of the Factors stayed behind to help him." He went on to say that they'd taken a land route to reach Hooghly, hiding from the Nawab's soldiers and robbers on the way, carrying with them these huge sacks containing ledgers and other important Factory paperwork.

I served them a large meal and made sure they had all the necessities, but I was even more anxious. For long hours afterwards we continued to talk of the trouble that had besieged us. It fell upon me to find housing for them, arrange for their meals, get them comfortably settled, and store the documents, while still looking for every opportunity to get the latest from Cossimbazar. We were a family now, bound by our love for a life we had left behind and loyalty to the Company. If only Job and Idris were here, I lamented frequently.

Sahira helped me at every step, constantly reminding me that I mustn't toil too hard. "If you run around so much, your baby will get restless, too," she said. "You don't want that. I was the same way before my first-born."

Less than a month after the arrival of the Factors, the courier I had sent to the Council of Directors in Surat finally returned carrying a sealed document. My fingers slipped a few times as I opened the document. The first half said that Job should call for a truce with the Nawab. As if I hadn't thought about that already, as if I had a way of reaching him. The second half declared that the Council gave me permission to open a new Factory in Hooghly. They'd made the decision based on Hooghly's rising prominence as a port and the fact that it had far bigger potential for trading than Cossimbazar. The Council was ready to send financial help. In the absence of Job, the directors wanted me to be in charge.

"We're cognizant of how much you have already done for the Cossimbazar Factory," the letter said. "We trust you'll be able to bring this new venture to fruition as well until Job Charnock returns." I clutched the letter and felt the weight of the paper, as well as the confidence the Council had invested in me, yet a corner of my mind fervently wished Job was a part of this new venture with me.

A week later, the Factors assembled in the drawing room; I presided over the meeting. I read the letter from the Council and waited for everyone's reactions. The air was heavy with their resentment, the goodwill of the past few weeks dissipating instantly. The room vibrated with murmurings.

"They could at least have chosen someone who speaks proper English," Francis said.

Hurt, angry, and embarrassed, I could feel my cheeks blushing, my eyes blazing.

"Perhaps they preferred someone who speaks proper Bangla?" Gordon interjected. "It's after all the language of those with whom we wish to trade."

Francis' face reddened.

My hands were steady; I held my head high.

"You will do well to consider your good fortune, gentlemen," Arthur said, with barely concealed anger in his voice. "Many independent traders will be more than happy to take your places, should taking direction from Maria prove to be an insufferable burden. They may still do so if this insubordination continues."

"Allow me to outline for you the tasks that need immediate attention," I said. "Someone must go across town to apply to the local Court for permits, and then keep going back until the process is completed. Visit local merchants and artisans and set up meetings, several per day. Rent space to warehouse the goods we receive."

"The Council believes in Maria," Gordon said eventually. "And they've given her the authority. Whether you all agree with it or not, it is their will. We'll be happy to carry out your orders, Maria-ji, our respected Factor."

"These are difficult times," I said. "I need your support. In turn, you'll have mine."

Though most were still skeptical, they acquiesced in order to keep their positions secure within the Company.

I plunged into the arduous task of establishing a new English Factory in Hooghly. On the ground floor of the house, I set up an office from which we conducted most of our trade. Soon the local brokers began visiting me. My pregnancy was visible now through my sari layers and I needed to rest often.

There was still no news from Cossimbazar.

Slowly, the Factors began to fall in line, but I was still not fully used to the rigors of being a leader.

One day, hearing footsteps at the door, I rose from my desk by the window and went to answer it.

As I opened the door, I almost staggered back from the shock and joy of the sight I beheld. Job stood, pale, gaunt, and shivering, Idris behind him.

"My love." I clung to Job. "Welcome back."

He smiled faintly, his eyes dark-rimmed, his breath warm on my cheek. "My dear heart." As I led him inside the house, he asked, "Our baby. Three more months?"

I nodded, breathing in the staleness of his tattered linen robe. My courageous husband. His hair was disheveled, his shoes mud-crusted, a finger-nail was missing. There was a deep purple scar on his right hand. I could only imagine the intrigue behind his escape, the harrowing journey, the secrecy he had had to maintain at every step. How many more such scars might he be concealing beneath the stained clothing?

Idris followed us at a respectful distance, his clothes soiled, face filthy with dust, the lines on his forehead deeper than I'd ever seen them.

After they had bathed and eaten, we lounged in the garden under swaying palm trees as Idris related the sad news about our magnificent mansion in Cossimbazar. The army had confiscated the furniture, artwork, and our store of saltpeter, looting it all with glee. As a last act, they'd torched the building. Within hours the Factory had been reduced to a smoldering skeleton, with only a few blackened columns standing witness to the turbulence. Every inch of the ground was strewn with stones, charred wood, and ash. The trees were scorched. Wild dogs prowled the area, growling menacingly.

The marble-white beauty of the mansion existed only in our memory.

Idris shook his head. "We lost five dear friends, five brave souls." Jas and Pratap were no more. Both had died fighting to keep the army from advancing to our mansion. Their bodies had been thrown into the river by the Nawab's soldiers.

I sat stiffly. Lines of misery etched in the corners of his eyes, Job's gaze seemed to search the past. I could see he was mulling over his plans, decisions, and actions time and time again.

"The sahib fought with his sword and killed many enemies," Idris said.

"Still, I couldn't save five of our courageous people," Job said.

"I saw them acting as a shield from behind a barricade," Idris said. "I shouted out a warning, but it was too late. They were trampled by that evil man's elephants and died on the spot."

"My wounds bother me far less than their deaths." Head down, shoulders hunched, Job sobbed. I'd never seen him shed tears before. He groaned as though in protest, sounding utterly desperate, covering his eyes with a handkerchief.

He stood up suddenly. "I'm going to the punch house."

"When will you return?"

He didn't answer me. He spent the rest of the afternoon and much of the evening in that dark, noisy, and rowdy place, which he had shunned in the past, and returned late in the evening. That night in bed, Job showed me the wounds on his body, at least ten, deep and purple. Wincing, he touched the gash on his upper arm.

"How did you get that one?" I asked.

Eyes swollen with tiredness, he said, "When I severed the iron chains placed across the river by the evil Nawab. You see, he was trying to stop boats from leaving."

I woke up in the middle of the night. Job wasn't in bed. I peeked from the top of the stairs and saw him pacing about the house, a ghost in his white nightclothes.

In the next few days, as we mourned the loss of our staff, the air remained heavy with grief, the days bereft of their zest. Had Job given in to the Nawab, our staff would still be alive and the Factory would still be standing.

In due time, when our moods had lifted a bit, I asked Job about the incident of the metal chains. "What exactly happened?

"Oh, I severed them."

"How?"

"With blows from my sword. I was determined not to be held down."

Idris, who stood nearby, joined in the conversation. "It happened at dawn, with the sun as a brilliant witness to what we were about to do.

Residents of our town who happened to be on their way to the mosque or the temple gathered and watched. They were on our side."

"I took off my turban and waded into the river," Job said. I could picture the scene as he described it, even the way his body shivered in the cold water. He unsheathed his sword, gripped it, bent it at an angle, readjusted it, and went after the chains. He struck time after time. A huge clattering sound followed as the chains began to fall into pieces. One struck him on his upper arm. Onlookers also jumped into the water. Some helped him stop the bleeding while others began collecting and removing the metal pieces.

"Where was the Nawab?" I asked gleefully.

"The bastard was probably resting in his bed, a smug smile on his face, dreaming he still had his English enemy locked up in the Factory." Job paused to catch his breath, looking decidedly smug himself.

"Who would dare to wake up a blood-thirsty ruler?" Idris added. "Pity the poor fellow who brought him the news the next morning. His was probably the first of many heads that had rolled. By then, Job sahib and I were long gone."

I stared at Job. "Where did you find such strength?"

"Why, from you, dear! I pictured your beautiful face and that helped me strike the chains time after time, even when I thought I could strike no more."

"The rest of the journey wasn't easy, either," Idris continued. "Our boat took us to a tiny village where we hid for a few days." He paused, as though urging Job to speak. In saving each other from death, they'd formed a bond.

"I couldn't eat or sleep or speak with anyone for fear of being found out," Job said. "Oh, the pain of having to flee your own Factory, your own mansion, like a common thief. To lose your possessions and your status. I wanted to slit that bastard's throat. Only now I realize I was ill-prepared and too proud to see my shortcomings." Job met my eyes and added, "You were right."

I drew closer and held his hand.

With what seemed like grudging respect for the Nawab, he added, "His forces were far better organized and led than I ever thought possible. They fought well."

"But the sahib will forever be remembered by the townspeople for his valor," Idris said after a while. "In the next few days when we were far away, we began to talk to local people. No matter where we went,

I heard the story repeated. 'You're Job sahib?' people would ask. 'You defied the tyrant who taxes us into poverty? You're our Prince of Swords.'"

Sad, depleted, haunted, Job stared into space. "I am told Charles had a hand in it. He'd conspired with the Nawab against me. He certainly had enough inside knowledge to give the Nawab the upper hand. If I ever get my hands on him . . ." His eyes flashed, and for an instant he was the Job of old. Then his shoulders slumped and he transformed again into a broken man.

"Charles can't get away with this," I said. "Where's he now?"

"From what I hear, he's on his way to England, where he'll be perfectly safe. Oh, how wrong I'd been about him, despite your warnings."

As though to change the topic, Job looked up at me. "I must tell you how proud I am of you, dear. You've done all that is required to get a new Factory started single-handedly. The Council gave you the authority, but it was your knowledge and tenacity that made it happen."

A beautiful day bloomed about us and we snatched a few moments of happiness together. Then Job stood unsteadily. "I'm off to the punch house now."

Many hours later, he entered through the front door, unsteady on his feet, looking past me, as if I wasn't there. He didn't hold me or kiss me. His ardor toward me had cooled; the desire I used to see in his eyes had been replaced by an unfocused expression devoid of any emotion.

"Please tell me what's troubling you," I said, lying in bed next to him. "And if I've done anything wrong. I am your wife. I love you and want to help."

"Oh, I'll be fine," he said, his voice raspy. "I just need time."

In the next few days, some color returned to Job's cheeks, though not the keen look in his eyes. His hair was newly streaked with gray strands.

"Should I order some new clothes for you?" I asked. "Have a tailor take measurements?"

"Yes, but no tunic and trousers for me. I want to dress like an Englishman, in doublets, capes, and breeches."

I was preparing to give birth to our baby and needed Job's help to shoulder the responsibility for our new Factory. It would also divert his attention from the humiliation of defeat at the Nawab's hands.

"Would you like to pay a visit to Anwar, the clove merchant?" I asked him one morning. "Make sure he fulfils his promises. And, while you're at the bazaar, could you look for a new source of indigo dye? The old broker has gone on a pilgrimage to Varanasi. And Job, please darling, put on some clean clothes."

A gray curl fell over Job's eyebrows. The eyes beneath them were vacant. "As you wish, my dear."

A few days after that, Anwar stopped by to visit me. "I've been meaning to send someone to you for a fresh supply of cloves," I said.

"But Maria-ji, I haven't been paid for last month's delivery."

How could Job forget this?

"A minor oversight," Job said later, sounding impatient and weary. "I can't be expected to remember everything."

The following week, I noticed a few more 'oversights'. There was no supervision, records weren't properly maintained, the taxes weren't paid, and the cargo wasn't loaded onto ships on time. During one especially long and tiring discussion, I tried to make him realize that given the stiff competition, we couldn't afford such mistakes. We operated from a cramped space, nothing like what we had in Cossimbazar, the scope of our business was far more limited, our position more tenuous.

Scowling, Job rose from his chair, his hair greasy, his doublet creased. "Idris! Boy! Bring me a peg."

Where was the Job Charnock who had once lived for the Company, when his voice boomed in the meeting hall, when he had wanted to form his own trading enterprise? He had changed in so many ways, even in the way he spoke to Idris, the man who had helped save his life.

We're English. We don't like to lose, he'd said. The rest of the Factors noticed Job's behavior and offered me their support in helping him, but no one knew exactly what to do. The Council began to correspond with me directly, knowing they were no longer able to count on Job to get any task done. He was the Chief only on paper.

In the ensuing days, the fever Job had succumbed to in the past returned. His skin burned at night under the covers, yet he wouldn't allow me to summon a physician.

On the 3rd Day of the Bengali month of Kartik, on a night dedicated to the Moon God, our baby girl was born. She had Job's oval face and blue-green eyes, my olive skin and dark hair, peach-blushed cheeks. When Job held her, shortly after her birth, his face shone with a light I hadn't seen in a long time. We named her Mary Moorti Charnock in recognition of our different backgrounds.

Mary filled my heart with joy. Cradling her in my arms, inhaling her faint milky smell, I felt a certain power. Both Rani Mata and Teema came to meet Mary. These two dear friends filled our house with excited chatter, if only for a brief period.

The shine on Job's face at Mary's birth was short-lived. His features sagged and the fever tormented him intermittently. I remember the day when I saw him bending low over his desk, dressed carelessly in a soiled doublet. Light shone on his papers through the open window, and his eyebrows furrowed in concentration as he looked at them. As I entered the room, his eyes passed over me, unseeing. Once so vigorous, he now slouched, as though shriveled into a brittle husk.

"Where is my damn hat, Maria?" he shouted. "Where did you put it, woman?"

I struggled to keep my voice low and peaceable. "I haven't seen it, but let me look."

"Don't bother. You seem quite able to keep track of all the business details, but when it comes to your husband's hat . . ."

"Job, please tell me what's wrong."

He remained silent.

"We have a Factory, not a big one, but it's a start," I said. "We have each other, and we have Mary. We can rebuild our life."

Job rubbed his chest. "Not so easy for me to make a fresh start. Have you forgotten how I was robbed and beaten by that scoundrel Nawab? We English don't suffer such humiliation lightly."

"My stomach sickens every time I think about it. But this is a different town, a different year, and we're under a different Nawab."

"I'd thought we were a superior military power," Job mused, eyes momentarily closed as though in a dream. "It'd be a simple matter to defeat a rabble of natives, even with a handful of us Englishman."

In the silver light streaming through the room, I prepared myself to speak the truth. My eyes were fiery; my voice low. "It had always bothered me how poorly the Factors treated us and not merely because we were servants. We were deemed inferior because of the color of our skin. The Nawab wasn't taken seriously, either. But he won! Do you now see that my people have enough courage, enough strategy, and enough training to offer resistance? Do you now have a bit more respect for us?"

Job cringed and sat back for a few moments. "I do see," he said finally, a light flickering in his eyes. "Painful as it is for me to admit it, I saw the beauty of Hindustan, but made the mistake of underestimating the people. From now on, we shall have to deal with them as equals. No more denying it. That's the bitter lesson I've taken away from this war."

THIRTY-FOUR

What a relief it was to see that our new Factory was finally operating fully! The buzz of activity returned, bringing in a minuscule profit. In the three years that had gone by, lacking commercial space, we let the ground floor of our Hooghly residence function as its headquarters. Although the regional administrators looked favorably upon us, we were as yet small in comparison to the Dutch. I had heard rumors that the Dutch were helping build the Mughal navy and were also suppliers of sailors and troops. As a result, they were given tax concessions, which conferred upon them significant competitive advantages. They often tried to lure the local merchants away from us by offering bigger bribes, as did the independent English traders. We had other worries as well. We could never be sure that either the Nawab of Cossimbazar or Charles, from his perch in London, would sit still, without taking further revenge.

Still, I spent little time worrying. I had a bigger goal in mind, of acquiring more land for business so we wouldn't be cramped, and in case we needed to expand in future. I would imagine a wide open space in which to build our Factory, proximity to the river to help in transporting goods. I talked at length with the kitchen help, asking for their suggestions; from experience, I knew they always had their eyes and ears open to developments and possibilities.

Idris, who had relatives living outside the town, suggested that I visit a trio of villages, only a few miles' journey from Hooghly. Though he didn't name the villages, he said, "Plenty of available land, cheap too, away from the bustle of our town. The villagers are gentle. The area is close to the river where boats can anchor. And you like being near water. Worth a look, wouldn't you say?"

The next day, sitting inside a palanquin, I peeked out to see grass plains, an occasional swamp, and scattered, sparsely inhabited villages. Job sat next to me, lost in thought. Soon the scenery changed a little; the plains were replaced by marshlands and rice fields, which would surely be flooded during the hightide.

Before long, I spotted a tiny hamlet located on the east bank of the river. A flat riverine land, fields dotted with ponds, translucent sunlight, and birds calling raucously from the treetops, just like my birthplace.

I asked the porters to stop. As the palanquin was lowered to the ground, Job and I climbed out. Insects whirred noisily around us.

"We're approaching Sutanati," one of the porters announced. "It is also called 'The Swamp'. Do you wish to break your journey here?"

"I do," I said.

We walked past marshland reeking of decaying vegetable matter and strolled toward the village. A vista of mud walls, thatch roofs, palm trees, wind-swept meadows, and ponds matted with water lilies spread out before us, the air ripe with the smell of fresh vegetation. A frog hopped out of its mud nest. A peasant cut through the trunk of a neem tree with a hatchet. A young girl plucked a lotus blossom from a pond's surface. Women carrying earthen waterpots on their heads paused to look at the new arrivals. A man tended his buffalos. Somewhere a wild dog barked. It all seemed familiar, comforting. In my mind, I could see the possibility of establishing the Company headquarters in a place like this, but I had to consider all business angles and also find builders and artisans here who could work for us.

"What do these people do for a living?" I asked a porter.

"Forty or so families live here; my cousin is one of them. They fish, grow crops, make salt, raise their children, take care of their livestock, and sell what little goods they make."

"I suppose there are a few craftsmen among them," I said.

"Oh, yes, quite a few. They don't have much work, only what's needed locally, even though some of them have real skills."

"Is this place safe enough to live?" I asked.

"Not by any means," the porter replied. "Occasionally, a tiger finds its way here. Sometimes the residents are able to capture the beast, but most of the time it gets away. Then there are crocodiles in the river which float to the shore and prey on the children. During the monsoon, stagnant water makes this the ideal home for mosquitoes. And at any time, bandits can break into a house, steal what they see, and abduct a woman or a child. It's a pitiful existence. Still, the villagers don't complain much. They assume it's their fate."

Abduct a woman or a child? My two brothers had also been abducted and later killed. "Doesn't the zamindar who owns this village provide protection for his people?"

"No. He sends a revenue officer to collect his taxes, which must be paid on time or else the householder will be punished."

"Suppose we lease a patch of land from the proprietor," Job asked the porter. "Drain those marshes, reclaim the forest areas, use the land for our Factory, and offer protection to the people living nearby?"

The porter nodded. It made me happy to see Job's mind working and our thoughts proceeding along the same lines. He was willing to give up his visits to the punch house for hours of pleasure to relocate in a rural setting like this. I could hear the enthusiasm in his voice. Finally, he seemed to be closing the door to the past behind him.

Job must have read my mind. "You know, this reminds me of the time when I was first transferred to Cossimbazar. Everything was new, many doors open, and I had a big vision. Still, things slipped away from me. This time I'll act more slowly, more cautiously, but it'll be just as exciting, if not more so."

Delighted, I turned to the porter. "Could you show us the other two villages?"

The porter led us back to the palanquin. In minutes we were on our way, and soon passed through Govindpur, a village similar to Sutanati, with its water, marshes, and greenery. A short time later, we arrived at Kalighat. A village loomed before us and familiar sights greeted my eyes. A group of villagers squatted on the bank of a pond, washing clothes, while a few others harvested brinjal and kolmi greens from their plots. Children ran back and forth. A cow rested under the shade of a tree, its tail twitching, its hooves, horn, and forehead smeared with ceremonial red dye.

As we approached the outlying huts, the porter pointed to a small temple. "That's the famous temple of Mother Kali, and this is the hour of worship. People pour in from neighboring areas to receive her blessings."

Indeed, a stream of pilgrims, people of all ages, sizes, and shapes strolled toward the temple. My father's words came floating to me from the distant past. *We have a life beyond the life we live and that should be attended to in sacred places.*

"Even Emperor Aurangzeb is afraid of Mother Goddess," the porter continued. "He has razed countless Hindu temples and replaced them with mosques, but not this one. You see, she's not a piece of black marble, she's infinite energy." The porter pressed his palms together. "Goddess Kali is kind and loving, but should you displease her, she'll destroy you with a single blow of her sword."

"I must visit the temple," I said to Job. "Will you come with me?" Job looked away. "I'll wait for you."

I mounted the steps, walking alongside a woman hauling a wicker basket of fresh marigold flowers, and a family with several boisterous children, each carrying a coconut. Once I reached the main entrance, I was directed to an inner sanctum reserved only for women and children. Although nearly every inch of space had been taken, I managed to squeeze in. In the center of the sanctum stood an altar containing a statue of the dark-faced, four-armed goddess, her tongue protruding, her hair long and wavy. Standing, I offered my prayers before the altar. At first, the sight of the statue filled me with a sense of dread. I wanted to leave. A woman playing cymbals paused as a saffron-robed priest entered and shut the door.

Taking his seat on a floor mat, an earthenware lamp with nine lighted wicks before him, the priest began chanting sacred hymns, his voice gentle but powerful, soaring high. This was what made people's lives bearable, journeying here to receive a blessing from the powerful goddess, to be transported to another realm. More than a mere place of worship, this temple was the heart of this locale. It gave meaning to many otherwise dreary lives, the will to go on.

For the pushpanjali, the flower offering, I picked up a petal from a large platter, approached the statue of the goddess, and placed it in front of her. Then, still bowing, I went out of the room. As I descended the steps, a vision formed in my mind in bits and pieces, floating clouds accumulating. To build an entire town around this temple for the betterment of the people. To give the villagers better opportunities to earn a living. To set traps for the tigers and crocodiles, banish the bandits. To provide safety for the people so no abductions would take place so people could live without fear.

Job was waiting for me at the foot of the steps. "Did Kali win you over?" he asked, his voice flippant.

"She did and she gave me an idea. Instead of renting a piece of land from the proprietor, suppose we buy all three villages and string them together to build a settlement? Our Factory will be a part of it, of course. We'll also establish pathsalas for children to study with a teacher, workshops for artisans, a market and other amenities, with the temple being at the center of it all. It'll be lively and peaceful."

Doubt clouded Job's face. "That's a big proposition, which will require our full commitment and occupy all our free time."

"Have you forgotten how much you once adored Hindustan?" I asked sadly, nostalgically. "How you loved the rivers, the trees, the fertile fields, the harvest, the people? How you wanted to live nowhere else? Don't you think this project will be much more worthwhile than simply building a Factory to benefit the Company?"

Job looked me full in the face, as though expecting me to say more.

"I haven't been able to forget the abduction of my brothers, how horribly their life ended, or Bir's murder. How can anyone get away with stealing children from their families to use for slave labor and doing away with them? How can someone murder a man and receive no punishment? Whatever power I have, I intend to use it to remedy the inequity."

Job smiled faintly; for a moment his forehead caught the ruby-colored rays of the sun. "It is a worthwhile idea. Mind you, we will not only need permission from the Council but also their financial backing. That might not be easy to get." In a more casual tone, he added, "What should we name the settlement? It has to be a name we English can pronounce easily."

"Goddess Kali has already named it for us. Kalikata—the Place for Kali."

"Kalikata," he repeated after me. "The Council won't object to that name, I should think."

I smiled. "You're so loyal to the Company, dear, but do you have to defer to them at every step? I would fight the Council, if I had to."

As soon as we reached home, Mary came running into my arms, nearly tripping on the threshold. My heart melted at the sight of her lively eyes.

"Mama, Papa, did you find a house for us?" She was almost four years of age; her chubby cheeks reflected the color of her red-orange dress.

I kissed her cheek. "More than a house, darling, we're going to build a brand new town."

In the weeks to come, I consulted with local architects and money-lenders about our plan and how to go about it so as to least disturb the residents. The advisors' assessment was that first, the zamindar must be willing to sell the villages and all the rights to us; second, the project would require the labor of hundreds of people, take decades to finish, and cost a considerable sum.

Would the Council back us financially? Would Job help me?

I went back to visit the villages several times, gazed longingly at the green fields, gem-like ponds, and groves of fruit trees; held long conversations with the locals and inquired as to what they needed the most.

"Houses, jobs, tools," they sang out, "a place where children can study with a teacher."

Although Job declined to accompany me on these strenuous visits, Mary did. She loved to ride in the palanquin. Upon arrival, she'd stoop down to touch the water lilies in the ponds, taste the freshly harvested palm syrup, play hide-and-seek with the local children. If Job had his doubts about this project, staying non-committal when I asked about it, I never did. Finally, my planning was complete.

A rider on horseback picked up the long document containing my full proposal to the Council. It would be weeks before I heard from them, and so I resigned myself to a period of anxious waiting, my pratikkha.

THIRTY-FIVE

Weeks went by. There was no response from the Council. Each day seemed interminable; the hours hung heavy, punctuated only by the clock's monotonous ticking.

One morning, a rumor about the Dutch East India Company, a far bigger and more established trading company than ours, reached my ears. They had acquired more land in Chinsura to build a fort, augment their trading presence, and exercise judicial power. I sat at my desk in shock. Not only did I have a grudge against the Dutch for abducting my brothers and possibly murdering them, but I also feared they would run the Company into the ground with their cut-throat competition. We were only a fraction of the size of the Dutch EIC. If the Council delayed our plan, we might soon be forced to close our doors.

Midday, I went upstairs with Mary in my arms. My darling child was sick. Her mouth half-open, her ever-alert eyes closed, she whispered. "Mama, I miss you when you go away." She looked lovely in her white chemise and stockings; her glossy black hair was matted and damp from the fever, the flower-petal eyelids half shut. I lowered her onto the bed and covered her with a warm quilt. Had I done the right thing by taking up this mammoth project? Was it worth being away from my daughter for long periods of time?

My gaze fell on the side table on which rested an oversized official letter written on fine heavy paper. I recognized the Council of Directors' stamp on it. Breathless with anticipation, I picked it up. It had arrived three days ago and had already been opened. The first sentence read:

"We, the Council, do not approve of the stated plan to build a large settlement near Hooghly."

The members of the Council further proposed that instead a fort be erected. ". . . a walled fort, a White Town, for the English only."

My mind empty, fingers numb, I finished scanning the rest of the missive; it contained further justification for their decision, justification with which I disagreed.

Job swooped in, carrying an umbrella. He was pale, with a yellow cast to his eyes. "I'm going to the punch house." He turned away.

"Please wait. I'd like to speak with you. You haven't mentioned this important letter."

He shrugged. "Oh, I must have forgotten," he said in a breezy manner.

I struggled with his casual response. It was affecting my mind and body. My ashen-faced reflection in the mirror bothered me every time I stood before it. My body ached, I felt exhausted all the time. Yet, it was important that I continued to dream about expanding our business, to plan for it.

His face blank, Job half-turned towards the door; he didn't seem to care.

"Did you read the letter?"

He turned toward me. "Aye, looks like they've changed our plan."

Why was his voice so bland, lacking even any hint of frustration? I stood still, perplexed. "How can the Council possibly dictate that the villagers will not be allowed inside the fort?"

"Quite obvious I'd say, after our experience at Cossimbazar. You will of course be a part of it. You're my wife, you speak English, and you're like us. We could employ the locals, but they'd have to put up their huts at a considerable distance. A high thick wall would surround our compound for safcty's sake. We will not allow any outsiders to enter."

I couldn't believe my ears. "That's preposterous! Those villagers are bound to their land. They've been so for generations. Even if we buy land from the zamindar, it's really theirs."

"Higher authorities than you have decided otherwise."

"You can't possibly agree with such a scheme," I said, my voice hesitant, sad.

"You must have noticed that our Factors are not comfortable around the locals." A note of bitterness crept into Job's voice. "After what we went through in Cossimbazar, they've become wary. Surely, you've also noticed how glad they are to let you handle all the local contacts. They want to live in a place where there will only be English people, and possibly other Europeans. Word of their feelings has gotten back to the Council, hence the decision. I think it's eminently fair."

There was more, I suspected. *No mixing of colors*, Sal's voice echoed in my mind from years back, as did Teema's; *there's a color bar*, she'd said.

"This land belongs to us, the Hindustani people," I shot back. "You can't build a White Town and shut us out. Such a plan is doomed to fail. Over time people will see the inequities, the barriers keeping them out, and they'll rise up against the Company. Without the support of the populace, the Company can't expect to succeed in any commercial venture, especially when the Dutch are in the picture."

"Why are you so bent on helping those peasants?"

It was as though I'd been slapped in the face. My outrage flared into open anger. "You forget I am one of them! Who grows our food crops, supplies our trade material, and helps facilitate the transfer of goods? We wouldn't live in such comfort were it not for them. They deserve a portion of our profit. They deserve to live better. People say particularly of the silk spinners that they dress others but their children go naked." I softened my tone, "Let's try to offer a counterproposal to the Council."

"No. As you surely must understand by now, their word is final. A castle for the English, that is as far as they'll go."

I took a deep breath to collect myself. "Well, apparently they haven't heard about the latest development then." I informed Job about the Dutch plan of building a fort in Chinsura. "If we want to offset the Dutch advantage, then we must motivate people to support us by offering them economic benefits, superior to what the Mughals have done, superior also to that of the Dutch. In fact, we should show them how we're different from our competition by building a settlement open to all. Give them a reason to come to us and I have no doubt they'll support our venture and help it succeed."

Job's expression made it clear he remained unconvinced.

"I must contact the Council and try to change their position while there is still time," I continued. "Don't you think that would be the most appropriate course of action?"

"No. I won't permit it! I too am opposed to your plan, as I have been from the beginning. It is bound to fail."

I stared at him, open-mouthed and hurt. "But Job," I said, my voice shaking, "Why didn't you try to change my mind earlier, discuss with me? Have you no respect for my feelings, my dreams?"

I watched him lean away from me, his arms tight around his chest, the air in the room thick. I couldn't take it anymore. An unbridgeable chasm had opened between us. "I am going to contact the Council on my own,"

He snatched the letter from my hand, the force of the action momentarily unsteadying me. "I forbid you." His voice was thick with anger and frustration.

"Then I will resign from the Company." He stood stunned.

"Listen to me, Job. All these years, I've obeyed you, even when I believed you were wrong. No more. The time has come for me to stand up for my own rights and those of my people. I love you, Job, I always will. I have never loved anyone this deeply, never known as much happiness as I have with you, but now I must sacrifice that life. This is a higher calling and I must respond to it. Once you claimed to hear that call, but it is clear you no longer do."

He remained silent, staring off into the distance. I wanted to clasp his hand, touch his face, lean in to his chest, and feel the real answer inside him. Why couldn't he look at me? How had it come to this?

My voice broke. "If that's how you feel, then I . . . I should leave."

He stirred, came closer, tossed the letter to the floor, gripped my shoulders, and shook them violently. "What did you say?"

I simply couldn't figure out what was going on in his mind. Then a dreadful thought occurred to me: His illness had taken over his mind and caused him to toss those cruel remarks at me. I stepped closer, gazed into his eyes, and tried to put my arms around him, but he resisted and stepped back a few paces.

Humiliation, anger, and sorrow flooded my insides, followed by dread. The man standing before me was no longer the man I had married. I'd seen a tendency toward violence in him before, but it had never been directed at me. I peered at him, a flicker of hope inside me that I would still be able to reason with him.

His eyes turned icy blue and he replied in a harsh voice, "Don't you understand, it is not your place to tell the Factors or the Council how to run the Company? I am in charge. You're my wife and I expect you to follow my instructions."

"But, Job, what I don't understand, what I really don't understand, is why you're speaking so horribly to me. Could it be that your illness has spread? May I please have Idris summon a doctor?"

His eyes flared in indignation. "I am just fine, thank you. I don't need a doctor. What I do need is an obedient wife. I won't have you going against my wishes, is that clear? You must do what I tell you to do. There will be consequences if . . ."

"Our marriage vows made us equal partners," I replied. "I can't live under those restrictions. I am leaving you and taking Mary with me."

"Don't ever try that, Maria."

Maria. The name he'd bequeathed me, the name that still sounded so fresh, so glorious, the name that had helped me stitch a new quilt of life. Despite that catch of emotion in his voice, I could tell he did, indeed, prefer that I leave. I wanted to close my ears to the message he so clearly spoke with his stern mouth, his cold back, his dispassionate eyes. What had happened to the man I had married? Had his illness so changed him? In front of me, I saw the ruin of a man, the destruction of a marriage, the toppling of what we called our kingdom, years flying away like stray petals in the wind.

My limbs shaking, his threat ringing in my ears, I again studied Job. He was no longer a robust man, but could he hurt Mary? I took a few steps closer to the bed and wondered, with a lurching stomach, if Idris and Sahira were downstairs. Could they hear us? Would they respond if I shouted for help?

"Mama! Papa!" Mary cried out from the bed; she tried to prop herself up, then fell back again. "Mama, why is your face so red? Papa, please don't hurt my mama."

Shamefaced, Job turned, glanced at Mary, and stomped out of the room. I heard him running down the staircase, slamming the front door. I leaned over the bed, scooped Mary up into my arms, drew her close to my chest, and held her tight, her safety my biggest concern. For a moment she nestled snugly, innocently, soft to the touch, then opened her eyes. "Why are you crying, Mama?"

I pictured the three guns Job had in his drawer; gleaming, malevolent weapons primed and ready to kill. I held Mary tighter. My stomach lurched; there was little time left. Mary peered at me, as though trying to grasp what had transpired, and then she closed her eyes again. I put her back to bed, picked up the letter from the floor, put it back on the side table, and quickly descended the stairs.

In the hallway, I found Idris, his face a mask of concern tinged with panic.

"Are you all right?" I asked.

"What has come over Job sahib?" He asked in a low voice. "He pushed me out of the way for no reason. I'd have tripped on the carpet, except . . ."

"I am sorry, Idris."

Idris faced me, his eyes brimming with compassion. "I must now see you to safety."

I got hold of myself and thought quickly. "Mary and I will go to Rani Mata's fort. Please arrange for a palanquin, and please, keep my where-abouts secret from Job."

Idris wiped his eyes. "I surely will."

"Will you be alright here alone in this house with him?"

"With Allah's help, I'll manage. The sahib and I have seen each other through the worst of times when we escaped from Cossimbazar. If I have any destiny at all as a servant, that is now tied with the sahib's. He's not well; I must take care of him. I'll return shortly with a palanquin."

In a cold, unsettled mood, I packed only a few necessary items. Then I spent the next half-hour preparing my letter of resignation for the Council. I stated my reasons and also gave them an account of the increased competition from the Dutch. I asked Idris, who had returned, to have the letter dispatched to the Council immediately via a courier.

I asked Sahira if she would accompany me.

"Oh, yes, my mistress," she said. "I'll go with you. It doesn't matter where I work, as long as I get to see my husband." She paused. "I am a simple woman, I say what I think. Your husband doesn't spend time with you. His eyes have a bad color. I don't envy you anymore. Mine is an ordinary laborer, but every night he holds me and says I am his guiding star."

Long ago, Job used to call me his guiding light, his ruby, his queen.

I slipped out the front door with Mary and Sahira. The palanquin and the white-vested porters waited at the gate. We said our farewells to Idris as he helped us into the conveyance. As we started to move away, he kept waving at us, a lonely figure among the trees. Misty-eyed, I glanced around at the familiar surroundings—the house, the garden, the balcony, the gray-blue waves of the river. Crowds of people chanted, meditated, oiled their bodies or bathed on the ghat, as though nothing had changed.

"Where are we going, Mama?" Mary asked after a time.

"To Rani Mata's house. It's big. You'll like it."

"Is Papa not coming with us?"

For Mary's sake, I had to stay strong.

In the two months that followed, in spite of the hospitality Rani Mata extended to us, I still found myself torn by love, fear, and emotions I couldn't name, tormented day and night. I played with Mary and helped Rani Mata in her administrative work, but I missed Job. Day and night, my thoughts centered on him; he trailed me like a shadow. I missed our house in Hooghly and the constant clamor of trade activities. I felt as though a part of me had been amputated.

One afternoon, I sat with Rani Mata by the window, a bowl of red hibiscus flowers between us. The golden shimmer of the sun accentuated the yellow of her silk. Her abundant hair was caught up in a loose bun and a necklace formed of red gems encircled her throat. Her eyes were wide with concern. Although she feared an invasion of her fort by the Nawab's forces, she maintained the confident pose of a queen who lived for her people, who would pick up the sword at a moment's notice.

She pointed to a plate of freshly made coconut rounds garnished with almond bits. Mary picked up a round, examined it, and began to nibble on it. As I watched her, my face softened. How much she resembled Job; those river-green eyes, the way she stood. The ache in my heart would not be eased until I saw him again.

"You're not eating?" Rani Mata asked me.

"I am not hungry."

"You fret too much," Rani Mata said. "You're so young. You have many years ahead of you to make your hopes and dreams come true."

"I gave so much of my life to Job and the Company. Did I make a mistake?"

"Mistakes can be corrected. You can choose a different arena to play, if you so wish. Consider the current political upheavals. All across our land people are rising against Mughal rule. The Marathas, who are a tough bunch, have set an example. In the meantime, Emperor Aurangzeb is in the South, with his cavalry. Foolish man, he won't ever fully win there. To my mind, he's already finished. Small kingdoms like mine might, after all, get a chance to flourish."

In this beautiful, sun-drenched room, this news weighed on me like a physical burden. "Ah, so," I sighed. Then after a pause, I said, "You want to keep me here, I suppose."

"I have wanted that to happen from the very first time I met you," Rani Mata said. "Call me selfish. I know that you've given much of your life to Job and the Company, but I'd caution you. Please reconsider your course. The English don't consider us as their equals. What do you hope to get by working for them? Surely, the Mughal rule will fall and leave a vacuum, and the English, the devious ones, will fill it. If they gain power, they will stay a long time, although it'll not be an easy win. You'll have blood in your hands by causing your people to . . ."

"You're asking me to leave my husband and the life I've built with him?"

"What brought you here?" Rani Mata asked. "Why are you not by your husband's side?"

As I pondered her severe questions, a manservant entered and bowed. "Someone is here to visit you," he said to me excitedly. "His name is Idris Shah. He's waiting outside. He says it's important. Do you care to receive him?"

I stood. "Oh, yes! Send him up."

"He says he prefers to speak with you in private."

I excused myself and rushed through winding passageways to reach the entrance to the fortress. Idris stood under the canopy of a peepul tree. I examined him from a distance. Not only had he grown thinner, but he had also aged in the last two months. Strands of silver streaked his gray-black hair. His bowed head betrayed a sense of resignation.

"Idris!" I called out, drawing near.

He raised his eyes to mine. "You must come home at once, Maria. Job sahib is not feeling well."

Worry twisted inside me. I couldn't trust my eyes to see clearly. I held onto a branch of the tree.

"This morning when the sun had been up for several hours and he still wasn't up, I went to his bedchamber. Eyes shut, he was lying there. 'Sahib, sahib,' I called, and put a hand on his forehead. It was slightly hot. He woke up and said he'd be fine, just needed more rest. Still, I decided to come and get you. Sahira is taking care of him and the household in my absence."

"Did you call a doctor?"

"No, the sahib asked me not to."

Typical Job. Never cared to see a doctor.

"Has he ever asked for me?"

"Oh, yes, the sahib talks about you constantly. I can tell how much he wishes you were with him. He hardly has any vitality left. I planned on visiting you sooner and persuading you to come back. How much I regret not doing that."

I heard Mary's sweet voice behind us. "Where's Papa?" she asked. "Mama, what's wrong? When is Papa coming to visit us, Idris?"

Idris opened his arms and Mary ran to him, throwing her slim arms around his neck.

Rani Mata stepped forward to my side. She had obviously heard my conversation with Idris. She held my hands and we spent a few moments face-to-face in silence. "Anything you need," she told me gently. "Anything at all, Maria. You have to go now, but remember that my doors will remain open for you."

Back at the house in Hooghly, I left Mary to play with Idris outside while I ascended the steps to the second floor and walked into our bedchamber. Job was asleep, his body covered with a white quilt; he looked pale and slightly emaciated. It was a shock to see my husband, a seaman, trade pioneer, adventurer, and leader, so frail and vulnerable. I did not disturb him. Walking past the desk, I saw the draft of a letter lying on it. It was written in Job's familiar curly script on creamy official paper and dated almost two months ago. I picked it up. Job was responding to the Council's order. The ink was dark, Job's handwriting firm. I went downstairs with the letter.

As I began to read it, I could hear Job's voice filling the room.

"In my years of service for the Company, I have come to love Hindustan and her people. Therefore, I must reject your ill-considered proposal of an English-only settlement and follow the dictates of my heart."

I clutched the letter to my breast, its message dizzying me even more as I read further. Job warned that he would remove his Factory from the Council's jurisdiction and run it as a separate enterprise in order to erect a town that would include the native population as well, one that would eventually become a thriving commercial center. There, all could prosper from the new Factory's trading activities.

I read on. Even more stunning, Job had proposed that I become the Chief Advisor, sharing equal responsibilities with him, that this new position would have more authority than those of the other Factors. "Had I heeded her counsel, we might have avoided the disaster at Cossimbazar. She is the only one among us who understands the locals, their language, and their customs, and as such she is an asset to the Company."

This decision, this recommendation, Job had insisted, was final.

Idris shuffled in. After taking a few moments to compose myself, I asked, "Did Job ever mention this letter?"

"Yes. He worked on it for days, trying to get it right, then had it dispatched by courier. Arthur-sahib and I were the only ones with whom he shared it. The other Factors had no inkling. Shortly afterward, Arthur sahib left for Surat on an errand." Idris paused, his voice thinning. "Job sahib's eyes were filled with anxiety when he explained to me what he had proposed. It made him anxious to think about the Council's reaction, what punishment they might impose on him, even the possibility of a bloody gruesome battle, should they send an armed contingent to crush his insubordination."

"I suppose that's why he didn't want me to be here?"

"Exactly. But given that the Council hasn't yet responded and the sahib is sick, I felt it was necessary to bring you back. I did it on my own, without the sahib's knowledge. Did I do the right thing?"

"Yes, I am very glad that you did. You are a wise and loyal man, Idris. With your help, I shall be able to nurse him back to health."

"It grieves me to say this, Maria, you were like a daughter to me, but I must now say goodbye. My duties here have ended. I am growing old and it is time I returned to my village, to spend more time with my family." He smiled faintly. "Perhaps I shall even master the flute."

I put out a hand to stop him. "But Idris . . ."

He shook his head slowly, but resolutely. "There was a time when I thought I'd relocate my family here and be able to see them more often, but then I decided against it. This town is big and prosperous, but there's so much scheming for power, so much unhappiness, danger at every step. I have had my fill of it and will not expose my family to it. In my advancing age, if I am to have any peace of mind, I must . . ." His voice choked; he abruptly turned and walked out the door.

Standing in a state of shock, I absorbed the silence about me. A bullock cart clattered by outside the window. I simply couldn't imagine this place without Idris.

I returned to our bed chamber and put the letter back on the side table. I was about to tiptoe out when Job called out. "Darling!" He was half-rising and propping himself up on the pillows. "You're back!"

"Yes, Idris fetched me from Rani Mata's." I drew close, sat on the edge of the bed, and noticed the sheen of perspiration on his forehead. His face held a bright light as he drew me close and kissed me. I tried to hide my concern, and asked him, in as level a voice as I could muster, about his health.

"It's only a low fever. I already feel much better." He paused. "I can't tell you how terribly I missed you and Mary. In the end, the pain in my heart made me ill. You're my whole life."

"It broke my heart as well. I didn't want to leave you, but you didn't leave me any choice. Oh my love, my life, how I wished I had known the truth. So much suffering, so many sleepless nights. Might there have been another way?"

"I didn't want to drive you away, either. But I suppose you've read the letter and hopefully you will understand and forgive me. Those dangerous times, all I could think of was keeping you and Mary safe, even if it meant tearing my heart to pieces."

I nodded. Yes, I understood better now. He had only pretended to take a position opposed to my own. How hard we'd argued, voices rising, our words like spears, remarks meant to wound. By design, Job had worked to make me furious, so consumed with frustration that I'd walk out the door. Job Charnock. Ever the strategist, he had worked towards driving us away, far away from him, out of harm's way should the Council decide to take action against him. He wanted to face the consequences alone. "How cleverly you assumed the role of an opponent," I said to him, holding his hand. "How bravely, too." We laughed together, drawing closer than ever in relief that the ordeal was over, at least temporarily.

A day later, with Job feeling much better, we sat in the garden, beneath a neem tree. The day's heat had subsided somewhat; a breeze rustled the leaves. Insects hummed, pigeons cooed, and a white heron flapped laboriously skyward. We discussed our life together, the events that had brought us close, those that had estranged us—from the time he had rescued me from a burning chita to the arrival of Anne memsahib in his life, to the time we got married, and then to the most recent episode in our lives.

Gradually, our emotions spent, our thoughts and feelings expressed like never before, we went back to the most pressing matter at hand.

Curious about his recommendation that I be appointed to the position of Chief Advisor, I asked, "Does that mean you take my work seriously?"

"Much more than that. You're my equal in every respect, darling. In fact, you're better than me when it comes to figuring out those nuanced situations that we so often face. Would we even have a Hooghly Factory without you? I doubt it. Back in Cossimbazar, you advised me against confronting the Nawab. I didn't listen to you and I paid for it. I only wish I had told you all this earlier."

A kite fluttered up into the sky. I watched its ascent with pleasure. "If I ever have to override the wishes of the other Factors, will you support me?"

"Rest assured, I will."

The Council hadn't yet replied to Job's letter. A frown formed on his forehead at the mention of this situation. I shuddered as I considered the potential consequences should the Council reject his idea. The Crown could ask the Council to dispatch a military force, arrest Job, burn our house down, execute both of us, and confiscate all our assets.

"Your love makes me stronger," Job said, his gaze fully on me. "I will stand my ground, however the Council replies."

"Please don't ask me to leave again, my darling. I'll share your destiny. Yes, I will. I'll send Mary away to Rani Mata's as soon as I sense any trouble coming to us, but we will face it together."

He nodded. I could see that he was ready to face whatever might come his way. He'd done that once before when he had rescued me from my first husband's funeral pyre.

A week passed. Once again, we were happy together. The mood was light and bright, the days full. Only occasionally would I be seized with worry.

One morning, I hired a palanquin and took a solo trip back to Sutanati, to once again survey the land I so wished to acquire. As I got off the palanquin and lingered by a pond, a village woman whom I'd met on a previous visit approached me.

"Mother Maria, we've been waiting for so long. Our people are thankful in advance for the work your Factory will offer them. Even our children are asking when they'll be able to study with a teacher. We have never had much to look forward to; our days are but one long grind. You're our only light."

Looking into her hope-filled eyes, I stayed silent for a moment. Then I assured her that somehow, with Job's help, I would strive to make that dream a reality, no matter what it cost. I reached out and squeezed her hand.

While my mind leapt ahead with the plans for this settlement, doubts about financing such a massive project crept in, as well.

A few days later, the Factors gathered in our house. Although I'd officially resigned from the Company prior to fleeing to Rani Mata's, they asked me to rejoin them. Job, back to his vigorous self, presided over the meeting.

A knock on the door and Arthur appeared, carrying a rolled-up document. He'd just returned from a journey to meet with the Council in Surat. Everybody in the room was quiet, anxious. Despite the lines of fatigue on his face and the dirt and grime on his clothes, Arthur looked animated. He took a seat, placed the document on his lap, and gave me a faint smile.

"How happy I am to return." He looked around the room, and then his gaze settled back on me. "And how happy I am to make this announcement. We missed not having you among us, Maria. Our Factory, let me just say it wasn't being managed as well as it might have been. We didn't know where you'd disappeared, and Job didn't feel well enough to handle his duties. The best I could do was to take a trip west, appear before the Council in person, and seek their advice."

"Such a strenuous journey!" I replied breathlessly. "What result did it yield?"

"The best possible. Let me break the news to all of you."

Arthur unrolled the document.

"I went before the Council and asked them what they would do to get our Factory back on its feet. I also argued your case. It took some time, but they heard me out, and threw away your letter of resignation. Allow me to read a few sentences from this document which they've signed and asked me to present to you and the rest of the Factors.

'Maria Charnock is hereby officially appointed the Chief Advisor of the Hooghly Factory. In that capacity she will work closely with Job Charnock, the Chief Factor, and be second in command. We have reconsidered our earlier decision. In expanding the territory of our Company, we see benefit for us and that of the people living in the trio of villages located near Hooghly.'

They ordered me to find you, Maria, and return you to our Factory. Their change of heart seems to have something to do with the Dutch and their plans for expansion, but now the Council wants to proceed with your vision, and that's what's important."

In the pause that followed, the Factors began to whisper among themselves. "Seniority," said William, "what happened to seniority?"

"The Council hopes all of you will accept Maria's authority," Arthur said to the agents present, "or else consider seeking other employment."

The Factors rose and went across to the window, whispering and complaining among themselves. A short time later, they returned to their seats and said in unison, "We agree."

Only Francis picked up his belongings and strode out the door. I smiled to myself at his departure. I stared at the harsh sunlight streaming through the window. I had no illusions about the Company's long term vision: expansion and an eventual takeover of our land. Still, it thrilled me, for they needed my services, and I wouldn't deny that I needed them as well to advance my own personal interests and those of my people.

My eyes roamed the room. I saw doubt etched in some faces. They didn't fully trust me; nor did I fully trust them. It would be important to have allies in the dangerous game I was playing. I imagined myself in the future, sitting across from Rani Mata, spending long hours discussing my strategies with her.

Job fixed me with a tender gaze. I could sense the love and support he would provide to fulfil my dream of establishing an open city. That city, after all, would be his loving gift to Mary and me, as well as to the people of Hindustan, a precious gift from a generous heart.

My reverie was cut short as I heard Job speak. "Now that the organizational structure is in place, we have trading to be done, the Dutch to deal with, and . . ." He turned toward me.

"And, gentlemen, we have a city to build," I said. "A town named Kalikata, a place where all are welcome."

See back of receipt for your chance
to win $1000

ID #:   7LOH5WJOHMZ

Walmart
Save money. Live better.

(219) 465 - 2799
MANAGER GARY SCHLECHTER
2400 MORTHLAND DR
VALPARAISO IN 46383

ST# 01479 OP# 009032 TE# 32 TR# 01370
LIBRTY CREEK 008500001129   6.98
               SUBTOTAL   6.98
TAX 1 7.000 %   0.49
               TOTAL   7.47
        CASH TEND   10.00
        CHANGE DUE   2.53
        # ITEMS
TC# 0803 8804 8805 5108 5

04/20/17   09:05
Store receipts on your phone. Walmart P
ay.

AUTHOR'S NOTE

Dear Reader,

Allow me to share with you the story of how this book came about.

Ever since my childhood days in Kolkata, when I studied its history in the classroom, I've been fascinated by the city's intriguing past. In particular, I yearned to learn more about Job Charnock, a faithful servant of the English East India Company in its early days, who was believed to have founded Kolkata (then known as Calcutta). Eventually, I immigrated to the States for graduate study, but I returned to Kolkata often on family visits and discovered that my childhood yearning was still very much alive.

I noted with great interest that the late 17th and the early 18th century was a time of great upheaval in India, with Calcutta at the epicenter. It was a period that afforded a preview of the bloody British occupation that would follow. The more I researched and learned about this period and about Calcutta, the First City of the British Empire, the more I dreamed of writing about it, especially how it was founded.

My research soon led me to the controversy that has in recent times surrounded Job Charnock. Did he really establish the foundation for Calcutta? Or did the credit belong to local Indians? With that as the starting premise of my novel, I asked myself the following question: What if Charnock and his Indian wife had jointly founded Calcutta?

His wife's life was never recorded in detail. All that is known for sure is that she was a village girl who was being forced to self-immolate on her husband's funeral pyre when Charnock appeared and rescued her. This historical vacuum provided ample leeway to give my imagination full reign. So I created Moorti, later to be known as Maria, a spirited woman equal to her husband in ambition, ability, and vision.

Although I have tried to stay true to historical facts wherever I could, Moorti is entirely a product of my imagination. So is Job Charnock, for the most part. Not only have I compressed the details of his life for readability, but have also fictionalized his personality and actions. However, there are a few exceptions. I've stayed true to one of Charnock's character traits noted by many historians, his loyalty to the English East India Company. I've also shown his interest in the Indians and their culture, unusual at the time, a point on which historians generally agree.

And finally, I haven't concerned myself only with kings, queens, and the high-born. I have tried to show how common people also lived, laughed, suffered, and even managed to thrive.

I thank you, dear reader, for taking part in this long historic journey with me.

Ever yours,

Bharti Kirchner
USA

ACKNOWLEDGEMENTS

I deeply appreciate the support of friends who have stood by me during the long years it took to write this novel. Their names (in no particular order) are: Margaret Donsbach, Ann Slater, Gail Kretchmer, Jo Ann Heydron, Barbara McHugh, Jean Akin, and Christine Z. Mason. I may have forgotten a name or two. You know who you are.

On the publishing side, I am fortunate to have the excellent guidance and brilliant vision of Priya Doraswamy, my literary agent, Sucharita Dutta-Asane, editor, the Severn House team, Bidisha Srivastava, editor, HarperCollins India, and Amrita Chowdhury, publisher, MIRA. I have enjoyed our collaborative effort.

Thanks to Deepa Banerjee, librarian. Much of the research was done at the Suzzallo Library, University of Washington.

Notable among the countless volumes I browsed there are: *Charnock and His Lady Fair* by Pratap Chandra Chunder; *Trader's Dream: The Romance of East India Company* by R.H. Mottrom; *Aspects of Indian Culture and Society* by Nirmal Kumar Bose; *Marriage, Religion and Society* by Giri Raj Gupta; *Travelers' India* by H.K. Kaul; *Maharaja: The Splendor of India's Royal Court* by Anna Jackson, and *The Romance of an Eastern Capital* by F.B. Bradley.

I am grateful to the following organizations for their partial support of this project: Artist Trust, City Artist's Project Award, and 4Culture.

As always and forever, my deep appreciation goes to my husband Tom. I couldn't have done this without you.